MW01267684

# Freedom's Menace

A Trevor Brice Novel

# Freedom's Menace

## A Trevor Brice Novel

*W. Laurence Willis*

Published by Hot Lava Publishing
233 Loggers Trail, Saint Louis, MO 63026

This novel is a work of fiction. Names, characters, places, and incidents either are the product of the author's imagination or are fictitious. Any resemblance to actual persons, living or dead, events, or locales is entirely coincidental.

Library of Congress Control Number:  2002101106


ISBN 0-9716765-6-9

Copyright © 2002 W. Laurence Willis
All Rights Reserved
Printed in The United States of America

HotLavaPub@aol.com
www.TrevorBriceNovels.com

*Dedications*

To Pam,
Samantha & Alexandra
I love you

**Special Thanks to:**

Shelley, Susan and Amy

# Preface

You are about to enter a tale of non-stop action, high adventure and political intrigue. In this story, you will explore one of the most fascinating places on earth, Hawaii. Freedom's Menace is set on the Big Island of Hawaii. As a result, the reader will encounter a number of words native to the people of Hawaii. To assist you in your interpretation of this marvelous language, I am providing a short list of Hawaiian words, which you will encounter and their pronunciation. Enjoy your journey!

The Hawaiian language is complex. In general, each letter is pronounced even when double letters occur. Hawaii is said Ha wa e e. The primary sounds consisting of only eight consonants, five long vowels and five short vowels. This is a meager list for such a significant language, but that's what makes it colorful and fun. The vowels in the following words are short.

Aloha – Hello or good-bye
Mahalo – Thank you
A'a – A type of lava.
Pahoehoe – A type of lava.
Hale – A house.
Lanai – A porch, balcony or veranda.
Nene – Sounds like naynay. A Hawaiian Goose.
Imu – Sounds like Emoo. An underground oven.

*Watch for the next Trevor Brice adventure*

*Coming - Spring 2003*

# 1

## The United States of America

We live in an uncertain world. The period following September 11th saw the United States and its allies waging a persistent and fearless war on terrorism. The cost in terms of lives, emotion and dollars was staggering. Military, diplomatic and covert operations along with self-protection initiatives drained the treasuries of the allied countries. The people of the world were tired, resources strained, stock markets anemic and still the terror continued, though dramatically slowed. No country was immune, no religion, no race. It was simply madmen run amuck, inflicting pain on an injured planet. Former President George W. Bush had declared the war was just and, "the only way to guarantee safety and freedom for our grandchildren." The world was not so sure anymore.

Economic strengths shifted, power bases were altered, the world order left in chaos. Unlike most wars, the enemy was not always obvious. Lesser evils like the virulent Islamic extremists from Malaysia, Indonesia and the Philippines rode the coattails of the stronger, more organized aggressors inflicted their own brand of skewed justice in small, painful doses. An old military adage declared that if the head of the snake were severed the body would die. But, this enemy was not a snake. It was a worm. Every time the head was incised, the body would slither beneath the earth, where a new head would grow. The revitalized vermin would then crawl up from the sewers to scavenge and spread their pestilence on the unsuspecting. As the global military machines chipped, chopped and hacked away at the cells of terror across the globe, the maggots rose from the ashes to fuel the fire of the jihad. Capturing world enemy number one, Osama bin Laden had been a surprisingly simple task. Actually, it was just dumb luck, a Delta Force team in the right place at the right time. Crushing the vast al Qaeda network had proven more difficult. With their leader imprisoned, the autonomous hoard of ugliness had been kept alive with a seemingly endless supply of funds from Iraq, Iran, North Korea and other similar thinking counties. Also included were wealthy individuals disgusted by the concept of freedom and hateful of any positive human condition.

The most troubling aspect, and the most frustrating, was the shear quantity of funds being channeled into these dark conspiracies. Billions of dollars had readily flowed into the coffers of the terrorist organizations, feeding the worms. Behind closed doors, world leaders knew the source. Smaller countries like Iraq did not have the wherewithal to provide the level of sophisticated support the terrorists were receiving. It was all too obvious who the true enemy was, but world leaders were unable to prove or halt the flow of cash. Only one country could afford such a hefty tab. The one country that had benefited the most from the madness was China. Diplomatic efforts endeavored to dam the headwaters, yet the money continued flowing. Their methods of distribution were just too many and too sophisticated.

# Freedom's Menace

President David Totten, a man of great resolve, campaigned on the earlier vision of President Bush to cleanse the planet of evil. The years, lives and billions of dollars spent were finally paying off. Intelligence told him they were finally turning the corner, starting to win. An end was indeed in sight. He felt they were at last over the hump. The people of countries most injured by the war, like Afghanistan, had turned their sympathies to freedom and peace because of the benevolence shown them. Northern Ireland was finally at peace. Israel and Palestine had settled their differences and were coexisting in peaceful accord. Islam, a religion of peace, fully embraced tolerance and respect for non-Islamic faiths and all people living together in harmony.

Finishing the war was going to be a direct result of what the United States does best, creating and utilizing technology. Technology and liberal surveillance laws allowed authorities to eavesdrop at will on the communications of those out to commit harm. Electronic mail intercepts were the greatest intelligence-gathering breakthrough since the Allies deciphered the German's secret code during World War II. Sophisticated tracking systems followed and diverted the flow of large sums of money in and out of sheltered accounts.

Somberly, President Totten stood behind his desk looking out the window of the Oval Office having concluded the daily meeting with his national security team. It was time to write the final chapter to this segment of history, close the book and turn out the lights. It was time to put this all to bed. America would indeed stand tall once again.

His planned trip to China would be the first non-war related major Presidential event in a very long time, but Totten viewed the visit with trepidation.

# Beijing, China

The dank vault buried three stories under the Ministry of Commerce in the heart of Beijing had not been entered in years. Three men stood at the entrance, in front of a massive steel door supported on hinges the size of a man's leg. One man carried a metal box, military green and worn from years of use. The enormous steel door groaned, and the rusted hinges creaked, as it swung open. A switch on an aging cobweb-covered electrical panel was thrown, creating a loud metallic clack. High intensity lamps flooded the area with brilliant white light. The green metal box was lifted and dropped onto the bamboo tabletop. Billowing clouds of dust rose into the air and spread through the small enclosure. The larger, and older of the three, dressed in a full-length robe of red silk trimmed with spun gold piping and polished gold buttons, watched intently. With a snap of his wrist, the newly installed Premier of China motioned the order for his aide to open the container. His large hand returned to its resting place atop his oversized belly.

In obedience, the second man cut through the padlock and lifted the hasp, but a disapproving grunt from the Premier stopped him from lifting the lid. With a toss of the head, the Premier instructed him to wait outside. The third of the group stepped forward, a small nervous English gentleman sporting a graying mustache, thick round glasses and wearing a dark pinstripe suit. He reached over and lifted the lid. The hinges groaned and the room exploded in a kaleidoscope of colors. As if shot from a thousand laser beams, painted light radiated out in all directions. An audible gasp sounded from the Englishman, and he took a cautious step backward. The Premiere's posture straightened. He stiffened at the wonder he saw inside the box, but allowed himself a tight smile. His head then nodded approval. Recovering, the diminutive character approached the bamboo table to have a better look inside. His gaze fell upon virgin white silk and the incredible object nestled in the center of it. Not a word was spoken for several moments. The man looked up at His Eminence.

"Sir," he said, "Only the Buddha could have created something as wonderful as this. It is astounding. But I must hold it in order to conduct my examination."

Premier Lolo squinted. With reluctance, he gave a slight nod for the man to proceed. Although the man's trembling hand was of average size, it could not fully encircle the colossal deep blue diamond as he lifted the stone and drew it toward his face. The diamond absorbed the white light from the overhead lamps and instantly reflected it back in rays of red, blue, green and yellow. From his jacket pocket he took out a loop. Setting his glasses on the table, he placed the loop over his right eye and studied the precious stone for several minutes. He set the diamond back inside the case. He removed the loop, replaced his glasses then removed them to wipe the lens. From his brow he dabbed away beads of sweat before turning to face the Premier.

"This is incredible! Astonishing! The stone is flawless! Perfect, it is perfect! And yet it is so very large." The Premier smiled again. This time it was a broad, relaxed, toothy grin spreading from ear to ear. "The clarity the stone possesses is unlike any diamond I have ever examined. And yet, and I repeat myself, it is so large! In all my years, I have never heard of a diamond of this size existing anywhere in the world. Can you tell me from where it came?"

The Premier sidestepped the question. "When I was but a small child the Buddha came to me in my sleep. Over the course of many nights he gave me instructions. With this stone and the others like it…"

"Others!?!" exclaimed the man.

"In just a few years time China will be a very different country, and the world will be very different as well. Thanks to our friends, the change is already well underway. As America fights the terrorists, a war, which will take many years, we shall plan for the future. This is the dawn of great happenings for our people and our culture. The diamonds will make the Buddha's wishes possible. No longer will the capitalistic ways of the West dictate to our people and the people of the world."

Premier Lolo reached over and closed the lid. The thousand tiny rainbows disappeared as quickly as they had formed.

## An Unexpected Find

American Airlines Flight TW1 was two hours away from completing its daily non-stop flight from St. Louis to Honolulu. Occupying a third row seat in first class was Trevor Brice, a St. Louis businessman. Brice stared out the window studying the cloud formations hovering above the Pacific Ocean. The plane was passing over several clusters that looked as if they were islands floating in the blue waters. Clouds, like most things in nature were a favorite form of inspiration to him. What wondrous natural effects God has provided for us, he was thinking while studying the different shapes, patterns and contrasts of clouds with the sea. A talent for design was his most prominent trait. Everything from buildings to consumer products carried the hallmark of his work. The 15-person design firm he ran enjoyed a worldwide reputation and was the hallmark for design excellence. His life as a businessman was one of international acclaim and provided an excellent façade for a man who had a need to freely roam the globe without suspicion.

The soft vibration from the alarm in his wristwatch brought his mind and eyes back into the cabin. After a thoughtful moment to clear his head, he bent over and lifted the black leather briefcase from under the seat in front of him. As he placed it on his lap, he glanced at the passenger in the seat to his right. She was fast asleep. They had chatted during the first hour of the trip. She had introduced herself as Martha Gielow, a Yahoo marketing executive. She was on the second leg of a journey that started a day earlier in Milan, Italy. St. Louis had been a stopover in route to the Hawaiian Island of Kauai for a long overdue vacation.

Brice flipped the briefcase onto its top and popped open the compartment hidden on the bottom. Martha Gielow shifted in her seat. He gave her another look. When satisfied, he lifted the lid of the compartment.

From inside he removed the familiar blue folder with its red security ribbon and the words "Your Eyes Only" in block letters fanned across the top. The seal of the President of the United States was embossed in the center. Again, Brice checked on Gielow and then up the aisle for a roaming stewardess or other passenger. Satisfied he could view the documents free of wandering eyes, Brice reached into his pocket and retrieved his Swiss Army knife. With the small blade, he cut through the red security ribbon.

Inside he found a single sheet of the President's letterhead and underneath it, a photograph. His instructions were written in the President's own hand.

# W. Laurence Willis

*From the Desk of David S. Totten*
*President of the United States of America*

*Mr. Brice:*

*Thirteen months ago, the Kilauea Volcano experienced a major eruption that blew the top off of the Pu'u 'O'o vent. The eruption uncovered a second large opening right next to the active lava tube. Experts thought it was only a dormant lava conduit probably formed centuries ago. The vigorous volcanic activity around the vent has limited their observations to aerial surveillance. Last week a team of vulcanologists finally got a look at the site firsthand. The lead member of the team, a Dr. Samantha Allison from the Hawaiian Volcano Observatory, supervised the lowering of an electronics and camera package into the old conduit. Prior to this effort the old conduit had been considered a bottomless pit. Scientifically, what Dr. Allison discovered was an ancient lava tube or conduit as it is called. The shaft was measured to a depth of about 4,000 feet, or down to sea level. At the bottom she also discovered a very large cavern, with an equally large pool of water inside it. The interesting part is, her camera snapped the attached photograph. As you can see, it is self-explanatory.*

Trevor flipped up the page and there, to his amazement, on crisp four by six-inch Kodak paper was the conning tower of a submarine. The insignia appeared to be Chinese. After a moment's contemplation, he went back to reading the note.

*Fortunately, Dr. Allison had the good sense to hide this finding from her other colleagues. Using local connections, she got the photo to Rear Admiral Hanover at Pearl Harbor, who forwarded it to me. Our intelligence has confirmed this is in fact the conning tower of a Chinese, Han class, nuclear attack submarine.*

# Freedom's Menace

*Trevor, I want you to confirm that there is in fact a submarine hiding in a cavern beneath the United States and, if so, answer the obvious question. What the hell is it doing there?!?*

*You can find Dr. Allison at the Hawaiian Volcano Observatory. I prefer not to have anyone else, except for the two of you, know anything about this, but do what you have to do. As you know I will be traveling to Beijing in only a few days. Our relationship with China is already strained and this does not help. Speed is essential. I need to know about the sub.*

*Exercise extreme care!*

*Good luck, Trevor, & God Speed,*

*David*

Trevor slowly closed the cover of the binder and stared straight ahead at the back of the seat in front of him. His mind became an instant blur of runaway thoughts. Mindlessly, habitually, he reopened the folder, quickly folded the letter and dipped it into his water glass. The special notepaper dissolved in an instant. The photo, he slipped it into his breast pocket. He again glanced over to the adjacent seat. Martha was still asleep. Good! He returned the folder to the secret compartment and closed the lid. He then sat back and shut his eyes. His fingers drummed lightly against the top of the leather case.

He tried to imagine an underground cavern with a submarine inside. The ability to envision a cavern was easy as picturing a submarine, but melding the two images together just wasn't working.

"How does a nuclear submarine, a Chinese nuclear submarine, find its way into an underground cavern 4,000 feet below and a good five miles inland of the Big Island of Hawaii?" he thought.

That was a huge question. An even bigger question was, what was it doing there? His mind was firing like spark plugs in a Porsche. He could almost feel the electrical impulses flash through his brain. He noticed his head becoming warm and his heart started to race. After a deep breath and long sigh, he turned to look out the window once again.

America had not forgotten the lessons that the Japanese taught her in World War II. Our Navy knew every square inch of the islands from Hawaii to Midway and the ocean floor below for 100 miles in all directions. But they did not seem to know about this cavern. If they did, the entrance would have certainly been mined. Ok, so our Navy doesn't know about the cavern. How the hell did an enemy attack sub get past the constant patrols and find the damn thing? In some ways the Hawaiian Islands were better protected than the mainland. Where was the entrance to this place? Was the sub now trapped, or could it still come and go? And was it still coming and going at will!?! A billion-dollar submarine? Sitting under the world's most active volcano? Why? What else could possibly be down there? Is the attraction something that they found or are they building something there? Nothing made any sense.

Half an hour passed and resolving this issue mentally was never going to happen. He finally decided to put it aside until he made contact with Dr. Allison. He turned the briefcase over and pushed it back under the seat. Again, he stared out of the window.

# Freedom's Menace

Seven hours earlier, he had kissed his wife and two daughters good-bye when they dropped him at the front entrance of St. Louis – Lambert International Airport. His final destination on this day was Hilo on the windward side of the Big Island of Hawaii. As far as anyone in his office knew, the five-day trip was intended to provide him an uninterrupted opportunity to study the active lava flows of the Kilauea Volcano. This was not his first trip to the Big Island. He and his wife had traveled here on their tenth wedding anniversary. He had maintained a good mental recollection of the volcano and its surroundings, but needed to refresh his memory and study the details.

The Blue Hawaiian Hotel & Casino was in the very early stages of design. Las Vegas had already brought New York, Venice and Paris to its famous strip. The beaches, fishes, rainbows and sunsets of Hawaii would arrive within three years. The main entrance was slated to wind through a massive man-made lava field with hot bubbling ooze, radiating heat, steam vents and sulfur cones. Brice's firm had won the contract to design what was promised to be the most ambitious hotel project in the world. Awards and letters of praise covered the walls of his office, but this project was going to top them all.

The unexpected jolt of the landing gear touching down on the runway in Honolulu caused him to jump. He took a long, deep breath and composed himself. A quick search of his briefcase located his itinerary; Aloha Airlines flight 48 to Hilo, departing 6:45 pm, Hertz rental car, convertible, of course, and a suite at the Hilo Hotel. He looked at his watch. He had a little over an hour until his connecting flight. Great! It would be nice to stand up and stretch a bit.

W. Laurence Willis

# 2

## Tian'an Men Square

Once the sole economic superpower of the world, the
United States could only sit back and watch in disbelief as
China's economic machine roared ahead, putting increasing
distance between them and the free world. So large had
China grown that the combined gross national product of
the Group of Seven Nations had almost fallen to second
place behind the Panda Republic. For years, the world's
focus had been on war, but world leaders had become
increasingly aware the sleepy Asian giant had finally
awakened. They remained circumspect as they watched and
waited in anxious anticipation of Beijing's next move.

Across the globe, major newspapers recycled headlines,
reading; **"CHINA'S GDP GROWS EVEN LARGER,"**
**"UNITED STATES PRESIDENT TO VISIT BEIJING,"**
**"CHINA TO UNVEIL THE DIAMONDS," "WHAT**
**DOES CHINA REALLY WANT?" "CHINA, WHAT**
**NEXT?"**

Freedom's Menace

It had been seven years since the discovery of the incredible diamonds. Diamonds China had used as collateral to eclipse the most powerful economies in the world. With the expeditious and suspicious rise in this country's economic strength ever present in the minds of the world leaders, the very appearance of the President of the United States, David S. Totten, in this city, in this country, raised conflicting passions around the globe. The stated purpose of the President's trip was to meet with the Chinese leaders for an economic summit. The leaders of the free world were growing increasingly concerned, but China had made no outwardly aggressive moves or any unrealistic demands as they methodically purchased buildings, prime real estate and corporations across the planet. But they knew it was only a matter of time before the other shoe would drop. To most people the President's trip was simply a pretense for viewing the recently opened public display of the finest of those astonishingly colossal super diamonds. However, only Totten knew that he had been summoned there, not invited. The other shoe was about to hit the floor with an emphatic thud.

## The Diamonds

The diamonds were beyond belief. All were deep blue, green and the rarest of all, red. Each stone was flawless and possessed exceptional clarity. The largest was called Bian Zhe Shi, meaning "All of the World." Its weight was 1,820 carats when cut. One diamond! And they were all real, natural and priceless.

Scottish archeologist Sterling P. Scott reportedly discovered the stones at a site that was exceptional from an archeological perspective. While much was known about China since the days of Genghis Kahn, the centuries previous to that were only a random blur to historians. Scott had spent 25 years helping to clarify an important part of world history. The day had been a long one and the river was difficult, a brief respite was in order. While taking much needed rest from their travels down the Huang He River in central China, 100 miles east of Lanzhou, Dr. Scott and his party made a startling discovery. Eventually this incredible find would garner worldwide attention and become known as simply the "Library."

In the process of seeking some privacy for the purpose of relieving himself, one particularly shy member of Scott's party found an opening in the cliff face next to where they had come aground. The opening was shielded from view by a very large boulder. In fact, the boulder had appeared to simply be an outcropping from the adjoining cliff. Dr. Scott found it particularly amusing that after all his years traveling up and down this tributary and, on many occasions, making camp at this very spot, no one had ever walked behind the giant rock. He concluded that the historic lack of spring rains and consequential lower water level in the Huang He contributed to the find by allowing someone to walk around the boulder on the riverside and stumble on this most amazing and unexpected discovery.

The stunning ruins in the eastern edge of the Shaanxi Province consisted of the temple, a crypt and the Library. All were virtually untouched by the effects of time. If one were to believe in UFOs, this place would certainly strengthen their argument. Its organization and documentation were amazing. The catalog system they found was centuries ahead of the famous Dewey Decimal System, but equally effective. The diamonds, 80 in total and none under 875 carats, were reportedly found somewhere in the Library. Each had been expertly cut, arranged, cataloged and named by an ancient people centuries ago.

# Freedom's Menace

Dr. Scott would instantly become world famous, for this was a find of legendary proportion. Six weeks after the initial discovery, Dr. Scott was ready to remove the cloak of secrecy and to share his findings with the world. Unfortunately, he died en route to the scheduled press conference in Hong Kong. The military cargo plane, which had been supplied by the Chinese government, mysteriously crashed into the Dongting Hu, one of China's largest lakes. The Dongting Hu was hundreds of miles off their planned route. The weather on the day that the plane went down was reported to have been clear skies with light winds, excellent for flying. No bodies and only a minimal amount of wreckage were ever recovered. The Chinese government was not willing to perform an extensive recovery program. This was in mild defiance to a United States offer to help fund such an effort. As a result, all of Dr. Scott's records and photos were lost with the plane. Family members could only grieve without bodies to bury. The strange fact that his entire exploration party with all their possession and records were also on board with him was never explained. This most unusual situation raised tremendous international speculation. But to what end? There was never any effort by the Chinese government to hide the archeological findings. In fact, the Chinese were uncharacteristic in their openness and permitted Scottish and United States crash investigators to join the search. After a six-month investigation, it was finally termed a freak and unexplainable accident. The Chinese publicly were thanked for their openness and assistance.

A year followed before archeological teams from around the world were invited back to evaluate Dr. Scott's landmark discovery. Six months after that, the diamonds were revealed to the world and the Chinese economic expansion began. The United States team was lead by then 19 year-old Alexandra Wilson. Ms. Wilson, a graduate from MIT at age 17, was the daughter of a Chinese-American

father and a Chinese mother. She had taken the
archeological world by storm at the tender age of 13 with
her breakthrough work in a Mayan history project that had
its roots in her middle school science project. Before
entering college, she had completely rewritten the book on
those mysterious Central American people. Following a
four-month sabbatical after leaving MIT, which mostly
involved sailing the Caribbean on a friend's 45-foot yacht,
Alex had spent the last two and a half years in China
working with Dr. Scott. A month-long trip home to attend
her sister's wedding had caused her absence from Dr.
Scott's announcement to the world of this most famous
discovery. It also had spared her life.

Alex was present when the site was discovered, but had
not seen the diamonds. They were not discovered while she
was there, nor was there any mention of them in phone
conversations with colleagues just days before the crash. As
soon as there was a hint that the Chinese were going to
reopen this find to the world, Alex was on the phone
petitioning academic and government officials to allow her
to lead the United States effort. The loss of her friends and
colleagues was very personal. The fact that the entire team
had left the site and subsequently died had an awful stench
to it. For an entire team to leave a major dig under
anything but the most critical of circumstances was
unheard of in the world of archeology. Not being the timid
type, Alex Wilson vowed to find the truth. And she knew
that the truth lay inside The Library. After weeks of
political wrangling and a certain amount of less than
honorable tactics, of which she was not particularly proud,
she received the appointment to lead the team.

## The Grand Hall of the People

The setting was the Grand Hall of the People, Tian'an
Men Square. Seventeen perfect diamonds were majestically

placed on polished gold platters, sitting atop small pillars of pure silver. Each pillar was a different height and randomly arranged. The platforms slowly rotated over a bed of blue silk. The sight was stunning. The effect was mesmerizing. The total sense of awe was the only thing that prevented anyone from reaching out and picking up one of the unguarded crystals. The Smithsonian would never consider displaying the Hope Diamond like this, in the open air within arms reach of the public. But the dozens of armed guards seemed to be an effective deterrent. Funny thing, the Hope Diamond had now become an almost insignificant bauble in comparison.

President Totten led by Chinese Premier, An Lolo, stepped into the viewing line along with, and as one of, the thousands of ordinary tourists who had been waiting to view this spectacle. For the two weeks the stones had been on display, an unceasing stream of curious people flowed nonstop, day and night, through the gallery. As the President's gaze first fell upon the stones, Premier Lolo spoke softly into his ear, "With these diamonds, sir, we will soon own your country! With collateral like this, it will not be too hard to finance the domination of the United States of America." The chill that fell over Totten was close to overwhelming. As he jerked to face his Chinese counterpart, his mind went blank for several seconds while his breathing halted. "Come, Mr. President, let us now talk," said Lolo, leading his guest to a side exit.

The silence inside the presidential limousine was deafening as the official motorcade made its way through the crowded streets of Beijing, heading toward the Summer Palace. The President had ordered all of his aides and staffers to ride in separate cars. He rode alone with his thoughts and the requisite three Secret Service agents. It was the first time that this former Navy Seal had ever experienced the feeling of this much uncertainty. "Mr.

President," asked Agent Donaldson "are you alright?"
Totten did not even move so much as an eyelash. The other
two agents in the car with him looked at each other with
obvious concern. What the hell had the Premier said to
him? Usually, they heard everything. It was their job. All
three had been within normal earshot, but Lolo's whisper in
the crowd had escaped them.

Premier Lolo was close to giddiness as he escorted the
President of the United States into the overstuffed red
leather chair that was situated in the study of this opulent
Palace, overlooking Kunming Lake. The two identical
chairs were facing each other, only three feet apart. An Lolo
sat with the thought, "This man before me and all that he
controls is now the property of the People's Republic of
China." This was the moment that his people had patiently
awaited since the beginning of their time on earth. They
were the chosen ones and they now would now set the world
on its proper course. "Mr. Totten, let me explain to you my
instructions. What will be required of you over the next 72
hours is critical to the lives and well being of your people."
Totten was instantly on guard and desperately trying not to
guess what the Premier was going to say next, although his
mind was racing in all sorts of directions. An Lolo spoke
calmly and with the authority of a parent instructing a 4-
year-old to clean his room. "First, you will relinquish
control of your nuclear missile system including the launch
codes. Second, you will provide me with the computer
passwords that allow your Federal Reserve Banks to
operate and transfer funds internationally. Finally, I want
control of the entire gold and oil reserves of your country.
You will no longer need them. Once these transfers are
complete, my people will move in and assume control of the
governmental functions. Not much will change, at least for
the immediate future. Your people can continue on with
their day to day lives, with some exceptions."

## Deep Within China

The bright Asian sun was making its ritual afternoon descent over the western horizon. The brilliant orange ball sat on the hilltop directly in line with the dirt road leading from the small village of Hankou. It was little wonder that villagers called the road "The Path to the Sun." As the day drew to a close, the inhabitants of this village of mud and straw huts, chickens, goats, cows and carts drawn by oxen gathered together in the village circle as they did every day. As the children scampered about laughing and squealing with the effervesce of youth, the women caught up on daily gossip, and the pipe smoking men ruminated about the women wasting too much time on idle chatter. Not much had changed here for more than a thousand years. Seldom did anyone grow up and leave. Even less frequently would anyone come to visit.

"Look, mama," said a child.

A din of silence swept over the village as all, hands shielding their eyes, looked up the road that was slowly swallowing the sun. Framed by the ball like a magnificent halo was the head of a woman just appearing over the horizon. The silence slowly subsided, giving way to the soft buzz of curiosity. A visitor! It had been a long time since a stranger had graced their humble village. Predictably, the men were wary, but the excitement generated by the women and children softened their unfounded concerns. As the sun set, the stranger seemed to rise out of the earth. Her long raven hair fell over her slender shoulders. She was quite tall for a typical Chinese woman. She had a striking presence, which grabbed the immediate attention of the younger men and adolescent boys. One of the elderly women thought there was something very familiar about the stranger. She was the first to step from the pack and toward the young woman. "Who is she? What is it that seems as though I know her?" she thought. As the girl approached, the woman moved closer as well.

Finally, as the girl's facial features sharpened through cataract-muted eyes, the old woman recognized the smile. It was the smile that had been passed from her own daughter to her child. This was her granddaughter. The old woman shrieked with joy, throwing her arms into the air. She raced toward Alex Wilson as fast as her frail thin legs would take her. As soon as the older population realized who the stranger was, the entire village broke out in celebration.

A fat pig was slaughtered, and a great feast was prepared. A mighty bonfire was erected in the village center. The gala and reunion lasted well into the night. Alex easily fell asleep on the straw mat spread across the floor of her grandmother's hut, but the old woman was too restless from a combination of elation on finally meeting her grandchild and worry, worry over Alex's mission. The reason she was there. Alex was like her mother, headstrong and defiant.

# 3

## Hilo, Hawaii on the Big Island

As was typical for the wettest city on the planet, it was raining in Hilo. The article about Hawaii in the *American Airline Ambassador* magazine reported that Hilo also experienced some of the largest raindrops in the world, 6 to 9 mm in diameter. The sound of the landing gear being extended for landing at Hilo was followed by an unpleasant announcement. The Jetway ramp at their assigned gate was broken and could not be maneuvered to permit its use for deplaning. This was going to necessitate walking down a mobile staircase and then crossing the tarmac into the terminal. As a courtesy, umbrellas would be provided and all passengers should exercise extreme care. There would also be gate personnel available to assist those that needed additional help.

As the weary travelers filed out into the pouring rain, the elderly lady in front of Brice slipped on the fourth step down. He instinctively bent over to help break her fall. The bullet that was meant for his head entered the soft abdomen of the gentleman behind him. It exited, tearing through the metal side of the stairs and into the cockpit of the plane. The wounded man fell forward, sending him, Trevor and the woman crashing down the wet steps to the ground. Trevor found himself sandwiched between the woman on the bottom and the bleeding man on top. Trevor's keen senses had recognized the sound of the bullet punching through the steel staircase. He immediately extracted himself from the tangle of bodies and took cover behind the mobile stairs. The second shot missed his head by only a fraction of an inch as it ricocheted off the handrail. Pandemonium set in. The elderly woman had seen the blood on her arm as she tried getting up and began to scream. Other passengers had rushed down the steps to assist, still not knowing that an assassination attempt was in progress. Aloha Air ground agents were rushing to the airplane and fought to get through the huddle of passengers that were all dripping in the pouring rain, a rain that was falling with such force that it stung their bare skin on contact.

After the second shot and not waiting for the third, Brice reached out and grabbed his briefcase. Looking around, he found his route of escape. He ran underneath the belly of the plane. He dove into the last wagon of a passing luggage cart that was heading to the baggage handling area on the lower level of the terminal. As the cart entered the cover of the building, it passed a maintenance shed and several cargo containers. Brice rolled out and hid behind the cargo containers. In one hand was his briefcase and in the other a suitcase belonging to one Jason Cahill, Pompano Beach, Florida. "I hope he's my size," he thought slipping into the shed and quickly opened the suitcase. Inside was the wardrobe of someone who had obviously lived too many years in a south Florida trailer park. He looked around and all seemed normal. "What a stud the old guy must be," he said just under just breath. Within minutes, Trevor was sporting white pants, an awful

Bermuda shirt decorated with orange, red and purple flowers, light tan shoes with red soles and a Panama hat that read "Bahama Mama's Bar & Grill" across the pink band. "Well, at least I'm dry and somewhat camouflaged." he thought.

The sound of another approaching baggage cart was a welcome noise to his ears. He dove into the third cart and headed for the carousel. The baggage handler was shocked, to say the least, when he flung open the canvas cover and the "well dressed" Mr. Trevor Brice hopped out, said thank you, stuffed $20 in the man's shirt pocket and jumped onto the baggage carousel, disappearing into the terminal. Once inside, he made his way toward a tour bus he had spotted idling next to the curb. A large group, obviously part of a charter tour, was milling about giving instructions to the skycaps about how to handle their luggage and then loitering in front of doorway. As he made his way to the bus, he stole a glance at a rather dapper gentleman loudly complaining to one of the skycaps about his missing luggage.

With his head hung low and the hat covering his face, he hurriedly brushed past several of the silver- and blue-haired waiting bus passengers and climbed onto the motor coach. He worked his way toward the back and slumped into an aisle seat. A survey of the many tourists that were filing out of the baggage area did not reveal anyone who seemed suspicious. Still, he kept his head low as he tried to will the bus to leave. At 7:10 pm, the big diesel engine roared to life and the driver slowly pulled away from the curb. The bus driver and his entourage drove down the gentle curve of the Hilo airport roadway and made a right turn onto Highway 11. A minute later, he turned left onto Highway 19 followed by a right on Lihiwai Street and onto the historic Banyan Tree Drive. Less than 10 minutes after departing the airport, the tour bus arrived at its destination, The Naniloa Hotel.

Trevor had tried keeping an eye on the traffic behind them as best he could without the aid of a rear window. He felt certain that the bus was not being followed. Yet his intuition told him to stay put. The incident at the airport was far too unexpected. No one should have known who he was. How someone had known his identity, not to mention the details of his mission, was of grave concern. The only information he had received was the "Your Eyes Only" folder and the first class airline ticket that had been hand delivered by a courier who was familiar to him. Before opening the folder on the plane, all that he knew was he was flying to Hawaii, at the request of the nation's President, of course. It was a mystery, a mystery that would have to be solved. The President was not going to like hearing this one.

The rain had now slowed to a light drizzle, so the windows in the bus were not as obscured as before. While the others slowly made their way to the door, all clamoring with the excitement of finally reaching their destination, Trevor slipped into the rear bathroom. "Now what?" he thought, lifting his briefcase up to the sink. Inside was a black leather case about the size of his laptop computer. This was a standard CIA issue makeup case. One never knew when one must change appearances. Considering his limited clothing options and the time constraints, Brice decided that his life, at least for now, should be spent as the Reverend Dr. Samuel Spencer, the retired black minister from Bude, Mississippi. This was certainly going to be a stretch, as Trevor possessed no black facial features that would validate the tone of color that was quickly covering his exposed skin. Brice, a 38-year-old with sandy blond hair and 195 pounds on his six-foot athletic frame, was an unassuming individual despite incredible good looks. His clear, almost transparent blue eyes always caught people's attention. Thankfully, there were contact lenses in the case that allowed him to alter his eye color as well. An electric clipper reduced his blond hair to a buzz cut and with a little bit of hair dye he looked just like, well hell, a white guy in black face. The reflection in the mirror confirmed the feeble attempt. At least it was night and the surrounding area was quite dark. Finally, realizing the lily-white pants would cause him to stand out like a sore thumb, he took out a tin of black shoe polish and streaked the white pants as best he could. Not perfect, but it would have to do. The Banyan trees would provide good cover for him to make his way through the park, across the golf course and onto the highway, about a half-mile away.

After 30 minutes passed, the last of the tourists had gotten off the bus and claimed their luggage. As the hotel bell staff was scurrying around like an army of ants, no one noticed a young woman who walked up and slipped a large Pullman into the baggage compartment under the belly of the bus. She then closed the compartment door, latched it and slipped off into the crowd and eventually into the night. Once again, the large bus engine roared to life and pulled away. Next stop, the tour company's terminal to put the bus to bed and then home for the night, or so the driver thought. The bus had traveled about 200 feet when Trevor/ Dr. Spencer exited the restroom and slipped quietly into one of the rearmost seats on the right side. As the driver made his way down Banyan Drive to the intersection of Highways 11 and 19, he did not notice that the rear emergency window of his bus had been pushed out and had fallen to the ground, followed immediately by a dark figure with a briefcase. Trevor hit the ground, rolled once and slipped off into the shadows of the Banyan trees. He took a quick look around and then 10 seconds later, running through the shadows of the trees, was knocked off his feet by an incredible explosion. Now lying flat on his back on the rain-soaked ground, he looked over to see only the burning chassis of the bus. The entire coach section, from front to rear, was gone. The burning hulk was still rolling. It came to rest 50 feet later, after jumping the curb and coming to rest against a large coconut palm. For several moments Brice did not move. He studied the area for any sign of the person responsible, but nothing. People from the hotels and condominiums were running to the scene. A Hilo police officer who happened to be in front of the adjacent hotel left his car and was doing his best to keep the crowd back. He had the presence of mind to realize that there was no point in calling the fire department, as half the island could see the flames and had heard the blast. While the confusion and chaos grew and sirens filled the night, Trevor slowly crawled on his belly toward the golf course. When he reached the drainage canal at the edge of the Banyan grove, he turned right and headed toward downtown instead of left toward the heavily wooded park. This was contradictory to logic, but with any luck it would also be unexpected.

## The Summer Palace - Beijing

President Totten was instantly incensed on hearing the Chinese leader's demands. He sat up erect, both hands gripping the arms of the chair. He leaned forward and asked, "Just whom the hell do you think you are speaking to? May I remind you, sir, that my country, the United States of America, is the most powerful country on this planet? I am not about to hand over all that you ask for, or any part of it for that matter. Where do you get the audacity to even think such a thing?"

Premier Lolo relaxed into his chair and curled up one side of his mouth in a faint smile. "Correction, sir," scolded Lolo "the United States *was* the greatest power in the world. The People's Republic of China now assumes that position."

"Why you arrogant..." Totten started to raise his voice, but was cut off by the Chinese Premier.

"Darnestown, Maryland? I am sure that you are familiar with that wonderful little town," said An Lolo. This got the President's immediate attention. "The people who are in charge of your well being have just completed the new security bunker for you and certain other leaders of your country. That bunker is, as you well know, 60 feet under the center of that lovely town."

Lolo looked at his watch and smiled. "I believe that you are having what your people call an Open House there today with many dignitaries and other important visitors. I suppose that many of your country's leaders are in attendance. Oh, and I believe that the town is also having some type of festival. A homecoming, I think it is called. It is most unfortunate that the elimination of that facility has caused so much devastation to such a wonderful community." The Premier's words were terse, biting and extended a very strong note of finality.

Totten just stared at the Premier wondering how he could have possibly known of the top secret Darnestown Project and just what he meant about it being destroyed. His mind was racing; all of this was too much to digest in just a short amount of time. Lolo just sat there with a look of complete satisfaction covering his face. Totten's secure satellite phone had been vibrating in his pocket off and on for the past 20 minutes. Lolo was waiting for something. The continuing vibration in his left coat pocket and Lolo's veiled threat forced him to finally reach for the phone. With great trepidation, he first pressed in the security code then placed the phone next to his ear.

"Jaymar, has something happened at home?" he asked.

An Lolo sat back in his chair and folded his hands, watching as Totten's eyes grew wide and his mouth fell open.

"You son-of-a-bitch," he shouted at Lolo, in a shaky voice, "there were 25,000 people living there! What the fuck is the matter with you?"

The phone fell from his hands and bounced onto the mosaic tile floor as he lunged forward and wrapped his hands around the neck of the Chinese leader. The palace guards reacted almost as quickly. Totten was subdued, pulled away and thrown roughly to the floor. He sprang to his feet and whirled around, only to find that he was staring into the muzzles of eight Chinese machine guns. He then heard a strange sound coming from the hallway just on the other side of the doors. It was a sound he could not identify, but unnerved him nonetheless.

Out in the hall, just 40 feet away, the Presidential party waited in the company of the Palace Guards while Totten and Lolo met privately. The sounds of Totten's pained ejaculation on learning the news from home caused Secret Service Agent Donaldson to react just as he was trained to react. With weapon drawn he bolted for the door. Three of the guards stepped in to stop him and a brief struggle ensued. The other agents had already been stopped by the heavily armed patrols.

An Lolo rose, adjusted himself, rubbed his neck and walked over to where Totten now stood. "You have 72 hours in which to comply with my demands, Mr. President. After that, I am afraid, another one of your charming little communities will suffer a similar fate."

# Freedom's Menace

At that, Lolo turned and calmly walked from the room through a side door. The President could only gaze down the barrels of the guards' guns. A small, strange looking man whom Totten had not seen enter the room approached, reached down and picked up the phone laying next to the balcony doors. He handed it to the President and motioned him toward the door. With this, the guards lowered their guns and backed away. For several seconds, Totten just stood there in stunned silence.

"Your car is waiting," said the man in very good English, again gesturing toward the door.

Entering the Grand Hall from the study, he found his Secretary of State, General Persi, four aides and seven of eight Secret Service agents huddled in the middle of the room, surrounded by a squad of armed palace guards, weapons at the ready. He quickly surveyed the group and in a measured tone, asked, "Where is Donaldson?"

The looks from the others caused him to turn and look over his left shoulder. There, in a pool of blood, lay Steve Donaldson, 38 years old, father of four and a 10-year veteran of the Secret Service. Suddenly, Totten's head, face and neck seemed to be on fire. He had never felt rage like this before. He shut his eyes and took in several deep breaths. He walked over to the body and bent down. Behind the left ear was a single bullet hole. He searched through Donaldson's pockets and removed all of his personal effects: wallet, gun, badge, wedding ring, wristwatch and radio. He then walked over to the strange, little man and said, "Would you please arrange for his remains to be delivered to my aircraft? I will be leaving in two hours."

The little man bowed politely and stepped back, providing President Totten clear passage. He approached his party and motioned for them to follow him. The guards

lowered their weapons and a confused and saddened group
of Americans walked out of the Summer Palace and into
their awaiting limousines. Inside the limousine, Totten
gave but one instruction: "Not another word until we are
aboard Air Force One!"

# 4

## Darnestown, Maryland

The giant 112,000-square-foot security bunker that had
been built under the Greenbrier Hotel in White Sulfur
Springs, West Virginia, was now a hotel tourist attraction.
The massive underground facility had been built at the
height of the Cold War in the early 1960s under the veil of a
hotel expansion project. The bunker was staffed and
equipped to serve as an emergency Capitol for both Houses
of Congress and other government leaders in the event of a
nuclear attack. It had been shuttered in the early 1990s on
the pretense that the Cold War was over, but in actuality,
the secret of its existence had been leaked to the press.
President Bush had approved a new facility to be built
under the quiet community of Darnestown, Maryland,
about 20 miles northwest of downtown Washington, D.C.
This state of the art hideaway was designed to serve the
country for at least the next 100 years. At quarter mile in
diameter and eight stories deep, the facility was a crowning
achievement for the Army Corps of Engineers. They were
particularly proud of the entrance, the #3 loading dock at
the newly built Wal-Mart Super Center. This was the only

retail establishment in the country that was, with the exception of the manager and assistant manager, 100% staffed by government agents. All proceeds from the store went toward the operation of the underground city.

The series of explosions that imploded it started at the lower levels and worked upward to the top floors in a matter of milliseconds. The collapsing structure caused a chain reaction all the way to the surface of the earth, 60 feet above, to the doomed village of Darnestown. The result was a sinkhole that literally swallowed the town. All that remained was a crater, one mile wide and more than 100 feet deep. This was the information that Chief of Staff Jaymar Jones had relayed to the President as he sat three feet in front of Lolo. At the time, the information was only 20 minutes old and had not even been picked up by CNN. Most of the world would not know for some time that this apparent natural disaster was the result of terrorism.

## Downtown Hilo, Hawaii

Within five minutes of the bus explosion, Brice had made his way across Highway 19 to a gas station where, for $20, he convinced a local resident to give him a lift to the airport.

"So, bro," said the local, "why you dressed and made up that a way? If you are trying to look like a native, just spend a few days on our beaches."

Trevor just laughed and said that he was playing a joke on a friend who he was to meet at the airport. By the time he was dropped off in front of the Alamo desk, the downpour of rain had resumed. He learned that the only available vehicle was a minivan (yuck!). He offered the clerk Dr. Spencer's driver's license and credit card. She was too preoccupied with her *People* magazine to even give much consideration to the picture and the person standing at her counter. As she finalized his car rental contract, a large Hawaiian, about 20 years old, entered from the back door. Joey Chan was a local college student who was working his way through school as the company's car jockey. He dropped several sets of car keys onto the desk and said that this was the last of the available cars. Trevor turned and looked through the sheets of rain across the roadway into the terminal where he spotted his suitcase still sitting next to the carousel, in open view. He turned to the young man and inquired as to his interest in earning an extra $20 for retrieving the suitcase. He was going through $20 bills as if they were water. Of course Joey was interested. The bright orange L. L. Bean duffel with the initials TCB was not hard to spot.

"I'll bring it to your car, sir, what slot are you in?" he asked.

"Slot 21, the green minivan. And Mahalo," said Trevor.

As Joey braved the rain to get the case, Trevor went in the opposite direction to the van. The van was parked on the far right side of the lot, near the entrance gate to the rental car lot. Thankfully, the van had been backed into the slot, giving an unobstructed, forward-facing yet distant view of the baggage area. Trevor reached the van and started the engine just in time to see Joey pick up the suitcase. He did not get more than 10 feet before three men of Asian descent fell in behind him. This was all Trevor needed to know. He threw the gearshift into drive and, as he started to pull out, spotted a rental car coming through the entrance to be returned. As the car passed, he pulled the minivan forward and interrupted the electric sensor, thus preventing the gate from dropping back down. The sign on the right stated in large red letters, **"DO NOT ENTER SEVERE TIRE DAMAGE WILL OCCUR."**

Knowing that this would only happen if he were going too fast, he slowly and deliberately pulled the van forward up and over the spikes. A quick left and then a right put him heading out of the airport against traffic, in the pouring rain. Several hundred feet ahead the road became two-way again, and he sped away. The headlights of the van were not turned on until he turned left onto Highway 11.

About a mile down the road, he made a quick left into the parking lot of Hilo Hatties, the Hawaiian clothing and souvenir shop. Brice pulled in between to other two rental cars, got out and went into the store. After leaving and tossing his purchases into the van, he walked across the street to the local Wal-Mart. Thirty minutes later he was back in the van heading south with several more changes of clothes, a small gym bag, personal hygiene supplies. For dinner he treated himself to a couple of hot dogs and a Coke from the Wal-Mart snack shop. With any luck he had gotten out of the airport without being seen. Considering that someone obviously knew too much about his covert life, he had to assume that they knew a great deal about his personal life as well. The minivan should provide good cover, considering it was nothing like what he would drive in real life. He was now heading south to the Volcanoes National Park. It was only a 20-mile drive, but he thought it wise to assure himself that he was not being followed. He had disconnected the brake lights before leaving the shopping center, a risky move on a rain-soaked darkened highway. The macadamia nut groves along both sides of the highway provided excellent cover, as he would occasionally pull off and wait for a period of time, to survey the parade of passing cars. Two hours later, he pulled up to the park entrance, advised the ranger that he was going to the Kilauea Military Camp and paid the $10 entry fee.

The Kilauea Military Camp had been built during World War II as an R&R facility for service men stationed in the Pacific region. The camp remained open for current military personnel, as well as former service men and their families who are visiting the area. The camp consists of single room cottages, a recreation hall and a mess. But like all military facilities, it was an excellent place to store a wide variety of military supplies. If the United States military does nothing else right, it certainly plans well for contingencies. Brice secured his cottage, took a quick shower, just to rinse off, and hit the bed. Sleep was the only thing that he could think of at that point. The dim green number from the clock radio sitting next to the single bed read 1:54 am, 5:54 am St. Louis time.

The morning fog was burned off by 9:30 am. Trevor awoke when the first sunbeam fell across his face. Taking in a deep breath, he sensed the faint odor of sulfur that emanated from the numerous sulfur cones around the Kilauea volcano. His mind quickly reviewed the events of the previous night. It was the first chance that he had to reflect on the magnitude of the fact that someone knew his identity and the reason he was really there. It was going to be a busy day, but first he had to get a cup of coffee, some of that wonderful Kona coffee that grows on this island. But even that had to wait until the good Dr. Spencer was washed down the drain and Charles Reidelberger of Schenectady, New York, took his place. Mr. Reidelberger was a free-lance writer of hiking and backpacking adventures. He was in Volcanoes National Park to research an article for *National Geographic Explorer* magazine. An article that would detail the thrill of hiking over an active volcano should sell quite well.

On entering the mess hall, he spotted the base commander sitting with a group of older veterans and their wives. He grabbed a cup of coffee and ordered a breakfast of pork chops, eggs, toast and brown rice. The table next to the commander's was vacant, so he grabbed a seat and waited.

He had finished eating and was on his second cup of coffee when the Commander bid his guest farewell and rose to leave.

"Colonel Kwiatkowski, may I have a moment?" asked Trevor. The Colonel glanced at his watch and said, "Only a moment."

He extended his hand as he sat down across from Brice. "I am in need of a few necessities that I believe you have available," he said softly as a thin black leather wallet was placed in front of the Army officer. Kwiatkowski opened the wallet and studied the contents, a picture ID on one side and brief statement signed by the President stating the person on the facing photo reported directly to the Commander-in-Chief and should be granted complete cooperation. His left eyebrow rose, then his right brow, followed by a long stare at Brice over the top of his glasses.

"This is all very impressive young man," he said, "but this don't mean shit to me. What else you got?" Brice reached over and retrieved the wallet. From the back he pulled out a small business card and handed it to the colonel.

"If you will please take the time to call that number, I think that all your questions will be answered," said Brice.

"Ok, if this all checks out, I'll pick you up out front in 10 minutes," he instructed.

The colonel left, and Trevor finished his cup of coffee before stepping outside to savor the day. It would likely be his last opportunity for a while. The sky was clear and the air cool, as is normal at 4,200 feet above sea level. The immediate area around the camp was wooded, with mounds of the rough, lumpy 'A'a lava and long dry grasses dotting the landscape. Just beyond the sparse spread of trees to the south was the Kilauea Caldera, the most active volcano in the world. This was truly one of the most spectacular places that he had ever visited. Too bad he was not going to get to enjoy it this trip.

"Danielle and I will have to bring the kids back here sometime," he thought.

The squeal of the brakes from the Colonel's Humvee broke the trance. Trevor ran around the back of the Humvee and hopped in next to him. Off they sped, toward the back of the camp, and disappeared around the mounds of lava that formed a small natural boundary.

"You didn't tell me that phone number would be answered by the Big Man himself. I almost wet myself. Want to tell me just who the hell you are?"

Brice just gave him a look and a grin.

Since being plucked from the ranks of his Air Force ROTC class at Cornell 15 years earlier, he had always appreciated the opportunity to use his gifts and skills to serve his country. For the past 10 years, he had served as a special "advisor" to three presidents. So secret was his existence, the outgoing President would privately brief the incoming chief executive of Mr. Brice and his unique services. The new President also learned of the other four individuals who were at his beck and call, like Brice, each one possessing broad-based talents that served the country quite well in times of need. This unique group, consisting of three women and two men, had the full backing of the office of the leader of the free world. They also had access to the latest and greatest innovations and information that our government could provide. Only four other people even knew of this group's existence: the directors of the CIA and

FBI, the speaker of the House of Representatives and the vice-president. Only the President knew their names and the method of contacting them. They each had the President's direct telephone numbers and his private, secured website address. The vast funds required for supporting this group of specialists was a simple, inconspicuous line item entry in the operating budget of the recently completed Super Conducting Super Collider, a giant atom smasher buried under the state of Texas.

The area they entered was filled with sulfur cones. The stench of rotten eggs almost caused him to lose his morning meal. They made a quick right and drove about a quarter mile. Just past a large mound of 'A'a lava, they approached a small area surrounded by mounds of lava, long grass and covered in camouflage netting. An armed military guard stepped forward and requested identification. On inspecting Kwiatkowski's ID, he relaxed his posture, stepped back and gave a high sign. A second guard walked over to a small metal box that was mounted on the side of the lava wall and retrieved a set of keys. He then unlocked a door that was built into the side of the 20-foot-high mound of lava. The guard entered the dark doorway and seconds later flipped on a light switch. The light illuminated a set of steps that lead down to another door about one story below ground.

"Do you require assistance, Colonel?" asked the guard.

Kwiatkowski waved him off, and he and Trevor made their way down the steps. Trevor glanced around at the sound of the outside door being shut and locked behind them. Colonel Kwiatkowski possessed the key to the second door. Inside was a 15,000-square-foot military warehouse, filled mostly with survival gear, as well as the necessary guns and ammunition. The small arms cabinet was the first stop. Brice chose a Glock 9 mm, four spare clips and several boxes of ammunition. His own gun was still inside his suitcase.

"Is this weapon really Army issue?" he queried.

The only response was a twinkle in the eyes of the Army officer. Next a backpack, hiking boots, compass, first aid kit and a canteen. Finally, some mountaineering gear. If he were going to get a good look at that submarine, he would have to rappel down to it. Everything just fit into the backpack. Sixty pounds of gear, but it was all necessary.

"Oops! Almost forgot. What do you have in the way of satellite location devices? I have one on my phone, but I'd like a back up."

"Anything that you want," came the response.

Three raps on the outside door and the guard opened it. The two men stepped into the sunshine and loaded the Humvee. The first guard politely wished him good luck as they drove away.

"Thanks for everything, Colonel," Trevor said, when dropped off in front of the cottage. He was impressed at Kwiatkowski's professionalism, as he had not inquired about the nature of the assignment.

It was now noon, making it 4:00 pm in St. Louis. He called home on his secure satellite phone to tell Danielle and the kids that he had arrived safely and all was well. "Better late than never," he thought. He described the small, but comfortable cottage with its stained glass rear window. All the cabins had original and unique stained glass windows, not what one would expect at a military camp. He did not know whose idea that was, certainly not the Army's, but he liked the touch. His family was happy to

hear from him, as they had heard about a bus that blew up
in Hilo, killing the driver. The shooting incident at the
airport had not yet made the national news. This was likely
because the gunshot wound was not discovered until the
victim had been treated in the Hilo hospital. Having
occurred at an airport, the FBI was now involved. This is
not the kind of thing that they liked to make public if at all
possible, but the news would seep out soon enough,
regardless. Secure in the knowledge that all was well at
home, Trevor loaded the minivan and headed off to the
Hawaiian Volcano Observatory, which is located next to the
Jaggar Museum and less than a quarter mile from Kilauea
Military Camp. It was time to meet Dr. Allison.

Freedom's Menace

# 5

## Hawaiian Volcano Observatory

The Hawaiian Volcano Observatory is not a public facility and therefore, does not have what one would call a main entrance. Access is only available through an unmarked metal door that operated via a credit card style scanner, much like a modern hotel room lock and key. Luckily, in this day and age, people are forced to come outside to have their necessary smoke. The first one to need his fix was one Don Rogers. "Excuse me," said Brice, walking toward the man. "I'm looking for a Dr. Samantha Allison. Do you know if she is in?"

It took Rogers several attempts to light the cigarette as he studied the stranger. "Sir, I'm sorry, but this facility is off limits to the public," replied Rogers, nervously puffed on the burning weed.

"I understand, but if she is in, would you please tell her that there is someone out here that would like to talk to her about submarines?" asked Trevor with a smile.

41

"Submarines? Dr. Allison is a vulcanologist, not an oceanographer. Why would you want to talk to her about submarines?"

Forcing a small chuckle, Brice smiled wide and said, "The truth is that we went to college at Cornell together. I'm visiting Hawaii for a few days, and I just wanted to say hello."

The man just stared at him and finally said, "Oh, I get it. Submarines, submarine races. Ya, ya! I got it." He dropped the half-smoked butt into an urn next to the sidewalk. "Sam's not in!" he said sharply. He turned, swiped his key card in the scanner and disappeared behind the door.

Damn, some people! "Well," he thought, "she has to go home sometime. I'll just wait until she does." He was heading up the path to the parking lot to get something to read when the sound of the observatory door crashing open caused him to stop and turn. Out the door came a most attractive brunette, five foot four, late 20s or early 30s, wearing khaki shorts, hiking boots and a gray tee shirt that was emblazoned in red with the words "Lava Lover" across the chest.

"Who the hell are you?" she demanded. "How dare you tell that twit Rogers that my old college lover is out here waiting for me! Who the fuck are you? And what do you want?" she persisted. "I've never seen yo…"

Trevor raised his hands and in a pleading voice said, "Hold it. Let me get a word in edgewise and I'll tell you."

Her dark brown eyes burned right through him as she said, "You have 10 seconds before I kick your ass!"

He smiled, reached into his shirt pocket and pulled out the picture of the Chinese sub. She felt her heart skip a beat when her eyes fell on the photo, a photo that she had taken just days before. Her mouth fell open and instantly went dry. Her eyes widened, as she looked straight into his.

"Maybe we should go somewhere and talk," he suggested. She gave a slight nod, her mouth still agape, held up an index finger to say wait one minute, and disappeared back into the concrete block building. Seconds later, she emerged with a backpack, sunglasses and a bottle of Naya water.

"I'll drive," she said, matter of factly. She hurried past him, moving toward her burnt orange and brown Jeep Wrangler. As she tossed her stuff into the back seat, she gestured for Trevor to get in. Trevor grabbed his gear from the back of the minivan and they were off.

The convertible top of the Jeep was off and the sun warmed his face in the cool air as she made a left turn and headed down toward the volcano's southern rift zone. At first, not a word was spoken as they drove through the volcanic wasteland. Again he marveled at what a spectacular place this was. Most people, when thinking of Hawaii, imagine palm trees, white beaches and tropical rain forests. This part of Hawaii was the exact opposite. Yet it was equally as unique as any other place on these islands. The silence was broken with Sam saying, "Well, you obviously know who I am. Who might you be?"

"My name is Charles Reidelberger," Brice began, "and all that I can tell you is that I work for Uncle Sam. I am here to see your submarine. Beyond that I cannot tell you much. Clearly, you understand the implications. Otherwise, you would not have taken the steps that you did in order to keep your findings quiet."

43

Sam looked at him and moments later she turned left as she wheeled the Jeep into a parking lot and climbed out. "Come on, Charles Reidelberger," she said, "First, I'll teach you a little bit about volcanoes."

They left the parking lot and headed for the Halema'uma'u trail. According to the signs, they were literally walking on top of the active Kilauea volcano. The ground was gray, barren and broken. It was all lava, with the exception of an occasional plant that was trying to reestablish itself in the rich soil that forms over time from the natural breaking down of the lava. Reading from the information signs, Brice learned that the last time a lava flow had occurred on this spot was 1940, but a few hundred feet away one could walk on lava from 1971, 1974 and as late as 1984. Dr. Allison began doing what she loved to do best, teaching about volcanoes.

"All of this in front of us is the Kilauea caldera. Centuries ago, when Kilauea was first formed it probably looked like most mountains would look to you, with a pointed top and sloping sides. At least that's one hypothesis, obviously no one knows for sure. At some point in time, long before Adam and Eve, Kilauea blew its top. That's why the surrounding area is so flat. Not like Mauna Loa over there," she said pointing to the massive sister volcano. "A volcano is a lot like a bottle of champagne. If you gently remove the cork without shaking the bottle, the eruption is pretty mild. However, if you shake it up, all of that carbonated gas builds more and more pressure. When you pop the cork, all of those bubbles rush out at once. In the case of a volcano, the scenario is similar, but the pressure builds to the point that the cork pops all by itself."

Brice was listening but had stopped to look at a steady puff of white steam coming from a crack in the lava. He reached down and fanned the vapor, but before Sam could stop him he stuck his fingers into the crack. "Yeow!" he exclaimed, drawing back his burned fingers. "Son of a bitch! That's hot! Shit!" he cursed.

With a laugh the vulcanologist said, "You silly man. You wouldn't stick your hand inside a tea kettle would you?" Trevor felt a bit stupid and just shook his hand to cool it off.

Sam continued, "Steam vents are quite common. These natural teakettles form when rainwater seeps into the cracks on the surface and encounters a very hot layer of rock only a couple of meters down. The water boils and produces the steam. In some places, the steam brings sulfur to the surface and deposits it in mounds. Those are called sulfur cones. As I am sure you have noticed, the rotten egg odor permeates the air in some spots."

They were heading for the Halema'uma'u crater. Dr. Allison continued her lesson, "This place is sacred or *kapu* to the traditional Hawaiians. Frequently, you will see the native people performing ceremonies at the crater's rim. It is believed that this place is the home of Pele, the Goddess of Fire. When we get to the observation point, you will see the many flowers that have been brought to Pele."

After 10 minutes of stopping to permit Trevor to examine every loose piece of lava along the path, they finally reached the observation area. In front of them lay a crater that was more than 200 feet deep and a little more than a half-mile wide. The floor has been steadily rising due to the pressures of the molten magma underneath the surface. "In the 1920s, this was an active, bubbling lava pool. The surface cooled in the 1920s and solidified 800 feet below the rim. It has risen almost 500 feet in the past 80 years, and it is still moving upward. Just under all of that ashen gray surface lies a lake of molten rock."

"I understand that the lava is not flowing here on top of the volcano, but rather at a place called the Pu'u 'O'o vent, which is where the submarine is located. Would you explain that to me?" Brice asked.

"Sure," she answered, "the Pu'u 'O'o vent is on the Kilauea volcano. Volcanoes here are very large and spread out. We have two active volcanoes side-by-side, Mauna Loa and Kilauea. Mauna Loa is the largest mountain on the planet and is still growing but it is not producing lava. At least not right now. The last time it produced was in 1984. It is twice as tall as Mt. Everest if measured from the ocean floor."

"What changed to cause Mauna Loa to stop producing lava while Kilauea has been so prolific for so long?" asked Brice

"The answer, in part, is simple," answered Samantha. "The path of least resistance is one reason. The other reason is that the earth's crust rests on tectonic plates. The plate that we are on is moving sort of northwest at a rate of about three inches each year. The center of the magma chamber, or hot spot, happens to be under Kilauea right now. In several thousand years, it will be under Lo'ihi," she explained.

"Lo'ihi? Where is that?" he asked.

"Oh, about 20 miles that way," she said, pointing out to sea. "You see Lo'ihi is already a sizable and active volcano, but it is still 3,000 feet under water. Someday, a very long time from now, people will visit its splendor just as we are here today, enjoying the Island of Hawaii. Pretty cool, don't you think?" A smile came over her face.

"Back to our lesson on lava flows," she continued. "When the column of magma begins to work its way to the surface, think of it as a giant oak tree. The trunk of this tree emanates from the main reservoir, which is about two miles beneath us. As the magma raises it follows the path, or paths, of least resistance, creating branches of cracks and fissures in the ground. We call them rifts. Kilauea has southern and eastern rift zones. What we call the vent is the location where those branches break through the surface. The branches are conduits for the lava to flow through to the surface. Today that path of least resistance takes the lava to the Pu'u 'O'o vent, which is almost 15 miles away along the eastern rift. Let me clarify what I mean by today. Pu'u 'O'o has been running continuously since the early 1980s. This has not been, nor will it always be, the case. At some point, the magma chamber will recede and the lava flow will cease, at least for a while. Pu'u 'O'o may even seal itself. At some other point in the future, the pressure in the magma column will build again and Kilauea will once again erupt. When and where that will occur no one can say with any certainty."

W. Laurence Willis

# 6

## The Birth of an Island

"If you are ready, we can go to see a real lava flow, up close and personal," she said, turning and starting for the parking lot. "The lava flow from Pu'u 'O'o travels down the face of Kilauea for a little more than five miles until it reaches the coast. At that point it flows over a cliff, like a giant quarter mile long waterfall, and drops down over 100 feet into the ocean."

The drive down Chain of Craters road was about 25 miles. Brice was here to learn about the submarine and this was a good time to start. "Sam, tell me about the sub," insisted Trevor.

After a long sigh and a shake of the head to indicate continued disbelief, Dr. Allison began to tell her story. "As we discussed earlier, Pu'u 'O'o has been actively producing lava since the early 1980s. About 18 months ago, the flow started to subside. Within about 4 months, the flow rate was down about 85%. All of the experts, including myself, had decided that the magma chamber was receding and that Kilauea was going to be quiet for a while. From a vulcanologist's perspective, this had been a great run. We really have learned a lot over the last 20 plus years. In fact, there was an air of sadness around the office. Anyway, the flow leveled out for about a month and then one day, a year ago September, all flow suddenly stopped, as if the conduit had become plugged.

With the cessation of flow, we started to get significant seismic activity in the area around Pu'u 'O'o. Most of the people on the island thought of it as just another set of temblors, but the coincidence of the stoppage of lava flow and the temblors was too significant for us to dismiss so lightly. Today our thinking is that part of the conduit that feeds Pu'u 'O'o collapsed and had been collapsing over that seven month period. The final collapse was like putting the cork back in the champagne bottle and then shaking like hell. Thirty-six hours after Pu'u 'O'o stopped flowing, the damn thing erupted again. Luckily, the seismic activity told us to get our people away from the area, which we did.

"The most recent eruption expanded the size of the crater in the vent to three times its previous diameter. Being lava lovers, this was like a wet dream. We had people all around the vent, doing what we do, within hours, but it was spewing lava over a wide area. We could only get so close, even wearing our protective gear. By close, I mean one-half mile away. One of our first objectives was to get as many aerial photos as possible, in order to record the event. The early photos weren't the best due to the volume of steam, gas and magma being expelled. As things settled down the photos showed us that there was what looked like a second conduit in the crater, about 15 feet wide, next to the active vent. But, since there was no lava flowing from it, we assumed that the eruption had just blown a large hole in the ground, which seemed perfectly normal. Three weeks ago, we finally got close enough to examine that crater without the cumbersome protective gear. What we found was that the second crater looked like a bottomless pit. Of course, it is hard to determine the depth visually since it got dark about 15 feet down. It's also hot as hell in there. We again donned the metallic high temperature suits and used metal shields to deflect the heat, but that is still only partly effective. Anyway, 10 days ago, after we first determined that the hole might have some depth to it, three of us decided to find out what was down there and how deep it went. We have, or had, an electronic package that included a video camera that was designed for use in high temperature areas. It was equipped with a sophisticated lighting system, as well as the ability to take infrared photos and record temperatures. It was a great tool, on loan to us from the Navy."

"You keep talking about it in the past tense," noted Trevor. "What happened to it?"

Dropping her head and shaking it she said, "The damn volcano ate it. The cable system got too hot and melted away. The whole thing is lying on the bottom somewhere. That's why you don't have a better photo of the sub. That's also the reason there are only a few of us that know about what was captured on the photograph. In case you were wondering, that is the only photo of the submarine that I got before I lost the camera."

"Who else knows about the sub?" he demanded.

"To my knowledge only me, you, and Admiral Hanover. I developed the photos myself. How many people may have seen it between the time the Admiral saw it and you did, I have no idea," she responded.

The brakes on the Jeep were suddenly locked up, tires smoking and squealing as they skidded to a halt. Twenty feet in front of them was a family of goose-like fowl nonchalantly walking across the road. "Damn, Nene!" She cussed at the birds. "That is the state bird of Hawaii. Any wonder why they're endangered?"

She laid on the horn and the birds just stopped and looked at her with complete indifference. She continued her rant, "This is why we have so much trouble keeping them alive. They'll just stand there and get run over. Well, Mr. Reidelberger, consider yourself lucky! Most people never get to even see a Nene." Samantha got out and shooed the birds off to the side and they continued toward the lava flow.

Ten minutes later they pulled up to a dead end, where the road was closed by earlier lava flows. There was a long line of cars on the left side of the road, which belonged to the tourists who were there to make the long trek out to the flow. The National Park Service had built toilets, an information booth, a ranger office and a turn around at the end of the road. Sam turned the Jeep around and headed back up the road until she found a parking spot about a quarter mile away.

"This will be the easy part of the hike," she said smiling and hopped out. "It is hot today, so you will need water and a hat. We have to hike in about one and a half to two miles. Bring a camera if you have one. This is a spectacular experience. Oh, and watch for cars. People have a bad habit of not paying attention to their driving along here." Her words of caution did not come a moment too soon as a car with three large Asian men swerved, forcing them to jump between two of the parked cars. "See what I mean."

Brice did not dismiss the event as easily as she had. After all there were three Asians who jumped the car jockey who had gone to retrieve his suitcase. Brice paused and watched as the car pulled ahead and disappeared over the hill.

"Let's go," Sam said. "They were just tourists that didn't have the balls to make the hike. It's their loss."

Trevor wasn't so sure, but turned and followed her down the road toward the path that would take them to the flow area. She had been right about the first quarter mile being the easiest. He was somewhat amazed at the number of people out here ready to make the difficult trek to the flow. The lava-covered ground was much different here than on the Kilauea Caldera. The flow patterns seemed to change every few feet. The smooth, rope like texture of the Pahoehoe lava quickly changed into the rough, uneven and mounding layers of 'A'a lava. The lava was also much darker here, quite black compared to the gray color he had experienced before. The patterns and colors were amazing, he thought, recalling that he was also here as a designer seeking inspiration for the Blue Hawaiian Hotel project. One certainly does not have to look far for inspiration.

"Why are there so many different colors?" he asked as he picked up a broken sample which displayed gold, blue, purple and red against the black, once melted rock.

Dr. Allison was obviously enjoying her opportunity to teach someone about her favorite subject as she responded, "What you are seeing is the minerals and metals that mix with the magma deep inside the earth. Each material cools and solidifies at a different temperature. These materials plate out on the surfaces of the lava. The piece you have looks like the mold of someone's finger on the inside, long and hollow. That's the result of a large gas pocket. When the lava cooled, it left that hollow "finger" inside. As you can see the rock hardened first, then the minerals plated out later."

She then reached down and picked up some long fibers that were about four inches long and resembled blond hairs. "This," she said, "is Pele's Hair. When the volcano erupts and spews matter into the air, it will form long thin streams that solidify and are carried away by the wind. Look around, it's everywhere. We can find this miles and miles away from the source."

About three fourths of the way to the flow, Trevor was startled by the fact that the ground had become suddenly and distinctly hotter. "Whoa!" he exclaimed, "What the hell is going on here? Is this safe?"

Her answer was a little unnerving as she explained that although the surface was solid, the material just a few feet underneath was still molten. The thought of the surface breaking away and him becoming a human fondue was not comforting.

"Are you sure that this is ok?" he asked.

"It's fine," she said, laughing. "Come on and stop being such a wimp!"

They finally arrived at their destination. The hot lava could be seen flowing on top of older flows. The surface was a light ashen gray, similar to what he had seen at Kilauea. The air above the flow was very wavy and almost opaque due to the intense heat radiating from it with much more intensity than that of a backyard grill. In places, they could see the red-hot lava, in patches that Sam described as skylights, as it flowed past them toward the sea. She had been right. It was truly an astounding sight.

One hundred yards ahead, there was a group of about two-dozen people standing at the very edge of the cliff, only an arm's reach away from where the lava was cascading over the side. The two got in queue behind the group and made their way closer to the exciting view. Dr. Allison stepped to the side as they approached to give others the opportunity to see the actual making of an island. She got to see this stuff most every day and was enjoying watching the reaction of others seeing it for the first time. As is usually the case when a group of people gets together, everyone wanted to see the action at once. The normal crowding and bumping was taking place. When it finally became apparent that Trevor was going to get his turn at an unobstructed view, the pushing became a little more intense.

Suddenly, he got the sensation that this was not the normal bump and grind taking place behind him, but rather, he was being pushed forward. Then two strong vice-like hands grabbed his arms just above the elbows and he felt himself being forced closer to the 2,000-degree river of lava. His reaction was instant and instinctive. He let his knees buckle as his right foot shot out in front to provide some leverage. At the same moment, he let his full weight fall backward. The man behind him was briefly taken by surprise and loosened his grip as his momentum carried him forward, just slightly. But that was all that Brice needed. Instantly, Trevor reached up and behind, grabbing his assailant's shirt by the collar and then pitching his weight forward. The man's own weight and forward motion, combined with Brice's actions, carried him over the top of his intended victim, in summersault fashion. He landed four feet away, flat on his back atop the molten rock. The only sound he made was that of his last breath being inhaled as he went over the cliff. Even before the man's body went out of sight Brice had rolled twice to his left to get away from the edge and to position himself for another attack. Screams from the sparse crowd filled the air.

# Freedom's Menace

He regained his footing and stood upright while his right hand went for the Glock 9mm he had tucked into the back of his belt. But before he could get his hand on the gun, two other men grabbed him, pinning his arms to his side, lifting him off the ground. The men were massive, well over 6 feet tall, each weighing in excess of 300 pounds. The men from the airport! Without the benefit of touching the earth, Brice could manage only a modest squirm. He could touch the butt of the gun with his fingertips, but just barely. As the two men stepped closer to the precipice, ready to launch him over the side, Sam Allison took the only weapon at her disposal a three fourths filled bottle of Naya water, and slammed it against the ear of the assassin on Trevor's right. The momentary shock caused him to loosen his grip, just enough for Brice to finally grasp the revolver. He pulled it from his waistband and with it still behind his back, fired point blank at the man to his left. The bullet entered at the base of the sternum, just below the junction of the ribs, and it exited through the center of his spine, leaving a hole the size of a mango in his back. His body became a pillar of jelly. His head fell back, followed by the top half of his torso. His knees buckled and he fell backwards into the mix of boiling surf and lava.

The remaining attacker was too professional to be thrown off again by all this distraction, and he grabbed Brice in a bear hug. Brice's gun was being held tightly against his back, but his left arm and hand were still free. They were only two feet from the edge, a distance at which the larger man would easily be able to throw him over. A look into his eyes told Trevor that his executioner had the same thought and was on the verge of doing that very thing. But, when the man gave his victim a last look, he knew instantly that Brice had won. The next and last feeling the man experienced was the four-inch knife blade entering the back of his neck at the base of his skull. Brice leaned into the man assuring himself that they would fall away from the cliff and not to the same fate that the others had met. They hit the ground hard. Trevor stayed on top of the man's body, weapon raised, just long enough to check the area for other assailants. There were none.

The tourists were now screaming and starting to run. Many tripped and stumbled over the course lava and were coming up with bloody hands, knees and forearms. Trevor cupped his hands over his mouth and yelled at the crowd, "I am a federal officer! Do not panic! Everything is under control! You will only hurt yourselves if you try to run!"

This seemed to work; almost everyone froze in their places. Many were openly crying. They all stared at Trevor and then at the man that lay dead at the edge of the cliff. One tourist, a lone woman in her early 30s, slipped large dark sunglasses over her eyes and tucked her long brown hair under a Maui Stingrays baseball cap and slowly began backing away from the area. In the ensuing panic, no one gave her a second look. Ms. Gielow knew the wisdom of a graceful, swift retreat. There would always be other opportunities.

"Sir, drop your weapon and step away with your hands in the air!" came the commanding order from a park ranger. Brice looked to his right and saw the 60-year-old ranger nervously pointing her Park Service issue 9mm at him. In her 35 years with the Park Service, she had never drawn a weapon in the line of duty. He obeyed without hesitation.

"If I may?" he asked with his hands in the air. "I have identification that I can show you."

The ranger tensed at this and again ordered him not to move.

"Ranger Belew, remember me?" asked Sam. "I am Dr. Allison from the Volcano Observatory. I can vouch for this gentleman. If you like, I will get his ID out for you!"

The ranger looked them both over several times before saying, "Yes, Doctor, I do know you. Please get his ID for me."

Sam walked over to where Brice was standing, asked where he kept his ID and then slipped her right hand into his left front pocket and pulled out the black leather case. She carried it to the ranger, opened the case and held it up for examination. After several moments the gun lowered and Ranger Belew said, "This all looks quite official, but sir, you were just responsible for the deaths of three men. For now you're in my custody. Please have a seat."

"That's fine. But you best get on the radio and summon help," offered Trevor. "In addition to my ex-friend over there, there are a lot of bloody knees around here."

He then surrendered his gun to Ranger Belew and sat down cross-legged on the warm rocks. "May I take the cell phone from my backpack?" he asked the Ranger.

"I'll get it for you," she said. Without taking her eyes off him she unzipped the black nylon bag and began rummaging blindly through it. She finally felt something she was not entirely sure of, but she wrapped her fingers around it and pulled the secure satellite phone from the backpack.

"Is this it?" she asked holding up the odd looking device.

"Yes, it is. May I have it?"

She looked the phone over again and decided that there would be no harm in granting the request and tossed it to him.

"Thank you," he said as he began pressing a series of numbers on the keypad. Everyone watched closely as Brice apparently reached someone and began a five-minute conversation, spoken in such a low tone that no one could make out what was being said. He finally hung up and just sat there as if he hadn't a care in the world.

Within 15 minutes a helicopter could be heard approaching from down the coast. The Park Service copter landed only 150 feet away and out jumped five men. One was the chief park ranger and four were medical personnel. The chief ranger approached Ranger Belew and began what would be a lengthy discussion as Ranger Belew described the events that had just transpired. The chief walked over and examined the dead man. Both of the Rangers kept looking over at Brice and then at the cliff and back to Brice and then over to the body as they continued to discuss the situation. They did not seem to pay much attention to Samantha, but they did acknowledge that she and Brice were together. The sounds of a second helicopter came into earshot. As the rotary winged aircraft came into sight it became apparent that it belonged to the U.S. Navy. It landed next to the Park Service craft and out jumped two MPs and a Naval commander. The commander walked straight over to the two park rangers and flashed his credentials. Whatever he was telling the two was effective, as they kept looking at him in disbelief. Trevor finally sensed that it was time and stood up and said to Dr. Allison, "Come on Doc, we have got to go!"

He retrieved his ID and gun and packed them into the backpack and headed out over the lava to the Navy helicopter. They both boarded just ahead of the

Commander. Trevor thanked him for his prompt assistance. The MPs climbed aboard, and they lifted off. They skirted the coastline as the pilot flew back to the parking area and set down in the center of the turn around.

"Are you sure this is where you want to get off," the Commander asked.

Brice assured him that it was and said a final thank you as he and Sam hopped out. The area was full of astonished tourists, including a few who had made the trek back from the flow and the mayhem in record time. Trevor grabbed Dr. Allison by the left arm and started walking back to her Jeep.

They had just gotten out of ear shot of the tourists when Sam wheeled and grabbed his right arm, swung him around and demanded, "Excuse me, what the fuck just happened back there? Who were those guys? What are you doing with a gun? Why did the Navy just send in their rescue squad based only on a phone call? I did not come out here with you to get involved with James Bond and some kind of international incident. I'm a vulcanologist for God's sake. My life is all about working around lava. I don't do dangerous shit. What if those second two animals had decided to throw me over the cliff at the same time that the first guy was working on you?" She was now on her tiptoes and chest to chest with him. "What then? I want to know just what the fuck is going on and I want to know now!"

At this point Trevor cupped her mouth with his left hand. He said, "Settle down. We will discuss this, but not here and not now. Let's just get in the Jeep and get out of here." She pulled away and screamed, "You son of a bitch! What have you gotten me into? Damn it, damn it, damn it! This sucks!"

# 7

## Beijing Military Air Base

The Presidential motorcade pulled up along side the Boeing 747 that was Air Force One. Totten's feet were the first to hit the tarmac. He made a beeline to the rear of the plane, where the 30-member press corps was waiting to board. Questions immediately started to fly, although none were yet aware of the events at home. The President raised his right hand to silence the group and said, "I am sorry to inconvenience you, but there are pressing matters at home. You will each have to take the Air Force One backup plane to get home. There will be no press aboard Air Force One today."

With the members of the press left standing there in shock, he turned on his heels and headed straight for General Persi. In a low voice, he advised his top military commander to start planning an appropriate response to an attack on the United States mainland by China. Bounding up the steps of the giant plane with Press Secretary Jessica Bonsall at his side, he instructed her to get all of the leaders of NATO on a conference call immediately.

"This call with NATO will last at least two hours. After that, I will need to speak to a Mr. Trevor Brice. "Here," he said, handing her a card with an unfamiliar phone number scribbled on it. "But first get me the Vice President," he instructed.

She handed him a secure satellite phone and said, "He is already holding for you."

The captain and co-pilot of Air Force One, in their customary positions just inside the doorway of the plane to officially welcome the President, came to attention as Totten boarded. They were given two instructions; first, to expect the delivery of a coffin within the hour and to depart as soon as it was aboard. Second, to prepare for a non-stop flight back to Washington, D.C. The captain bristled at hearing this order because no one liked the idea of performing a mid-air refueling operation on Air Force One, especially with the President aboard, but the plane was equipped for just such a contingency. Plans were made for the non-stop flight.

After a brief conversation with his vice president, Totten settled into the executive chair behind the desk of his on-board office and began jotting down notes. Within an hour, he had moved into the video- conference room and was joined by the Secretary of State and General Persi; together, they planned Totten's address to the world leaders. The satellite conference to begin briefing the leaders of NATO, as well as the Secretary General of the United Nations, commenced 15 minutes after the President's plane left the ground.

"Ladies and gentlemen," President Totten began, "the United States of America has, within the past few hours, suffered from a savage act of terrorism at the hands of the

People's Republic of China. This is the culmination of years of supporting and funding the terrorism that has swept the globe. A massive underground explosion has destroyed the town of Darnestown, Maryland, which is located just 20 miles from our nation's capital. The loss of life is estimated at over 25,000 people. The government of my country has also lost many of its leaders in that heinous act. So far, we have confirmed that over 37 of our United States senators and representatives have died from this terrorist act, directed squarely at my country. Many of the dead, I believe, you all know. In addition, Premier Lolo has threatened another attack if certain demands are not met within 72 hours. Those demands include the total and complete transfer of power of our Federal Reserve System, the transfer of our gold and strategic oil reserves and, of course, the launch codes for our defensive missiles. Lolo has also demanded that we relinquish control of our government. He will certainly not get any of these. The very sovereignty of our country is being threatened. The purpose of this conversation is to advise each of you of that incident and of my full intention to depart this aircraft within 18 hours, drive directly to our nation's Capitol Building and, in an address to the joint houses of Congress, ask that war be declared against China. And war will be declared!"

For the next two and one-half hours, the leaders of the free world gathered more specifics, talked strategy, considered options, and promised all the assistance that they could provide. By the end of the satellite conference, the world leaders had virtually declared world war on China themselves. The task now at hand was to convince their respective governments and peoples that this action was a necessary and just thing to do. As for the United States, the immediate task was to decide on their response to An Lolo's demands. They now had less than 67 hours.

Freedom's Menace

## Atop Kilauea

The chirp from the satellite phone sent him scrambling into the backseat of the Jeep for his backpack. "Brice here," he answered after retrieving the phone.

"Mr. Brice, this is Jessica Bonsall. Please hold for the President of the United States."

Sam had been maneuvering around a particularly sharp curve and did hear the name, Brice. After ten minutes of silence Trevor finally spoke, "Yes, Mr. President, I am with Dr. Allison right now."

Samantha did an obvious double take, and her Jeep wandered off the right side of the road as she stared at her passenger.

"First, sir, so that you know, my cover has been compromised. There have been three attempts on my life since I arrived here 24 hours ago. I'm sure cable news has made you aware of the shooting at the Hilo airport and the bus explosion. Those were numbers one and two. The latest was just within the hour at the Kilauea volcano." Brice filled him in on the details of his flight and the events surrounding the attempts on his life.

"That's not good news," said the President. "Are you alright?"

"Yes, sir, I'm fine."

"I'll pass this information along. We need to find out where the leak came from, but you and I need to move on to more pressing matters. What about the damn sub? Have you seen the submarine, yet?" Brice's jaw tightened as he sensed the concern on the Chief Executive's voice.

"No, sir. I plan to start making arrangements to get down to the sub tonight," he said and then paused. "Sir, it will take a few days. After my conversations with Dr. Allison, this is going to be a lot more difficult than I first anticipated. I will have to secure the necessary equipment to deal with the heat of the volcano. It is 2000 degree at the mouth of the opening."

"Brice, this country does not have a few days. I need to know something by 6:00 pm tomorrow, Washington time," barked Totten. He then softened his voice and said, "Listen, Trevor, I'm planning to leave China very soon. The bastards have bombed the United States. There are dead all over the palace. I am very concerned about the next 48 hours. China has become too big, too powerful, and Lolo is crazy. I know that damn sub has something to do with all of this. I need to find out what it is. Considering the attempts on your life, I will see to it that your family is protected, and we will uncover how they found out about you. Good luck! The country is depending on you." The phone then went dead.

"Was that THE President?" asked Samantha in awe.

Trevor nodded affirmatively as he dialed a phone number that was stored only in his head. When the party on the other end answered, Trevor spoke in an almost mechanical voice, "Command code – Alpha, Tango, Epsilon slash 378245, Identification confirmation – Omega Red." He paused, then.

"I need to speak to Admiral Hanover at Pearl." Fifteen minutes later he hung up the phone after having been connected to the Admiral and advising him of the operation and discussing what personnel and equipment he would require. The Jeep kept running off the road. Sam's attention was more focused on the conversation she was overhearing than on her driving.

"Doctor, are you married? Do you have any obligations at home that require your immediate attention?" Brice inquired.

"Well, I ... I do have a dog that needs to be fed. I suppose that my neighbor could watch her tonight, but..." she answered, uncertain of where this was all going. "Wait one damn minute! I want to know who you are and what is going on here."

The events of the past few hours were rushing home to roost. Her head was now swimming with thoughts. Less than an hour ago she witnessed an attempted murder and the deaths of three strange men. Now this stranger, whom she had known for only a few hours, was riding in her Jeep, with a telephone that allowed him to talk to the President, Navy Admirals, and Lord knows whom else. And now he was planning a full-scale military assault on a volcano. What the hell was going on?! Finally she found her voice and in a stammer said, "Look, I do not know what is going on here and I don't care. It seems to me that you have everything under control. Why don't I just drop you off at your car and I'll go home to my dog? I promise to forget all of this, and I won't tell a soul. Really!"

Trevor looked at her with empathy, but just shook his head. "I'm sorry that you've gotten mixed up in all this," he said gently. "Unfortunately, you have now been associated with me and your life is in danger. I've been damn lucky so far, but no one can be lucky forever. I cannot let you go back home right now, not alone. It just would not be safe. What I can do is get you off this island and over to the Naval Base at Pearl. You will be safe there until all of this is over. We can also make arrangements for your dog."

There was way too much going on in her mind to answer right away. She was obviously distracted by all of this and thought it wise to pull over so that she could better concentrate on what was going on.

"Samantha," Trevor continued with, "My real name is Trevor Brice. Charles Reidelberger is just an alias that I occasionally use..."

A look of severe skepticism crossed her face. "That is the truth, just let me finish. I work on special assignments for the President. The submarine you found is of great interest for obvious reasons of national security."

As they sat there at the roadside pull out, he explained all that he could and avoided the rest. She was too smart to think he had given her the entire story, but she also knew that he could only say so much and had probably offered more than he should have.

She sat in silent contemplation for several minutes. Finally, without even looking at her passenger, she turned the key to restart the Jeep, depressed the clutch, threw the stick into first and burned rubber as she sped away. Ten minutes later, they approached Crater Rim Drive, and she took a right. She didn't know why, considering that the observatory and Brice's minivan were the other direction, but she did not want to go any place that those people might be looking for her.

"Lest I forget, I really wanted to say thank you for saving my life. Seeing you swing that water bottle was the most welcome sight I've ever had." She smiled a weak smile and nodded in acknowledgement of his gratitude.

"Hungry?" he asked. She looked over at him as if he had three heads. "Hey, it's been a long day, and besides, we have to eat," he said with a smile and then added, "and you need to relax. Everything really *is* going to be alright."

This did not ease her mind at all. She let go of a long sigh and mumbled, "Well, if I'm going to die, I might as well go out with a full belly." She cleared her throat, gave another long sigh as she wheeled the Jeep into the entrance of the Volcano House Hotel. "This place is really very good," she said. "Next to lava, food is my second passion." After another sigh, she said in a nervous voice, "Besides, this place has a great bar, and I really could use a drink. But are we safe here? I really don't know where else to go."

"This is going to be great. And, yes, we will be safe here. We left all of the bad guys at the volcano," Trevor said to offer her some peace of mind. In reality, he knew that this was not a game they were involved in and any assumption could be deadly.

The Volcano House Hotel sits on the bluff at the north rim of the Kilauea Caldera. Built in 1877, it sits on the site of the original volcano observatory. Professor Jaggar of MIT established Kilauea's first formal scientific team from this site in 1912. For well over 100 years, the hotel has hosted scientists, world leaders, vacationers and curiosity seekers from around the world. Brice and Dr. Allison entered through the main doors and proceeded to the bar off the left side of the lobby. Trevor ordered a beer, while Sam had a beer and a shot of Jack Daniel's. She downed the shot immediately. The bartender held up the bottle to offer another shot, and she pushed the small glass toward him. She downed the second shot as well, but waved off the offer of a third. Grabbing their beers and leaving the empty shot glass and a $20 bill on the bar, they headed out past the gift shops to the rear exit. Trevor looked in his wallet, thumbing through the dwindling number of twenties.

Along the back hallway hung a number of old photographs which provided a pictorial history of the hotel, including one of Samuel Clemens standing on this very spot as well as one of him standing next to the boiling Halema'uma'u crater. Forty feet beyond the door, a stone wall separated the hotel grounds from the giant caldera below. The pungent fragrance from the white Plumeria, the colorful Bird of Paradise and the lush greenery from the vegetation that grows along the wall provided a stark contrast to the natural devastation that lay beyond. Out to the south they could see the Halema'uma'u Crater. All around the area, one could see the small steam vents releasing into the air. The continuous cloud of sulfur dioxide rose from the crater and spread over the area. Los Angeles has its automotive smog, while the Big Island of Hawaii has its volcanic vog.

"The primary reason that plant life has not returned to the caldera in great abundance is due to the vog producing acid rain, which falls back down onto the area. It literally poisons most anything that tries to grow out there," said Sam.

Walking down the path she pointed out turn-of-the-century concrete pillars that remained on the grounds. "These were the original supports for the measuring devices that were first used in the study of this geological wonder. We moved to our current location in the 1930's."

As they stood there taking in the splendor, the day began to wane. The evening was cool and peaceful. The clouds were starting to change into their nightly shades of red, orange, blue and purple as the sun began to set over the Pacific Ocean. "Is there any wonder why people love this place?" Sam asked.

Trevor smiled and said, "This has always been one of my favorite places." He took her bottle and walked their empties over to the trashcan and tossed them in. "Let's eat," he said as they headed back into the hotel. "And to answer your question more fully, no, I cannot image anyone who would not love it here. I have always found this place to be exceptional. Rain forests, volcanoes, deserts, mountains, and black sand beaches, all in one place. The diversity on this one island is incredible. I can go snow boarding on Mauna Kea and then be sunning myself on the beach an hour later."

As the two entered the dining room, Brice, being ever vigilant, surveyed the crowd. He consciously sensed the presence of his pistol, secured in the back of his belt. After the events of the past 24 hours, this was no time to let his guard down. Yet his calm, relaxed manner did not reflect any sign of his wariness and caution. They were shown to a table for two next to the large windows that over looked the caldera, but he opted for the lone table along the wall and in the back of the dining area. He preferred an unobstructed view of the door and windows to his left. Looking out from across the room, the sky was now ablaze in color.

Looking over the top of her menu, Samantha began offering recommendations, "On the Big Island, we are known for our beef. The island is the home of several large cattle ranches that are on the north end of the island. In fact, one of the largest cattle ranches in the United States is located right here. You can't go wrong with the rib eye. However, being from the mainland you can usually get a great steak anytime. You are now in the middle of the

Pacific Ocean and the fish here is incredible. I would recommend the Opacapaca, the Ahi or the Mahi-mahi."

The waiter delivered their drink orders and sat the wine list on the table between them. "May I?" she asked, as she picked up the leather bound listing. He responded with a nod and a grin.

The waiter returned to accept their order. Trevor's choice was wok seared Ahi tuna with a medley of young vegetables and new potatoes, all on a bed of island greens. Samantha decided on grilled Mahi-mahi served atop a mound of garlic-mashed potatoes, with a black bean mango salsa as garnish. The wine she selected was an expensive bottle of Opus One at $145.00.

Brice was familiar with the wine. "Planning on this being your last meal?" he asked.

"No. I just decided that since Uncle Sam put me in this position, He was going to feed me well."

"And, what makes you think that I'm picking this up? You're the one who chose this place."

"I am also the one who hit that goon with my water bottle and saved you from something that I don't even want to think about."

"You're right, no more argument. And again, thank you very much. So tell me about yourself. How did you get interested in volcanoes?"

"Oh, who knows? I've always liked the outdoors. My parents tell me that on any nice day I was always out the door first thing and I wouldn't come back in until they made me. I considered oceanography, biology, and stream management. I stumbled over volcanoes in college and then took a trip here during my sophomore year and, well, you know."

"Where did you grow up?" Trevor asked.

"Monterey, California. Have you ever been there?"

"You bet I have, what a great area; Monterey, Carmel and Big Sur. I love the Monterey Bay Aquarium. I have a huge jellyfish poster from there hanging on my office wall. I also really like Point Lobos. It's just too cool for words."

The rest of the dinner was filled with mostly small talk about families, work and such. Trevor wanted her to relax before he released the next bolt from the blue. As they were finishing their second cup of Kona coffee, which accompanied a decadent desert of sliced bananas, chocolate and vanilla ice cream in a caramel basket, Brice spotted a rugged looking Marine who had just entered the dining area.

"Looks like the cavalry has arrived," he said. Trevor dropped Charles Reidelberger's American Express card on the table and, as they walked out, he told the waiter that they would be waiting in the lobby.

# 8

## The Plan

The marine, Captain Reginald Jones, was black, about 30, at least six-foot-four inches tall and weighed no less than 235 pounds. He was built like a linebacker for the Green Bay Packers. The look on his face was deadly serious.

"Mr. Reidelberger?" he asked as Trevor approached.

"Yes, I am," responded Trevor.

"Identification, please," Jones asked coldly. Trevor handed him Charles Reidelberger's New York driver's license, which Captain Jones took and examined carefully. "Do you have any other form of ID, sir?" Jones questioned.

With that, Brice extracted the black case from the left front pocket of his jeans and handed it over to the officer. The marine's brow furrowed as he examined the documents. "Very good, sir," he said returning the black case and driver's license. "The name is Reggie Jones, sir. I have orders to assist you in any way that I can," he explained. "The rest of my team is outside. Shall we..."

The waiter interrupted as he approached with the bill. Trevor signed the check, provided a generous tip and thanked the man for his gracious service.

"I suggest we get going, sir," said Jones. "Will the lady be accompanying us?"

As they stepped into the chilly night air, Brice looked over at Samantha and said, "Yes, she will. In fact, you, me and the rest of your unit are going to be joined at the hip until this is all over."

At this Sam's head began to swim and she felt slightly faint. "Now wait a minute," she protested, "you said that I could go to Pearl Harbor or somewhere else and that you would protect me. Isn't that what you said?"

"Yes, Doctor," said Trevor, "that is what I said. But that was before I realized just how much I need your expertise."

As the two argued, a U.S. Marine Humvee pulled up. A sergeant hopped out and saluted Jones. "Sergeant, you will take the lady's vehicle, and they will ride with me," said Jones.

"Where are you taking my car?" Sam asked.

"Don't worry, Dr. Allison, the Corps will take very good care of it," answered Jones.

Suddenly, Dr. Samantha Allison felt as though she had lost all control of her own life. And in many respects she was right. Jones climbed in behind the wheel, as Brice slid into the passenger seat next to him. Sam was left standing alone in the middle of the parking lot.

"Doctor, get in." Jones barked, "We are leaving!"

Captain Jones and the two new members of his team turned left out of the hotel parking lot and headed toward the Kilauea Military Camp. Sam looked back and saw the lights of her Jeep disappearing in the opposite direction. As they passed the visitor's center three more Humvees fell in behind them. The convoy drove down the road to the camp entrance. They drove through the camp and out the back, as Trevor and the Commander had done earlier in the day. This time, they made a left turn and drove about half a mile. Jones made a quick left turn and seemed to head straight into a lava mountain when, suddenly, a number of bright white lights came on and a large camouflaged door opened up in front of them. The Humvees raced through the opening. Just beyond the entrance, the roadway dropped away and the group found themselves entering an underground bunker. Trevor immediately realized that the warehouse he was in this morning was on the east side of this sprawling subterranean complex. The underground facility covered almost four acres. Missionaries had discovered the cave in the 1700s. Centuries before that, King Kamehameha I had used the hidden cavern to mount surprise attacks on enemy tribes. Uncle Sam found it to be the perfect place on which to build a military camp for the rest and relaxation of weary servicemen. Things are just never what they seem.

Once inside, Jones arranged for a female corporal to see to Dr. Allison's needs. He and Brice then disappeared through an unmarked door. It was now 9:00 pm. Sam was shown to a bunk in a room that served as the sleeping quarters for four other female enlistees. She took a very long, hot shower as she tried to reconcile the events of the past 12 hours. Exhausted and simply too tired to think anymore, she climbed into her assigned upper bunk and fell fast asleep.

Colonel Kwiatkowski, meanwhile, joined Brice and Jones in a small conference room that was connected to a well-equipped communications center. Jones started, "Mr. Reidelberger, I do not know who you are, but as I told you at the Volcano House, my orders are to see to your every need. I have a team of 12 of the finest men the Marines Corps has ever produced. What is our mission?"

Trevor relaxed a little. This was exactly the type of man he needed to pull this off. "Gentleman, to start, my authority comes from the top. My real name is Brice, Trevor Brice. At this point, I do not have a lot of details about our assignment. But I can tell you that our country's relationship with the People's Republic of China is souring and tensions are high. Our superiors have reason to believe that there are answers lying 4,000 feet below Kilauea. We are going to retrieve those answers."

Jones interrupted, "I beg your pardon?"

Brice reached into his shirt pocket and removed the picture. "The only way I know of to make this mission a success is for you to know everything I know." Brice continued, as he slid the photo across the table, "Dr. Allison took this last week through the dormant volcano lava conduit that was uncovered when Pu'u 'O'o erupted last year. Due to the high volume of lava the vent has been producing, no one could get close enough to study it until recently. Intelligence has confirmed that the sub is real. We have every faith that Dr. Allison is not playing games with us, and this thing is or was down there. What we don't know is whether or not it can come and go at will or if

possibly it was trapped during last year's eruption. Our
mission is to answer that question."

Jones frowned and shook his head with uncertainty.

Kwiatkowski demanded, "Exactly what are you asking
us to do, Mr. Brice? You already sent a camera down there.
Why the hell don't you just do that again?"

Trevor leaned forward, placing the palms of his hands
flat on the table, while rising slightly from his chair. With
his stare frozen on Kwiatkowski's eyes he sternly said, "We
are not here to discuss options. We are going down inside of
that damn volcano. Our purpose here is to figure out how
we do that."

Rising from the table, he walked over to the white
board at the far end of the room, picked up a black marker,
and continued, "The camera failed because the heat melted
the support cables. Our challenge is to overcome that
situation, so we can get our men down there. So that I can
get down there." He began sketching a scene of the volcano,
the cavern and the submarine as he proceeded with his
briefing. "We know that the Chinese sub is a Han class
nuclear attack vessel. It is about 60 feet shorter than our
Los Angles class submarines, but the displacement is about
the same. At this point, we do not know where the entrance
of the cavern is. I have already been in contact with
Admiral Hanover; the Navy has crews out there right now
searching for the entrance. This is particularly perplexing
due to the shear size of the sub. Another thing we cannot
answer is why they would risk one of the few jewels of their
fleet and park it under an active volcano. There is no
strategic military benefit. Given the metamorphic rise in
the Chinese economy over the past several years, I am
personally very suspicious. If they have funded their
economy on the backs of something that was taken from the

# Freedom's Menace

American people, I want to know about it. The President
wants to know about it!"

At this, Captain Jones spoke up, "Alright, enough of
this. We now know the what. Let's figure out the how. With
your permission, I would like to bring in the rest of my
team to start planning."

It was 3:30 am before Brice, Kwiatkowski and the 12
Marines under Captain Jones' command had developed
their plan. It would take some time for all of the supplies to
be collected and transported to the site. The next 24 to 48
hours were going to be very strenuous and Brice wanted the
crew rested and in top shape. They adjourned for sleep and
agreed to regroup at 10 hundred (1000) hours in the mess
hall of the underground bunker.

As they were filing out, Kwiatkowski's voice rose above
the clamor. "What about the girl? What do we do with her?"

Brice was at the door and without turning around, he
paused and said, "Dr. Allison is the foremost vulcanologist
on the island. She's going with us. I need her down there.
Why? I don't know yet. We'll answer that question when we
get there."

At 0930 Hours, Samantha was awakened by one of her
female roommates. At first she was completely disoriented,
but then, through the cobwebs, she remembered. "Oh shit,"
she said, slightly under her breath and pulling the covers
over her head. "Yesterday really happened, didn't it?" She
peaked out from under the sheet and looked at the private.

"Yes, M'am, and you are expected in the mess hall in 30
minutes. We took the liberty of retrieving some personal
items for you from your house; thought that you might need
them."

Sam looked over the edge of the bed and saw her green duffel sitting on a chair. She also saw the happy, anxious face of her golden retriever. "Busch," she yelled as the dog tried his best to jump up to the top bunk.

"We will take very good care of him for you," assured the private as she left the room.

Jumping down from the bed, Sam played with the animal for 10 minutes until the private returned and advised her of the time. She opened the duffel and found everything she required. Obviously, another woman had packed it for her, thankfully.

Ten minutes later, she found herself at the mess table situated between Marine Corporal Polumbo and Trevor Brice. As the group ate, Captain Jones reviewed the plans that had been put together just hours before. When he got to the part about rappelling down into the conduit, she almost choked on her scrambled eggs, sending a shower of pale yellow particles flying across the table. After recovering from the coughing attack, she looked around the table and asked, "Are you all fucking nuts? I'm not going down there!"

Corporal Polumbo nudged her with his elbow and said, "Don't worry, M'am, it will be just like a walk on the beach."

The rest of the group roared with laughter as she cupped her head in her hands and asked out loud, "Why me, Lord?"

The Humvees had already been loaded with all of the necessary equipment the base had to offer. The very specialized equipment they would require in order to safely rappel into the cavern was being flown in from Pearl, the helicopter would meet them at the Pu'u 'O'o vent. Colonel Kwiatkowski wished them good luck and the convoy roared out of the underground bunker with Jones, Brice and Dr. Allison in the lead. The distance to the Pu'u 'O'o vent was relatively short, but because there were no roads, they had to travel over the rough, uneven lava. The trip was arduous at best and took more than an hour. The group assembled on the north rim and immediately began unloading equipment and setting up a command post. The first of two helicopters arrived 20 minutes later. Six large wooden crates were lowered to the camp below. The copters were then ordered to return to base and pick up the remaining supplies. A half an hour later, a Medivac helicopter arrived and landed about 300 yards away. The medical team quickly set up their first-aid tent and equipment. In the mean time, Jones, Brice, Allison and the five other Marines who would be entering the conduit were being briefed on the use of the specialized climbing equipment and making ready for the descent.

## Washington, D.C.

Air Force One touched down at Andrew's Air Force Base north of Washington, D.C., 17 hours after leaving Beijing. The news of Donaldson's death had been broadcast 12 hours earlier. The Presidential limousine was waiting on the tarmac to take Totten directly to the Capitol. The remaining members of both Houses of Congress were already waiting. All the major world news networks were on hand, each speculating about the nature of this hurried and most unusual convening of the Congress of the United States. Did this have only to do with Darnestown? Or did something else happen in Beijing as well? How was the Secret Service agent killed? Why did the Presidential press corps not return on Air Force One? The past 20 hours had been filled with coverage of the tragedy in Darnestown and speculation surrounding the President's unusual behavior.

# W. Laurence Willis

The nerves of the nation, as well as those around the world, were frayed. The entrance to the Capitol's underground garage was heavily guarded as the President's limo pulled in. Totten exited the vehicle and started making his way to the chamber of House of Representatives. He dispensed with the usual courtesies that he would normally extend to those Capitol building employees who always litter the halls whenever he was present. The news anchors took immediate notice of the grim and somber expression cemented on his face. He hurriedly entered the House chambers and was half way to the podium before the band could even start playing the customary "Hail to the Chief." He took up his position and politely waited until the music stopped. But before the traditional round of applause could start, he began speaking.

*"Ladies and gentlemen, citizens of the United States, I stand before you this day with grave news from China. The giant sinkhole that swallowed the town of Darnestown, Maryland, was no freak accident of nature, but rather a direct attack on this country by the People's Republic of China. Premier An Lolo has threatened our country with other acts of terrorism if certain demands are not met within the next few days. Their demands would, in effect, turn control of the United States over to the leaders of the People's Republic of China. I stand here before you to provide you with complete assurance that their demands will not stand.*

*Clearly, Premier Lolo and his government do not understand or appreciate the enormous value that we, the citizens of this great country, place on our freedom. They have not learned much about us over the past 200 plus years. They do not understand that, as in the past, we have and will fight to the death for the rights that our forefathers died for and that we have inherited and work so hard to preserve. The rights granted to us as citizens of this great country, the United States of America. The Chinese have committed an act of war. I ask our Congress to reciprocate by issuing an immediate Declaration of War against the Chinese government, their leaders and the military machine that carries out their agenda.*

*I regret that I also have to ask our citizens for some extreme sacrifices. I will not discuss these openly due to the sensitive nature of the request. However, all involved will receive notification of what is being asked of you within 24 hours. I am also issuing an Executive Order to halt all foreign travel into and out of the United States until further notice. Additionally, it will also be necessary to impose certain limitations on interstate travel within our borders. The reasons for these extreme measures will become clear in the following days. These sacrifices are absolutely necessary in order to prevent the loss of any additional lives to Chinese terrorism.*

*Tonight, I ask that each of you sit at home with your families and reflect on the blessings and benefits of being a citizen of this great country, and pray that we once again turn back those that threaten our liberties and the liberties of others.*

*Keep the faith and believe in your country and its leaders. Freedom and human rights have and will always prevail. Good night and God bless each and every one of you."*

With his brief address concluded, Totten was off the platform and headed toward his car for the White House without the normal glad-handing that traditionally occurs. The country sat in shocked and stunned silence. The CNN and ABC anchors began to cry as they struggled to repeat the words that the President had just presented. Mothers and fathers around the country openly wept as they tried to comfort the children that were frightened by the reactions of their parents. The magnitude of the uncertainty that lay before them came into focus. United States military troops stationed around the world slowly began to rally and prepare to go into battle. Local authorities from 85 towns around the United States, each with a secret military connection, were starting to receive faxes and e-mails advising them that their towns were likely targets of a Chinese attack and that evacuation was to begin at once. They were also told that the evacuations were top secret. The National Guard and State Police were being mobilized to help, and interstate transportation would be halted to aid in those efforts.

General Persi had just reached the war room under the Pentagon as the President concluded his address. The Joint Chiefs were already in attendance. Each having been briefed from Air Force One, they were all ready to present their recommendations. They had about four hours before Persi was to make his recommendation to the White House.

When President Totten arrived at the executive mansion, he went straight for the Oval Office. Other leaders of the free world were already on the phone awaiting his arrival. Although many non-essential White House personnel had been asked to leave, the place was in bedlam. The chief of staff was at the door to greet him. Inside was the director of civil defense, the attorney general, directors of the CIA and FBI, the secretaries of defense and state, along with countless aides and technicians. Totten had authorized the presence of one member of the press, with the stipulation that no cameras or recording equipment be allowed. The reporter was only there to observe. The nod, of course, went to the CNN correspondent. Two hours passed and C-Span reported that Congress had declared war on China. Similar reports went out over all of the other networks within minutes.

# Freedom's Menace

Halfway across the globe, Premier Lolo had flown to his mountain retreat near the city of Changsha, two hours north of Hong Kong. He stood, overlooking the mountainous view with the ice blue waters of the Dongting Hu lying placidly in the valley below, with his three top advisors and that strange man who had led Totten from the Summer Palace just some 20 hours before. His name was Yang Wu. They too got CNN and had heard Totten's speech.

"The fools!" the Premier said. "Do they really not appreciate what we can do to their country? China is now the mightiest country on the planet. How dare they defy us?" Turning to Wu on his left, he suggested that the second targeted city should be destroyed.

"But Premier, you gave them 72 hours. They still have time to comply. We have already angered them. Should we not keep our word?" he cautioned.

"They are not going to comply," said the assured Lolo. "Yet, I did give them 72 hours. We will wait. It is my sincere hope that they will foolishly try to send one of their nuclear missiles to destroy us. That way they will learn of the technology that we now posses to prevent such an attack. It will be a hard, sad lesson, but one that they will never forget. But you are right. Another few days will not matter."

# 9

## The Pentagon

In the war room, deep below the Pentagon, the military leaders had already briefed General Persi. An attack on China had already been planned years before and was continuously being refined just for a situation as this. Right now they were trying to determine why the Chinese would launch such a brazen attack. They know that we have nuclear first strike capability and can hit them from numerous launch sites around the globe, including the four Trident attack subs that are continuously patrolling their waters. Army General Jalbert sat back in his chair and slammed his briefing folder on the top of the table. "Gentleman, something here smells really funny. There are no signs that the Chinese are in any way preparing for war. All of our intelligence gathering sources, including the satellites, aircraft and personnel on the ground are telling us that they are doing nothing unusual. There are no troop movements, no ship movements, no nothing. That bothers me. It bothers me a lot!" he exclaimed.

# Freedom's Menace

From the back of the room came the squeaky voice of 19-year-old Seaman First Class, Anthony Rivecco, an aide to Admiral Packard. "Sirs, excuse the interruption, but I had a thought," he said. The room went dead quiet as all of the top military officers turned to stare at him, as if he had just spoken heresy. Seaman Rivecco went stiff with fright.

"Go on, son, speak up. We ain't got time to fool around. If you got something to say then say it," General Jalbert ordered.

"Well, Sirs, I was thinking that, well, if, er..."

The general slapped his palm on the table and shouted, "Goddamnit, we don't have time for this shit." They all turned to resume the business at hand.

Rivecco, now sporting a loud, commanding voice that surprised even him, again interrupted by saying, "Sorry, sirs, but I think that the war is going to be fought electronically."

General Jalbert, now frustrated with the seaman, said, without turning around, "Admiral, you need to send this young man back to kiddygarden. He seems to think he knows more about the Chinese computer capability than we do."

Before the Admiral could admonish his young aide, the seaman took another step forward saying, "Maybe I do, sir. The Chinese have over 75 million personal computers in their country. And most are less than four years old. With the right network programming, you can build one hell of an Internet super computer, sir."

He then froze, knowing that he had just over-stepped his bounds. General Jalbert slowly turned in his chair and

faced the frightened man before him. He lowered his
glasses over his nose and stared out over the top of the rim.
Before the general could speak, Persi interceded.

"Tell me what's on your mind, son," he said in a soft,
kind voice. Clearing his throat, the young seaman told of
Internet attacks that had occurred a few years back, on
major websites like Yahoo and CNN. "The results of these
attacks, or hacker incidents as they were categorized,
resulted in an overload and subsequent shut down of the
affected system. These were major events to the systems
that were targeted. Lone hackers accomplished the shut
down using one or two computers that belonged to someone
else, a college or university. First they hack into the
college's computer and program it to go after the bigger
target. If a hacker or, in this case, an enemy government
had 75 million computers at their disposal and the
sophisticated programming needed to run it, well, the chaos
they could cause would be unimaginable. Power plants,
radio and television stations, national and international
banking as well as phone companies would be crippled.
They could potentially black out the entire nation." Seaman
Rivecco paused to let the impact of his words take hold.

The eyes of the Joint Chiefs of Staff darted around the
table at each other. General Jalbert rejected the argument
by discussing the vast and independent communications
system that the United States Military had in place.

"But, sir," pressed Seaman Rivecco, "they are not going
to attack the military directly. First, they will be attacking
the population, the people. Our daily lives. Then, with the
country's infrastructure incapacitated and the people in
panic, the military will not be able to support itself for
long."

# Freedom's Menace

"How the hell are they planning to turn back our missiles and planes? What about that?" demanded the general.

"I don't know, sir, but that would seem to me to be a key element. They have to assume that we are not afraid to launch our missiles at them. They seem to know that and have devised a way of avoiding or withstanding our attack. They only have to hold us back just long enough to let the effects of the collapsed infrastructure take hold," asserted Rivecco.

Jalbert turned back to look at his peers and then back to the seaman and said, "I did not get to where I am by being too stupid and too vain to think that I always had all of the answers. I do not think any of us have given this concept you have proposed any serious consideration before now. The idea is, or was, simply too wild. But you could be absolutely correct. How would you handle this?"

Stunned by this request, Seaman Rivecco felt as though he was going to faint, but quickly regained his composure. The strategy he suggested was simple: determine how they were going to undermine our missile attacks by launching one at them. Then they could devise a counter measure. This would return first strike capability to the United States. In the mean time, the major Internet providers need to prepare for a massive influx of messages, all intended to choke their systems and freeze America's computers. Consideration should also be given to overloading them, the Chinese, first. The room was quiet for several minutes as each man wrote down his thoughts.

Finally, Persi, recognizing the situation, began giving orders in rapid-fire succession. Persi looked at his Navy admiral and said, "Jason, I want you to make preparations for the launch of an unarmed missile toward China. A

Tomahawk should do. I, personally, will issue the order. I want it aimed so to appear that it is heading directly at Beijing, but be prepared to adjust the trajectory at the last moment so that it will over-shoot and ditch in the Sea of Japan. If you launch from a location in the Indian Ocean, it will be hard for them to determine the actual destination until it is well on its way. I want to see want happens, how and if they have a response. But do not do it until I give the order. I want to discuss this with the President first."

The Air Force general spoke next, "Ok, let's assume that they have a way of preventing a ballistic missile attack. Then what? What about their ability to respond to more conventional methods of attack? If they can do that, then what other capabilities do they have that we do not yet know about? I think that we should try several approaches to see what happens."

Most of the officers agreed and plans were made accordingly. They all assumed it would be easy to determine China's response. The United States already had available spy satellites positioned over their country while several others made routine, scheduled passes and still others could be diverted as required. The room soon emptied as the admirals, generals and their aides left to perform their assigned tasks. There was now only one hour remaining before Persi had to brief the President. As Rivecco gathered the admiral's belongings, he felt a hand on his shoulder and heard Persi saying, "Tony, you have performed extremely well today. Thanks to you we may now be headed in the right direction. I want you with me when I go to the White House."

With that, the chairman of the Joint Chiefs of Staff patted the aide and his newest advisor on the shoulder and left the room. A proud Admiral Packard, standing in the doorway, gave his young aide a congratulatory wink.

# The Oval Office

Totten's primary concern, at the moment, was the health and well being of the people of the United States. A list of 83 towns that could be potential Chinese targets, due to little known military or government presence, had been made during the flight over from Beijing. That was the easy part. The ability to predict beyond the obvious was always much more difficult. Those original 83 communities had been warned, and evacuation plans were in progress, a fact not yet well known, nor would it be if they could keep the lid on it. The citizens of these towns were to be transported and housed at nearby military bases or at other secure locations. Communications from within the towns was being intentionally compromised before the commencement of the evacuations to maintain as much secrecy as possible. President Totten had two immediate goals. One, to stifle widespread knowledge of the evacuations and potential for future attacks, in the hopes of preventing public panic. Second and most important, to prevent the Chinese from seeing any action on the part of the United States and moving up the clock to strike before the 72 hours expired. Time, they needed time, and it was quickly evaporating. He wanted to convince the Chinese, and the world, via television that he was seriously working toward meeting their demands. But even harder than that was preventing the news media from locking onto this story and creating widespread panic. He only needed a little more than 48 hours.

Within the ranks of the military and his cabinet officers, it was generally believed that China could not pull off more than one operation the size of which destroyed Darnestown. The next attack would likely be on a much smaller scale, but still quite deadly, such as a toxic biological release or multiple bomb blast. The survivors, the

press and the world would immediately recognize it as a
terrorist act. He was certain that the next attack could not
be hidden from the country. They had taken out
Darnestown to get the attention of the country's leaders.
Next time they would be seeking attention from the world
populous. The United States did not need a string of crises
at home, on top of the one that was developing in Asia. It
was imperative that the citizens of the country think that
they were out of harm's way, even though the President
knew otherwise. Totten knew instinctively that a massive
disinformation campaign would be required to keep the
Chinese off-balance and protect American lives.

This is why CNN had been invited into the Oval Office
to "observe." Their reporter, Dixie Makepeace, was a 25-
year-old, Native American who had graduated from Yale
University's School of Journalism three years earlier. She
was on temporary assignment while the regular White
House correspondent took a weeklong vacation. With the
President in China, it was to be good experience for the
bright, talented young reporter. Unknown to her, as she sat
in the Oval Office witnessing first hand the actions of the
government in crisis, CNN was frantically trying to contact
her. They were going to advise her that a more seasoned
journalist was being flown in to replace her, in
consideration of the circumstances, of course. What CNN
did not know was that they would be receiving a phone call
from the White House, within the hour, requesting that Ms.
Dixie Makepeace be allowed to continue her assignment to
the White House until further notice.

It so happened that the talented Ms. Makepeace had a
penchant for writing tales with a folksy bend. Her stories of
fictional small town America and its interesting, but quirky
inhabitants had won her a great deal of critical acclaim.
Anyone else with the story telling ability she possessed
would have easily enjoyed a very successful writing career.

# Freedom's Menace

Yet her heart was in television journalism. The fictional stories were simply her source of funds for college tuition, and, now, her creative outlet. Unbeknownst to her, that ability just won her the role of chief disinformation officer in charge of fooling the Chinese.

President Totten sat on the edge of the great oak desk, which had been built by his grandfather, to address Ms. Makepeace directly. "Ms. Makepeace. Dixie, may I call you Dixie? I have particular need for your special talents."

Adjusting his wristwatch, which was sticking to his clammy skin, he began to explain to her how important it was for the public to maintain a secure peace of mind during the upcoming days and weeks.

"Sometime within the next 48 hours, the Chinese may once again attack the United States. Right now we are forcing the evacuation of the communities that we feel are potential targets. The list is 83 cities long. We have a formidable task ahead of us. I want the American people, and most importantly, the Chinese, to believe that this is not really happening and that everything in those little towns is perfectly normal. I want you to take that wonderful story telling ability of yours and produce the scripts of the dialog that you will be having with the town's people when you interview with them. These will be wonderful, hard working Americans that are overjoyed, but somewhat skeptical, to have a big time TV station like CNN visit and report on their little town. Your cameras will pan around the town and show the people milling about, wondering what all of the excitement is about. And ..."

He was interrupted when Makepeace clutched the arms of her chair and jumped to her feet. "You want me to do what? Are you joking?" She started pacing awkwardly around the room, bumping into chairs and people as she held her forehead in the palms of her hands in disbelief of what she had just heard.

She started rambling. "Mr. President, with all due respect, what you are asking is, well… unethical. No, I cannot possibly use my position to lie to the American people. That's contemptible. How dare you even ask that of me? I can't believe this. What are you thinking, sir. And on top of everything else, I'd lose my job and my career. No, sir! No, I will not. I won't do it. I cannot!" Her resolve strengthened as her anger grew more intense. The emotion was clearly present in her voice.

President Totten just stood by and let her go. He wore a smirk for a grin and nonchalantly walked behind his desk and started to arrange some papers, all the while listening to the young woman's tirade. After several minutes of hearing disjointed opinions about the First Amendment and how he was abusing his power and how the American people deserved more respect than he was giving them, she slowly began to calm down at least verbally. At this point, Secretary of State McKeckney walked over to the shaking, young, idealistic reporter, placed an arm around her shoulder and walked her out into the hall to offer a few words. Tears were rolling down her face, like sweat from a glass of iced tea on a hot summer day, and her jet-black hair was plastered against the bright red of her puffy, damp cheeks. After 10 minutes of listening to McKeckney's perspective on the issue, she turned to the secretary and nodded her acceptance of the role that she had been asked to play.

They stepped back into the Oval Office, where with a voice that shook like a Jell-O jiggler in the hands of a child she muttered, "You son-of-a-bitch. It isn't really supposed to be like this."

# Freedom's Menace

With his head still down, looking at the top of his desk, Totten rolled his eyes up to the top of their sockets to see her. Then looking back down to his papers he said, "I'm sorry, Dixie, but this is the real world, and these are the things that we must do to keep our world free and our people safe."

He then lifted his head and made eye contact with the journalistic neophyte and said, "You will not get to publish all that you have learned here, but I promise that you will get to report on the story and with plenty of detail. Your superiors are being advised of your actions and your willingness to serve your country. As distasteful as it may seem, this is actually going to save lives, a great many lives. You will get to tell the truth about that later. Thank you for joining us. And never call me a son-of-a-bitch again."

Walking back from around the desk, he approached and guided her back to her seat. He pulled up a chair to face her and continued with his instructions. "Now for the tough part. We currently have camera crews scattered around the country, filming all aspects of those towns that we feel are targets. Those towns are now being or will soon be evacuated. News of this is going to leak out despite our best efforts. We will request that the other media suppress their knowledge of the evacuations for a few days. What I need you to do is to begin a Charles Kuralt-style, small town America series, just like you have done in your written stories, but this time for television and this time with real people as the characters. Each will focus on one of these towns and provide your viewer with the homey story of the communities and the townspeople who live there. If their community is attacked, I do not want the whole world knowing about it, at least not right away. To the eyes of the world, thanks to your journalistic and creative abilities, the towns will seem to still be occupied. You will file a "live"

report from the site showing that all is well. You will
interview the people as they go about their daily routine.
Viewers will see the kittens and puppy dogs playing in the
yards with their young owners as well as the cantankerous
residents who will complain loudly about all the disruption
from the darn television people."

He sat back in his chair to give her a moment to absorb
what he was asking her to do. "This will be the biggest
weapon we have in keeping the Chinese off balance. We
want them to be confused. We want them to question the
effects of their initial attack. We want them to think that
we scuttled their plans. They cannot suspect that we are
doing anything other than what we have been instructed to
do."

Totten rose and returned to his desk where he reached
over and pressed the small green button on the control pad
next to his phone. A moment later his personal secretary
came into the room. "Mrs. Sutton, would you please escort
Ms. Makepeace downstairs and introduce her to Robert
Townsend and his team," he asked.

Dixie furrowed her brow, stared at all of the other
occupants in the room, retrieved her notepad, briefcase and
purse and walked out of the room. As the two left the room,
Totten turned his attention to the next issue on his agenda
the status of the evacuations and the next stage of that
process.

# 10

## Oblong, Illinois

The scene in front of Fred Ethridge's Feed Store would have appeared in a photograph as that of a guided tour being organized. Hundreds of people, each wearing backpacks or carrying duffel bags, some with only large paper bags, were all waiting impatiently in long lines to board buses that were destined for some adventurous place. But this was not like a field trip at all. It was not fun. It was not exciting. It was scary very scary! Everyone was afraid. The tension-filled air could be cut into slices like the slabs of beef down at Clancy's Market. There were military personnel and vehicles all about, more buses than you could shake a stick at and 10 or so people with video cameras roaming up and down their streets. The worst part was that there were only vague explanations being provided, although everyone was being assured that this was all for their own good. No one believed it, but they all helplessly obeyed.

The only thing that the people knew was that they had been cut off from the rest of the world after the U.S. Army had roared into their lives at 1:30 am, six hours earlier. It started with the barking of the neighborhood dogs. The occasional pooch yapping in the wee hours was normal, and most people just slept through it. But this night was different. All the dogs were barking, and the barks were frantic sounding. Next came the drone of trucks, Humvees and bus engines moving through the town. Deep sleep was already interrupted when the inharmonious sounds of sirens filled the night, each different in pitch and intensity, causing the residents of this sleepy place to raise to half consciousness. The flashing emergency lights that poked through the slits in the window coverings of their bedrooms was the final straw. Damn! Sheriff Dan must have gotten himself a speeder. But suddenly the sounds of unfamiliar voices seemed to surround their homes. This preceded the sharp raps on the front doors. Up and down the streets and throughout the town, homes were waking up and becoming illuminated. It looked like the closing credits from the *Flintstones* cartoon show. As the women groped for their bathrobes and house slippers, the men in boxers and old tee shirts grabbed their shotguns. The households came alive.

A member of the U.S. Army dressed in camouflage greens and standing at near attention, greeted each resident from the other side of their tattered screened doors. They all heard the same rehearsed speech, "Sorry to trouble you folks, but we have an emergency situation, and for your safety an evacuation has been ordered. There is no need to rush or get excited; as everything is under control. But you must leave for your own well-being. You will each need to pack one small bag and meet in front of Ethridge's Feed Store no later than 6:00 am. Everyone has to go, there can be no exceptions."

What the hell was goin' on? The worst thing that ever happened here was when that truck load of chocolate, that one that was heading for the Heath Bar plant in the next

town over, collided with old man Clark's hay wagon and all
that chocolate spilled out all onto Highway 33. It made
quite a mess. The first reaction was to call someone and
find out what all of the commotion was about. Blurred eyes
and sleepy, confused minds were quickly replaced by wide-
awake fear. A lonely, isolated kind of fear resulted when,
after trying to phone friends, neighbors and family, they
discovered that the phone lines were dead. Communication
with others was impossible. Even the cellular system was
down. The ham and CB radio operators could only raise
static. The sense of helplessness came on so quickly that it
was almost overwhelming.

"I'm sorry. But we have to get you out of here. It's for
your own safety. Now, if you will just get your things in
order and report to the buses," was the standard reply that
came from the Army privates, corporals and sergeants that
were leading the evacuation when asked what was going
on. That was it. That's all they knew or, at least, that was
all they would tell. That's all anyone seemed to know. They
had been forced out of their beds and now had to leave their
homes and possessions and board some damn bus for Lord
knows where.

"Mommy, I want Mrs. Wiggins to go with us, too. Why
do we have to leave her at home?" asked 4-year-old Melissa
Yager as she stood in the long bus line on the dusty parking
lot with the scores of others.

Her mother, Amanda, tried her best to sooth the
confused child over the low groan that was coming from the
big diesel engines of the 15 charter buses parked in the lot
of Etheridge's Feed Store. The chatter from the hundreds of
voices almost enveloped the bus noise. Adding to the
discomfort and frustration was the all too familiar moaning
of Margaret Fitch, known around those parts, rather
unflatteringly, as Miss Fitch the Bitch. The 92-year-old life-

long resident was the self-appointed matriarch of Oblong. In all her days, she had never heard of such a thing as having been told to leave her home. If only her husband was still around. He would give them a piece of his mind. It was obvious to her that the men directing the operation were just impudent Army privates, just snot- nosed kids. And, by God, she was going to call her congressman, David Hatch, whom she had met at the county picnic last year... or was it 1999? And what about her cats? All 14 of 'em. Who was going to feed them? Not these Army brats, she was sure of that. They wouldn't know what to do. Poor little creatures were gonna starve, that was for sure.

Ben and Angela Summers and their four kids were huddled together in prayer, while the Hardin family, waiting to board bus #34, searched through their backpacks for fresh batteries for the Gameboy that was occupying their son Scott.

Mrs. Perkins, standing behind the Hardin's, knew that this was all due to them Simon boys. They was always up to no good.

"Mommy, I want Mrs. Wiggins," demanded Melissa, stomping her foot in clear defiance.

"Who's gonna feed them kitty cats?" shouted Mrs. Fitch, at no one in particular.

Amanda bent over and touched her forehead to that of her daughter's and said, "Mrs. Wiggins has to stay and watch the house. You decided that Baby Sara would come with us, remember? There are only so many things we can bring with us, sweetie."

Army Private Robinson excused himself from the verbal grasp of Mrs. Perkins and stepped over to Melissa and her mother, interrupting their conversation. "Who is Mrs. Wiggins and why is she not here?" he asked.

The younger Miss Yager offered the explanation as she held up a 12-inch tall, redheaded doll sporting a pastel summer dress and lace apron. "This is Baby Sara. Mrs. Wiggins is Baby Sara's grandmother. And she is at home watching our house because *you* won't let her come with us. And that's not fair!" said Melissa as she continued her protest.

The startled but amused private lowered himself to one knee so he could address the complainant on her level. He then gently explained how important it was for Mrs. Wiggins to stay behind. He assured her that everything would be all right and that when she and her mother come back home, Mrs. Wiggins just might have cookies baking for them.

With her hands placed firmly on her hips, Baby Sara dangling from her left hand and that curly blond head cocked to one side, Melissa sniffed. And with all the indignity that only a 4-year-old could muster, Melissa said with a sigh, "Sir, Mrs. Wiggins is only a doll. Dolls cannot bake cookies."

The now pie-eyed private, having lost this battle, stood, tipped his hat to Melissa and said to her mother, "I think it best that I retreat now, ma'am." And off he went shaking his head and laughing at the fact that he had just been done in by a 4-year-old.

With new batteries powering his Gameboy, Scott ran off to play with his friend, Mark, who was two bus lines over. This sent Mr. Hardin chasing after him. As soon as Scott and his dad broke rank several of the other anxious kids broke away to find their friends. They were just burning off some of the excess energy that was boiling up inside of them, but the result was chaos. This immediately got the attention of the Army personnel. They came rushing over, in an attempt to maintain control. One corporal almost tripped over a child who had bolted away. Unfortunately, he did not miss the girl's mother who was right on her heels and knocked the woman hard to the ground. Her husband, in a feeble attempt to defend his wife's honor, tried to cold cock Corporal McAfee, but landed only a glancing blow. McAfee responded by deflecting the next roundhouse blow, grabbing the man by the right arm and swinging him around. Then, with the nightstick held tightly across his throat, the husband and father realized that his struggle was only the result of extreme frustration and stopped his resistance. The sight of the two men struggling caused all of the morning's frustration to boil over. Several others, both men and women, decided that enough was enough and came after McAfee and any of the other enlisted men that were within an arm's reach. The Army personnel struggled to free themselves without striking back as the fists and kicks that were being sent in their direction were finding their mark.

The ensuing melee was cut short by the unmistakable sound of a gunshot. With her .45 raised high in her left hand and a bullhorn gripped tightly in her right, Sargent Mariann Hughes made her way through the crowd, demanding order. "Ladies and gentlemen, stop this now!" she exclaimed, her voice blasting through the bullhorn. "This is not the time to lose control. We are here because your health and well-being are at risk. We do not need injuries from fighting amongst ourselves. Please stop this, and stop it now."

The gunshot had gotten the attention of the entire crowd. Everyone was now standing around looking sad and embarrassed. With words of apology oozing from under their breath, everyone involved moved back to their original positions in the bus line. It would have been some comfort had these people known that this same routine was being played out in Magnolia, Arkansas, Milton, Pennsylvania, Page, Arizona and 23 other small towns currently being evacuated throughout the country. But Sargent Hughes could not tell them this, because she, too, was unaware.

By 8:00 am, the town of Oblong, Illinois, was abandoned. That is, with the exception of the military personnel stationed five miles out of town in each direction on Route 33, as well as on the smaller rural roads leading into the town. And the camera crew that was hurriedly filming the next chapter of Dixie Makepeace's "Tales from an American Town."

# 11

## Pu'u 'O'o

The area around Pu'u 'O'o was a beehive of activity.
One group of four men had just finished stretching a 1-inch
diameter steel cable across the vent. From this cable, they
would hang a curtain made of a special heat resistant
material. The curtain would act as a heat shield to protect
the team from the radiant heat of the Kilauea volcano's
river of lava that was only a few feet away. This would
allow them to set up the necessary rigging in preparation
for their descent into the open conduit. A remote device,
similar to the one that Dr. Allison had lost before, was
being prepared. This time, there would be two heat
resistant cables securing the costly government
surveillance equipment. A 20-foot-high tripod made up of 6-
inch I-beams was being erected above the ancient lava
conduit, the opening through which the surveillance device
would pass, followed by Brice, Allison and six others. The
tripod also provided a sound structure from which to secure
all the rigging that was necessary for the descent party to
use as they rappelled into the volcano.

# Freedom's Menace

The decision was already made as to who would be making the descent. The lucky volunteers were Trevor Brice, Sam Allison, Captain Jones, three members of an elite Special Forces team, Private Phillip Horner, Private David Weaver and Corporal Wayne Benson and finally a submarine officer and an engineer Commander William Ocker and Seaman Bradley Davidson. The descent team began the process of inspecting and trying on the air-cooled, heat-resistant suits, moon suits as they are called, which they would wear as they rappelled down the old lava conduit into the cavern. The air temperature only 25 feet down into the opening was 1,100 degrees. Each of the members of the descent team would also have to wear a 35-pound Scotts Air Pack on their back. The Scotts Air Pack is similar to a SCUBA diver's air tank and is frequently used by firefighters when entering burning, smoke-filled buildings and in "clean room" chemical rescues. Additional Air Packs would have to be lowered along with them for safety, as well as for the return ascent. The suits were bulky and awkward. Maneuvering in them was going to be difficult at best. The sharp, irregular edges of the lava could easily snag their plastic, metallic-like material at each opportunity. This was going to make the descent extremely hazardous.

Luckily, the suits were relatively easy to get into and out of, with a little assistance. Considering this fact, the descent crew practiced removing the suits while hanging 10 feet in the air on a nearby lava mound that was to simulate the conduit wall. It was decided that if the opportunity arose and with any luck, they would be able remove some of the burdensome protection after dropping below the heat-affected region and leave them hanging on the cliff face. A more than 4,000-foot decent was going to be taxing enough. Of course, they would have to get back into the suits to ascend back to the surface. They practiced for this possibility also. It was decided that they would remove the suits and redress in them, until it could be done flawlessly. And then, 10 more times, just for good measure. The act of changing clothes while hanging from a single rope was a daunting task. Samantha's agility and feminine sensibilities about dressing became a tremendous asset. After only three tries, she broke the code of undressing from the rope and nimbly relieved herself of the protective garment. Even with her guidance, the seven men in the group continued to struggle, but eventually, they each grasped the concept, after 10 or 12 attempts.

"You boys always make fun of us girls for playing with Barbies, but it sure paid off," she quipped as she stood firmly on the ground looking up as the guys tried to finish their requisite 10 perfect trials.

The biggest unknown was the size of the opening in the conduit. It was plenty big at the surface and as far into the depths as they could see. It was assumed that it got even wider the deeper it went, but this was only an educated guess offered by Dr. Allison. This was not something that she had been looking for the first time. The remote unit would help to determine this before they started their descent. Thank God for technology. The combination of the baggy suits and the Air Packs would make it almost impossible to squeeze through a tight opening.

"Captain," said an approaching Navy technician, "we have the remote unit ready to deploy. At your command, sir."

"Dr. Allison, it is time for us to go see what we're up against. Meet me in the control tent in five minutes and we'll start making ready for the remote's descent," said Captain Jones.

# Freedom's Menace

"Excuse me for a moment," said Trevor. "I have to advise the President of our progress." Walking out of earshot, Brice typed in the secure phone number that would ring the President's phone in the Oval Office. The conversation was brief and to the point.

Sam took the moment of downtime to survey the activity around her. There were about 50 people, all military, scurrying around performing their assigned tasks. There was no one barking orders. All seemed to instinctively know just what needed to be done and in what order it was to be performed. Everyone's efforts appeared to be well planned and rehearsed. However, what was being done had never been done before and never would be again. She stood in awe and amazement at their skills. The steel I-beam tripod that was centered over the conduit in which they would descend went up in less than 90 minutes. A communications hut and operations room had been erected 50 yards to the north of the vent. Surrounding it were several satellite dishes that were pointing in various directions up toward the heavens three 20-foot-tall radio towers that resembled the old style TV antennas and a variety of other strange looking devices that she assumed were also some type of communications apparatus.

The control center for the remote descent unit was housed in a small 10-foot by 10-foot open-sided tent that looked like a back yard barbecue shelter. The mess hall and the field hospital were situated about 100 yards further to the north of the operations hut. Next to them, the sleeping barracks and sanitation facilities were being erected. To the west and only about 100 yards away were three diesel powered electric generators, two of which were screaming for all they were worth as they pumped electricity through the miles of electrical cable that lay scattered across the top of the volcano. Last, but not least, the helicopter pad with its mini weather station and windsock was situated 300 yards to the east. The heat shield curtain separating the Pu'u 'O'o vent from the dormant conduit was almost in place. Samantha was amazed at the transformation this area was undergoing. Just last week she was here taking lava samples, with a metal cup attached to a long metal rod, dressed in a protective, metallic suit with heavy heat-resistant gloves and boots. That was the same day that she lost the remote.

Incredibly, this group of 50 people had literally built a small village in a matter of only a few hours. Again, the men and women of the United States military were demonstrating their superior training, preparation and ability to respond to all contingencies. It was all happening while steady streams of the familiar Blue Hawaiian tourist helicopters were buzzing overhead. Much of the time, the Pu'u 'O'o vent is shrouded in clouds. But when the sky is clear, as it was now, this was a prime spectacle for the tourist crowd, and the helicopter operators were only too happy to accommodate. Certainly there was much wonderment above them, as the throngs of tourists circling above in the blue helicopters tried to ascertain what was happening around the world's most active volcano.

"Sam, we're ready," came Brice's strong voice above all the noise and activity. Sam took a last moment to review the activity around the remote unit that was now hanging from the steel tripod above the opening of the fissure. The remote device was about the size of two of those popular rolling airline suitcases. There were lights pointing in all six directions, various sensing elements protruding from the sides and it was wrapped in a special heat resistant cloth, similar to that which the descent team would be wearing. A one-inch electrical cable was attached to the top of the unit in the center. As a precaution, a battery back-up pack was added and suspended two feet above. Two independent heat resistant steel cables secured the device.

Both the suspension cables and the electrical power cable were special, water-cooled cable systems. Cool water was pumped through a metal shield that surrounded the outside of the primary cable and then back to the surface through a hole in the center of the cable. The cables ran through a special pulley, down separate legs of the tripod and then went in opposite directions for 150 feet, and curled around giant capstans that were anchored to the front ends of two Humvee all-terrain vehicles. From there, the cables ran to a point midway between the two Humvees. There stood a large, elaborate contraption that coiled the cables onto large spools and provided the pumps and the supply of cooling water. A small water tower sat next to the spool system and cooled the heated water as it returned from the center of the cables. The electrical cable had a similar system sitting nearby. Everything seemed to be in place.

Inside of the control tent sat an electronic console that was the size of an executive desk. There were four large computer monitors, two on each side. In the center were numerous dials, switches and gauges that provided the operator with information about the cable systems, such as temperature of the water inlet and outlet, the voltage and amperage of the electrical drive systems, and how much stress and strain was been applied to the support cables. It also contained all the buttons for the operation of the lights, cameras and sensors as well as the communication equipment. The monitor on the upper right was segmented into four quadrants, each showing a different camera angle. Considering that there were six cameras, the pictures from the top and bottom views showed continuously, while the four side views rotated every 10 seconds. The lower right monitor was for displaying the temperature measurements that the remote would be transmitting on a continuous basis. An atmospheric sampling device monitored the air quality and was depicted on the lower left screen. The screen on the upper left provided the operator with a constantly changing view of the mechanical systems for the tripod, the two capstans and spools, and the cooling water system. It also served as the monitor for the infrared camera, if needed. A normal looking keyboard and computer mouse sat in the center of the console and provided all of the control that was required. A microphone arched across the center of the keyboard.

"Sir, I am ready to begin," said Marine Corporal Jessie Reynolds, the operator sitting at the console. "All system checks have been completed, the water cooling system is a go, and the capstan wrenching system is on standby. On your orders, sir."

"The command is given. Let's begin lowering the unit at a rate of six inches per second," ordered Captain Jones, adding, "Stay alert, we don't want to loose this one." He glanced at Sam in time to see her roll her eyes to the heavens. When she looked back, he gave her a wink.

"Just one of life's little moments," she said.

"At this rate it will take about two and a half hours to reach the bottom," said the operations officer. "That's based on the fact that we are about 4,000 feet above sea level. At the opening of the crevice, the air temperature was 110 degrees. Twenty-five feet down, the temperature had jumped to 1,100 degrees. At 50 feet, the side cameras were showing that the wall adjacent to and common with the Pu'u 'O'o vent was glowing a dull gray red."

"It is amazing to me," observed Dr. Allison, "that the wall did not collapse during the last eruption. I really don't like the looks of this. We see this same coloring on the surface flows. That wall cannot be more than several inches thick, a foot at the most. The slightest impact would break whatever bond is holding it together, and the lava flow would rain down on top of us."

Brice coldly chimed in, "Well, we just have to be sure that we don't bump into anything."

Everyone in the room just looked at him in uncomfortable silence and then turned their attention back to the screen. The lower left monitor showed that the air quality was quite toxic, with sulfur being the primary pollutant. At 100 feet, the conditions improved slightly. The color of the lava rock walls had returned to their normal jet-black, and the temperature had dropped to less than 1,000 degrees. Conditions improved even more dramatically at 135 feet below ground. The path of the conduit had started to veer away from the Pu'u 'O'o conduit, air quality was improving, and the temperature was a tepid 285 degrees.

Thus far the size of the conduit remained fairly steady at 15 to 20 feet in diameter. The slope of the cavity continued to fall away from the active vent, but only at a very slight angle. But at some point the cable system would start to rub against the sides of the walls. The rate of descent would have to be slowed to prevent damage to the unit and to the support and electrical cables. Conditions suitable for humans were finally reached just past 210 feet. The temperature was 105 degrees and the air quality was acceptable. The team considered this, but decided that with the exertion of rappelling in combination with all the obstructive equipment, it would be best to find a more suitable elevation at which to remove their burdensome gear. The desired conditions were finally found at 675 feet. There was also some good news discovered with the aid of the cameras, a ledge at 680 feet. Not a big ledge, from what they could see, but certainly large enough for two people to safely stand while removing the protective suits and air tanks. This would make the remainder of the descent much,

# W. Laurence Willis

much easier if in fact they could exercise this option. The descent unit continued dropping into the vast abyss of ancient lava flows.

Freedom's Menace

# 12

## Changsha, China

There were now 36 hours until the deadline for the ultimatum was to expire. An Lolo dismissed two of the three advisors and stood on the third floor balcony, off the study of his mountain retreat, with Mr. Wu. The air was cool, crisp and sweet. The beauty that lay in front of him was beyond description. A waterfall to the east, cascading down the mountain, formed four pools at different elevations as it dropped more than 2,200 feet. The river that was formed at the base of the falls traveled southeast through the plush green valley. Although winter was approaching, it felt like spring to the Chinese leader. "Soon," he thought, "the world will be a new place, a new world order, and I, An Lolo, the son of a peasant farmer, have been selected to lead it."

"Premier Lolo, sir," said a voice from the study. "You have received a message from your source in the United States. Would you like to read it now?"

# W. Laurence Willis

Lolo turned and extended his hand for the papers that were being offered by one of the guards. Mr. Wu dismissed the guard as Lolo read the message. After a few minutes, he let his right arm and hand, the one clinching the paper, slowly drop to his side. With his left hand, he removed his reading glasses and in thoughtful speech he said, "Those stupid Americans are so arrogant. They wish to defy me. This, of course, is completely expected. It is my belief that they will even try to attack us in an effort to 'set us straight,' as they are so fond of saying."

He stepped to the door of the room. "Sung, I will have tea now." Sung, the young servant girl from the nearby village, bowed politely and scurried from the room. After the young woman had left, his lone advisor, Mr. Wu, asked, "What if the Americans attack? How can we protect ourselves? How do we stop them? We have no missiles that can defeat theirs."

With head bowed and eyes looking only at the floor, the servant woman reentered the room with a tray of tea, biscuits and cakes. She poured the tea and presented it to the two men and then, bowing frequently, she retreated to the back corner of the room that was her place until summoned again. She was new to the premier's personal staff and was very willing to please.

Sipping the delicate green tea, Lolo turned to face the mountains and valleys that lay before him. "Mr. Wu, the Americans win by shear force and technology. They are too predictable and no longer freethinking. What they will do first is to decide to fight. Then a massive military build up will begin. There will be hundreds of planes flown in and ships sailed into our region. But this will only occur after the weeks that it will take to convince all of the world's governments to support their plan. Then additional weeks and possibly months as they move troops and equipment into the area. All the while, there will be a lot of strong talk and saber rattling, for they never strike until all plans are in place. Once they make their decision to attack us, they will do so by first throwing scores of cruise and ballistic missiles at us. This will be followed by strategic air attacks. All of this will be necessary in order to render our communications inoperative. If we are blind and deaf, how can we possibly strike back?"

The Chinese leader paused for a long breath and reached for one of the biscuits that lay on the tea tray. Yang Wu stood there with his heart pounding and his mind racing, waiting for An Lolo to complete the story. There certainly had to be more. Lolo's relaxed posture spoke volumes. He was quite assured that all contingencies had been covered. Taking a sip and savoring the warm brew, Lolo motioned for his aide to help himself to a snack.

He then continued. "You are wondering why I do not fear this. The Americans, you see, are quite good at war, they learn their lessons well, but I remind you that they are no longer freethinking. The Americans will be most surprised when they find that their missiles will never land on our soil. Rather they will simply and harmlessly fly out to sea. With any luck on our part, some may even land in Japan or, better yet, Taiwan."

"But how is that possible?" asked Wu.

"Technology, Mr. Wu, technology," answered Lolo. "We will beat them at their own game." A broad grin formed on the lips of Premier Lolo. "You see, the Americans have learned to guide their missiles from great distances using lasers and radio waves beamed from distant aircraft, ships and satellites. Our scientists have learned that we cannot shoot down their missiles, but we can distract them. By detecting the incoming enemy missile on radar, we can then send up our own missile to intercept the enemy. Our intercepts are small, fast and powerful, but carry no explosives. Rather they contain very strong lasers and radio signaling and receiving devices. It does not have to strike the enemy, just get close. The radio receiver picks up the enemy's incoming instructions and simply plays it back, only at a much louder signal. The enemy projectile is now getting two redundant signals at different strengths only milliseconds apart. This creates great confusion for the electronic mind of the missile, but just for a moment. We then change our signal to try and alter the enemy's course. It will not work, but it creates even more confusion. With their superior technology briefly befuddled and our missile continuously sonding it conflicting signals, the American missile will enter a fail-safe condition. At that point, it will enter a straight and level flight condition while it tries to verify the information. Again, it will get two signals at different strengths. The missile goes into permanent fail-safe condition and it just flies harmlessly out to sea with our missile in the lead. The laser-guided bombs are even easier. We just shine our laser on it, and it follows us wherever we want it to go. I wish that I could look into the faces of their military commanders as they try to figure out what we have done."

A light mist had started to fall from the mid-afternoon clouds that roll in this time each day. The two men moved into the adjacent study and continued their conversation. Neither had noticed that Sung had moved to within earshot of the conversation and was quickly returning to her place. As they entered the room all was normal. They found two comfortable chairs and continued their conversation. "I believe there are things that you are not telling," said Wu with a hopeful smile.

"Actually, you are right, Mr. Wu. If all goes well, there will never be a shot fired from either side. It is important

that someone knows of our plan in the unlikely event that
something happens to me. You, my friend, are the chosen
one. This information will not make you the next leader of
China, but it will provide you and your family with a good
and generous life. There are others, government and
military leaders, that know of my plans, only not in their
entirety. You will be the key to unlock the unknowns if that
becomes necessary."

The young woman standing quietly in the corner, with
head bowed and eyes fixed on a spot on the floor, shuddered
at what she was hearing. She almost lost her composure as
she felt as if she had just been immersed in ice-cold water.
But she held it together, maintaining her subservient
posture as she listened intently, every word committed to
memory. Sung was the maiden name of Alexandra Wilson's
mother. Her grandmother lived in the small village only a
few miles from this mountain retreat. Her one daughter,
Alex's mother, was an exceptionally bright child who had
eventually been sent to the United States to continue her
education. She had met Alex's father, a Chinese-American,
and elected to remain in the Unites States, eventually
becoming an American citizen. Little did Alex know that
when she had committed to learn the secrets behind the
death of Dr. Scott and his party that she would stumble
into the planning of world conquest by her ancestors'
government. She was also thinking that this was the
stupidest thing she had ever done and that her life was now
in serious jeopardy. "Stay focused," she said to herself, "just
stay focused!" She then let her mind go back to the
discussion in the opposite corner of the room.

"My plan is to create so much anxiety for the American
people that their government will become incapacitated and
anarchy will result. We plan to attack their small towns in
order to create terror and panic. Following that we will
sever their communications by flooding their computers

with a most sophisticated computer virus. This war will mostly be fought and won with the aid of that wonderful Internet, which, of course, they perfected. As you know, and with much thanks to your efforts, we have already destroyed that one little town outside of Washington. I did that with President Totten sitting just three feet in front of me. His feeling of hopelessness was so strong that he even attacked me. It was a wondrous event!"

"I have even considered striking once more, just to make sure he understands completely."

An expression of concern crossed Wu's face and he said, "Did you not give him 72 hours?"

The premier nodded.

"If you strike too soon it may appear to the rest of the world and to our own people that you are an untrustworthy leader. The upper hand now belongs to you now, and they know that. One more day, it will not matter."

"The hell it won't," thought Alex, her head swelling with anger. She was starting to fidget, but caught herself. A fidget could be a death sentence.

"You are right," said Lolo, throwing a quick glance at the young woman. "Another little fact that the Americans are unaware of is that we now have 12 Russian-made Bars class nuclear submarines at our disposal. Eight of them are within striking distance of the United States mainland as we speak. The other four are patrolling our own waters. We have three each off the Pacific and Atlantic coasts and two in the Gulf of Mexico. We have our sights trained on New York, Washington, Newport and Charleston in the east, Pensacola, Houston, New Orleans and Corpus Christi from the Gulf and finally, San Diego, Los Angles, San Francisco and Seattle on their West Coast. From these positions, we can launch a preemptive first strike if forced to do so. We will make Pearl Harbor look like a training exercise."

Relaxing a little and settling back into his chair, Yang Wu gave careful consideration to all that he had just learned. There was something here that made him uncomfortable, but he could not identify the feeling. Several moments of silence passed, and An Lolo rose from his chair, but indicated that Yang was to stay seated.

Lolo walked over to the young woman. He reached out with his left hand and cupped it under her chin. He slowly raised her face to meet his. Leaning in closely he said, "You are a very beautiful young woman. I hope you understand how fortunate it is for you to be here serving me. A position like this is not only good for you, but it assures that your family remains in good health as well."

"Oh, shit," she thought as her eyes widened, "just what does he want from me? Thank God he has no idea that I switched places with that girl in the village."

Then placing his right hand on her left breast he quietly said, "I must return to Beijing tomorrow. The next many days and weeks will be very stressful. I trust you will comfort me tonight and ease all of my tensions?"

With that he smiled, turned and walked back to his chair to continue his conversation with Wu. Alex's head lowered, and she regained her docile expression while staring at the floor, but her thoughts were on rapid fire.

"What the fuck, now?" she wondered, "Do I have to screw the old fart? Oh, shit! Oh, shit! How in the hell did I ever talk myself into this? And if I don't play along what happens to me? What happens to the girl in the village?

117

...and to her family? Oh, my God! I have really screwed up this time! I really have to get out of here. Ah, shit! But how?"

Pleased with himself, Lolo sat back down and addressed Wu once again, "As you have figured out by now we are hitting civilian as well as military targets. They will be so thrown off by all of this that their entire society may even collapse."

Yang said, "You talked about the computer virus and an Internet war, but now you speak of rockets and bombs. Pardon me, sir, but I do not understand."

Tilting his head back and staring at the ceiling for a moment, Premier Lolo pondered the question. "My friend, the submarines and their rockets are not our first option, although, I personally would enjoy using those weapons against the Americans. And we will use some destructive means as an offensive move. As we have already destroyed the one town, we will destroy a few others just to raise the anxiety level. Even their prized Disneyland will not be spared. It will not take much; four or five devastating attacks will do. Then the computer virus. Our scientists advise me that the computer virus we will launch will disable all of their systems in a matter of hours. We will shut them off from virtually all means of electronic contact. Their anxiety will already be at fever pitch, and then all of the unfounded fear that resulted years ago from Y2K will become reality on a grand scale. With luck, we will even shut off their lights. When the plan is fully implemented, the United States will become paralyzed. America is a country that has become too soft, too complacent, too accustomed to the comforts of their bountiful lives. The experience we are going to provide will be devastating."

# Freedom's Menace

Handing Wu a thin stack of papers, Lolo indicated that the specifics and targets for the terrorist and submarine missile attacks and the approximate location of the submarines were listed on it. Mr. Wu was to commit this information to memory and then destroy the notes. This was an easy task for Mr. Wu, his mind was like a camera, recording everything he read and retrieving it at will. Alex knew she had to see what was on that paper. But after Yang Wu read it carefully, he walked over to the desk in the corner of the room and dropped it into the shredder. Alex's heart sank. Both men were now on their feet and heading for the door.

Lolo looked over to his planned evening guest and said to her, "You will join me for dinner at 7:00?"

The young woman simply nodded and bowed, head down, her eyes never leaving that point on the floor in front of her. The door shut with a loud bang.

Alex instantly sprinted across the room toward the desk. Of all the dumb luck, the only thing in the plastic bag below the shredder was the shredded pieces of the notes that Wu had destroyed. She yanked open the top drawer of the desk and quickly found an envelope, which that she filled with the hundreds of quarter inch squares that were once the top-secret note. She knew that she did not have the time to even begin to reconstruct it, but if she could get it to someone else then maybe a disaster would be avoided. She tucked the envelope into the front of her camisole and headed for the tea tray. She reached it just as the door swung open. Appearing to collect and arrange the china service she stopped and acknowledged the guard that had come to escort her back to the kitchen. Grasping the tray with both hands she hurried toward the door and down the hall to the back stairs. The guard shut and locked the door and followed his charge to the kitchen.

On entering the kitchen, the head of the servants approached her. A stone-faced woman of 50 years who was built like a fireplug grabbed Alex's face and squeezed her cheeks.

"My dear," she said, "as you know you will be entertaining the Premier this evening. If all goes well, he may even invite you to accompany him back to Beijing. You should know that this is a great honor. You should also understand that it is necessary for your health and the health of your family." The Chinese have always had a subtle way of convincing people about what was required of them.

"I am very honored to have been asked to provide for the premier, although I do not feel that I am worthy. I am but a poor village girl and do not have proper clothing. How can I dine with a man in his position dressed as I am, in my working clothes?" Alex asked.

In the voice of an empathetic pit bull the woman said, "My dear young woman. We will get you clothing. You will not be sent before the premier looking the way you do. You will be taken to the village. The women there have many very nice silk fabrics with which to dress you. You will be bathed, dressed and prepared in every way to be received by the premier. You will be returned to the emperor's retreat by 6:00 pm. Is that understood?"

Alex politely bowed.

# 13

## Alexandra's Date

"Guard," barked the woman, "take the servant to the village so that she can prepare for the premier's dinner tonight."

The guard grabbed Alex from the back, his long, muscular fingers almost encircling her neck, and pushed her toward the rear door. She stumbled and fell on to the wet tile floor. She scrambled to her feet just in time to miss the kick that the guard made for her right thigh. She ran to the door, opened it and, all the while continuously bowing, she held it open for her armed escort. A two-passenger, Chinese Jeep-like vehicle sat 20 yards away. A second armed guard sat in the driver's seat smoking a cigarette. She climbed into the unpadded rear cargo area and made herself as comfortable as possible. The floor was littered with an odd assortment of things; a night stick, several boxes of ammunition, a pair of boots, a first aid kit and hand tools like wrenches and pliers. She shoved as much of it under the front seats as she could. Fortunately, the village was only a 20-minute drive away, but it was over the same old wagon road on which she had entered the village just days before. The first guard swung into the passenger seat, and they were off with a jolt. Clearly the driver was making every effort to make the trip as uncomfortable as possible for his human baggage.

When they finally reached the village and pulled to a stop, the obligatory "welcoming" crowd circled around the guards and their Jeep. Alex stood and tried to step out of the vehicle but found herself sprawled face down on the ground as a result of a forceful shove from the driver. Both men roared with laughter as several women raced over to help Alex to her feet. While the first guard explained to the mayor what was expected, the driver went over to taunt Alex even further. He grabbed at her camisole, tearing out the left shoulder, exposing her breast. He then scolded her, explaining how she was not worthy enough for even the son of a laborer much less for the premier himself. He reached out for the dangling scrap of material and yanked it toward him. The force swung Alex around 180 degrees. The envelope fell out from its hiding spot in the tuck of the garment and fluttered onto the ground. One of the women in the group immediately stepped over the off-white rectangle, hiding it from the driver's view. The driver pulled at her right arm in an effort to turn her back around, but several of the women stepped in front to shield her nakedness and to prevent a further attack.

One of the older women stepped forward and said, "The premier will not like for his mistress to be damaged."

With that, the senior guard ordered the driver to move the vehicle to the village center and to wait there. Alex and several of the women disappeared into a nearby hut. The women undressed her and tended to her wounds, which consisted of only rug burns and minor scratches on her knees and forearms. She was dazed, but unhurt except for possibly the bruise on her tailbone caused by the rough ride to the village in the back on the Jeep. Looking through all of the confusion, Alex saw the envelope being handed to her. She had not even realized that it was missing. Suddenly, she regained her focus. What was she going to do? It was 4:00 pm, only an hour and a half before she had to return to the emperor's retreat and her "date." The guards were goons and could be easily overtaken, but then the entire village would be punished. She could run, but the girl she had replaced would be killed as well as her family. No options, she had to follow it through.

The hot bath that the women had prepared was heavenly. She allowed herself to relax to clear her head as the women bathed her and shampooed her hair. They cleaned and trimmed her fingernails and toenails. Another was showing her bolts of silk for her dress. The sad fact was that this had all transpired before; the women had a routine for this. They all knew just what to do and how much time they had to do it. A young woman was being dressed for the slaughter. This was the village of her grandparents and everyone knew who she was. Her surprise visit was not nearly as unexpected as her volunteering to trade places with the other young woman, the 18-year-old daughter of the town's elders. They were particularly solemn as a result. Alex's mind was beginning to whirl again. She handed the envelope to her grandmother, asking that it be well hidden. She gave instructions that if she was not back for it by sunrise they were to get the information to a friendly American or Brit or, if possible, send an e-mail to the White House in the United States. Luckily, as China was preparing to enter in the 21st century, even the more remote villages could gain access to the Internet. Not the easiest thing to do, but doable just the same.

As she was being fitted for her gown, she asked a question that was completely out of order for this culture, but she needed to know. "When your day has been long and you are very tired but your man orders you to lay beside him at night, what can you do to prevent it?" she asked.

Dead silence filled the room as all of the women sheepishly looked at one another, not knowing exactly what to say. Soft giggles began to fill the hut, and then outright laughter followed. One of the women left the hut as the others simply went along with their business of fitting the red silk gown. A few minutes later the woman returned and offered Alex a small black silk pouch.

"A spoonful in the premier's wine will cause him much embarrassment," she said, as the room once again filled with knowing giggles. "Of course," she continued, "after he drinks, you must then spend much time assuring him that he is still a worthy man and that all will be better tomorrow." Once again the drab little hut was aired with joyous laughter.

The makeover was now complete. Alex stood in the center of the room wearing a red silk, form-fitting, floor-length gown with black silk slippers. Her hair was up and held in place with chopsticks colored in black and gold. Her fingernails were painted in a bright jade with silver sparkles. A wrist bag hung from her left arm and the most important smaller, black pouch was safely tucked away in a hidden fold just above her waist on the right side. She was ready, and not a moment too soon.

The guards came bursting into the hut, shouting orders that it was now time to leave. The sight of Alex stopped them cold. Their mouths fell open, and they just stared as a rush of warm blood filled their groins. Their obvious physical change caused the older women to giggle, clearly embarrassing the two. They grew stern, stepped from the door and indicted that Alex should follow them. The senior guard ordered the driver to sit in the cargo space while he drove. The driver immediately protested, but the sight of the other man's pistol trained at his forehead persuaded him to reconsider, yet he grumbled as he climbed into the tight space behind the seats. Alex climbed into the passenger seat and waved good-bye to her grandmother and friends. The driver let his eyes run up and down the curves of her body before starting the engine and speeding off toward the emperor's retreat. Throughout the 20-minute jostling ride the two men talked non-stop about how much they were going to enjoy the young woman's pleasures after the premier was finished with her. It was also made clear that after they were through with her, she would then be shared with their comrades. Alex just sat and listened, all the time knowing that there was no way in hell that that was going to happen. They pulled up to the front entrance of the emperor's retreat, where they were greeted by the female fireplug.

"You will do quite nicely. The premier will be quite pleased. Follow me, please," she ordered.

The emperor's retreat was more than 400 years old, large and in the opulent architecture typical of the Ming dynasty, but it had been built during the Qing dynasty in the 17th century for Emperor Qianlong. As Alex climbed the marble steps, the eyes of the guards were fixed on her. At 5 feet 9 inches her height was somewhat rare for Asian women, and the men all found this quite appealing. She was led upstairs and into the state dining room that was centered along the east wall. The room was simply grand, with ancient Chinese art and sculpture, hand woven rugs, fine 17th century furniture and sparkling gold leaf trim all around. The ceiling was at least 30 feet high and dripping with gold and crystal chandeliers. A large fireplace filled a

portion for the outer wall and glowed with a brilliant fire.
Doors on either side of the fireplace lead to separate
balconies that overlooked the eastern mountain range and
surely offered an impressive view of each morning's sunrise.
In the center of the room sat a hand carved marble table. It
had been set for dinner with flowers, wine and the finest
silver and china place settings.

"Man, if I could only be here with Mel Gibson," Alex
thought.

She was so taken with the splendor of the room that
she almost didn't notice all the activity happening around
her. The servants were preparing everything as if it were a
state dinner. There were also guards stationed all around,
two at the main doorway, one at each balcony door, one at
the serving area and two more on either side of a closed
double door on the north wall to the left. There was one
woman who was sampling all of the foods and wines. She
was followed closely by another man who Alex knew to be
the chef.

"Poor woman must be the guinea pig. If someone tries
to poison the old goat, she gets it first," she said under her
breath.

A soldier behind the taster was likely there to ensure
that she did not poison the food after sampling it. Suddenly
the room became very quiet. Everyone moved to what
appeared to be his or her pre-assigned spot.

The guards had opened the two doors on the north wall,
and there stood An Lolo, in all his glory. The robe he was
wearing had to have been spun from pure gold. It was the
most amazing sight she had ever seen. He entered the room
and walked toward her, all the while examining her every
detail. She felt incredibly uncomfortable. Without a word he

bowed and directed her to the table. She stood while he was
seated. She then sat down.

   The next several hours were a complete blur. The
events of the five-hour festival whirled past her in a fury of
color, movement and mystical sound. It was like dining
center stage at a Fosse musical. There were more dinner
courses served than she could count. Lolo was becoming
drunk and the night was growing late. He finally rose from
the table escorted her out to one of the balconies to see the
stars. In the absence of city lights the night sky was ablaze.
She knew what was coming next as she felt his hands on
her waist. He then slowly and gently lowered them down to
her hips and thighs, then back up to her shoulders and
down her arms. She felt his fat belly against her butt as he
tried to make contact with his manhood. She had not been
able to slip any of the magic powder into his drink. The
guards were always too close and too watchful. She turned
to face him and pressed her body close to his. His reaction
was as expected. Then tossing him a coy smile she slipped
from his grasp and stepped back inside the room. To her
amazement he had dismissed the entire staff, including the
guards. The room was completely empty! Walking over to
the wine service, she began to pour him another drink.
While outside, as Lolo was distracting himself by feeling
her up, she had slipped her fingers into the pouch and took
a good thick pinch of the powder between her thumb, index
and middle fingers. The powder had now dissolved into the
wine.

   Now to just get him to drink without first calling on his
taster to sample the wine. She glided across the room to
where he was standing and pressed herself close, the glass
of wine at chest level. First gazing into his eyes she raised
the glass and took a long sip. Having had no idea what the
powder was, she knew this was risky, but she figured that
it was worth it. Lolo took the glass from her hands and

downed the remaining contents. Then with the flair of
Sandy Koufax tossing the final pitch of a no hitter, he sent
the expensive, crystal goblet sailing into the fireplace, a
scene he had viewed on American movies. The shattered
particles glistened in the flames as they showered down
upon the hearth. He placed one arm around her waist and
drew her closer, moving his other hand to her backside in
the process. His advanced state of arousal was immediately
obvious. She tensed, but tried her best to play along.
Having made his point, he backed away and took her right
hand in his. They were now walking toward the doors at
the north end of the room. The two doors opened into what
seemed to be another planet.

They stepped into a world of even more splendors than
the one that they were leaving. Elegantly carved marble
columns highlighted with jade, precious stones and gold
supported the 30-foot-high ceiling of the round room.
Windows covered about a third of the wall space and
centered on the view of the great waterfall to the northeast.
In the center of the room was the bed, if one could call it a
bed. It was huge, looking like someone had grafted together
four American king-sized mattresses. At each corner was a
marble column that rose 20 feet into the air. From the
column-like bedposts hung the finest of silks. They formed
the canopy and draped to the floor. There was neither a
headboard nor a footboard; all sides were open. Pillows and
coverings of more fine silk were spread over the sleeping
area. The ceiling was a deep blue and decorated with stars
of gold leaf and diamonds. Alex walked to the room's center
and slowly turned, taking in all of the finery that the room
had to offer.

She felt Lolo's approach but was too taken by the
splendor to pay much attention. The golden attire that just
moments before adorned his body was now laying across
one corner of the bed. When she finally turned, she found

him to be quite naked and very aroused. He stepped
forward and placed his hands on her shoulders and pulled
her in close. His hands then became heavy weights on her
shoulders as he forced her down to her knees.

"Ah, shit," she thought. "I really don't want to do this."
But at this point she had no choice, and she knew it. The
price of refusal would be death. Not only for her, but also
for some of the villagers as well.

She took his penis in her right hand as she conceded
defeat. Almost on cue, as if someone had flipped a switch,
the blood flowed from him like air from a burst balloon.
Lobsters being plunged into a pot of boiling water do not
even die that quickly.

"Oh, thank God," she thought, almost saying it out
loud. She wasn't quite sure that she hadn't said it at an
audible level, but it did not matter because Lolo shrieked
and stepped back 8 or 10 paces. He stared down at himself
in shock and terror. Not knowing what else to do, Alex
began sobbing and apologizing profusely. He started to yell.

"What have you done to me? What evil do you possess?
Aargh!" he screamed.

The sounds of Lolo's anguished cries alerted the
guards. Four of them burst into the room, two from each
door, machine guns cocked and ready to fire. They found
Alex still kneeling next to the bed, begging and pleading
with Lolo for forgiveness. Their leader, An Lolo, stood only
10 feet away, completely nude and holding himself with
both hands.

"Get this devil woman out of my sight!" he bellowed.

W. Laurence Willis

# 14

## Alexandra's Escape

At first the guards just stood there, mesmerized by the sight that they were witnessing. Lolo's continued bellows and Alex's profuse pleas for mercy finally snapped them back.

"Premier, what shall we do with her?" asked one of the guards. "I don't care. She is yours. Do with her what you will. Just get her out of my sight, out of the emperor's retreat and, and … Just take her away!" Lolo yelled.

Alex started to rise, but was grabbed by the hair on the back of her head and dragged out into the hall. She was thrown face down and felt the barrel of a machine gun being wedged between her legs.

"By the time we finish with you, you will wish that we had just shot you down here instead," laughed the guard, jamming the rod of cold metal into her crotch.

# Freedom's Menace

The guards were accustomed to getting the women that Lolo discarded after he was through with them, but this one... This one would be special, a treat. Untouched, fresh and clean. And they also did not have to be concerned with harming her, because she had clearly become the focus of his wrath. Two guards lifted Alex to her feet and herded her toward the main staircase. The others went to shut the doors to the premier's bedroom. Looking inside the room as they pulled the tall ornamental doors closed, they saw Lolo standing naked in front of the 12-foot-high mirror desperately trying to restore that which he had been so pleased with just minutes before. Shame and embarrassment were clearly written across his broad face.

Halfway down the main stairs, the two guards were already planning the sexual romp they would be having with this beautiful Lolo reject. Suddenly the sight of their superior officer at the bottom of the steps stopped them cold. Alex looked up and into the face of the senior guard, the same one who had taken her to the village earlier that afternoon. The same man who had described in graphic detail the encounter that he would be having with her when Lolo was finished. The thought crossed her mind that there was not enough of that magical powder in all of China to stop what was about to happen.

One of the guards spoke up, in a nervous voice, "Look, sir. Look what has been given to us by the Premier."

Their superior just looked at them with an unemotional stare. "Thank you for bringing her for me," he said coldly.

The other guards considered protesting, but realized that it would be to no avail. They reluctantly released their prize. Better to get the leftovers later in the night than to miss out on a bite of the plum altogether.

The superior ordered his driver to take the girl to his Jeep.

"We will return her to the village," he said.

The two guards that had lagged behind to close up the room were now joining their comrades on the stairs. All four men instinctively knew that they would never see the woman again. Their boss had a nasty habit of taking the castoffs for himself and rarely sharing with the others.

The Jeep was parked on the front drive of the emperor's retreat. The senior officer's driver picked Alex up by her waist and tossed her, like a bag of dog chow, into the rear cargo compartment. She landed hard. Most of the impact was taken up by her tailbone, which was already sore from the earlier drive. Her throat tightened and tears welled up in her dark brown eyes even before her head slammed down on the floor of the Jeep. Her legs were sticking straight up into the air and flailing wildly as the engine sputtered to life. Still stunned and laying flat on her back, she felt someone else climb aboard. With a jolt and loud backfire the Jeep lurched forward. As they left the grounds of the retreat and pulled onto the old wagon road, she was still desperately trying to right herself. The bouncing was making the task especially difficult. Her tailbone screamed in pain while the back of her head throbbed in the unrelenting cadence of a John Phillip Sousa march. The lump in her throat and tears in her eyes were joined by an overwhelming sense of helplessness. The Jeep was traveling at a much higher rate of speed than earlier in the day. Her two captors spoke in loud, jovial dialog, but in a strange Chinese dialect that she did not fully understand. The language she did not know, but the intention was only too clear. She was going to be fucked and then killed. It was just that simple and just that crude.

# Freedom's Menace

Struggling for composure, she finally adjusted herself so that she was now sitting upright. When the tears from her eyes dried enough to allow her some degree of clear vision, she found the muzzle of the senior officer's gun was only four inches from her face. She contritely slumped back down, but only slightly. Her right hand was desperately searching underneath the car seats to find something, anything that could possibly help her out of this situation. All she could find were the few boxes of bullets and an old boot, no gun, of course, and the pliers that she had shoved under the seat earlier.

"This is really useful," she thought. "There has to be something else in this pile of crap."

An order was given, and the driver made an abrupt right turn, maneuvering the Jeep between two larger boulders. The rocky path they were now driving on made for an exceptionally bumpy ride. The driver was holding onto the steering wheel for dear life while his passenger held a white-knuckle grip on the crossbar that was attached to the dash in front of him. Alex was on her own, her already sore rump was now numb and the guards did not seem to care whether or not she bounced out. The officer screamed at his driver to slow down and to watch out for the edge of the cliff. The driver happily obliged and slowed to a crawl. The Jeep settled to a continuous, but almost comfortable, jostle. There, up ahead, was a small clearing. The two men had finished another brief exchange when the senior officer turned to Alex to advise her of the fate that awaited her in the clearing just ahead. After he, and then his comrade, finished their turns at enjoying the pleasures of her body, it would be he that would have the enjoyment of throwing her body off of the cliff.

Alex just saw red. As his hardy laugh quieted and a broad grin spread across on his face, he turned back and

133

faced forward. The grin diminished only slightly when the blade of the screwdriver entered the base of his skull and imbedded itself six inches into his brain. With the terrain still very tenuous, the edge of the cliff only a meter to the right and several hundred meters to go until they reached the clearing, the driver was totally focused on the task at hand. He was completely oblivious to the fate of his, now dead, superior officer. A few more bumps and a few more bruises later the driver lifted his foot from the accelerator, and the Jeep began to slow. He announced their arrival. This was a familiar place, a place where the two of them had frequently taken their "dates" for a night of lovemaking. For the women, a night of terminal lovemaking. But not for this woman, not on this night. The driver finally turned and looked at his passenger. His eyes were huge, almost bugging out of his head. His mouth dropped open. The driver gasped when he saw his partner's faded smile and then the handle of the screwdriver sticking out of the back of his head. That was the very last thing he ever saw. The orbed end of a ball peen hammer found its mark just above his left temple.

Whether he was dead or just unconscious was irrelevant. Alex placed the calves of her legs over the edge of the Jeep, arched her back and lifted her torso and bruised butt up with her arms. She swung her legs and hips over the back of the still-moving vehicle.

"What's one more bruise? All's well that ends well," she said in Chinese, as she pushed off from the back of the Jeep and into the night. And finally all was well. All except for the sharp metal fragment that was protruding from the back of the moving death mobile. That small, jagged piece of metal had a firm grip on the hem of her red silk gown.

Breath exploded from her lungs as her shoulder blades hit the rocky ground, her hips and legs being held high

# Freedom's Menace

above her head by the fabric of the dress. Her shoulders bounced over the lumpy, rocky surface as the Jeep and its passengers pressed onward. She struggled to lift herself so that she could reach the short train of the gown. The pain was excruciating as the rocks continuously stabbed at her shoulders and the back of her head. The Jeep continued forward, only 10 more meters to go to her first ever skydive. Her mind was going a million miles an hour.

"Have to get out of this dress. Where is the tie? Somewhere in the back." Bam! Her head struck a large rock. Disoriented. "Have to get free," her mind screamed. "Oh, shit. I don't want to die. Not like this. No, I won't. I will not die this way!" And then the fabric tore loose, her hips and legs fell. Her heels stung as they landed on the hard ground.

With her head still spinning, she managed to look up and see the headlights dip into darkness. The red glow of the taillights kicked up a bit and then dropped quietly out of sight. There was no more sound. Only silence. She lay there waiting for the crash and the explosion. It did not come, at least not for her ears to hear. However, 1,200 meters below was a scene straight out of a Bruce Willis movie. The Jeep and its two passengers slammed onto the top of a giant boulder and burst into flames. The burning gasoline splashing out, illuminating the skeletal remains of their previous victims. For Alex, the Jeep had just disappeared into the night's dark cloak.

She just lay there for several minutes in the cold mountain air. The pain in her shoulders, head and tailbone had spread their numbing sensation throughout her body. She could not move. Tears filled her eyes, and she cried openly. With the constellation Virgo casting down its gaze, she started to tremble in the biting cold. She had to get up or face death from the elements. After the night that she had had, she wasn't about to go out lying on the ground and staring up at the stars. She had to get to the village, had to get the envelope and the shredded message to the authorities in the United States.

"Cannot just lay here and die," she thought. "I have to get up and get going."

Rolling over onto her stomach, she raised up on her hands and knees. She got to her feet, adjusted her dress, fixed her hair, took in a deep breath and she started back to the road. The tears that continued streaming down her face turned icy cold as they rolled down her cheeks. She began slowly at first; the pain in her hips made her feel like a granite statue that had just come to life. With each step her determination grew, the stiffness subsided and the pain diminished. Ahead, on the path lay a strange-looking mound, barely visible in the darkness of the moonless night. Reaching it, she bent down and picked up the first aid kit she had found under the seat and had tossed out as she desperately searched for the weapon she used against her captors. She tore open the box, and inside was an emergency blanket. Wrapping herself in the lightweight thermal material, she made her way back to the road, turned right and headed for the village.

"Well, at least I'm not wearing fucking heels," she said out loud and in perfect English.

# 15

## The White House

The entrance of General Persi and Seaman Rivecco into the Oval Office of the White House was not even noticed by the throng of people inside. The President and his national security advisor, Fredrick Ott, standing next to the windows behind and to the right of the President's desk, were in deep discussion. In three of the four chairs situated in front of the fireplace directly across from the desk sat Attorney General Marshall Turner, FBI Director Denise Ripply and California Governor Mathew Pope, also a former Navy Seal and former presidential advisor on urban terrorism. The current advisor on urban terrorism, Arthur "Buck" Jacobs, was hospitalized in Costa Rica after being attacked by a monkey while on a family vacation walking the canopy of the rainforest. He was scheduled back in Washington by the end of the week. Behind this group were the secretary of state, the secretary of defense and three experts on Chinese affairs from the Brookings Institute. Add in the usual complement of aides, staffers and Secret Service personnel, and the room was very crowded.

Ott was the first to spot Persi and indicated to the President that the country's top military leader had joined them. With him was a young Navy seaman that no one seemed to recognize.

"Richard, welcome," said Totten, extending his hand to the general as he walked across the room. Turning to the young seaman, he said in a voice too busy to really care, "Hello, young man. Anthony Rivecco, isn't it? Aren't you assigned to Admiral Packard's staff?"

Rivecco was momentarily stunned. "Yes, sir. It is a pleasure to see you again, sir," he said, now standing at attention.

He had been introduced to the President at the launch of the USS Seawolf, the country's newest attack submarine, but he had been one of hundreds of sailors there that day. They had talked of him being from Oregon and that he liked to fly fish, which the president had said he enjoyed as well. The conversation could not have taken more than 30 seconds, and that was 15 months ago. "Whew, this guy is good," Rivecco thought.

In the center of the room, numerous other conversations were continuing without hesitation. No one even appeared to notice or even acknowledge that the others had joined them. "David, what have you got for us?" asked Ott.

"Relax," whispered Persi to Rivecco, out of the side of his mouth.

"Mr. President," began Persi, "all of our intelligence, including the satellite observations, are not showing any unusual troop movements or posturing. We know that despite their phenomenal economic rise their military is still third rate. Why they would launch a major terrorist attack with their troops in a stand down mode is real curious. What concerns me is the question of whether they have developed some capability that we are totally unaware of? We know that the Russians have been up to something at the Severodvinsk Naval Yards. The number of Bars class, Akula submarines they produce has increased over the past few years. That we know as fact. And we can account for and know the present location of each one of them. But there is an enigma. We are aware that the amount of materials the Russians have been shipping into the yards does not coincide with the number of subs we know they have built. I have strong reason to believe that there may be more Bars class subs out there than we know."

Ott jumped into the conversation, interrupting the general and said, "The CIA is telling us there may be as many as 10 Akulas out there that we are not aware of."

Bobbing his head to indicate at least partial agreement, Persi said, "Our assessments agree with that, but maybe not 10. Certainly seven or eight."

It was now Totten's turn. "You are telling me that the Russians could have built ten nuclear attack submarines, but you are not sure. They may be out there, but we just aren't sure of that either? Gentlemen, help me out here."

His voice then rose to the point that all of the other conversations in the room abruptly stopped. "Are you trying to say that the Chinese could be in possession of ten Russian Akula submarines? Just what the fuck is that all about?" he screamed, turning red in the face.

"That is exactly what we suspect," said Persi. "I have ordered Admiral Packard to find them. The first place we are going to look is in the waters around the continental United States."

Nodding agreement, Totten mockingly agreed that was a good first step.

"If they are out there, we will find them," Persi assured him.

"Be damn sure that you do," said the angry President, "and if you do find them, sink 'em. Immediately! I don't care whose waters they're in. Is that understood?" Without so much as a curled eyebrow, Persi let the Commander-in-Chief know that his orders would be carried out.

Having now turned to face Seaman Rivecco, Totten said, "Ok, son, it's your turn. Why are you here?"

"Mr. President," said Persi, "Seaman Rivecco has some interesting ideas I thought you should hear."

The seaman's eyes shot straight at Persi as if to ask permission to speak. The general gave a slight nod, and Rivecco looked the President straight in the eyes and began his epistle. "Well, sir, in the absence of any conventional troop movements or build up, I suggest they are about to play out this war using the Internet, using our very own computers as ammunition."

He paused as the others in the room gathered around to listen to his hypothesis. Everyone in the room was now huddled around the four men at the right side of the President's desk. Taking a deep breath, Anthony continued, "With all of the wealth that they have amassed over the past few years, they have the financial wherewithal to hire all of the computer programming expertise that they need."

# Freedom's Menace

FBI Director Ripply interrupted by saying, "But we know that their super computing capability is still limited and somewhat in the dark ages."

"Yes, ma'am, but they have more than 75 million personal computers. More than adequate to launch a formidable hacker attack," said Seaman Rivecco. That set everybody's mind into motion.

"Well, Donald, what do you think?" the President asked.

"Hum... On the surface it sounds like pure fanciful. Something that a paperback novelist would come up with," said Ott. "But the Chinese are very obedient people. If the government tells them to run a software package on a certain day, at a certain time, it's likely to happen. What Rivecco here is proposing is possible and goes a long way toward answering many questions."

Totten surveyed the facial expressions of his top advisors and asked, "Ok, folks. How do we defend against it?"

Attorney General Turner had been standing back and quietly taking this all in, but now said, "Wait a minute. Darnestown was not a computer virus. It was real. Real explosions and real death. Not a simple inconvenience."

"Marshall, you're quite right," said Persi. "But we do not believe that they are capable of another hit of that magnitude. It took years of preparation for them to pull off Darnestown."

"How the hell do you know that?" interrupted Turner.

Before the debate could even get off to a good start, Governor Pope stepped in to support Persi's position, saying, "I agree. That was a gargantuan task. It was just our bad luck or their good luck, or some combination of the two that the damn thing even went off in the first place. They could never pull off something like that again. But we cannot dismiss the possibility of smaller attacks. There are a lot of ways to kill a lot of people without using big bombs. Remember the gas attack in the Japanese subway?" That was pulled off by a small cult, not a government the size of China."

Ripply said, "I think that I agree. Their intention was a major slap in the face, a provocation and probably a diversion. But, I agree with the governor, they could still have smaller attacks planned. This is no time to let our guard down."

"Hold on, everyone," said the President. "Let's not get off track. I want to finish the discussion on this Internet attack possibility. What's the potential, and how do we deal with it?" Everyone looked at each other, wondering who was going to respond.

"Sir?" said Ripply. "Give me a couple of hours, and I'll get back to you. We have to study this a bit."

"Ninety minutes. You have 90 minutes," said the President. Ripply and Pope hurriedly gathered their things and left the room, cell phones glued to their left ears.

"Anything else, Richard?" the President asked Persi.

"Yes, there is, sir. The Chinese know that we can bomb their asses back to the Ming Dynasty if we so desire, but they are not making any preparation to defend themselves. We think that they have some method of avoiding a direct missile attack, but we don't know what it is." As a result of this surprise revelation, the group spent almost an hour in discussion.

"All right, I've heard enough. What do you proposed?" asked the Totten.

"A trial balloon," said Persi. "We shoot an unarmed Tomahawk cruise missile from the USS Ohio, which is sitting in the Indian Ocean, and watch to see what happens. I have already ordered three additional satellites be moved into position over China. The CIA is cooperating with us. The more eyes the better." Ott looked at Totten, who looked at Rivecco, and they all looked back at Persi.

"What's the target?" asked Ott.

"Beijing," said Persi. "At least that's what we want them to think. I do not want to land a missile in their country just yet. Why provoke another attack on the United States at this stage? Just flying one over them will be risky enough and is certain to piss them off." *He paused before continuing.* "So, if they have no new defensive capability, then it just flies out of the country and crashes into the Sea of Japan."

Nodding his head in approval, Totten said, "Let's do it, and do it soon. Just give me a half hour heads up before launch."

Ott cleared his throat and shook his head. "I don't know about this, sir. Richard is right about one thing. They will be pissed."

Letting his head hang to the point that his chin was almost resting against his chest, Totten said, "I know... I know. But we are inside the 48-hour window. We have to start making some decisions. If we wait two more days, they will hit us again anyway."

He raised his head and walked over to the fireplace. After a thoughtful moment, he turned to face the room.

"War is not my first choice in resolving this matter, even though my emotions are telling me to bomb the shit out of them. This war, as with all wars, will just mean more death on both sides. Keep in mind that they have innocent citizens in their country, too." After a long pause and with the room dead still, he spoke again. "Ladies and gentlemen, it is the job of everyone in this room to protect the lives of all innocent people. We are going to do just that, and we will do it by using our good minds and attitudes to determine what they are up to and how to stop it. This is not going to be about retaliation, but rather about the rights and freedom of people. Their people and our people. This is not just our world! We have just about 48 hours in which to accomplish our objectives."

A door to the left of the fireplace opened and in walked Chief of Staff Jaymar Jones. "Have Ripply and Pope gotten back yet?" he asked, just as the FBI director and the governor reentered the Oval Office from the reception area.

"What's going on?" asked Denise Ripply. "Why did you call us back here in such a rush? What have you got?" Standing in front of the President's desk, he motioned them over with a wave of his hand.

"I have reports on Oblong, Illinois, and on Darnestown," he said. Opening his black leather folder, he pulled out a white piece of paper and began to read from it. "I'll start with Oblong. The evacuation is done. It went pretty well all things considered. A lot of anxiety, a little commotion, but nothing serious. Thankfully, there were no medical problems. Right now our people are searching the place from top to bottom. Nothing to report so far."

"Hopefully, it is not a target after all," said Governor Pope.

"Hope not," said Jones. "Now, as for Darnestown. One of the chief project managers for the excavation contractor apparently has ancestry that runs straight to downtown Shanghai. Same old sad story; a wife, kids and a house in the suburbs along with a mistress, booze and a passion for the craps tables. And like all of the others, we missed it in the screening process. Some day we just may get it right." People were either looking up at the ceiling or down to the floor.

"What else, Jaymar?" asked Totten, impatiently.

"Well, sir, the Corps of Engineers is thinking that the bombs that took out the bunker and, subsequently, the town were a series of individually operated devices that were buried in the rock walls throughout the excavation. They were there for years, just sitting as the project was being built. Detonation was likely accomplished with individual timers and, possibly, coupled with acoustical switches. One or more of the devices went off and then the next device, closest to it, detected the sound of the explosion, and it went off. A classic daisy-chain reaction. In all likelihood they blew out the outer supports, and then everything else simply collapsed in on top of it."

Totten took a deep breath to let the information soak in. He then asked, "Who was the project manager, and where is he now?" Jones picked up his folder and flipped through several papers.

"The man we suspect is named Yang Wu. He was the project manager for the excavation contractor. Once the hole was done, he was off the site. And it seems he returned to Shanghai to visit relatives six months ago. He's back home in China, sir." Jones said.

"God, damn it!" was uttered from several voices in unison.

Holding both hands in the air and waving them from side to side and shaking her head like a three-year-old refusing a bath, Denise Ripply said, "Whoa. Wait one minute. I don't buy this for one second. How could they possibly get so many devices in there and hide them so well and for so long? Someone had to notice. You don't just carry a hundred bombs into a top-secret military bunker. And besides, they inspect for those things on a regular basis."

Seaman Rivecco piped in, "I may be able to shed some light on that. If it was the excavation contractor, it was probably fairly easy, with care and a good deal of luck. Before my family moved to Oregon my dad was a mining engineer in the trona mines of western Wyoming. You can excavate only so much at a time. The crews are always working in very close quarters, so they will always dig out a series of small side tunnels as they go. They use the spaces to store tools and equipment. They can also serve as their dining hall. It's hard to go out for lunch when you are 1,500 feet under ground. Anyway, the side tunnels are never filled in. They are just abandoned."

He glanced around to see if everyone was buying this. They all seemed to be interested, so he continued. "My guess is that the excavation took about 18 months. He just hid the devices on a random basis, long after the crews moved on to other areas. With today's battery technology and considering the small amount of power that would be required to operate a small timer and acoustical switch device, it was duck soup."

Pope spoke, extending the thought, "The inspectors would be looking for devices in the building materials, not virtually out in the open under a few scoops of dirt. Son-of-a-bitch, that's clever."

"Hold it, hold it, hold it!" said Totten in a loud voice. "Darnestown is gone. We will deal with the hows and whos later. Right now we have a more immediate threat. Lolo has threatened other American towns and more American lives. While it appears we are all in agreement that it's not likely that we are facing another disaster the likes of Darnestown, we are still dealing with a very viable threat. What are we going to do about it?" He looked at the governor and said, "Matt, this is your area, and, until Jacobs gets back, you're the man."

Inhaling deeply, Pope stepped forward and said, "Mr. President, I am in agreement with most of what I've heard here. Yes, Darnestown was a major undertaking, the likes of which we will not see again. On the other hand, I agree that the threats are real. I've reviewed the list of potential target cities and the reasons they were selected. It's a good list, and I think we should stay the course for the evacuations and inspections. The quicker that we move up the timetable the better. If we can expand the list, let's do so ASAP. As we speak, we are doing all that we can."

The door from the reception area opened, and Mrs. Sutter stuck her head inside. "Ms. Makepeace is on CNN," she advised.

Jaymar walked over and retrieved the remote that was sitting on the front edge of the President's desk and clicked on the television. While watching a 30-second commercial

that asked the imposing question "Do you Yahoo?" Jones
sat on the edge of the desk, flipping the changer over and
over into the air. It landed upside down onto his large palm.
Staring up at him were the words "Made in China." "Shit,"
he thought, laying the changer on top of the desk.

The commercial faded to black and the pleasant,
smiling face of Ms. Dixie Makepeace filled the 42-inch
screen.

*Good Afternoon, everyone," came the cheery voice. "My
name is Dixie Makepeace, and I will be your host for CNN
Travel Weekend for the next several weeks. Unfortunately,
Angela Summers is on leave due to difficulties with her
pregnancy. Our prayers are with Angie and her husband
and their unborn child. We all look forward to the healthy
birth of their child and to her return to this station and to
this program very soon.*

*I am not here to replace her or to even try and fill her
shoes, so we will be taking a slightly different tack from the
style of reporting that you are accustomed to from Angela.
Just a few days ago, we lost a small town in Maryland at
the hands of an enemy outside of this country. To honor
Darnestown and its people, we are going to visit some other
small towns across the United States. I have intentionally
picked towns with unique names just for the fun of it. This
afternoon we will visit Oblong, Illinois. The residents have
the distinct privilege of living in the only Oblong in the
country. Stay tuned. We will be right back to visit the folks
of Oblong, Illinois, and hear their stories."*

Totten reached for the changer before Jones could get
to it and hit the power button. The TV went dead. "Good!
Very good," he said.

# 16

## Camp Pu'u 'O'o

"Ok, everyone," said Trevor, "it's time to start the pre-descent briefing. We will gather in the command tent in 10 minutes."

As the team gathered, they found Brice and Captain Jackson in front of the white board discussing the plan. Captain Jackson took the lead. "We will be descending in groups of two. The first group will be Brice and Weaver. They will get to the ledge at the 680-foot mark, where they will set up the rappelling equipment for the remainder of the descent. If the ledge is as large as it appears to be, they will be able to get out of the protective suits and switch from the water-cooled cables to standard mountaineering gear. The thinner ropes will be easier to handle and they are what you are most accustomed to using. Once that position is secured, Messrs. Brice and Weaver will continue down to the bottom. At that point, they will go in on *dark* conditions. They will be equipped with night-vision goggles. If they see any movement at all, they will halt their descent and report. Mr. Brice is a civilian, so I cannot give him orders. Mr. Weaver, on the other hand, you belong to me. I want your weapons ready to fire, and you have permission to fire at anything that moves, if required. But I hope it doesn't come to that. The weapons are for your protection, and I know that you each have the good judgment to know when to use them. Is that clear?"

The two men looked at each other and then to Captain Jones and nodded an affirmative.

Then Benson asked, "Uh, sir, to change the subject, I'm confused on one point. Where is the fresh air coming from down there?"

Even before the clueless look could cross the faces of Jackson and Brice, Sam spoke up, "I have been trying to figure out the whole origin of the cavern. Oxygen is not a big mystery. The entire surface of these islands has the texture of Swiss cheese. There are all sorts of cracks and crevices that go on forever. Water and air pass through very easily. My guess is that the cavern connects to the sea and the air at sea level. The tides help by creating a bellows effect, sucking in the air at low tide and blowing it out when the tide is high. Personally, my biggest question is how did the cavern form in the first place? But we will have to deal with that later."

Satisfied that her answer was acceptable to the group, Jackson continued. "After you have safely reached the bottom and reported that your position is secure, the rest of us will begin our descent, two at a time and at 200-foot intervals. Dr. Allison and I will be second, followed by Benson and Horner and then Commander Ocker and Seaman Davidson."

Sam looked skeptically over to Captain Jackson, and he looked at her, smiled and winked. Benson suppressed a laugh and said, "Dr. Allison, he's the best that there is. He trained all of us. I only wish that he were my partner."

Sam looked back to the captain and considered that, while it was a comfort that he was so well thought of, she really wasn't relishing this.

Interrupting the distraction, Captain Jackson broke in. "All of us will be wearing lighting packages on our arms and legs. With the exception of Brice and Weaver, we will all be illuminated during the decent. Each of us will also have radio headsets capable of transmitting to each other as well as to the surface."

Clearing his throat and bowing his head, Jackson turned his gaze away from the group, his hands behind his back. With his gaze directed only toward the floor, he openly expressed his concerns about the mission. "Each of you understands that your country asks a lot of you. You also understand the pride that goes with serving your country. Today your country is asking that you step forward and go above and beyond the normal call of duty for this mission. I cannot offer you any guarantees of success. Nor am I predicting failure. This is strictly a volunteer assignment. Some of you have families to consider. There will be no shame for backing out."

He raised his eyes and scanned the room, where stern looks of determination responded to his offer. There were no dissenters. "Each of you is well trained and possesses the superior attitude that is required to complete this mission. I wish you all well."

Commander Ocker stood and said, "I know that each of you is a faithful person. Shall we take a moment for prayer?" Everyone in the room stood and bowed their head as the submarine commander led them in a brief, but poignant prayer. Eager to begin, each person left the room to collect their gear. Brice and Jackson went straight to the control tent for an update of the status of the remote.

At 2,500 feet below the surface, the remote continued on its uninterrupted descent. All was well. The sloping lava conduit had transitioned to a straight vertical drop at the 1,800-foot level, and it appeared this condition would exist through the remainder of the descent.

"Kill the lights and activate the infrared camera array," said Trevor. "I want the rest of the descent to be 'dark.' Why let anyone that may be down there know we are coming?"

Reynolds leaned over and pressed several buttons and typed in some commands. The monitor to his left reflected the eerie change in the view from the lens of the infrared camera. Actually, there was very little heat in the conduit so the picture was mostly black. 3,000 feet. 3,500 feet.

"Stop!" instructed Brice, "Let's just watch for a while."

Ten minutes passed, and there was no sign of any life or of the operation of any machinery detected by the infrared night vision system. "Ok, drop the remote another 200 feet," Brice said.

Still there was no sign of any human activity. Brice and Jackson conferred with the operator of the remote and elected to let the device slowly drop until it struck something solid land, water, whatever. At 4,075 feet, it struck the hard ground, but the cameras still did not reveal any sign of life. They raised the camera to 40 feet above the cavern floor and let it swing there, staring at the room with its infrared cameras. Nothing. Fifteen minutes later they decided to shut down the infrared and fire up the incandescent lights. Directly below, bathed in the white light, they could see a wooden walkway with handrails and lined with large round spotlights that resembled those used by highway construction crews. To the north and east was a blind wall of lava. To the south and west, the long lava walls stretched out and then curved to form a circular shape. To the southwest was a pool of black water and a submarine. *The submarine?* Trevor pulled the photo from his breast pocket and held it up to the screen. The markings on the conning tower, or sail as it's sometimes described, matched. The lights on the remote unit were not powerful enough to illuminate the entire cavern, but they were powerful enough to reveal the 350-foot-long submarine.

"Let's adjust the camera angle to 30 degrees and make another sweep around starting 180 degrees from where it's now pointed," said Trevor.

Along the closest wall were boxes, a lot of boxes, of what looked like food. Possibly gallon-size cans of vegetables and fruit. The cases were stacked 10 high and were 12 across and four deep. Sweeping clockwise, they discovered additional provisions and what possibly was the mess tent. Between the walkway below and the sub was an equipment storage area. A wide assortment of shovels, picks, jackhammers and wheelbarrows were stacked neatly against wooden racks. Several crates were discovered that looked like storage for smaller hand tools. To the right were two electric generators and an air compressor. The walkway wound around the water's edge and disappeared into the darkness.

"Uh, sir, where are the people?" asked Reynolds.

"Good question," said Ocker as he joined the group. "A nuclear submarine that big and complex has to have a complement of at least 120 men. Make another sweep." The next sweep produced nothing new.

"This is all very strange, very strange indeed," said Jackson. "I have assumed up to now that if the sub was trapped down there then everyone just died of starvation or something. If the sub could come and go at will then there should be people down there. But there are no bodies, alive or dead. So did they leave somehow?" He looked at Brice and Ocker and saw the same look of puzzlement that he was sure was written across his own face.

"The only way that we are going to solve the mystery is to go down and have a look. But I am not taking any chances. We will approach the cavern as if there are Chinese troops down there," said Brice. "I don't want to get my butt shot off." He tapped Reynolds on the shoulder. "Can we get hard copies of the pictures we are seeing?" A few clicks of the keyboard and the soft hum of the HP color laser printer behind them answered the question.

"Good idea," said Jackson. "I want everyone to know what they can expect when they get down there. I agree with you, it makes me even more nervous that there is no one around. I do not want to lose these guys to an ambush."

Grabbing the pictures from the printer tray, the three men headed for the staging area next to the tripod that sat over the old volcano opening. Weaver and Benson joined Brice, Jackson and Ocker. Together they walked to the staging area next to the conduit. Dr. Allison was already making preparations for her descent. Brice and Weaver suited up. An ingenious Marine corporal had made a platform to be used in conjunction with the water-cooled cables that would serve as their rappelling ropes down to the ledge at the 680-foot mark. The platforms were made of small square metal tubing that had been welded together to resemble a pogo stick. The platforms had then been attached to the rappelling control mechanism, which allowed for control of the rate of descent. The benefit was that they would have better control and would reduce a lot of the swaying by standing upright. This was going to be particularly useful as they passed the hot spot on the adjoining wall. A final check of the Scotts Air Packs and the radio transmitters was performed. Jackson advised them that the remote had returned to the 680-foot-elevation and would be waiting there for them with its lights on.

# 17

## Into the Mouth of the Volcano

Jackson and Benson, assisting in the preparation, saluted Weaver just as he and Brice confidently swung out over the 10-foot opening of the 4,000-foot drop. As agreed, Brice went first, and Weaver followed 50 feet behind. At first the men dropped slowly as they developed a feel for the equipment. Brice contacted the control room to report that all was well and that the platforms and rappelling devices were working well. The two figures increased their speed and disappeared from view into the darkness. The lighting system attached to the outside of the protective suits provided adequate illumination for the men to have a clear view of the surrounding walls of the conduit.

Brice reported in, "Control, Brice here," he said in a voice that was showing signs of sudden tension, "it's really warm down here. I can see the hot spot coming up, and I'm starting to feel like a boiled crawfish in Paul Prudhomme's kitchen."

# Freedom's Menace

The rest of the crew was huddled around Corporal Reynolds as he worked the controls. They each felt the heavy wet blanket of concern drape itself over them. Reynolds broke the tension when he said, "Mr. Brice, I don't know if you are from Louisiana or not, but you sound just like a Cajun. All they talk about is food."

"Mr. Reynolds, when I get back up there we gonna fix us some crawfish etoufee, jambalaya and a whole skillet of my momma's cornbread," said Brice in his best southern drawl.

"Brice to Weaver, this is really nasty down here. I'm going to let up and free fall past all of this shit."

"Alright, I'm with you, Brice. Just let me know when to slow up so I don't run you over."

Brice squeezed the handle of the rappelling device and began the rapid decent. Below he could start to see the glow of the hot spot on the wall. He was now sweating profusely and was becoming light headed. The wall glowed its dull red and pulsated like charcoal on a grill. The spot was larger than he had expected, 20 feet wide and 30 feet long. The temperature inside the suit was approaching 120 degrees. The heat was burning his skin just as if he were standing in the middle of an asphalt driveway on an August afternoon in Atlanta. He now knew what it was like to be a chicken on a spit. Perspiration filled the lower potion of the Scotts Air Pack mask. He passed the lower edge of the glowing rock wall and knew that he would reach the cooler 135-foot mark in only a few seconds.

To the group standing helplessly in the control room, the seconds ticked away as if they were hours. Everyone's expression showed grave concern mixed with hopeful anticipation of hearing the voices of their two team members. Finally!

"Weaver? It's Brice, are you still with me?" The three seconds that passed were agonizing, but Weaver responded in a strong clear voice. He was fine.

"Control, this is Weaver, we made it past the worst of it. I'm staring to slow. Mr. Brice, I suggest that you do the same. Do you copy?"

"I copy," said Trevor.

Cheers arose, and high fives were pasted all around the control tent. Reynolds contacted the descent team. "Brice, this is control. Good work guys! You relieved a lot of stress up here."

Sam leaned over Reynolds' right shoulder so that she could speak into the microphone attached to his headset. "Trevor, this is Dr. Allison. I have a question. Where the hell are you going to get crawfish in Hawaii?" Laughter from both men flowed out over the speakers.

"Motivated Seafood Company, New Orleans, Louisiana. They pack those yummy little creatures in ice and airfreight them to you the next day."

"I may not be Cajun either, but I do make a mean Hawaiian seafood gumbo," she said.

"Doctor, it's a date," said Brice. "Just be sure that our other friends bring the beer."

The tension that had gripped everyone five minutes earlier was now gone. The two men continued to report as they descended. Their protective suits had done the job as intended. The air from the Scotts Air Packs that flowed through the suits and the masks had cooled them down, and they were now relatively comfortable.

"Weaver, this is Brice. I have the lights from the remote in sight. Why don't you slow up and let me check things out? Did you copy that, control?" Reynolds confirmed that he had.

Brice reached the 680-foot elevation. The conduit was a little wider here, and the ledge was in clear view. It was also 20 feet away. "Weaver, hold your position. Control, I've reached the first stop. The remote is at just the right spot. Thanks for the extra light. One small problem though, the ledge is 20 feet away. I am going to have to swing over to reach it. The good news is that the ledge is a little deeper than we thought, so it will be much easier to maneuver around on it." A pause before he continued. "Ok, guys, here goes. I'd do my ape man yell, but I'm afraid I'd hurt myself."

Arching his body like a kid on a swing, he pushed forward, and the cable began to sway. Brice twisted his body and began to turn in a slow circle as he swung back and forth. He wanted to be sure he did not bump into the wall on the opposite side. The bulky suit and heavy cable made the process difficult, but he slowly gained momentum. A few inches at first, then a foot, then three and four. Unfortunately, the opposite wall was closer than the ledge. As he swung into the wall he pulled his feet up to his chest and let them land up against the side. With a mighty push, he swung back toward the ledge while allowing himself to drop another two feet. It was a good effort, but not enough. The wall came screaming back at him, and he stuck his feet out to cushion the blow. As he swung away, he rechecked his safety line. It was going to be too short for what he was about to do. He loosened the knot and let out another five feet of rope. Using the footholds on the little platform for

leverage, he increased the arc of his swing. The wall came
rushing at him and he again lifted his legs and pushed
away with his feet. But his left foot slipped, and he began to
spin wildly. "Shit," he screamed as he made a wide circle
and crashed backward into the wall.

"Trevor, are you ok?" asked Weaver, too high up to even
see the lights from the remote yet. He began to lower
himself to Brice's position.

"Wonderful. Simply fucking wonderful," crackled the
voice of frustration over the sound system. He let the swing
slow to regain his bearings and control before starting
again. This time he positioned himself to face the wall and
started over. Slowly and deliberately he got back to where
he would stop just a couple of feet from the wall before he
would swing back toward the ledge. Looking over his
shoulder, he picked a spot to land. With a strong push to
reach the wall on the other side of the conduit, he tucked in
his legs and pushed away with all the strength that he
could muster. He planted his feet back onto the pogo stick
and prepared to jump. As his swing reached apogee and he
neared the ledge, he pushed away with his feet and
released his grip, flying through the air for the final eight
feet and landing backward two feet inside of the edge. He
came to rest in a sitting position atop the coarse lava.

"Control, Lava One here, the moron has landed."

"What was that?" asked Reynolds.

Trevor didn't bother to answer. He just got up and
pulled at the safety line to reel the cable over to the ledge.
"Mr. Weaver, it's your turn, pal." A minute later Brice could
see the shadow of Weaver descending toward him.

Stopping at a point that was even with the ledge, Weaver asked, "Now what?"

Brice exhaled a short chuckle and said, "If I can make it certainly you can, too." But then, shaking his head with laughter, he flipped his own cable out to where Weaver could reach it. He then pulled him over to the ledge. "Control, this is Brice. We are now both on the ledge. If you could raise the remote about 10 feet it would help."

"Lava One, control. Copy that," said Reynolds as he pressed the button to raise the remote.

For the next 15 minutes the two men removed their suits and air packs. Retrieving the bottled water from their fanny packs, the two took a well-deserved 10-minute break. They discussed how to make the descent easier on the others and radioed control with their suggestions, including increasing the airflow in the suits. They also requested that the equipment bags be lowered. After a brief repose, they began setting up shop on the small precipice. First, they removed the pitons and hammers from the fanny packs and secured safety lines into the cliff face. Attaching themselves to the safety lines, they hung the suits and air packs off to the right side just as they had practiced.

"Hey, guys," said Reynolds into their headsets, "look up. Your luggage should be arriving at baggage claim 3."

Indeed, the six-foot by three-foot nylon mesh bags were just coming into view. They stopped at eye level when Brice gave the signal. Weaver had attached himself to one of the cables and safety lines. Brice guided him as he swung out to where he could retrieve their supplies. Once back on the ledge with the equipment, the men hurriedly unpacked the contents. A change of clothes and black makeup for their face and hands was on top. In the layers that followed they

found their packs of food and water, utility belts for the
ammo, cameras, flashlights and other small essentials, two
machine guns each, a 9-mm side arm, a dozen hand
grenades and the night vision goggles. In the second bag
was all of the necessary mountaineering equipment: ropes,
harnesses, hammers, pitons and clips. By the time the two
had finished dressing out in their commando gear, they
looked like the poster boys for a Navy Seal ad.

"Control, this is Brice. We are ready to proceed."

"Acknowledged," said Reynolds. "Hold your position." A
minute passed before Reynolds' voice came back over the
headsets. "Brice, this is control. Gentlemen, you have the
green light. Good luck!"

They checked and rechecked all their gear, and then, as
a wise precaution, they checked the harness attachments of
the other man. Together, Brice and Weaver stepped
backward off the ledge and descended once again into the
darkness of the dormant volcano conduit. The lights on the
remote dimmed, as it did not follow. It was necessary for
the two to start adjusting their eyes to the darkness. The
dimmed light from the remote disappeared about 250 feet
down the shaft. Soon they found that they were forced to
grope in the total darkness. The conduit had started to
slant even more. The slope was a problem because it was
not steep enough to "walk" down, but steep enough to
prevent them from just slowly dropping past it. They kept
banging into the rough, uneven surface. Many times one
foot would land on the wall with good solid contact while
the other foot slipped into a void. They frequently lost their
balance and fell sideways and backward onto the jagged
rock. By letting out on the rappelling rope in practiced
three-foot increments, they were able to estimate the
distance they had traveled. After what seemed an eternity,
they finally reached the 2,200-foot mark. This was the point

where it had been determined that the straight vertical descent began. They continued down until they reached what they estimated to be 3,000 feet. The time had come to assume the position. They adjusted themselves into a head-down attitude. This would afford them the best attack posture if they had to defend themselves.

"Ready?" whispered Weaver into the necklace microphone that rested against his throat.

"You bet," said Brice. "If I stay like this much longer, I'll turn into a bat." Slowly, methodically, they lowered themselves further into the darkness. At an estimated 100 feet above the cavern floor, Brice gave the whispered order to halt.

"I think we should drop some 'fireflies', Brice said, "Four should do the trick." The men reached into a pouch that hung on the right side of their utility belts and removed two clear rubber spheres, about the size of tennis balls. Molded into the center of each ball were a battery and four small light bulbs. When the ball bounced the bulbs lit up in a random, flashing manner that lasted about 15 to 20 seconds after the ball stopped bouncing. When used in conjunction with the night vision goggles, the light from the balls would illuminate a surprisingly wide area. As a bonus, the combined effect of the flashing lights and the bouncing ball would confuse and distract anyone hiding in the darkness. The balls were actually children's toys. A Miami DEA agent whose son brought one home discovered that they to be an excellent device for flushing out drug dealers during nighttime raids. The DEA would shut off the power to the building they intended to raid, usually a large warehouse, and toss in a few dozen of the flashing balls. Invariably, the surprised drug dealers would just start shooting randomly and wildly, wounding and killing their own people. The agents let the bad guys do the dirty work and then they went in to clean up the mess. It wasn't long before the military had them in their arsenal as well.

Brice gave the agreed-on signal, and each man released one of the balls and then the other after a two count. They then reached for their weapons and waited for the light show to begin, ready to open fire at anything, aside from the balls, that moved. The fireflies did the job. Through the night-vision goggles, the area appeared to be bathed in light. The eyes of the two darted all around. Behind boxes, next to the generator, on the walkway. But there was no one to be seen.

"This is really creepy," said Weaver as the bouncing balls came to rest and the flashing lights finally extinguished.

"This is control. What's going on down there?"

"Control, Brice here, there is no one at home. At least not out in the open."

# 18

## The Cavern

Reynolds looked to Jones for instructions. "This is control. At your discretion, you are to proceed to ground level."

Fifteen seconds later, the two were standing back to back, feet firmly planted on the ground, scanning the area, guns at the ready. Still nothing. At this point each of the men reached into their utility belts and retrieved several chemical light sticks. They squeezed them to break the glass vial and mix the two light-producing chemicals. The light sticks were tossed around the area, and the soft lime-green glow they produced provided adequate illumination for the night vision goggles so they could maneuver about.

"Let's check out the sub," Brice said.

They made their way across the improvised wood plank gangway. The topside hatch covers were closed and latched. They climbed the conning tower from opposite sides and peered over the edge onto the bridge. Still nothing!? With weapons at the ready, they raised the main hatch cover and stood back. There was no visible light coming from below. Brice edged forward and gazed into the opening. He then flipped the switch to turn on the flashlight, with its powerful krypton bulb, that was built into the front grip just under the barrel of his automatic weapon. Weaver and Brice just looked into the emptiness below and then to each other.

"Care to flip to see who goes down first?" asked Brice.

"No thanks. You can go ahead," Weaver quipped.

Without hesitation, Brice stepped down to the first rung of the ladder. When his upper body passed through the hatch, he let go and fell the final eight feet to the floor of the submarine's control room. He immediately swept the room with the gun's blue light. Wherever the light went, the muzzle followed. His right index finger was firmly planted on and was partially squeezing the trigger.

"It's a freakin' ghost town down here," he reported.

The interior of the submarine was pitch black. None of the instrumentation was operating. No lights, no illuminated dials or gauges, none of the computer screens. He breathed in deeply. The stale, sour air confirmed that the vessel had been abandoned for some time. Weaver dropped down next to Brice, and the two decided to search the ship. But first Weaver climbed back up so that he could make radio contact with the surface and report. His radio signal would never pass through the three-inch-thick steel walls that made up the outer skin of the massive boat. Commander Ocker had provided several good suggestions as to where to look places the two may not have considered on their own. It was, after all, a big ship. The Han class nuclear submarine was 350 feet long and 35 feet wide.

# Freedom's Menace

There were a lot of places for someone to hide. The search took more than an hour, and as they had already surmised, the big boat was empty. They had expected to at least find a body or two. It was inconceivable that they did not leave anyone to watch over the place. There was a huge sigh of relief in the control room when Brice finally reported in.

"You know, the only thing I saw that was unusual was the fact that most of the life rafts are missing. Apparently, they have escaped by water."

"All right, gentlemen, the rest of us are going to join you," said Captain Jones. "Dr. Allison and I will start our descent in 15 minutes. See if those generators still have fuel. If they do, fire them up and turn on the lights. Try not to disturb too much, but do have a good look around. If you can determine why the crew abandoned their ship, so much the better. We will see you down there in a while."

The two Chinese-made electrical generators were very similar to those made in the United States and in Japan. Despite all the instructions being in Chinese, Brice had little trouble understanding how to operate the devices. They checked the fuel tanks and found them to be mostly full. A fuel storage tank sat 50 yards away, and it too had an adequate supply remaining.

"Those guys just turned off the lights before they left," observed Weaver. "Obviously, they were not in a hurry and probably thought that they would be coming back. And maybe they are."

The first generator started like an old reliable automobile. It smoked and coughed a little, but after a few seconds the large diesel engine roared to life. The sound was deafening. Luckily, the Chinese had been nice enough to leave behind a few pair of ear protection muffs sitting on

167

top of the control panel between the rumbling electrical beasts. To the left of the two generators, mounted on a wooden stand, was a gray electrical panel. Inside were 15 circuit breakers, seven single and eight double breakers. Weaver reached in and flipped the top, left breaker to the ON position. Four 100-watt light bulbs, mounted on a wooden, overhead trellis, lit up the immediate area where they were standing. He looked around and then flipped on two more of the black breaker switches. The area along the wall where the remote had located the stacked boxes of canned provisions and the mess tent was now illuminated. The last four single breakers controlled the lights lining the boardwalk, leading from the submarine to an area 500 or more yards away that was still bathed in darkness. Guessing the big double breakers controlled the highway-like construction spotlights, they flipped them on one at a time. Seven of the 12-foot-tall, eight-bulb light towers started up. First there was the faint, dull yellow-blue glow that emanated from the center of the bulb. Slowly, over several minutes, the glow from each bulb grew in intensity until the bluish light finally coated the entire cavern. For the first time the two were able to appreciate the sheer size of the pseudo-Chinese submarine station. They were in awe.

"Damn!" said Brice. "This looks just like the inside of the Superdome. Except that the Dome isn't this darn big."

Weaver just walked away, staring around in complete amazement. The area on which they were standing was at least an acre in size, shaped like a giant crescent. "This is bigger than my yard, including the house," he said.

The room was slightly egg shaped, with the spot where they were standing at the fat end, the cavern roof rising more than 300 feet above their heads. The lake or pond or lagoon, or whatever one wished to call the body of water in which the sub was resting, was large enough for the 350-foot underwater boat to completely turn around, with room to spare.

"Let's get a good look around," said Brice.

W. Laurence Willis

# 19

## USS Ohio - Somewhere in the Indian Ocean

The USS Ohio, the Navy's first Ohio class Trident
Ballistic Missile nuclear submarine, silently sailed the Gulf
of Martaban off the Burmese coast. Captain William C.
Hopson sat in his quarters reading his newly received top-
secret orders. They were direct from Admiral Packard at
the Pentagon and had been confirmed by his submarine
squadron, SUBRON 17, located at the Ohio's homeport of
Bangor, Washington. The orders were short and simple:

*At 0200 hours, the USS Ohio will launch an unarmed
Tomahawk UGM-109 land attack missile at the heart of
Beijing.*

There was no explanation. Not that it was unusual for
Pacific Command to issue blind orders, but this time
Hopson was going to launch a rocket at the heart of the
capital of a foreign and unfriendly government and it was
to be unarmed? That was very different. Before going to the
wardroom to brief his senior officers, Hopson took the most
unusual step of taking his ship to periscope depth to

establish a satellite link directly with the Pacific fleet commander submarine force, COMSUBPAC. He took this action only to reconfirm the authenticity of the orders, not to question the orders. After the briefing, he and the executive officer made their way to the control room of the submarine, the CONN.

"Torpedo room, CONN. Load the Tomahawk in tube number1," ordered Hopson.

The torpedoman mates did as instructed. Once the Tomahawk was loaded into the torpedo tube, the "A" data cable was attached and the breech was closed and sealed. Confirmation of this was displayed on the fire control officer's computer monitor and on the screen of the BSY-1 computers in the control room. The fire control officer, from the large console in front of him, loaded the mission guidance information through the "A" cable into the guidance system of the missile.

"CONN, fire control. Tube number 1 is loaded, sir."

Hopson checked his watch, and at 0155, he issued a familiar order, "Fire control, CONN. Make tube number 1 ready in all respects, including opening the outer door."

The sound of the outside torpedo door sliding into the open position could be heard throughout the ship. Any other submarine within 50 miles of their location could also hear the distinctive sound. The clock was now ticking. Everyone waited. The BSY-1 continually processed the targeting information and updated the computer screen. At precisely 0200, the captain gave the signal and the executive officer issued the order to fire. A loud whoosh of compressed air could be heard as the missile was shot from the submarine. The Tomahawk swam forward and up; 30 seconds later it broke the surface of the water. A few seconds after that, the guidance fins and wings deployed and the missile's self contained turbine engine roared to life. The Tomahawk began its journey, heading to Beijing at 100 feet above the surface of the water. Captain Hopson thanked his crew and gave the order to close the outer torpedo door. The Ohio then turned to port, diving to 500 feet at flank speed and disappeared into the safety of the dark waters of the Indian Ocean.

Sitting in his customary chair in the center of the Pentagon War Room, General Persi received the satellite confirmation of the missile launch. He sat listening intently to the conversation around him and, with paper and pencil in hand, doodled the cartoon character, Mr. Squiggles, which his 6-year-old grandson had taught him to draw a few weeks earlier. The artistic doodles that Persi created were known far and wide since first emerging during his days at the Academy. He alternately drew and thumped the eraser end of the pencil on the pad, waiting for his AWAC, airborne radar planes to pick up the flight of the dummy tomahawk. The planes were flying off the aircraft carrier USS Enterprise, which was now cruising the Formosa Strait. Two additional AWACs backed up the three AWACs from the USS Enterprise from the Air Force base on Okinawa. In addition, the military and the CIA had three spy satellites watching overhead. The radar signals from each aircraft and satellite were being fed directly to the six-foot monitors in the War Room of the Pentagon. Persi rarely looked down at the paper. His eyes were focused on the screens, his ears on the voices in the room. He was not even aware that he had developed the ability to draw a pretty darn good likeness of Mr. Squiggles. A voice over the PA advised that an AWAC operator had made radar contact with the Tomahawk. The center screen flashed, and a red line tracing the flight path of the missile was overlaid on the map of China. The missile was over the town of Kunming. So far, so good. All was normal. Twenty minutes later, satellite warnings rang in Persi's ears. He looked over to the screen on the lower left and saw the blue circle form around the mountain village of Xi'an. A satellite was reporting the detection of a missile launch from the site. The presence of the second rocket was confirmed by one of the AWACs out of Okinawa.

Persi looked at his Air Force general and said, "I know that we have already been through this, but don't you even tell me that they have an anti-missile system."

The general swallowed hard before responding. "No! We know for a fact they do not have that type of capability. Shit, sir, our own Patriot system doesn't even work that well. At least not yet."

Persi removed the $10 reading glasses he had purchased from the local drug store just hours before, pinched his nose and squeezed his eyes shut. He then looked back at the screens as the eyeglasses swung back and forth cradled between the middle finger and thumb of his right hand. A blue line now marked the path of the Chinese missile. They were on the same course, but the Chinese missile had overtaken and passed the Tomahawk and was now in the lead. The Chinese rocket settled in about two miles ahead of the Tomahawk and maintained an even distance.

"What the hell is going on here?" asked Persi to no one in particular, as he slipped his glasses back on and hopped out of the chair, dropping the sketchpad and pencil on the floor next to it.

He stepped through the crowded room toward the giant screens and stood next to the operation's officer, resting his right forearm on top of the console. The rest of the Joint Chiefs and the others in the room just looked at each other,

but no one responded. Persi stared down at the console
keyboard and then back to the screen. As his eyes moved
from one place to another, so did all of the eyes in the room.
The operator had programmed a yellow line on the screen
to show the point where the missile had been programmed
to turn east toward Jinan before turning north for its final
run at Beijing. The Tomahawk turned as programmed, but
it turned a little too far to the east. It was now on course for
the town of Xuzhou. The Air Force general was on the
phone speaking directly with the missile guidance control
officer aboard the lead AWAC.

"Sir," said the missile control specialist, "I don't get it.
I've tried to overwrite the GPS signal, but nothing is
working. It's heading out to the Yellow Sea, and I cannot
stop it."

"You had better stop it," ordered the General. "I want
that damn rocket to land in downtown Beijing, or I'll have
your butt. Do you understand me?"

The shrill sound of the satellite warning filled the
room. A second satellite launch detection warning was
being sounded, followed by radar reports confirming that a
second Chinese missile was heading for the Tomahawk.

"Hang on, sir," said the airman, "I have one more trick.
I am going to shut down the GPS receiver and manually
guide the missile in from my position."

The radar screens indicated that he had been
successful. It also showed that the first Chinese missile
maintained its original heading and was now approaching
the coast. But with the second missile, the scenario played
out as before. The second Chinese missile rapidly overtook
the Tomahawk and positioned itself about two miles ahead.

# Freedom's Menace

The two missiles then turned 120 degrees and headed out toward the Yellow Sea, west of Japan.

Before the General could utter a single word, the voice of the missile control specialist came on and he said, "Sir, my butt is yours, I guess. I'm sorry, but there was nothing I could do."

There was a long pause. "That's ok, son," said the general, "that was a test of the Chinese, not of you. You did just fine."

"Thank you, sir. But sir, I don't get it. I know that our missile got my signal. The feedback downlink acknowledged the commands I sent it, but it then went off with that lady rocket and totally ignore me after that."

A voice came over the PA and interrupted all of the conversations that were now buzzing throughout the room. The voice identified itself as an Air Force communications officer on board one of the AWACs flying over the Yellow Sea and also monitoring the test.

"I think I've got it, sirs. I think that I see what's happening. I was monitoring the signals to and from the missile and plotting an electronic trace on my computer screen. I kept getting a repeat signal, like an echo. At first, I dismissed it as static, but it was just too consistent. It seems that it was coming from the Chinese rockets. I am not 100% certain, but it sure looks like both of the missiles are receiving the guidance command signals from the GPS satellite and then the Chinese rocket is replaying and broadcasting the information it just received. But then, the Chinese missile starts to alternately send true then false commands to our missile. When we switched from GPS to AWAC control, the second Chinese rocket started to repeat everything we sent it, just like the first one did with the

GPS signal, only now the signal was more powerful. It then sent out a command signal of its own. Our rocket's interpretation of the second and third signal created a conflict in its programmed flight information. We temporarily restored the correct commands, but the second rocket caused it to alter course and then our missile just went into a failsafe mode. From there it locked onto a straight and level flight and kept going until it ran out of gas."

Persi, again sitting in his chair, said thank you and took the airman's name, which he wrote down on his tablet next to a picture of Mr. Squiggles coming out of a trashcan. "Gentlemen, what do you think about this?" he asked of all present.

The Army lieutenant, operating the communications console and big screens, swiveled around in his chair and said, "Sir, I don't know much about how our missiles work, but I do understand encrypted radio signals. It is perfectly plausible that the Chinese rocket could be receiving and then echoing our signal back to our own missile. This could happen in a matter of nanoseconds. Our rocket gets the same instruction twice, maybe three times in a fraction of a second. I think this is all ok with the Tomahawk as long as the message remains the same. As far as their rocket interpreting our codes, and changing the instructions to our rocket, it cannot happen. However, what may be happening is that it is only sending a portion of our signal. So the Tomahawk is getting two identical signals virtually at the same time and then a partial signal a few milliseconds later. That could be causing our missile to change course and then finally just going into the failsafe condition."

The room fell silent as everyone considered the possibility. "I agree," said Admiral Packard, "and we can deal with that possibility. Nice plan, but it's not going to

work. Someday the goofs in this world will stop
underestimating the United States military and its
capability."

He picked up the phone in front of him and pounded in
a number. Packard had more knowledge of missile guidance
technology than the rest of the room combined. As he spoke
to the party on the other end of the phone, the officers and
staff in the room considered all that they had been privy to
for the past two hours.

Packard hung up the phone and turned to address
General Persi. "It seems we have a good handle on this. I
suggest that you ask the President to authorize one more
test just to be sure. Sauce for the goose, as it were."

The remaining members of the Joint Chiefs nodded
their agreement. Persi reached for his phone and pressed
the small blue button above and to the right of the keypad.
This rang directly on the President's desk.

# 20

## The Oval Office

Chief of Staff Jackson burst into the Oval Office. "Mr. President, An Lolo is on line 2, and he is not happy," he said.

Totten set his jaw, picked up the black plastic receiver and placed it to his right ear. "This is Totten," he said in a firm voice.

"You have sent one of your American missiles to bomb my country. How dare you!" exclaimed the Premier of China. "Do you wish that I destroy another of your pretty little towns or perhaps more than one?"

"Premier Lolo, I was about to call and apologize for that errant missile. I just learned about it myself. It was fired from one of our submarines as part of a training mission. It seems that one of our sailors mistakenly programmed in the wrong coordinates into the missile guidance program. I hope that no one was hurt? Did it land on your soil? I was led to believe that it crashed in the Yellow Sea. Is that not true?" queried Totten.

"Mr. President, you and I both know that this was not an accident. It was intentional, an act of war against my people. You aimed that rocket directly at Beijing and at my people. You will pay dearly for this!" said Lolo, his voice just slightly below an angered scream. "You have only 36 more hours in which to meet our demands. I will ignore this incident for now, but if it happens again your time will be up."

"Premier Lolo, if anyone can speak with authority regarding of acts of war..." he started to say, but the phone went dead.

Totten withdrew the receiver from his ear and held it in front of him as he considered the exchange he had just had. As he stood there contemplating his next move the telephone rang again, and the blue light signaling an incoming call from the Pentagon flashed. Totten, receiver still in hand, pressed the pulsating blue button. "Yes?" he said.

Persi, on the other end of the phone, began advising the President of the results of the missile test. "We were right. They do have a system to evade our missiles, but we know how they accomplished it. I am certain we can overcome it."

Totten listened intently before saying, "I just hung up from a conversation with Premier Lolo, himself. He is mad as hell that we fired on his country."

"Bullshit, he's lucky that I didn't shoot one up his fat, yellow ass!" barked Persi. "That son-of-a bitch is happier than a pig in shit right now. Their little plan worked like a charm. They think they have us beat. But we know how they pulled it off, and we are prepared to challenge them. I need your authorization for one more test."

Totten praised the general for his work, but explained, "General, I agree that a second test is warranted, but the situation with Beijing is just too sensitive right now to risk it. You may have to perform the second test in an actual war-time situation."

Persi persisted, "Sir, Lolo thinks that he is on top of the world right now because his plan worked. He deflected our missile attack. I want to take some of the air out of his sails. I have to try again to show him that we can beat him at his own game."

"Absolutely not," bellowed the President. "You have your orders. Do not fire a second missile without my express permission. Is that understood?"

"But, sir," pressed the general. "You cannot not expect me to go into battle not having 100% confidence in how my weapons are going to respond. I have to do the test."

"Listen, Persi," barked Totten, "don't forget that I am the Commander-in-Chief, you report to me, and you will do as I say." His voice then softened, "Richard, I need 36 hours. After that you will likely get your test. Just not right now. Ok?"

"Very good, sir," Persi said. "I had to try."

Totten concluded the conversation with, "I know you did. I would have been disappointed if you hadn't. For now, I'm working to establish a relationship with a Chinese rebel group. The leader is a former general of the People's Liberation Army. He was banished by Lolo for insubordination. Actually, Lolo tried to have him killed, but

he escaped and now has a price on his head. I also hope to
have a man there, within the next 18 hours, to work with
them. We will need their help inside China. I have someone
coming to your office as we speak to brief you on this
development. Call me when he is done, and we will discuss
this further."

He patted the receiver in the palm of his hand a couple
of times before hanging it up.

## Hong Kong

It was 2:00 am when Alexandra Wilson walked back
into the village of her grandparents, tired, hungry, hurting
and cold. She was surprised to find a small welcoming
committee consisting of five of the village's elder women.
Having gone through this hell too many times before, they
had stayed up, praying that she would return. There were
some girls who did return, and others who never did. They
were overjoyed to see her. Taking her into one of the huts,
they grabbed for warm blankets to wrap her in. The dim
light from the candles cast their yellow glow onto the cuts
and scrapes and tears in the silk gown. Dark blue bruises
had already started to form. Looks of grave concern covered
the women's faces, but they only spoke to each other with
their eyes. Alex was trembling, and the blankets were as
welcomed as a hot tub on the beach would have been. One
woman brought warm soup, which Alex slowly sipped. It
helped. It all helped. She finally looked up at her
benevolent caregivers and smiled weakly.

"Do you still have the envelope?" she asked. This
surprised the others. Chinese women were not usually this
headstrong on such issues. "I have to take the envelope to
Hong Kong," she said, "It is very important!" She then
leaned against the woman on her left and fell fast asleep
from exhaustion and injury.

# W. Laurence Willis

"This is a very brave young woman," said one of the women. The others agreed. They laid her down and undressed her. Rolling her over onto her stomach, they cleaned and dressed her wounds and bathed her filthy body. Alex just lay there in silent sleep, never so much as twitching at the sting of the antiseptic as it was applied.

The cloth door of the hut opened and flooded the room with bright sunshine. Alex opened the eyes in her throbbing head and squinted to see what was going on, while her brain tried to figure out where she was. The smell of food flushed through her nostrils. She sat up and pulled the blanket up and over her bare shoulders. A young woman of about 20, carrying a bowl of rice and vegetables, was wearing a warm smile as she passed through the doorway.

"Good morning," she said. "The sun is very high in the sky, and still you sleep."

A soft giggle flowed through the hut. Alex managed a weary grin and motioned for her visitor to come and sit down. A small girl then entered and sat a pot of tea next to them and quietly left.

"There were soldiers here this morning looking for two of their officers and a young woman. It seems that none of them returned to the emperor's retreat last night," she said as Alex ate. "I will be taking you to Hong Kong," she then said in perfect English.

This startled Alex and she choked on a mouthful of white rice sending the fluffy kernels flying through the air. She composed herself quickly and just looked at the woman as she continued speaking. "My name is Soon Ki. My family is from the next village. One of the elders sent for me early this morning and said that they had someone that must get to Hong Kong. That is you, I take it?"

Alex nodded her head and then asked, "Why do you speak English so well? This place is in the middle of nowhere."

"I studied medicine at your John Hopkins in Baltimore," she explained. "The Americans offered me residency to stay and practice in the United States, but I wanted to come home and help my people. I made an agreement with my government to allow me to set up a practice in the village of my parents and to provide care for the other surrounding villages."

"But how can you get me to Hong Kong" Alex asked, "It's a long distance from here."

Soon Ki smiled and said, "Being a doctor in this country does not provide me with much wealth, but it does offer certain advantages. I have summoned a medical helicopter to come and pick up a woman with a severe head injury. With a little gauze and all of those cuts and bruises you have, we will not have any trouble fooling them. The helicopter will be here shortly. We must hurry."

With the envelope and its shredded contents securely taped to the small of her back, Alex and Soon Ki climbed aboard an ox-drawn cart, with its solid wooden wheels, for the ride to the next village. Alex hugged and kissed her grandmother and then waved goodbye to the people of her mother's village and promised that she would come back to visit. As the wagon lumbered along the rut-filled road, Alex relived the previous night and shook her head in disbelief that she had survived. The straw-filled wagon did nothing to cushion her badly bruised butt, and she swore never to ride in anything without springs, shock absorbers and padded leather seats ever again. She and Soon Ki filled the time with discussions about America. Soft chocolate ice cream, VH-1, Maryland crab cakes and guys in tight blue jeans. They arrived at the village right on schedule. The sounds of the helicopter rotors beating through the mountain air greeted their arrival. With the phony bandages already in place, Soon Ki asked one of the villagers for the small sheepskin cask that had been prepared earlier.

"Wine?" asked Alex, puzzled and just a little hopeful.

"No, no. Goat's blood. Now lay down and moan a lot," said Soon Ki as she spread the bright red sticky liquid over the bandages, her exposed hair and down the left side of her neck and robe.

"Thanks a lot! Whew! That stuff smells awful," whispered Alex to Soon Ki, giving her a wink. Soon Ki squeezed her hand, and four men carried her litter to the awaiting Korean War vintage aircraft. She was strapped to the landing pod outside the passenger door, and a wind hood was slipped over the head of the litter. A rush of anxiety filled her body as the craft lifted off, and the opening scenes from the M.A.S.H. television show rushed to the forefront of her memory.

Two horrendous, chilly hours later, the helicopter sat down on the roof of a downtown Hong Kong hospital. A team of doctors and nurses rushed to her side. A young, male doctor took charge and began to give orders as he felt around her neck and head. Someone stuck her restrained right arm with an IV needle and taped the plastic tube to her forearm. The doctor then forced her right eye open and flashed his pocket flashlight into it. Then he did the left eye. She flinched from the intense pain from the light. He closed and covered both of her eyes with his left hand. He then placed cotton patches over each eye and taped them into place. The pain slowly subsided, but she was now very disorientated. She felt the litter being disconnected from the helicopter and then being picked up. As they walked into the hospital she was wondering if someone was planning to perform surgery or something. Several minutes passed when a low, soft male voice whispered into her left ear, "I am a friend of Soon Ki. Just relax."

Thirty minutes later, with her eyes still covered, and after the doctors had performed a battery of tests, including the drawing of three blood samples, she overheard the instructions to take her to the X-ray room. She was placed on a gurney and rolled down the hall into the X-ray room. She was lifted from the gurney and laid on top of the ice-cold X-ray table. She heard muffled instructions being given, followed by footsteps leaving the room. Someone began removing the bandages that had been placed over her eyes. She squinted into the face of the young doctor who had met her at the helicopter. He softly whispered words of comfort to her.

"But we must go now. And hurry," he then said in a harsh whisper.

He supported her ankles and rolled her off of the table. Although her eyesight quickly became accustomed to the light, her mind was still mush as she found herself being guided to a doorway in the back of the room. Through it she entered a small, dimly lit storage room that was filled with X-ray film canisters, old X-rays and assorted other clutter. Her mind was just absorbing all of this when she found herself standing in front of a second door on the left side of the room. The doctor was struggling to slide open a heavy rusted bolt that secured the room from whatever lay on the other side. The bolt finally let go and slid open for the first time in years with a resounding *Pop!* He pushed open the door and forced her through it. They were now standing at the base of a staircase and at an emergency exit. From the vacant area under the steps, he retrieved a small, brown paper bag.

"Here," he said, thrusting the bag at her. "This is a change of clothes, some money and a small jar of cream and a rag to clean the blood off your face and neck. Now listen very carefully." Footsteps could be heard coming down the steps. "When you leave here, turn right and go three blocks. There you will find a public bathhouse. You can clean up there. When you leave the bathhouse, turn left, go two blocks and turn right. Then go straight for 11 blocks and you will find the American Embassy. Is that clear?" She nodded. Her wits were finally coming back to her. The sounds of the footsteps were growing louder.

"Hide," he said and pushed her to the area beneath the steps where the bag had been hidden. "And good luck." He stepped back into the storeroom and shut the door, and she heard the rusted bolt grind back into place.

The doctor ran back into the X-ray room and quietly opened the door leading into the hallway. Carefully checking in both directions he found that it was empty. He slipped into the hall and headed to the right. As he reached the corner at the far end, he looked back and spotted the X-ray technician turning the corner at the opposite end. He slipped around the corner hoping that he was not seen. With his back against the wall, he took a deep breath, exhaled slowly and started a 10 count. He then stole another glimpse down the hallway, just in time to see the white tail of the technician's lab coat disappear into the X-ray room. He gave it another 10 count before stepping back into the hallway to leisurely stroll back to supervise the X-ray of the female patient's head injury.

# Freedom's Menace

"How is she?" he asked as he entered the room.

The technician, standing at the X-ray light table examining a leg fracture, turned and looked at him in bewilderment.

"How is who?" he questioned.

The doctor put on his practiced furrowed brow and then arched his eyebrows and said with the open palm of his left hand pointing toward the door way, "The woman that is in there on the table to have the head and neck X-rays."

The technician gave him a strange look and walked around the protective wall and looked in at the X-ray machine and the empty slate-cold table stretched out below it. "There is no one in here," he said.

"What?!" the doctor exclaimed, rushing over to the technician's side so that he too had a view of room. "We brought her in here not five minutes ago. Where could she have gone?" The two men looked back at the empty table and then at each other. "Quickly, we must find her. She has suffered a severe head injury. You, go get the nurse," said the Doctor.

The technician ran from the room and down the hall. The doctor let out a long sigh of relief and then made his way to the nurse's station to aid the subterfuge along to its ultimate, baffling conclusion.

W. Laurence Willis

# 21

## UNITED STATES Embassy - Hong Kong

The late morning Hong Kong air was moist and hot.
Alex stepped from the emergency exit and found that she
was on a busy city sidewalk. Several of the hurried
pedestrians bumped into her as she stood outside the
hospital door, her eyes squinting in the bright sunshine.
She tried to get her bearings as she stood in the sea of
people. The envelope and her personal papers were in her
left hand, the brown bag in her right. Not having a purse or
fanny pack in which to carry it, she stuffed the envelope
down the front of her loose fitting cotton pants. She turned
left and started down the crowded sidewalk. After about 10
paces she whirled around, remembering that she was to
have gone right to get to the bathhouse. She fell in with the
pace of the crowd and covered the three blocks to her
destination in about five minutes. Once inside, she hid the
envelope and her papers in a crack along the wall next to
one of the toilets. She then disrobed and stepped into the
public bath. A great deal of whispers were generated by the
other patrons when they saw the cuts, scrapes and bruises
that covered much of the back of her torso. There were still

bloodstains running down her back and chest. Being the center of unwanted attention was not something that she was going to concern herself with at this point. The water was warm and relaxing. She allowed herself the luxury of a 10-minute soak and meditation before she got out and went back to change.

Back on the street, she walked down the two blocks and made the right turn toward the Embassy. The city was alive with midday activities. Street vendors lined the roadway with their stands, selling food, clothing, souvenirs and magazines. The streets were jammed with cars, taxis and delivery trucks, bicycles and rickshaws. Young businessmen sporting their finest black, hand-made silk suits artfully dodged those who were slower and less hurried. A black Mercedes limousine was honking at the throngs of people, as some obviously important dignitary was trying to make his way to the financial district for a luncheon engagement. People dressed in shimmering silks of red, blue, green and yellow scurried all about. It was like a carnival. There was a sense of electricity and energy in the air. Alex stopped and purchased a couple of pieces of fruit after avoiding the man hawking the grilled mystery meat on a stick.

Half an hour later, she stood looking through the gates of the American Embassy. She entered through the gate that was marked for people with passport issues. It seemed to be the easiest way in. Approaching the desk, she asked to see someone in charge of security. After a couple of minutes of answering the irrelevant and pointless questions, she was directed to a row of chairs situated on the left side of the room. Twenty minutes later, a woman of 30 something, wearing a navy blue suit and sensible shoes, obviously the uniform of the day, entered from a rear door and approached.

W. Laurence Willis

"Hi. I am Holly Atkinson. May I help you?" she asked.

Alex stood and extended her hand. "Yes, but this is complicated story. Is there somewhere we can talk?"

"Well," said Ms. Atkinson, "first, why don't you give me a little flavor of what you are here for?"

Closing her eyes and rubbing her forehead, Alex said, "This is going to sound nuts on the surface, so please let me get through it before you toss me out on my ear." Holly Atkinson was now very suspicious. She had heard the line, "This is going to sound nuts," too many times, and in each case it was correct. But being a diplomat is all about being diplomatic. She asked Alex to proceed.

"My name is Alexandra Wilson," she began. "Seven years ago, I was on an expedition with a Professor Scott. I was with his party when the Library was discovered."

Atkinson interrupted, "But everyone in that party died in the plane crash."

"Yes," acknowledged Alex, "everyone that was still there. I was back home for my sister's wedding. I came back a year later as the lead researcher for the United States when the Chinese reopened the site." She paused to let this soak in. "I knew from the start that something was wrong. I have spent all of my time since the accident trying to find out what happened. A few weeks ago, I worked my way into the Retreat at Changsha, posing as a servant. Actually, I allowed myself to be chosen from the village. I was making great progress. The premier took a liking to me and placed me in the position of his personal day servant."

Holly stopped her cold and led her to the rear door and into the private section of the Embassy. Once through the door she said to Alex, "Say nothing else. Our relations with China are very sensitive right now. The fact that you have been in close contact with Premier Lolo is of interest."

They entered a small lounge where Ms. Atkinson instructed her to stay put until she returned. It was a short wait of only about three minutes; Atkinson returned with an armed Marine guard.

"Ms. Wilson, Private Eardly will escort you from here."

She was led to an elevator and taken upstairs to the reception office of the United States Ambassador to China. A rather stiff, stately looking older gentleman greeted her at the door. He introduced himself as the assistant ambassador and chief of embassy security. "I understand you have been in the presence of Premier Lolo within the last few days. Is that accurate?" he asked.

"It is," she said.

"And just how did you happen to come in such close contact with the premier of China?" he asked, with skepticism dripping from his voice like ice cream down the side of a cone on a hot summer's eve. Alex repeated the story up to the point where she had left off earlier.

"And my dear, did you hear any of the Premier's conversations?" he asked.

"I heard plenty, and I will be happy to relate what I heard directly to the ambassador," she said, unfazed by his condescending tone.

This, of course, was not what he wished to hear. He stiffened even more, stood up, ordered her to stay and left the room. For the next two hours she waited. The assistant

Ambassador entered and exited the room several times, but never again so much as glanced in her direction. The final time she saw him, he leaned over to the secretary and said something Alex could not hear. After he left the room, the secretary walked over and told her that the Ambassador was unavailable and suggested that she should try calling for an appointment.

Alex reddened as the blood filled the capillaries of her face. She was pissed, and the secretary knew it. The two just glared at each other for several moments. Finally, Alex stood up, her nose only inches away from the secretary's face. The door to the ambassador's office opened, and several men came walking out. The dutiful secretary turned to greet them with a pleasant smile, a slight bow and a cheerful goodbye. Alex could see the ambassador standing in the doorway, his left hand pushing the door closed. She was at the door in a flash and pushed her way into the room, knocking the ambassador backward.

"What the..." he started to say, but was cut short by his Marine body guard throwing himself in front of him and covering his body with his.

A second guard drew his 9-mm Barretta semi-automatic and pointed it directly at her head. Two more guards rushed into the room and pinned her arms behind her back, while lifting her off of the ground. She kicked and screamed as they started to carry her from the room.

"Wait," she cried out, "I know about Darnestown and I know which towns are next. They have eight submarines sitting off our coast with rockets aimed at Disneyland. For God's sake give me just one minute. Just one minute, one damn minute." The guards exited the room and slammed the door behind them. Alex continued her verbal and physical protest, her legs flailing wildly as she was carried through the outer office. The door to the ambassador's office swung back open.

"Stop," ordered Ambassador Filsinger. "Put her down and bring her back in here. But do not holster your weapons."

The guards obeyed, lowering Alex to the ground and cautiously released her arms. "My sincere apologies, Mr. Ambassador, but what I have is very important," she said, shaking herself off.

"It had better be young lady, because you are only 60 seconds away from going to jail," he said as he turned to go back to his desk. Flanked by two very serious looking Marines and a third behind her, each with a 9mm aimed point blank at her, she walked briskly back into the Ambassador's sanctum.

He was already sitting at his desk wearing a look of extreme intolerance. He looked at his watch and said, "My dear, you now have 50 seconds."

She eyed the guards nervously and said, "Don't react, but I've got to retrieve something from the front of my pants."

Not buying this for a moment, the guard at her rear grabbed her elbows and tightly pulled them together behind her back. She winced in pain. The guard to her right lifted her white cotton shirt and reached his massive right hand down the front of her pants. To his surprise out came the envelope and the package of her personal papers. This also surprised everyone. He tossed the material onto the Ambassador's desk. The other guard released her elbows and she quickly got back to her story.

# W. Laurence Willis

"Sir, in the cream-colored envelope is the confetti remains from a letter that I stole from one of Lolo's men. I overheard them say that it contains the submarine locations, their targets and the locations of the other United States towns they plan to destroy."

Ambassador Filsinger took the envelope from the small pile of papers and carefully tore open the end. He peered inside and then, without even looking at her, he leaned over and pressed one of the many buttons lined up at the top of his desk blotter. Seconds later, a male aide of about 26 years old, also dressed in the navy blue suit of the day, entered from a door on the right side of the room. First folding over the torn corner of the envelope so not to spill the contents, he tapped it on the desktop and then handed it to the aide, saying "I need this put together in the next half hour." The young man took the envelope and hastily left the room.

Turning his attention back to Alex, he invited her to have a seat. He then said, "The premier's embossed seal on the flap was your salvation. It saved your ass. Now why don't you tell me who you are, what exactly you think is in that envelope and just how it came into your possession."

With that he interlaced the fingers of his hands, laid them across his chest and leaned back into his soft, overstuffed burgundy leather chair and propped his feet on top of the desk.

# 22

## 33 Miles, East-Southeast of Cape May, NJ - 300 Feet under the Atlantic Ocean

"CONN, sonar. Captain, could you step in here when you have a minute. I have something here, I think you will find very interesting," said the sonar operator, Seaman first class Kim Dawson.

Captain Jeffrey W. Wright, commander of the USS Seawolf, designated SSN-23 and named the *Jimmy Carter*, the Navy's newest fast attack nuclear submarine, was immediately curious. He was already well aware of the situation with China, and like his peers in the rest of the Navy's underwater silent service, he was actively scouting for any sign of the Chinese Akulas and anything else that seemed unusual on or below the water. His orders were quite clear, shoot first and ask questions later. Entering the sonar room, he found Seaman Dawson huddled over his computer terminal instead of, as expected, the BSY-2 sonar screen, Busy Two as it is called. He walked up and looked over his shoulder. Pictured on the screen was a

topographical map of the ocean floor, also not what he
expected.

"Find a new rift in the tectonic plates?" Wright asked.

Without looking up, the ace sonar operator typed a few
commands into the computer. He then said, "Sir, a few days
ago when we went to periscope depth to establish satellite
communications, I took the opportunity to download the
latest seabed maps from the National Oceanic and
Atmospheric Administration. The section we are looking at
was surveyed just five weeks ago. Let me show you
something."

The soft clatter of computer keys preceded the picture
of a large undersea mountain range.

"Now watch this," he said.

Taking the mouse he formed a small box around a
valley area to the right center of the mountain range and
clicked the right mouse button. The screen zoomed in on the
boxed area. He did this twice more until the image had
become a fuzzy, rounded "V."

"See this area," he said, taking the point of his pencil
and making a small circular motion around a soft
cylindrical figure that blurred onto the background. "I
realize that the picture is very blurred at this
magnification, but that shape is much too rounded to be
naturally occurring."

Captain Wright's eyes squinted as his face moved closer
to the monitor, still unsure of what he was looking at. He
straightened his posture slightly and looking down at his
sonar operator, he asked, "Akula? You think that's an
Akula?"

Seaman Dawson shrugged and said, "Well, sir, it's a long shot, but I'd bet my headphones that it's a submarine. And not a friendly one."

Wright straightened the rest of the way and paced the sonar room, his mind running in all directions. "Where is that? What's the location?" he asked.

"About 250 nautical miles from our present location. Specifically, about 20 km east-southeast of Atlantic City, New Jersey," answered Dawson. "Sir, that's way too close for a vessel with nuclear strike capability to be sitting. New York and Washington are sitting ducks from there," he added, clearly stating the obvious.

Wright reached over and took the microphone that was hanging in its cradle over the BSY-2 sonar console.

"CONN, sonar. Officer of the deck report to the sonar room immediately," Wright ordered. The OOD entered the room within seconds.

"Sir?" he said.

Wright, Dawson and the OOD spent the next 20 minutes reviewing and discussing the situation. The OOD returned to the control room where he issued the captain's orders. "Chief, take us to periscope depth and set your bearing to 215, two-one-five. All ahead full."

Captain Wright retreated to his cabin to consider the situation before establishing the satellite up-link that would allow him to report the situation to his superiors. Thirty minutes later, after a lengthy conversation with the Atlantic Submarine Command (CONSUBLANT), he ordered the boat to be taken back down to 300 feet. He then called his senior officers together in the wardroom for what could well be a pre-attack briefing.

Aboard the Russian-built Akula, the Chinese commander was relishing the fact that they had slipped in under the noses of the Americans. Although they had been in their present position for almost 6 weeks, in just under 36 hours he would get the opportunity to launch his missiles, in a surprise attack, at the unsuspecting enemy. The Chinese had purchased the Akula just 18 months before, the seventh Barr class submarine out of eight. This ship had been selected as the flagship of the Chinese Submarine Service. The Chinese crew serving aboard each of the Akulas was Russian trained and considered to be the best of the best. On board one of the Akulas in the Atlantic and one in the Pacific were Russian advisors, not that the Chinese commanders wanted them there, but politics demanded their presence. The Chinese captain was secretly happy to have the additional expertise aboard. This particular Akula now sat on the flat bottom of the Atlantic Ocean with its nuclear reactor at the lowest possible power level. Giving credit its due, their Russian advisor's information had directed them to the mountain range. It was proving to be the perfect hiding place, 800 feet below the surface and on the "dark" side of a 500-foot underwater mountain.

As was always good military practice in all countries, the commander kept his crew busy with a regiment of daily drills and tasks. His sonar operators were being rotated at twice the normal frequency to ensure that they were well rested. He decided that a fresh, well-rested sonar crew was his best defense from unannounced visitors. The sonar operators were good and had demonstrated their proficiency on a daily basis. The constant flow of merchant ships sailing to and from Europe and the United States attack submarines patrolling the area gave them plenty of opportunity to hone their skills. They had easily identified the NOAA survey ship. The commander knew all too well that the NOAA ship had "painted" them with its underwater side scan sonar, but he also knew that it would be at least 6 months before the information was processed and distributed. By that time, it would all be over and he would have returned to his native country as a hero. A promotion would certainly be in order, and then, in a few years, he could retire, never again to want for anything. Everything was just as it should be. The only wrinkle in his plans was, that what normally took months in his country took only days or weeks in the United States. While he reveled in his subterfuge, the USS Seawolf was only three hours away and approaching at 30 knots.

W. Laurence Willis

# 23

## A Battle Under the Sea

Captain Wright's briefing with his officers had been expanded to include the lead sonar operator, the chief of the watch (COW) and the OOD. The Seawolf would go the last 50 km at two-thirds power. The mountain behind which the Akula was hiding added to the complexity of the mission. On one hand it would help shield their arrival. On the other, it limited their maneuvering options. But it also eliminated one possible route of escape for the Chinese. Half a dozen attack strategies were discussed. Considering that the continental United States was the target, the Akula was likely facing to the southwest, parallel to the mountain range. After two hours of planning, a game plan was agreed upon. The Seawolf would approach the mountains to the southeast then swing northeast and come in on the stern of the enemy boat. The plan was set. The torpedoes would already be loaded and warmed up. To make this work, they would have to sneak up on them as quietly as a church mouse. The big question was whether or not the Akula was still there. If she were still there, she certainly would not be making any sounds that could possibly give away her position. Otherwise she would have been found by now. This would be to their advantage. For the Seawolf to find the Akula, it would be necessary to go to active sonar, thus giving away her own position in the process. Fortunately, the Seawolf's advanced spherical sonar could send out focused beams of sound. If there were any other unfriendly submarines in the area, which was being considered as quite likely, they would not hear the sonar ping. Wright dismissed his crew and each man went to his assigned post to make preparations for the attack. At 100 km from the target point, Captain Wright's voice came over the intercom and he addressed the crew.

"Gentlemen, as many of you already know, we are presently moving in on a position in pursuit of a Chinese Akula. Our orders are to engage it and to destroy it. I understand that for many of you this will be your first real combat experience. I understand what you are feeling right now, and I share in your concerns. I also know that you are the best that the United States has to offer. It is a distinct privilege and a pleasure to serve with men of your caliber and it's of great solace to know that I have you here watching my backside. Fighting wars is our job. Winning those wars is our responsibility. It is what we have all trained for. With God's will, we will do our jobs and do them well. I offer the next few moments for silent prayer."

Thirty seconds passed.

"Good luck gentleman! Good luck to us all!"

Wright then issued the order to go to battle stations. Flashing red lights lit up the interior of the submarine along with the drone of the audible alarms. If there was anyone that doubted the reality of what the Captain had said, they doubted it no longer. Men scurried along the narrow corridors and seemed to flow up and down ladders, like water through a hose, to get to their assigned posts. On the bridge, Captain Wright was once again reviewing the attack plans with the executive officer, lead sonar operator and the fire control officer.

At 50 nautical miles, the pace of activity picked up.

"Torpedo Room, CONN. Load tubes 1, 2, 3 and 4," ordered Wright. The torpedoman mates had already visually inspected the tubes using a process known as diving the tube, in which the skinniest sailor got the draw to crawl through the 21-inch-diameter gun-barrel-like pipes, looking for anything that might forestall the successful launch of one of the killer torpedoes.

The first Mark 48 ADCAP torpedo, with its 600- pound explosive package, was removed from its cradle and carefully slid into tube number 1, like a rifle bullet into the muzzle of a gun. The electronic feed or "A" cable was attached, and the BSY-2 computer immediately recognized the weapon and displayed the fact on the fire control screen. The wire control cable was then connected. This step was also confirmed by the BSY-2. The wire control cable was a 20-mile-long electronic extension cord, which allowed the fire control officer, the BSY-2 computer and the torpedo to communicate with each other. This sophisticated system allowed a torpedo to be launched and sent out as an unmanned electronic scout using its onboard sonar to seek out enemy vessels. The wire will also permit the BSY-2 and/or the fire control officer to guide the torpedo to the target. Once the torpedo's sonar acquired the target, the wire would be cut and the torpedo's self-contained guidance system would take over. One of the beauties of the Mark 48 ADCAP (Advanced Capability) torpedoes is that it is very hard to fool, despite the enemy's electronic countermeasures, noisemakers and boat-maneuvering techniques. Once a Mark 48 acquires its target, pity the unfortunate souls who will soon become its victims.

The Mark 48 was also an excellent choice for firing a snapshot, a term used to describe the firing of a torpedo in emergency situations or in close quarter operations. A snapshot can be fired without benefit of the BSY-2 computer-generated firing solution, and the torpedo will seek out the enemy with its onboard sonar system. All in all, the submarine and its weapons and electronics were a deadly deterrent to anything in the oceans of the world that threatened the United States. The torpedo tube breech was closed and the fire control officer reported to the control room that the loading operation was complete.

The USS Seawolf approached the mountain range from the northwest. With confirmation that the torpedoes were loaded and ready, Wright issued the order, "Make tubes 1, 2, 3, and 4 ready in all respects, including opening the outer doors. Slow to one-third and turn to port, bearing 060. OOD, make your depth 600 feet."

The massive undersea boat slowly turned northeasterly and began a slow dive from 300 feet. Without the aid of his active sonar, he wanted to give the mountain a wide berth, but not too wide to offer the enemy any advantage. In the center of the control room, two navigators were plotting their location on paper nautical charts. Wright reviewed their position and ordered a slow turn to starboard. This would bring them around the mountainside and directly behind where they hoped to find the Akula hiding.

"Sonar, CONN. Let's see what's out there," said Wright. PING! The submarine's spherical sonar sent out a burst of sound focused at what they guessed would be the enemy's most likely hiding place.

"CONN, sonar. We got him, sir. Bearing 255, 15,000 yards," said the operator.

"Firing point procedures," ordered Wright, with a tone of urgency in his voice. "Launch tubes 1 and 2."

"Commander," sounded the panicked voice of the Chinese sonar operator, "We have just been pinged by an American submarine, bearing 075, 16,000 meters and closing."

The Chinese commander immediately went to battle stations. The emergency sirens woke the napping Russian advisor, who fell from his berth onto the cold steel deck.

"Load all torpedoes," yelled the commander of the Chinese sub as he raced down the narrow corridor toward the bridge.

"Auxiliary power, all head full."

A rumble wafted through he sub as the big diesel engine screamed to life. The sound of the reactor cooling pumps could be heard as they came up to speed. It would take a while before the reactor was at a level that the power transfer could be made from the auxiliary diesel power plant. In the meantime, the Chinese skipper would press forward, turn the corner and get behind the end of the mountain to safety. The mountains to his starboard side did prove to be an advantage to the Seawolf because the Chinese Akula could not immediately turn to starboard and escape.

"Launch countermeasures and cavitate," ordered the Chinese skipper.

# Freedom's Menace

The electronic signal decoys shot out from the tail while the propeller spun at a rate that produced the tiny cavitation bubbles that created the sound of crispy rice cereal popping in a bowl of milk. All actions intended to confuse an enemy torpedo. The Akula rose from the sea floor and lurched forward, knocking many of the sailors off their feet.

The unmistakable sound of the two Mark 48's departing the Seawolf told Wright all he needed to know, even before confirmation came from the sonar room.

Once again he ordered his crew to open fire on the enemy sub, "Firing point procedures. Launch tubes 3 and 4."

"Ahead full, do not cavitate," he instructed his chief of the watch. *Whoosh, whoosh.* Two more torpedoes were in the water headed for the Chinese submarine that was scrambling desperately to get away.

"CONN, sonar. We have four fish in the water. All are swimming straight and true."

Captain Wright walked across the control room and looked over the shoulder of the operator in the center seat of the BSY-2 control panel. He checked the screen.

"CONN, sonar. The target is moving away. She is only making about 10 knots. Looks like she is on auxiliary power, at least for now. As for our fish, we have two minutes to acquisition and eight minutes to impact. The Akula has not returned fire."

Wright was pleased, but not complacent. The likelihood of other submarines in the area could not be ignored. His sonar crew knew this, too. Two of the operators were listening to the events regarding the Akula while the third operator was listening for anything else that might be out there. This was particularly difficult with all of the noise that the torpedoes, countermeasures and the Akula were making.

"Commander, I have two torpedoes in the water," came the report from the Chinese sonar room.

The Chinese commander lost his composure. Over the strenuous objections of the Russian advisor, now standing in the control room in white boxers and an unbuttoned white shirt, and his chief engineer, he ordered that the reactor turbines be brought on line and pushed to full power. It was too much too soon. The reactor could not keep up with the turbine's sudden demand for steam and the reactor SCRAMed, completely shutting down. It would take several minutes before it was back on line. He was forced to go back to the auxiliary system. This cost precious time, and he knew it, but he still had a shot at making the edge of the mountains, turning and ducking for cover. And in his mind, he knew that he would make it. After all, he had a promotion waiting for him at home and retirement. After slipping to safety behind the mountain, he would turn back around and fire his torpedoes around the corner, thus teaching those arrogant Americans a lesson.

"Commander, I have two more torpedoes in the water. There are now four torpedoes coming for us," said the 21-year-old sailor, in a noticeably shaky voice.

The first of two Mark 48s were closing quickly, but not quickly enough for Wright. As long as the torpedo guidance wires were still attached he could not close his outer doors and reload. He had already awakened one sleeping giant; he was not keen on waking another. If there was another submarine lurking out there, and it decided to shoot at them, they were a sitting duck. He was also pleased with the performance of his crew. Most of them were in their late teens and early twenties, but the calm, cool way in which they approached this mission was truly admirable and worthy of recognition. And he would tell them so, later.

"CONN, sonar. Torpedoes 1 and 2 have acquired," reported the sonar operator.

"Sonar, CONN. Acknowledged. Cut the wires, close the outer doors and reload tubes 1 and 2," he ordered.

The guidance system in the bellies of the two torpedoes took over. They knew their target and they were going home to mama.

"CONN, Sonar. Torpedoes 3 and 4 have acquired."

"Sonar, CONN. Acknowledged. Cut the wires, close the outer doors and reload tubes 3 and 4," said Wright.

Everything was now very quiet as they awaited confirmation that they had hit their target.

"Tubes 1 and 2 loaded, sir," reported the BSY-2 operator. Wright again ordered tubes 1 and 2 to be made ready in all respects, including opening the outer doors. He released a silent breath of relief.

"Right full rudder," shouted the Chinese commander of the Akula, as they reached the point where they could finally make the turn.

"Commander, we have the reactor back," came a voice out of nowhere.

"All ahead flank," the commander screamed.

BOOM!!! The first of the Mark 48s struck the Chinese boat in the stern, five meters in front of the starboard propeller. It was a glancing blow, but enough to blast a small hole in the submarine's side and damage the propeller thrust bearing. The crew was thrown about like rag dolls. The prop abruptly stopped turning, and the Akula started to take on water. The second torpedo struck about 30 feet ahead of the first and was dead on. A massive hole opened in the side of the boat. The Chinese sailors and officers did not have time to contemplate their fate as they were again violently thrown about. Most of them had fallen to the deck and were trying desperately to regain their footing when torpedo #3 struck at the junction of the conning tower and the hull. As if this were not the final death knell, the last Mark 48 followed number 3 into the hole it had already opened up and exploded 10 feet inside of the Akula. The force, literally, blew the Chinese boat into two pieces. The Chinese commander would not get his promotion, but he did get to leave a substantial monument to stupidity at the bottom of the Atlantic Ocean.

"CONN, sonar. I have one explosion, sir. I can also make out the sounds of running water. We put a hole in it. Second explosion! That was right on. The boat is, at the very least, out of commission. We still have two minutes until 3 and 4 get there," said the lead sonar operator.

"CONN, sonar. I have two more explosions. The last one was significant. *(a pause)* I can hear implosions and sounds of it breaking up. They are done for, sir."

"Good work, everyone." praised Captain Wright, "But keep your heads up and your ears on. We may have more work to do. Chief of the watch, bring the boat to bearing 120."

# Freedom's Menace

The Seawolf turned southeast with the mountain behind them, taking a defensive position in order to begin the task of searching the area for other submarines.

"CONN, sonar. We may have company. I cannot give you anything specific at this point, but I'm working on it," advised the operator.

The captain walked to the sonar room and watched intently from a distance. Fifteen minutes passed. The operator, instinctively knowing that his captain was standing there, turned and shook his head as a sign that he had no conformation of what he had first heard. He was bending over the console with his eyes shut and listening with all his might.

Suddenly, he sat straight up and blurted out, "Holy shit! CONN, sonar, I have torpedo doors opening, bearing 270."

Captain Wright ran back to the control room, shouting his orders as he moved through the narrow passage, "Hard right rudder, bearing 300, all ahead flank, do not cavitate. Fire control, prepare a firing solution."

The crew reacted without hesitation, just as they had done during the hundreds of training exercises. The big boat seemed to spin around like a car on an icy road and headed the opposite direction at full speed.

"Chief, bring your depth to 400 feet," he said.

The chief of the watch thought this was a strange order. Under normal procedures and circumstances, one would prefer to dive. In addition they were now heading straight for the mountain. But like every good sailor, he knew better than to question his commander, especially under these conditions. He would satisfy his curiosity later.

"CONN, sonar. I have two torpedoes in the water, bearing 080, 12,000 yards,"

"Prepare countermeasures. Sonar, CONN. Give me a mark at 8,000 yards," ordered Wright.

Wright looked at his watch and pressed the top button to start the stopwatch. The Seawolf continued on course at 32 knots. After two minutes and 30 seconds, he ordered the chief of the watch to take the boat to 450 feet. His intentions were now clear. He planned to skim over the top of the mountain and dive for cover on the other side.

"CONN, sonar. Torpedoes at 8,000 yards."

"Launch counter measures," Wright said. "Sonar, CONN. How far to the mountain?"

"CONN, sonar. 1,000 yards, Sir."

"This is going to be close," said Wright just under his breath, but loud enough for most of the control room crew to hear him. Several of the seamen turned and looked at him.

"Gentlemen, we have a job to do. Get on it!" barked the officer of the deck.

"CONN, sonar. We might want to climb a bit more, sir. This is going to be really tight."

Wright knew that this was true. He was also aware that it did not matter. If he lessened his depth, the climb would slow them down and the torpedo would catch them.

If he hit the mountain it would not matter anyway. This was their one and only shot.

"CONN, sonar. This is going to be close."

"Brace for impact," Wright warned his crew.

The first sounds of metal scraping against rock could be heard emanating from the bottom of the hull. One of the BSY-2 operators without looking up from his screen said to the captain, "Sir, you scratch this boat, and dad is going to be really mad."

The levity was unexpected, but appreciated because it helped everyone to refocus on the task at hand. The scraping was evidently minor and never grew any louder or slowed their escape, although it did considerable damage to the paint. They had just kissed the surface.

"Dive, dive, dive," ordered the OOD. The giant boat pitched forward as the helmsman pressed forward on the control wheel.

"Hard left rudder, cavitate and launch noisemakers," commanded Wright. The force of the boat turning and diving was violent, throwing men and equipment all about. Everyone held his breath.

"CONN, sonar. The first torpedo went after the noisemaker and the second just swam right past us. It's gone, sir." Everyone aboard exhaled at once, producing a sound like that of a torpedo being launched.

"Hard right rudder, bearing 120 and hold your depth at 600 feet," ordered Wright, "Sonar, CONN. What is chasing us now, mister?"

"It's a Chinese Han class. BSY-2 recognizes her."

That information would speed up the process of developing a firing solution. The mighty underwater battleship leveled out and turned back toward the attacking submarine that was somewhere on the other side of the mountain range. As the boat turned through a bearing of 120, Wright instructed the chief of the watch to come to 300 feet.

"Fire control, CONN. This will be tight. I need that firing solution ASAP."

The ballast was slowly released and the boat began to rise, 550 feet, 500 feet, 450.

"CONN, Fire Control. We have a firing solution."

Wright checked the firing solution on the BSY-2 screen. He then instructed the fire control officer to program torpedoes 1 and 2 to swim out in a straight line for the other sub. Torpedoes 3 and 4 were to go out at 40-degree angles and then would be guided back in once the target was acquired. At 400 feet, they cleared the top of the mountain.

The sonar operator came on at once, "CONN, sonar. They got off two snapshots. I have two torpedoes, bearing 300 at 5,000 yards!"

"Launch countermeasures and noisemakers. Firing point procedures," said Wright, still following standard Navy practices. "Fire tube 1." Thirty seconds later, he ordered tubes 3 and 4 to be fired. The three torpedoes were shot from the black cigar shaped vessel just as two enemy torpedoes were coming at it.

"CONN, sonar. Torpedo 1 is going to swim right between the two incoming enemy fish. Three and four are swimming out at 40-degrees, straight and normal."

"Firing point procedures. Fire tube 2. Fire control, CONN. When #1 gets three hundred yards from their fish, detonate manually. I want to take out those first two torpedoes. Chief, make your depth 500 feet, but do it slowly. We don't want to break the guidance wires if we can help it."

"CONN, sonar. I have two more torpedoes in the water. Looks like two more snapshots, sir. At least we caught them off guard. *(a pause)* Sir, I now have two confirmed explosions bearing 310, but I think there's still one out there. Hold for confirmation. Got it! It is still active and coming right at us!"

"CONN, fire control. Torpedoes 3 and 4 have acquired."

"Fire control, CONN. Guide them in. What's our depth, chief?"

"450 feet. We are just below the mountain top."

"Launch countermeasures."

"Torpedo 2 is still hot and swimming straight and normal," reported the fire control officer.

"CONN, sonar. The lone torpedo took the bait. It's heading out to sea."

There were still two torpedoes to worry about, but they had not acquired the Seawolf before it dipped below the top of the ridge. Most likely they would just pass overhead or crash into the rocky slope on the far side.

"CONN, sonar. I have two explosions bearing 300, and I hear sounds of the hull imploding. I think we got 'em, and we still have one fish to go."

Ninety seconds later, the sonar room reported the impact of the final torpedo. The Chinese Han was finished. Mark up two for the good guys! A pleased and proud Captain Wright once again congratulated his crew. They reloaded tubes 1 and 2 and decided that it was time to get the hell out of Dodge, find its submarine tender and reload. They also needed to report this incident to COMSUBLANT.

# 24

## Oval Office – The White House

The President sat around the coffee table in the center of the Oval Office, discussing the China situation with his closest advisors Chief of Staff Jamar Jackson, National Security Advisor Fredrick Ott, Chairman of the Joint Chiefs of Staff Richard Persi and Attorney General Marshall Turner. Also present was a Mr. Steven Wong, a third generation American, wealthy San Francisco operator of several chic restaurants and former college roommate and close personal friend of Chinese Communist Party leader Sin Bin Lu.

The President opened the conversation, "Gentleman, it seems that Sin Bin Lu has discussed with Mr. Wong, in private conversations, his concerns about the activities of Premier An Lolo. It seems that global domination is more a goal of Lolo and his military followers than it is for the Chinese Communist Party and the people as a whole. Unfortunately, Lolo has strong singular control and a faithful following, but a very weak organization. He's too much of a one-man band. Mr. Wong seems to think that if

Lolo were not in the picture then the rest of organization would quickly fall apart."

"In other words, gentlemen," said Wong, "if we cut off the serpent's head, the body, it too will die."

General Persi jumped at this, "I'm all for sparing the lives of the men that serve under my command. We have attack plans in place. We feel strongly that we can win a war with China, but the cost in terms of human life will be staggering. I have lobbied with all that I have, urging anyone that will listen to seek other solutions."

"I agree, Mr. President," said Ott. "The price we will pay to protect our national security by going to war with the Chinese will cost us equally in terms of damage to the very security that we cherish so much. The mental and emotional toll will be overwhelming. A war with China will make World War II look like Los Angeles fans celebrating the Lakers winning the NBA championship. Any other option would be preferable. If we can kill the beast by severing its head, then let's do so. We have operatives in China. I'm not suggesting that it will be easy, but it's worth a try."

"We do have a slight problem," Turner suggested. "Let's not forget the executive order that Gerald Ford signed in the late '70s. We cannot assassinate another country's head of state, no matter how tempting it might be. We are a great nation because we respect the law, not because we are outlaws."

Totten held up his hand to halt the conversations. "All of you are right. I'm not at all anxious to commit the citizens of this country to what would have to be a third world war. Mr. Wong has a proposal that might help... Mr.

Wong. I will remind each you that Bush rescinded Ford's executive order after the trade center attacks in 2001."

"Thank you, Mr. President." Wong said, "There is a faction inside China that has opposed Lolo for many years. Their leader is a General He. The general, Sin Bin Lu and I were roommates at Berkley. After graduation, I went on to the Culinary Institute of America, Sin Bin Lu followed politics and He went into the military, eventually becoming a general in the People's Liberation Army. About five years ago, Lolo started to pull together his life-long plans for taking over the world and returning it to, in his mind, the rightful people, the Chinese. I well remember our discussions during college. Lolo was of the mind that the Chinese were the first to inhabit the planet and, as such, they were the ones that should be in control. Lolo also disagreed with the western ways of life, the differences in discipline, lack of respect for authority, capitalism and the consumer life styles. An Lolo is truly a brilliant man, but in recent years, he has come to think that he is the chosen one. General He was not of the same mind, which quickly became apparent to Lolo. Lolo issued an order for He's assassination. Through circumstance that I am not aware of, General He escaped death. Along with a small band of loyal soldiers, politicians and with the support of Sin Bin Lu, General He has worked continuously on discrediting Lolo and seeking his removal from office. Party Leader Lu believes that if Lolo can be captured and taken to Taiwan, the current situation will quickly end through sheer lack of leadership. The Taiwanese have issues with Lolo, and they would deal with him appropriately."

"Thank you, Mr. Wong," said Totten. "If I could ask that you now excuse us?" Wong stood, shook hands with the President, bowed to the rest of the group and left the room.

After the door shut Totten said, "Mr. Wong has already put me in contact with General He. After talking to him, I think, with General He's help, we can extract Lolo and transplant him in Taiwan. There are other reasons, which I cannot discuss, for wanting Lolo out of China. I have an operative who I will be sending to Hong Kong to rendezvous with General He. In addition, there is this young woman, being protected inside our Embassy in Hong Kong, who has spent a great deal of time in the emperor's retreat near Changsha. As the saying goes, it is sometimes better to be lucky than good. She has provided us with a great deal of helpful information. With the aid of some papers she was able to smuggle out, we now know just how he plans to hurt us. I have already discussed that information with each of you based on your particular need to know, but I will summarize for all of you. Thanks to the young woman, we now know the locations of the United States towns Lolo has targeted, the locations of six Russian-built Chinese submarines that are lurking just off our coasts, and loaded for bear I might add. We also have information about their plans for a major Internet attack, which they plan to pursue. This, of course, confirms what Persi's man already proposed about an Internet war. And last, but not least, we have confirmation regarding how they intend to prevent and repel a missile attack on their country."

He reached over and took a drink of water before continuing, "Last night the crew of the USS Seawolf found one of the Chinese submarines off the coast of New Jersey. Both submarine and its escort were destroyed. We are looking for the others now, and with luck, they will suffer the same fate. Now, let's discuss my planned course of action. We know that Lolo goes to the retreat every Thursday and returns to Beijing on Sunday afternoon. It is a schedule he has kept for years. He is a man of habit and discipline. It is already Friday in China. Our 72-hour ultimatum will expire just as he is ready to return to

Beijing. He has to be captured while he is still at the retreat, and it has to happen this weekend. We do not have time to evacuate all of the towns, nor do we have any assurances that all of the Chinese submarines will be found and eliminated. If we don't stop him now... Look I am not even willing to think about the 'what if.' It's going to be a tall order, but I hope to have my man in place in 24 hours."

"Sir, who is this man? Do we know him? What branch of the military is he in?" asked Attorney General Turner just before a revelation struck, "Oh, wow! Uh, sir, the law does not permit you to have or use mercenaries!"

"Who said anything about mercenaries!" snapped Totten. "Who this man is and where he is and why he is is none of your business. As far as you are concerned, he does not exist. Understood? The very sovereignty of this country is in the balance. At this point, under these circumstances, I don't give a rat's ass about what the law allows! Are we clear?"

# 25

## The Cavern, 4,000 feet below Pu'u 'O'o

Before beginning their search of the cavern, Brice and Weaver began considering how long it would be for the remainder of the party to make the descent. Based on a descent rate of only five feet per second, it would take only a little less than 15 minutes to make the descent. Given the need to stop and shed the protective gear, Brice determined that the next group would be down in about 30 minutes and the entire party in about an hour. This allowed for a cursory look about. First stop was the mess tent and food storage area they had seen earlier with the camera mounted on the remote. It was the most obvious sign that the Chinese had set up housekeeping and turned this into a somewhat permanent base. Surveying the storage area it quickly became apparent that they had underestimated the amount food that was here. They discovered boxes upon boxes of canned goods and large canvas bags containing rice and dried pasta. Everything from Chinese noodles to Green Giant vegetables was stacked eight and 10 high in the area around the mess tent. There were also a number of cartons that had the descriptions marked only with Chinese characters. Weaver pulled one of these down, pried open the box top and pulled out a gallon-size tin can. Carrying it over to the mess tent, he found a can opener. "Thankfully, some things are universal," he thought.

"What are you doing?" asked Trevor.

"Eating. I'm starved," Weaver said.

"But, we just ate a few hours ago and besides we have a mission."

"Sir, I'm only 22, and after that climb, I'm hungry. Besides, the rations and granola bars we brought with us just aren't as appealing."

Trevor shrugged and continued his search. He looked up just in time to see the expression on Weaver's face go from one of hopeful anticipation to one that was a mix of anxiety and disgust.

"You, ok?" he asked.

Weaver grabbed a pair of tongs from the nearby sink, reached into the can and pulled out a pickled squid, holding it up for Brice to see.

"I vote that you go for the canned corn," Trevor said, laughing.

Dropping the slimy, multi-tentacled sea creature back into the can and replacing the lid was Weaver's signal that maybe he really wasn't all that hungry after all. He resumed assisting Brice in the search of the area and opened each of the three refrigerator units, which had been down for sometime. Proof of this fact was the awful stench from the spoiled food products.

"You know," said Trevor. "I find it funny that everything is in order, just as if they were coming back tonight. There are no signs that they left hurriedly or unexpectedly. Everything is clean and put away. Yet I would think that the refrigerators would have been emptied if they made an orderly exit and planned to return. Well, there is no point in dwelling on it. None of this makes much sense to me right now."

"I know what you mean. All the pots and pans are clean and hung up. No dirty dishes setting around, and the hand towels are folded and laid over the edge of the sink. Its like dinner was over, they cleaned up as always, and then they went away and never came back," said Weaver.

"What do you make of the fact that they set up a separate mess area? They have a first-class galley in the submarine. Why do they need this?" Trevor asked.

"I don't understand that either, unless they dropped off people here. Like there was a work crew living here," Weaver said.

"Well that's what I thought, at first," said Brice, "but there are no sleep facilities or bathrooms... Of course, how do you get a Port-a-John on a submarine?" He paused and exhaled slowly. "I don't know, maybe it was just for convenience. It would save the crew a lot of time by not having to climbing in and out of the sub just to eat and rest, but it doesn't matter. We're not here to answer those kind of questions."

"So, is the corn done?" Brice joked.

"I think that will be a while," said Weaver, walking out of the mess tent.

# Freedom's Menace

Before leaving the mess tent, Brice made one more search through the drawers and the boxes of cooking utensils. Something was not right. But when he opened a small, 12-inch-long cardboard box, it was all suddenly clear. "Oh, yeah," he said holding up a handful of chop sticks, "and I'm standing here looking for spoons and forks in a Chinese kitchen. Duh!"

Weaver asked, "How do you pick up a sliced peach with those things?"

"Do what my daughter does when we have Chinese takeout. You just stab it."

The two laughed and headed for what they perceived was an excavation area at the far end of the boardwalk.

At the entrance to what they could now determine was a man made tunnel, racks of digging tools, like picks and shovels and long steel pry bars were meticulously lined up next to the entrance. Behind the hand tools lay several jackhammers with air hoses neatly coiled all next to a large air compressor with its 8-foot-high storage tank. To the right of that stood several metal cabinets, two of which had decals pasted on the doors that bore the United Nations' universal symbol for explosives. The other cabinets contained a variety of mining equipment, including hard hats with lights mounted above the brim, fresh-air masks and work gloves. One cabinet had a few drills and drill bits, the type that would be necessary to bore the holes in which the high explosive would be inserted.

Thanks to Alfred Nobel, miners, from the 1800's to the present, were given the ability to use explosives to blast away large sections of rock walls. But first they must drill holes in a circular pattern several feet deep into the rock and then insert the explosive charges. They also drill one hole in the center of the round pattern. The explosives around the perimeter are detonated first, which breaks up all the rock within the pattern into very small pieces. Then, within only a few milliseconds of the first detonations, the center charge explodes and blows all of the broken pieces of rock out and onto the floor in front of what is now a nice, new hole.

"This does not seem to be a full complement of hardware," observed Trevor looking into the drill storage cabinet. "Too big a cabinet and not enough stuff to fill it and, yet it is arranged for additional supplies."

Weaver was not paying any attention. He had found a bolt cutter and was in the process of breaking into one of the locked explosive cabinets. With a very loud grunt, the handles of the cutter were forced together, followed by the loud snap from the shank of the hardened steel padlock. He swung the door open and found it to be virtually empty with the exception of a few mangled looking blasting caps. Brice was 15 feet behind him, and his mind was already sorting out different scenarios explaining the discrepancies in the amount of materials in the drilling and blasting cabinets. POW! The sound of the lock from the second explosive's cabinet snapping reverberated throughout the cavern. Weaver swung open the doors and found it to contain absolutely nothing.

"This is very strange," said Trevor, "They had everything in this place very well stocked, everything except for the drills and explosives. What gives?"

As he spoke Weaver was making his way toward the entrance to the excavation tunnel.

"Wait," shouted Brice, "not so fast." He walked over to stand next to his cohort. "I'm comfortable that the bulk of the crew is not here, but I had a sudden thought or maybe just a feeling. What if there were one or two sailors left to guard the place?"

Weaver reached around his back and produced two "flash-bang" grenades. "These will incapacitate anybody that may be in there," he said, handing one of the tennis-ball-size explosives to Brice. "Now, on three, toss these into the tunnel just like you're throwing a baseball. Aim at the far wall, and these little babies will bounce off like the cue ball on a pool table and angle to the back area. Three, two, one."

Both men tossed their spherical explosives into the tunnel and then flattened themselves against the black lava wall just five feet from the entrance. As soon as the two grenades went off, they rushed inside the tunnel with their semiautomatic weapons cocked and ready to fire at anything or anyone that moved. Both were relieved and not too surprised to find that the tunnel was empty. They stepped back out and allowed the smoke to clear. The Chinese had obviously been excavating for something. Their efforts were all centered on this hole in the ancient lava wall. Brice dropped to his knees and started sifting through the rubble at the mouth of the manmade cave.

"What were they digging for?" asked Weaver.

"I'm not sure. The President sent me to find out why a Chinese submarine was down here. It seems that this tunnel is the answer. They've been mining for something in here."

"Look at the rocks. Its just lava," Weaver observed.

Brice stood back up, cradling a handful of the crushed material that was scattered beneath his feet. He held it under the light mounted on the end of his weapon. It was similar to the stuff that he and Dr. Allison had walked over the day before when they visited the lava flow. It shimmered with the multitude of different colors from the various minerals, but beyond that it was not unusual, at least not to him. "Dr. Allison will be able to help us answer that question. That's why I brought her along," said Brice.

With the smoke thinning, the two men stepped into the entrance of the excavated tunnel. The gun- mounted lights swept the area as they slowly made their way into the depths of the black hole. It was a not small tunnel, 8 to 10 feet high and 12 feet wide and, as they soon found out, about 60 feet deep. The floor was littered with more of the loose rocky debris. It was like walking on a gravel road. Some of the pieces were as large as volleyballs, but most were only an inch or two in diameter. But there was nothing else inside, no tools, trash, nothing. The right side of the tunnel wall had also been excavated, with a chest-high section, two feet deep by three feet high and running the entire length of the tunnel.

"I don't know what they were digging for, but whatever it was it looks like they found a lot of it," said Weaver, his mind clouded by a lack of understanding.

Brice did not respond. He bent over and picked up a golf-ball-size rock that glistened under the beam of the flashlight. He held in the light and saw that it sparkled like a crystal. It was dirty brown with patches of thin black lava covering it like the skin of an onion. He tapped it on the side of the gun barrel and reexamined it. His mind was flowing like a raging river. The stream of thought that flowed through his mind was tossing information about like pebbles and stones rolling down a mountain brook.

Something told him that he understood what all of this meant, but the light bulb was just not coming to full illumination. The orb went into his right front pocket so he could show it to Dr. Allison, hoping that she could shed some light. He looked at his watch. It had been 45 minutes since Control had advised that Samantha Allison and Captain Jackson were on their way down.

"Let's go," he said. "The next party should already be here."

Brice and Weaver exited the tunnel and looked around. There was no one else in sight. Trevor grabbed his radio and called control to inquire as to the status of the others and to ask why they were late.

"I'll let them explain," reported the control operator. "You should be seeing them any second now."

And he was right; 15 seconds later Jackson appeared as he passed through the opening in the cavern ceiling. A few seconds later, he was standing on the cavern floor waving at Brice and Weaver. All three looked up expecting to see Dr. Allison, but she had still not appeared. They walked over to greet the Captain. Weaver saluted and Brice extended his hand.

"Are you alone?" asked Brice.

Looking up, Jackson just shook his head. "This has been like shopping with my wife," he said. "We had to stop every two feet all the way down so she could collect samples from the conduit walls. She then puts them in little plastic bags and labels them with a felt marker. I keep expecting her rope to break under all of the additional weight. All I know is she's dragging that shit back up by herself."

"Well, like I keep saying, she is the best. That's why I insisted she come along," Trevor explained.

"Hey, guys, this is great," Sam could be heard saying from overhead. They all looked up once again and saw the vulcanologist with her rock hammer in her right hand, chipping away at the edge of the conduit opening. She slipped the sample into a plastic bag and then into the pouch secured to the back of her belt. She then dropped down to join the rest of the party.

# 26

## Understanding

"I cannot wait to get this stuff back to the lab," Sam exclaimed. This has already been an incredible experience. I've never even had a dream this good."

She unhooked her harness and slipped the pouch, utility belt and backpack off and sat them on the ground in front of her. She detached the pouch from the belt and scooped up the hammer and headed off toward the cavern wall where she immediately started to chip away at more samples. Brice, Jones and Weaver just looked at each other in wonder and shrugged their shoulders.

"The next group will be about 20 minutes behind us," said Jones. "What do we need to do in the mean time?"

"Well," said Brice, "Let me first brief you on what we have found so far. As we expected, this place is completely empty except for us, of course. It appears that they left in an orderly, unhurried manner. All the equipment has been properly stowed. The submarine was shut down and closed

up. My best guess is that they are planning to return. All of
the lifeboats from the sub are missing, with the exception of
a few that we found in a forward storage compartment. As
you can see, we have electricity and lights. There was one
breaker that didn't appear to turn on anything. We don't
know where it's connected. We have plenty of canned
rations, complete with pickled squid and a kitchen to
prepare it in. Over there is a manmade tunnel where they
have been mining for something, but we don't know what.
Last and surely not least, we discovered that a great deal of
mining equipment and explosives are unaccounted for. That
is a far as we have gotten."

Samantha walked up with her sample pouch brimming
with her black shiny treasures. "Can I borrow someone
else's pouch? Mine is full," she said and dropped it to the
ground where it landed with a resounding plop. "You can
have mine," said Weaver, tossing the green canvas bag to
her.

"Ok, doctor, the fun's over for now," said Brice. "I need
you to look at this." The orb that he had picked up in the
cave was now in the palm of his extended right hand.

She took the rock and examined it. "Where did you get
this?"

He pointed to the excavation site. She then bent down
and rummaged through her backpack and pulled out a
small makeup mirror.

Brice looked at Jackson, winked and said, "At the risk
of sounding sexist, why do women always carry that kind of
shit?"

"Because you men couldn't get through the day if we
women didn't carry all this shit for them. It is the only

thing that keeps your butts out of trouble," she snapped, just before a broad smile formed on her face.

Taking the rock in her right hand, she slid it over the surface of the mirror. A long, thin scratch appeared from under the path of the rock. She looked at Brice, but stopped short of saying anything when she saw the look on his face. She knew he realized that this was a diamond. To Brice everything became clear. The submarine, the Chinese, the diamonds. The sudden and meteoric rise in the Chinese economy from diamonds supposedly found in the Library.

"Son-of-a bitch," he said in a voice that was just barely audible.

"What is it, sir?" asked Jackson.

"You can now stop wondering how the Chinese got so rich so quickly," said Trevor.

"How did they find this place?" Sam asked.

"We can go on all night speculating on that, but for now let's just assume that it was dumb luck. They stumbled on the cavern. Then they found the diamonds. The discovery of the Library was just coincidence and served as a convenient shield to hide the real origin of the diamonds," Brice explained. "But we have to put that aside for now. First, while we wait for the others, let's try to discover how the sub got in here and possibly where the crew went. Once the rest of the group gets down here, I will have to go back to the surface and report this. Ocker and his man will see to what it takes to get this sub operational. Dr. Allison, you are free to explore."

"Let's start over the... What the hell," yelped Jackson as a shower of fine rock rained down on top of them. They all ducked, covering their heads with their hands and rapidly backing away from the area. The first thought that went through everyone's mind was that the cavern was starting to collapse. Brice looked up and there hanging in the entrance of the conduit was Benson, a broad, mischievous smile covering his face. He was stretched out in an almost prone position and scraping his boots on the side of the conduit wall to break off the tiny peaks from the rough edges of the lava.

"Mister, you had better just stay up there if you know what's good for you," shouted Captain Jackson.

While Benson completed his descent, Samantha headed off to the excavation site to study the source of the diamonds. Brice and Jackson made their way toward the sub along with Weaver. On the platform that led to the gang plank, Brice spotted a black electrical cord, about one inch around, which ran along the water's edge until it turned and disappeared into the water, 30 yards behind the aft end of the sub. Brice asked Weaver to trace out the destination of the cable. Brice and Jackson climbed the gangplank and were standing next to the conning tower of the submarine when Weaver called out to them. "Hey, I just found two ends of the cable that are not plugged in. What do you want me to do with them?"

"Go ahead and plug them in," responded Brice, cupping his hands over his mouth to help project his voice.

As he walked past the two-story-high conning tower and now had his first unobstructed view of the backside of the cavern, two sets of the industrial lighting fixtures flickered on along the back wall, almost a football field distance away. The soft yellow glow slowly turned to blue as the bulbs warmed up. The sight before them brought Brice and Jackson to an abrupt halt.

"Well, this certainly answers a lot of questions," said Trevor.

"I'll say that it does," Jackson said. "We now know why they abandoned the sub."

"Yep! And I have an idea that once we get over there we will discover what happened to the missing drills and explosives," Brice said.

Before them, bathed in blue light, was the entrance to the cavern. Like a giant upside down cone, it rose above the water line for well over 100 feet. A monstrous wedge-shaped section of the right hand wall had at some point broken loose, fallen and jammed itself into the opening like a giant railroad spike. Only 15 or 20 feet of the black lava wedge remained above the surface of the water. Judging from the size of the gap left in the entry, there was a section at least 80 feet long jutting down into the water like a stony iceberg, effectively blocking the submarine's egress. Floating in front of the huge mass was a lone, yellow six-man life raft, oars neatly crossed in the center.

"You said that there were still two life rafts below?" asked Jackson.

"Yes, Weaver knows where they are," said Brice. "I'll meet you over there."

With that he dove into the dark brine and started swimming across to the cavern entrance, leaving a surprised Marine captain standing on the aft deck.

"Well, he's certainly very decisive," he thought with a chuckle and turned to summon Weaver.

Brice reached the natural obstruction in short order and found a small area with a flat surface onto which he could pull himself up and out of the water. The jagged surface made the climb to the top relatively easy. Once on top, he found exactly what he expected to find and a little more. The massive section of lava extended back into the opening at least 60 to 80 feet. The thinnest section of the obtrusive rock was on the left side, the word thin being relative; the section was more than 10 feet thick, and that was on the end he could see, the cavern side. The drills and bits were scattered along the surface next to the left-hand wall. Remnants of the wrappers that once covered the explosives littered the area. From the holes that were drilled in a straight line along the edge, it was obvious that the Chinese crew had tried to blast away at the section, hoping it would fracture and fall away to the point that the submarine could float past. There was a large area that was covered with small pebble-size pieces of lava that had been blown from the two-dozen holes they had successfully made. They were on the right track. In all likelihood given enough explosives, the plan might have worked.

"Too bad for them. They were making progress," Trevor thought.

The biggest irony was that they had numerous torpedoes loaded with high explosives at their disposal, but the warheads would have been far too powerful to detonate in such close quarters. There would have been a very significant risk, almost a certainty, damaging or possibly sinking the submarine. Not to mention the fact that the lava had already given way, dropping the wedge and closing the entrance.

"A major blast could have brought the entire cavern down on top of them. They were wise not to even try it," he thought.

# Freedom's Menace

He started to study the shape of the entrance as he walked along the top of the wedge, deeper into the mouth of the passage. He noted that the height and width appeared to remain fairly constant at least as far as he could see. The beam from the light towers was only effective for a few hundred feet. Beyond that, he could not make out anything else in the darkness. Voices from behind him came into earshot. He turned to see Dr. Allison and Captain Jackson walking toward him.

"What do you think?" asked Jackson.

"I think they didn't have enough explosives to finish what they were trying to accomplish that being to blast away the edge over there and hopefully drop this chunk of lava to the bottom of the cavern pool."

"Don't these submarines have torpedoes?" questioned Sam, joining the conversation.

"Yes, they do," said Trevor. "We just considered the same thing. The explosive package in a torpedo is very large. The concussion from the blast could sink the sub or collapse the cavern roof. Good question though. Now I have a question for you. What caused this piece we are standing on to break away?"

"My guess is that it fell during the earthquake that proceeded the Kilauea eruption last year. Considering the effects of time and the fact lava is very brittle, it just happened. I don't know that there is a good scientific explanation. In fact, I'm somewhat surprised that this entire cavern has survived so well."

Brice gave this several seconds of consideration. "Well, I guess that's that. Look, I need to get back to the surface. Doctor, what did you find in the excavation?"

"Quite a bit," she answered. "The floor of the excavation is covered with diamonds in the rough. I'm not an expert, but most everything I saw is probably industrial grade at best. There were some very large stones lying about, which I suspect are of poor quality and would only be good for industrial applications. Not that that is any thing to sneeze at. I did find these, though." She reached into the pocket of her jeans and pulled out three marble-size stones. "These could very well be jewelry grade, but, like I said, it will take an expert to make that determination. What I do know is that they have not mined out the vein. From the looks of things there could be a lot more in there."

The expressions on the men's faces went from acute interest in what Samantha was telling them to puzzlement and concern when both felt a wave of uneasiness overcome them.

"What the hell was that?" asked Jackson.

"It was just Pele. She must have gotten up on the wrong side of the bed this morning," explained Dr. Allison. But she could tell that the two men were not satisfied with the response, so she added, "Gentlemen, if you are going to live on this island you have got to get used to the earthquakes. They are just a way of life here."

# 27

## Command Center - Pu'u 'O'o Vent

The earthquake was felt at the surface as well.
Although it registered only as a slight sensation in
everyone's feet, it was enough to concern anyone who was
unfamiliar with the seismically active island. That included
most everyone at the vent site. The last of the descent party
was approaching the ledge at the 680-foot elevation.
Commander Ocker and Seaman Davidson had felt nothing.
They were unaware that the slight swaying that they were
experiencing was due to an earthquake. They were also
unaware of a far more serious situation. The red-hot section
of the conduit wall, 50 feet below the surface, had cracked
as a result of the small tremor. A trickle of lava had begun
to ooze from it and drip down into the older conduit. The
molten rock cooled as it fell, and by the time it reached
Ocker and Davidson, it was the consistency of fine sand.
They hardly even noticed the light mist that was raining
down on them. Ocker was already pulling himself onto the
ledge when the second tremor hit. It was not much different
than the first, but this time he felt it.

# W. Laurence Willis

"Command, this is Ocker. Did I just feel something?"

"Yes, sir," answered Reynolds. "We are experiencing some very minor tremors. I'm told that this is very normal and nothing to be concerned with."

Ocker took this in stride and began assisting Davidson over to the ledge. Six hundred feet above them the crack in the wall opened ever so slightly, and the mist of lava increased, but not to a detectable level. While they were in the process of removing their protective suits, Kilauea rumbled mightily. The staff at the Jaggar Volcano Observatory would find that their measurement devices had recorded the earthquake intensity at 6.8 on the Richter scale. Normally, this was nothing to be concerned with. The Big Island experienced quakes of that magnitude a few times each year. The vulcanologists from the Volcano Observatory were always happy to record and study new data. Of course, they never had to be concerned that a river of lava was about to pour down on top of them. The crack in the lava wall was now wide enough to allow the lava to freely flow. Like water seeping through a crack in an earthen dam, the more lava that flowed through the crack, the more erosion of the surrounding area it caused. The hole was slowly opening wider and wider and wider.

The force of the last quake knocked Ocker and Davidson off their feet. Davidson had fallen flat on his belly and was now clinging to Commanded Ocker's belt. The commander had slipped and rolled over the edge when the quake took them down. He was off balance and flailing wildly. He had just removed the Scotts Air Pack, but the protective suit was still hanging around his ankles. Davidson was slowly sliding over the coarse surface of the lava. It felt as if he were riding a porcupine as the scalpel-like surface cut into his skin. Ocker quickly gathered his thoughts and calmed down. He swung himself into a position that let him reach the surface of the wall and straighten to a vertical posture. With Davidson still supporting his weight, he pulled closer to the wall and found a couple of handholds. The shiny metallic suit finally came loose, and he kicked it off. It floated down into the darkness like a leaf falling from a tree. Luckily, rock climbing was a part of his training, and he masterfully climbed back up on top of the ledge. He and Davidson just lay there catching their breath.

After what seemed an eternity, Ocker finally spoke, "Mr. Davidson, I thank you. I owe you my life."

Davidson rolled over and sat up, revealing a shredded and bloody shirt. "And you, sir, you owe me a new shirt."

The men slowly got to their feet, still a bit winded from the experience and wondering what effect the quake had on those down below. They began the process of preparing for the rest of the descent. They also noticed, for the first time, the sensation from the falling bits of lava that was raining down in ever-denser particles. They dismissed it as dirt having been shaken loose from the long vertical conduit walls.

Brice, Jackson, Allison and the others in the cavern all found themselves on the ground after the temblor. "Damn, that was a good one," said Sam. "I don't remember us having one that severe in a quite a while."

Brice jumped to his feet. "I really don't like this. We need to figure out how to get out of here if something else happens."

Jackson was also on his feet and was assisting Sam in getting up.

"I want those two life rafts brought up here, inflated and ready to go. Just in case," said Brice to Jackson.

"Go where?" asked Jackson.

"That way," Brice said, pointing to the black passage behind them. "Doctor, if there is anything else that you want to do, I suggest that you make it quick."

Benson, Weaver and Horner were staring over to the rest of the party from the aft deck of the sub as it rolled gently from side to side. Jackson indicated they should stay put. He and Dr. Allison had brought along the two remaining rafts when they joined Brice.

"We can drag up one of the rafts, and I'll go get the others," Jackson said.

"Slow down, everybody," warned Trevor. "First things first. Number one, that could have been all there was. Right, Doc?"

Sam just looked at him and shrugged.

Trevor understood and continued. "We should have some food and water to take with us. A few weapons just in case. And light; we will need plenty of flashlights. Let's get the one raft up here, and then we can all go back together to collect supplies."

The three lifted the larger of the two rafts up the 20 feet from the water. Jackson and Dr. Allison drug the 10-person rubber boat to the back of the passage. Brice carried the remaining raft to the back of the passage, inflated it and left it setting next to the first. The three climbed aboard the lone remaining raft and returned to the sub.

# Freedom's Menace

On the deck of the submarine, Brice gave everybody orders on what to get and how much. Captain Jackson and the three enlisted men headed off to the mess area to gather food and water. Once Jackson and his men were out of earshot, Trevor decided to let Dr. Allison educate him a little about earthquakes.

"I'll admit that was a big one," she said. "Most earthquakes are the result of tectonic plate movement. In the case of a volcano, the situation is similar, but it's all about the island growing. We get several of these each year. Generally, they are weeks or months apart. Unfortunately, you just never know. I cannot possibly offer you any kind of prediction."

"Hey, Brice," shouted Captain Jackson. "Look at this." They turned to find him holding up the silver- colored protective suit that had fallen when Ocker was struggling for his life on the cliff face.

"Where did you find that?" Trevor asked.

"It was over by where that first remote landed. Looks like one of the guys coming down dropped it when they changed."

Captain Jackson's assessment of the situation could have been accurate, but that did not ease Brice's mind one iota. "Let's check out the sub," he said.

He and Sam started to make their way to the conning tower ladder in order to board the submarine to look for flashlights, flares and anything else that would be useful.

Ocker and Davidson had hurriedly adorned themselves in the rappelling gear and started the final descent. The lighting pacs strapped to their bodies were better than nothing, but left a lot to be desired. Reynolds, in the control tent, had advised that the last quake shut down the generator that was powering the cable drive system, and it was going to be a while before they could lower the remote and its high intensity lights. So they made do with what was at hand. They simply elected to complete the descent without the remote. It really was not a big issue. Depending on their rate of descent, they would reach the cavern in less than 15 minutes.

The shower of solidified lava was steadily increasing. When they first dropped away from the ledge, the size of the droplets had grown from that of fine sand to the size of BBs. They had now increased to the size of jellybeans and were not nearly as cool as the smaller pieces. The larger pieces did not dissipate the heat as quickly. As the lava flowed through the air and cooled, it formed into the shape of a pear. Native Hawaiians called those little nuggets Pele's Tears. The velocity at which they were falling, coupled with the temperature, was not making the descent particularly easy. The heavy rain of hot droplets was a lot like stepping into a hot shower immediately after coming in on a frigid winter's day. The particles burned and stung each time they made contact with exposed skin, but at this point, the experience was not too uncomfortable, just irritating. The two men were at the 1,500-foot level when the side of the conduit wall completely blew open, allowing a huge stream of hot, molten lava to flow from the active conduit into the old. The lava pool in Pu'u 'O'o, containing more than 250,000 gallons of the molten rock, was draining out of the basketball-size hole and into the old conduit. The jet of lava resembled the flow from a 100 fireman's hoses as the gushing stream of red-hot liquid blew through the opening with titanic force. The cables that connected the remote were instantly severed, and gravity took over.

# Freedom's Menace

The immense spray of lava hit the far wall with such force that it shot magma in all directions, including straight up. The upward flow exploded from of the top of the conduit. The Navy and Marine troops manning the operations around the tripod scattered for their lives as they heard the on-coming rush of liquid. Flaming masses of blazing fire shot 90 feet into the air, creating a fountain of fire all around the conduit next to the Pu'u 'O'o vent. A large semi-solid mass, the size of a refrigerator, hit the control tent, causing it to burst into flames. Reynolds just made it out by diving through the burning canvas and then dousing himself with the water in the reservoir next to the cable spool machinery. Multiple projectiles hit the mess hall and sleeping quarters, and both burned faster than a mobile home in an electrical storm. Eight soldiers died inside the inferno. The fireballs that landed next to the generator fuel storage tanks sent troops diving for cover. A basketball-size flaming rock scored a direct hit, creating a deafening explosion. One of the supply helicopters was hit and exploded within a few seconds, killing the pilot and two ground support personnel with shrapnel as they tried to flee the area. Ten people dove into a nearby Humvee, and it sped away only to have a glowing lump crash through the roof, killing all who were aboard and setting the vehicle ablaze. A nurse was hit in the chest by a fireball the size of an orange that burned right through her even before her body fell, face first to the ground. A soldier, running to safety, was sprayed by a molten glob that had landed just to his right side; his pant leg was now on fire as the hot liquid boiled his skin. A Marine staggered from the scene, his face completely burned away, his remaining hair smoking like the end of a fat cigar.

The scene was one of total mayhem, death and destruction. The opening connecting the two conduits was now the size of a city bus. The lava pool inside Pu'u 'O'o slowly lowered as the hundreds of tons of melted rock drained into the neighboring conduit and down to the cavern below. After more than 30 years, lava no longer flowed from Pu'u 'O'o.

It took less than a minute for the free-falling remote unit to catch up with Commander Ocker. The edge of the heavy metal case struck him on the shoulder, severing the right appendage. His death was instantaneous. His limp body was now dangling from the mountaineering rope that was attached through the descent device and secured by a stainless steel carabiner clipped at his waistline. As the belaying device was designed, it provided for a slow gradual descent toward the cavern floor below. Davidson, 15 feet above, had seen the large, black object fly past and then heard the impact, but in the poor light he could not see what had happened. He began to shout for his commanding officer. No response. He then began to panic as Pele's Tears turned into flaming golf balls. They streaked past him like fireflies on a summer night and stung like a swarm of angry hornets. He was now in a hailstorm of fire and could do nothing about it. He was dropping as fast as the rigging would allow. He bumped into Ocker and, momentarily, froze in horror at the sight. The scene was almost Biblical. While the smell of burning hair blanketed his olfactory senses, he was completely unaware that the back of his shirt was in flames. He was now swinging wildly from side to side while banging hard into the conduit walls and spinning at a dizzying rate. Above him, only 100 feet and three seconds away, was a bright crimson curtain of boiling liquid magma. The cremated remains of the two men rejoined the earth in grand Christian symbolism ashes to ashes and dust to dust.

Captain Jones was still examining Ocker's protective suit when the first traces of what was coming started to settle on his head and shoulders. He and the others looked up only to get a face full of fine dust. Wincing, they ducked their heads and wiped the debris from their eyes. Only when Pele's Tears began to fall did they realize that serious trouble was fast approaching. The remote unit suddenly appeared as it fell through the opening, smashing onto the ground just a few feet away. Jackson directed his men away and guided them toward the mess area so as not to be directly under the conduit opening. They had not, could not have fully considered what was coming next, even though they had been loosely warned. Tears from the Hawaiian goddess danced about the cavern floor in a spectacle worthy of a Fosse production. The mass of still molten lava quickly followed. It hit the ground with tremendous force, spraying the igneous blaze in all directions. The artificial light was no longer required, as the spray of red filled the area with the dull glitter of a room full of Christmas lights.

Brice and Dr. Allison scrambled up the ladder alongside the conning tower as the 2,000-degree fireballs dropped all around them. Samantha was in the lead. A ball of fire glanced off her right hip and exploded like a Roman candle on the steel surface next to her. The shower of sparks covered both of them. The red-hot pellets felt like needles against their exposed skin. Her jeans had started to burn where the fire had struck her. Brice reached up and swatted at the small patch of fire, extinguishing it. They reached the top and dropped over the side onto the bridge. Brice leaned over and yanked open the hatch. He grabbed Sam around the waist with his left arm and literally dropped her into the pitch darkness of the control room below. He then looked up and over the side to locate Jackson and his men. To his horror he found them huddled next to the burning mess tent, desperately looking for a way out. They were trapped, with no possibility for escape. The boiling goo was covering the ground between them and the sub. The wooden boardwalk was already being consumed, the flames shooting 10 feet into the air. Suddenly and without warning, the fuel tanks for the generators exploded, sending Brice ducking for cover. When he looked up again, he saw that Captain Jackson and his men lay dead, torn apart by the shrapnel from the disintegrating metal storage tanks.

"Oh my God! Oh, shit!" He paused, looking for any signs of life, but saw none. "Ah, damn it, just plain damn it," he said out loud. He stared out over the devastation, and just under his breath he said, "Better than being burned alive, I guess. Those poor bastards!"

# 28

## Trapped

Brice said a short silent prayer and looked, once more, over the side as the spray of flaming particles flew overhead. The flow of lava had now bridged the gap between the sub and the ledge. The bow was being covered, and the paint and rubber matting was burning off. Trevor gave a long sigh, and he climbed down into the sub, closing the hatch behind him.

Within minutes the lava crept over to the mangled bodies of Jones and the three others and quietly consumed them. The cardboard boxes of provisions started to burn and the metal cans of vegetables, fruit and fish began exploding as the intense heat boiled the liquid contents. The cylinders filled with propane cooking gas went next. The area had been turned into a war zone of proportions that no human could have ever imagined. Soon the lava began to mound against the cavern wall, with the sides rising up and forming a giant trough that funneled the entire flow of red into the water. The magma exploded as the tepid seawater quenched the fire. BBs of rapidly solidified lava and an unending fountain of scalding water sprayed the surrounding area. Splatters of liquid rock were being thrown 100 feet into the air. Billowing plumes of steam from the boiling salt water rose into the air and started filling the cavern.

Inside the total darkness of the submarine the sounds from the hot magma popping as it instantly cooled reverberated with almost mystical qualities. Incredibly, they could already start to feel the heat penetrating the once cold steel hull. Brice found Sam in the total darkness and took her in his arms. The two just held each other tightly, saying nothing for several minutes. The tentacles of fear had reached out and grabbed Sam while intertwining its prickly existence around her every nerve. A cloud of hopelessness had blanketed her with despair. She was shaking as she silently contemplated death in a way previously beyond comprehension. She started to cry. Trevor felt every twitch of her body as if they were one. Her tears wet his shirt as her fingers dug into his back.

In a voice quivering with anxiety, she said, "Trevor, I really don't want to die. Not this way."

The emotion of raw fear pasted over them like an icy vapor. He cradled her and kissed her forehead. The temperature inside the sub had already risen 25 degrees. Then, as if it were written in a script, his survival instincts took over. Trevor slipped his hands around her waist and gently pushed her away from him ever so slightly. He then cradled her face in his hands, her tears running down her cheeks and over his open palms.

"Samantha," he said gently, but with sincere confidence, "it's not over yet. We are going to get out of here." Tears began to trickle down his face, as the emotion of the moment briefly seized him as well. The sound of his breathing fluttered like the wings of a scared bird. She wrapped her arms around him and held on for dear life.

"As much as I would love to stay and dance with you for the rest of the evening, I do have a wife and two kids. They are the most important things in my life. I cannot and will not go out like this. I cannot fail them, not this way. And you, my dear, have a puppy waiting. We're getting out of here, and we are going to do it now!"

She raised her head as if she could see him through her swollen, wet eyes in this darkness, curious about his words but not really believing that escape was possible.

"If I have learned anything about life and death situations it is to worry about death later, when there is plenty of time to do so. Right now we have to concern ourselves with living."

"Ok," she said, her voice trembling as visibly as her hands. "What do we do?"

"We have to get from here over to the cavern entrance, but we will need to take along some supplies like, flashlights, flares, a few small weapons and, of course, water. Food, if we can find any. I saw bottled water in the mess earlier. It would also be a good idea if we could find the life jackets." He placed his hands on her shoulders and asked, "Can you make it? Are you ready?"

She nodded and, as she fought back the final tears, whispered, "Yes."

She was happy to know that even in the most dire of circumstances there were those who continued to reach out and grab hold of the only things that were important in this world, love of God and love of family.

"The bulk of what is flooding the cavern right now is coming from the lava pool that was in the vent. Once that drains, the only thing that will be falling is the normal flow. Right?" asked Trevor.

"Yes. But, and this is a real big But, at the rate at which Kilauea produces lava it would only take maybe five minutes to refill that pool. No, I'm sorry, but that stuff is going to continue raining down on us until the cavern fills up or something causes the flow to change."

"In that case, Doctor, we had better get moving!"

He lowered himself on hands and knees, feeling along the floor searching for the small waterproof flashlight that was once strapped to his left leg. It had fallen off as he climbed down into the sub. He found it in short order and held his breath as he pressed the small, rubberized button. The small but adequate beam lit up the darkness. He shone the light all around the control panels until he found the master switch. With the butt of his right hand he snapped the switch into the ON position. The submarine interior stared to glow with the blue hue from the emergency lighting system.

"Great, the batteries still have a little life left in them, but I doubt there's too much left. We'll have to hurry."

From his initial search of the sub, Trevor could still recall where most items of significance were stored. The captain's chair that sat in the middle of the control room had a powerful four-cell light mounted under the seat. He peeled away the Velcro strap and handed the light to Sam.

"This way," he said, starting out for the rear of the sub.

# Freedom's Menace

They came to a small staircase and climbed down to the lower levels. They turned and headed back toward the bow. Forty feet down the corridor and to the right were the crew quarters. Most everything they needed was there; flashlights, batteries, weapons and ammunition. They even found a case of bottled water someone had stored under his bunk. Not Evian or Naya or some other designer bottled water, just regular water. Sometimes one just has to rough it. They stuffed the supplies into two backpacks that they found stored above one of the hammock-style bunks. Trevor found a locker and pulled out a Chinese sailor's cotton shirt. He handed it to Samantha saying, "You look like you need this."

"Why?" she asked.

"Well, there is a burn hole about this big just between your shoulder blades," he said, extending his arms, his middle fingers and thumbs touching to form a circle.

Surprised, she reached back and confirmed what he had said. "Thank you," she said. "Now if I may have some privacy?" Trevor turned his back while Sam stripped off the old shirt and donned her new apparel. "I'm ready, but first I have to go back up to the control room and get my samples."

"The hell you do!" snapped Brice. "You brought those with you? Darlin', I have know idea what we are facing. We may have to swim our way out of here. You cannot possibly do that with 50 pounds of rocks strapped to your ass and that volcano firing red hot bullets at you!"

"No, I can't, but with you taking half of them I think we can both make it with the aid of these life jackets."

She barged past leaving him, life jackets in hand, standing there dumbfounded. After a moment, Trevor turned and followed her back up the steps and to the area where she had left the two pouches. She poured half the contents into her backpack and handed the rest to him. He just stared into the canvas bag for several seconds and then reluctantly filled his pack and slipped the burden onto his back.

"Can we go now?"

She looked at her watch and said, "Now's the time. Low tide is approaching. I'm not real keen about this place as it is, but I sure as hell don't want to be in that passage when the tide returns. Lead the way."

Trevor climbed the ladder to the bridge, grabbed the hand wheel, spun it open and gave a slight push. It did not move. He positioned his open palm just under the hatch and felt the heat of the lava that was now mounded high on top of the hatch and covering the bridge deck. He knew immediately that they were not about to get out this way.

"The hatch is hot and wouldn't open. We'll have to find another way out."

They climbed back down into the control room. He led her aft to the rear escape hatch. He climbed the ladder and carefully placed his hand on the metal cover to determine the amount of heat on the other side. It was warm, but not hot. He gripped the wheel and turned, causing the mechanism to twist and spin inward. Then, with a resounding click, the hatch popped open a few inches. His eyes were met by an eerie red glow that pulsated like a slowly beating heart. Slowly he pushed open the hatch. Above his head was the finest fireworks display he had ever seen. The spectacle of a million roman candles all aimed to form an arch over the sub in a brilliant display of color. His head rose above the opening, and he looked all around. The fireballs were falling everywhere. The cascade of burning pellets was too dense to try an escape from this position, at least not right now, maybe as a last resort. He climbed back down.

"Now, what?" she asked.

"Let's try the engineering section. Maybe they have an equipment hatch built into this thing. Head back that way."

As they made their way toward the back of the boat they felt a slight shudder.

"What was that?" Sam wondered out loud.

Trevor looked at her, clearly wondering the same thing. "Let's go back and look," he said as he slipped past her, heading for the escape hatch they had just left.

He scurried up the ladder, opened the hatch and looked out. Immediately he saw what had happened. The three-inch ropes that had secured the submarine to the side of the landing had burned through, allowing the boat to drift at will. The force of the lava and the boiling water was pushing the boat away, out to the middle of the cavern's lagoon. This was a good thing, as the shower of sparks would soon diminish. Except for being much further away from the mouth of the passage, escape was not nearly as risky now. He climbed on to the deck, hoisted up the backpacks and then assisted Sam. They gathered up their provisions and took a few steps toward the tail when the sight of the deflated, melting raft caught their eyes.

"Now I know why you wanted the life jackets," she said.

"Yep, looks like we're going to swim after all. I suggest that you leave your science experiment behind," said Trevor.

"Not on your life," she replied defiantly. "I'm taking these with me and you are taking yours with you. If you drop them, I'll kick your butt."

"Now wait one damn minute. Look at what's going on here. Do you see how far we are going to have to swim? It's raining little shit balls of fire all over the place. It's going to be hard enough dodging those things without a bag of rocks strapped to our backs, life jackets or no life jackets. I think that this time, science can wait."

"Just remember, you drop my samples, and it's your ass."

With that she jumped into the water and began the swim to the passage, 300 yards away. Trevor just shook his head, slipped on the pack and followed her in.

"This woman is nuts," he thought.

It only took a few seconds for Sam to realize that Brice was probably right, but she was not about to concede. She slipped out of the heavy burden, rolled over onto her back and laid the pack on her stomach. This seemed to work. She saw Brice jump into the water and sink beneath the surface. His head popped up and he started to cuss a blue streak, all directed at Sam and her "fucking" rocks. He started to kick frantically and was certain that he would never make it. Finally he spotted her and figured out what she had instinctively understood. He turned onto his back and started to kick with the backpack resting on his stomach.

# Freedom's Menace

"Why does it take you men so long to figure out the simple stuff?" she called out.

They took their time, frequently having to dive under the water to avoid a flaming lump of lava from landing squarely on top of them. After 15 minutes, they reached the passage and climbed to the top of the giant spike of lava that blocked the entrance. They held onto the small ledge and caught their breath. Trevor flipped the backpacks and rock sample packs up onto the ledge and then pulled up, out of the water.

"If you're ok, I'll just climb to the top with this stuff and come back down for you."

"I'm fine, go ahead," she answered.

Brice had just gotten the final piece to the top when he heard Sam say, "I'm three feet below you, just climb on up."

Standing atop the massive shard of lava, they stood and surveyed the scene they had just left behind. Lava continued to pour in, like steel from an iron foundry ladle. It was hitting the ground like water falling on a flat rock, sending spray in all directions. For a moment he mourned his lost comrades, his throat gripped in emotion as his damp eyes blurred the view. Slowly he came to realize what a truly beautiful spectacle this really was. The sight tickled whatever it was inside of him that gave him his gift for design. For several minutes he forgot where he was and contemplated the wondrous possibilities.

"How would this look in the lobby of the Blue Hawaiian?" he thought.

Sam tugged gently on his sleeve. As he looked at her, a small tear ran down the side of his nose and she wiped it away. Exhausted, but finally out of harm's way, they walked the 70 feet to the opposite end, where they had left the rafts. They tossed the packs down and sat next to each other on the edge of the larger of the two rafts.

Trevor mumbled, "Like my youngest daughter always says, 'That was none fun!'"

Sam laid her head on Trevor's shoulder and shut her eyes and for the briefest of moments, she fell asleep.

# 29

## The White House Situation Room

The President's secretary entered the Oval Office.
Totten, General Persi and Jaymar Jones were standing in
the center of the room discussing the success of the USS
Seawolf in finding and destroying the first of the Akulas. In
the past 18 hours, the country had had three subsequent
victories over other Chinese submarines, one more in the
Atlantic and two in the Gulf of Mexico. Four down, two to
go. One of the victories in the Gulf had nothing to do with
U.S. Navy superiority. The Chinese had chosen a derelict
oil platform to hide beneath. It was actually a great
strategy. Unfortunately, they were unaware that the Coast
Guard had planned to destroy and sink the structure as
part of a demolition-training program. A Los Angeles class
nuclear attack submarine that was scouting the area at the
time picked up the sounds of a diesel engine coming to life
just after the first sounds of the demolition explosives were
recorded. Each of the six legs of the massive superstructure
that supported the platform exploded like a string of
firecrackers from the bottom, up. The high explosives
attached to the platform segmented it into four pieces. In

less than a minute, the entire structure fell into the water
and down on top of the Chinese crew, crushing the sub like
a beer can under the front tire of an 18-wheel tractor-
trailer. The scope of the planned marine sanctuary had now
changed considerably.

Ms. Sutton hastily walked over to the TV and tuned in to
the CNN Breaking News event.

"Excuse me, Mr. President," she said, turning the
volume up, "but there is something on CNN you need to
see."

As the screen changed from black to white and then to
full color, the carnage from around the Pu'u 'O'o vent came
into view. At first no one in the room had any idea what
they were looking at. The glowing embers from the fires
were plainly visible. Newscaster Robert Michaels of CNN
affiliate KHNL in Honolulu was 1,000 feet overhead in
Hawaii Newscopter One, providing the live audio and video
feed.

Michaels described the scene, "Forty-five minutes ago,
several helicopters from Blue Hawaiian Tours based in Hilo
reported seeing a terrific eruption from the Pu'u 'O'o vent.
This followed on the heels of an earthquake that measured
6.8 on the open-ended Richter scale. As we reported
yesterday, forces from the Navy and Marines have been
conducting operations around this active volcano vent for
the past several days. Our sources from around the state
have only reported that the military was keeping quiet
about the nature of these activities. But it is obvious that
something here has gone wrong, terribly wrong. As you can
see, the ground is littered with bodies, and the tents and
portable facilities have already burned to the ground."

# Freedom's Menace

"Wait while we swing around... and there, coming into view now, are three emergency medical helicopters from Kona and Hilo that have just arrived on the scene. The white coated doctors and nurses are scouring the area searching for victims. The medical teams will be attending to what appears to be a number of seriously injured military personnel. As you can plainly see, this looks like a war zone! Most of the equipment, ground vehicles and aircraft have been burned beyond recognition."

"Most surprisingly, folks, the lava flow from the volcano has stopped. In fact, I cannot even see any lava in the vent at all. As most people know, when Kilauea erupted last year it uncovered a second conduit. It is my belief that the military presence had something to do with the second vent. But, wait... I'm receiving a message from the pilot. Ladies and gentlemen, I am sorry, but it seems that the U.S. Navy has asked that we clear the area immediately. They are declaring this a restricted site."

The picture abruptly changed to the CNN Newsroom in Atlanta where news anchor Maria Rosa picked up the story. "That was Robert Michaels from our Kona affiliate KHNL. Thank you, Bob. Now to summarize our breaking story from the Big Island of Hawaii..."

"David, What the hell is that all about," asked Totten.

"I don't know, sir. I do know that everything around that volcano is being coordinated by Admiral Hanover at Pearl at the request of your man Brice."

"That's not what I mean. I know about the damn operation. I want to know why we have burning equipment and dead bodies being flashed around the world. What the fuck happened over there? Where is Brice? Why hasn't Hanover kept this quiet? The last fucking thing I needed

was for the damn Chinese to learn that we knew that what
was under that volcano. Damn it man, you're killing me."

An aide stuck her head into the room and announced
that Admiral Hanover was on the phone.

"Charlie, this is Totten. What the hell is going on over
there?"

"I don't know yet, Mr. President. We just learned about
this on the cable news channel. Our link with the site
stopped working about the same time that CNN reported
that those tourist choppers saw the fireworks. We do know
they experienced a few earthquakes in the area; one was
pretty sizable. It's possible the active volcano somehow
merged with the ancient conduit we were using as access to
the submarine. Sir, I don't know shit right now. Give me 30
minutes. I've already got men on the way to secure the
site."

"Charlie, this is Persi. And I want your butt out there,
too! Understood? Call me back in 20 minutes."

"Yes, sir. I already have my chopper waiting. I'll call you
in route."

Persi turned to face the President, who was red faced
and ready to bust a gut.

"God damn it, Dick! I don't need this shit right now! At
this point, there is nothing we can say that the Chinese will
believe, other than the truth. So I want a complete
communications black out from this point forward. Do not
let another one of those news helicopters back in the area
without my say so. If anyone asks anything, I want the
answer to be, 'No Comment,' exclamation mark! Are we
clear on that?"

# Freedom's Menace

The President pressed a button next to his phone and shouted to his secretary, "Ms. Sutton, find Beckie and get her ass in here now."

Three minutes later White House Press Secretary Rebecca Hutchinson stepped into the President's office to find him in a heated telephone conversation. "Beckie, have you see CNN?"

"Yes, I have, and so has the Press Corps. They are very anxious to find out what's going on."

"Damn it!" exclaimed the President. "All right, here is the story line. The U.S. Navy, in cooperation with the Department of Interior and the National Parks Service, has been conducting a joint operation that involves the exploration of the Kilauea Volcano. At this point in time, we think that a series of earthquakes caused a significant eruption to occur, resulting in the catastrophic loss of life and injury to the exploration party. Our thoughts and prayers go out to all those who lost family members in the horrific natural event. Period, that's it. Don't give them any more than a 30-second sound bite and take no questions."

He turned to face Persi as Hutchinson left the room. "Alright, Dick, this whole thing may blow up. Lolo is likely to strike at any moment, so let's be ready. I still don't want to fire the first shot, but I sure as hell will fire the second one. You guys wanted to shoot a second test missile, so go ahead and do it."

Persi left to return to the Pentagon, cell phone cemented to his right ear. The only people still in the Oval Office were Totten, Jaymar Jones and two Secret Service agents.

"Jaymar, it looks like I have lost Brice and the rest of his team. He was my ace in the hole. I have a few other operatives at my disposal, but no one else with the expertise that Brice had. Damn, he was a good man. Poor guy. What a lousy way to go. I guess I'm going to have to call his wife and kids and tell them."

"Sir, why don't you wait, just to be sure? It's really not going to matter when they find out," said Jaymar.

"Be sure of what? You saw the pictures. The whole damn volcano blew up. He may not be dead, but he is certainly trapped down in that hole with no way out. So, he may already be dead or he may die tomorrow or the next day! He's still dead!!!"

"Forty-eight hours, sir, just give it 48 hours."

## Beijing

Wang entered the office of An Lolo. "Premier," he said, "that American volcano in Hawaii has erupted. Their CNN was showing pictures of some military operation on the surface above where our submarine is trapped. Sir, they may have found out about the diamonds!"

"Turn on the television," ordered Lolo.

As the two men watched, CNN reviewed the situation and the previously recorded videos. They interviewed a variety of expert witnesses, mostly ex-military personnel, all professing to know the true secrets about what the United States Government had hidden beneath the volcano. A range of vulcanologists, including Samantha Allison's boss from the Jaggar Observatory, discussed the unpredictability of nature's fiery wonder. The news of the fight between Brice and three goons at the lava flow had already reached the media, despite the best efforts of the Navy. The Head Ranger at Kilauea National Park was interviewed to try to establish some correlation between the two events. But through it all there was no mention, suggestion or even a hint that anyone had any knowledge of the cavern, the diamonds or the submarine. For the most part the consensus of opinion was that there was a hidden military operation that had been damaged by the eruptions and that the surface operation was a rescue mission.

"That's enough," announced Lolo after 75 minutes. The views and opinions from the long parade of experts had become repetitious, and he had seen the same video footage of the burning camp and charred bodies at least a dozen times. "The Americans know nothing. We maintain the strong hand. In less than two days their pitiful efforts will be over. China will assume its rightful place as world leader. We will make things to be as they should be. And I, An Lolo, shall rule the planet from this point forward!"

Wang's mind was suddenly awakened to the reality of Lolo's true plan. He had what would be the second biggest revelation of his entire life. The chill froze him to the very spot where he stood. For more than 25 years he had been a loyal servant to China and to the premier. The construction business, which he had built in America, provided his mother country with much valuable information through the government contracts it had secured over the years. Good business acumen and a bit of luck had provided the opportunity to work on the Darnestown project. He had provided Lolo information about this project only as a service to the country that he so loved. The same was true of planting the explosives that brought down the structure and killed all those innocent people. He had done all of this himself, many times working into the wee hours of the morning, so as not to be detected. He had smuggled the explosives and timing devices into the project by a sophisticated variety of means. It had taken months, but he had successfully honored the premier's wishes. After all, as Lolo had told him many times, it was the Americans who were out for global conquest. It was their fault that China was not as prosperous as it rightfully should be. Responsibility for the plight of the Chinese people lay squarely at the feet of the American capitalists. Lolo was only trying to do what was best for China and its people. The revelation that Lolo was actually mad was far more than his sensibilities could handle.

In a quivering little voice, he started to speak. "Lolo, you have done all of this so that you can become a god? None of this you have done for our people?"

"It is for the good of China! The Chinese are the rightful rulers. Simple people such as you cannot understand what is important. Now go do as I have instructed you."

"I cannot do this for you any longer. This is not for the good of the Chinese people as you said. This is only for you. This is not right. You cannot continue. I will not allow this."

"I am through with you. If you are smart, you will leave now."

"I still have friends in America. I can stop all of this, you know," said Wang as he rushed from the room.

As Wang slipped through the door, Lolo looked at the guard stationed just to the right of his desk. With a contemptuous toss of his head, he motioned for the guard to make sure that Mr. Wang caused no further problems. The guard bowed obediently, and with an ever so slight grin forming on his lips, he left the room. Wang was still at his desk gathering his few possessions and muttering to himself when the guard reached his side. Now the single

biggest revelation of his life occurred when the guard
placed his heavy hand on his right shoulder and squeezed
tightly, digging his fingers into the man's flesh and muscle.
As the blood drained from his face, his worn and faded
brown leather case fell to the floor with a resounding
thump. The guard led him across the room and through a
side door. To the others in the room, what was about to
occur next was only too obvious. Everyone immediately
returned to the appearance of work and did not so much as
look at the side door for the remainder of the day. The
heavy wooden door mercifully spared them from the bone
crunching sound of Wang's neck breaking as the guard
twisted his head three-fourths of the way around. The trash
incinerator behind the building became his final resting-
place.

Everyone in the outer office jumped when the buzzer on
the desk of Lolo's secretary screamed to life. The harsh
humming was unrelentingly as she jumped to her feet and
rushed into his office.

# 30

## Escape from Kilauea

Trevor took a deep breath. The noxious mixture of sulfur, steam and other volcanic gases had begun to fill the vast cavern.

"Sam, not now. You have to wake up. We have to keep moving."

She snapped back to consciousness and sat upright. He stood and walked over to the other raft and pushed it into the water, 20 feet below. It bounced once and landed upside down in the water. He then opened his backpack and grabbed a handful of flares and a second flashlight. He stuffed the flares into the side pockets of his cargo pants and wrapped the lanyards of the two flashlights around his left wrist. He then reached over and, with his right hand, pulled Sam to her feet. She stood, but felt as if she were in a complete fog. He wrapped the life jacket around her and secured the clasps, and then did the same for himself. Sam was finally coming around as he helped her over to the edge and shone the light down into the dark water. The raft had floated about 30 feet away and was still moving. He tightened his grip around Sam and stepped over the edge. The shock from the cool waters was all that was needed to bring them both to a full state of awareness. Sam coughed for several seconds after ingesting a mouth full of saltwater. They just bobbed there for several minutes, inhaling deep breaths from the small pocket of unpolluted air.

Assuring himself that Sam was all right, Trevor swam over to retrieve the raft and flip it over to the upright position. He hoisted himself aboard and turned his light over to where he had left Samantha. She was not there. Frantically, he swept the beam all along the base of the massive lava wedge. She was nowhere to be seen.

"Sam! Samantha! Dr. Allison! Where are you?" he shouted.

"I'm up here," she replied. Brice pointed the beam of the flashlight up to the point from where they had just jumped. There she stood 20 feet above the water with the two backpacks full of lava samples, one in each hand.

"She is one determined woman," he muttered, thinking that he had successfully left the burdensome weight behind.

He paddled over to a point just underneath her and stood to the best of his ability on the spongy bottom of the raft, as she tossed down the black bags that held her most prized possessions. She then jumped into the water next to the rubber boat and pulled herself aboard. Trevor secured the packs, handed her one of the paddles and began rowing away from the cavern and into the dark passage that lay ahead.

"You are a real piece of work! You know that, don't you?"

Sam said nothing, but smiled a triumphant smile that he did not see. She gripped the oar, leaned over the side and joined him in the effort to make their escape. Three hours later they were still paddling.

"Can we take a break? My arms are about to fall off," Sam said.

"I think mine already did," Trevor said.

Although they had flashlights, they had used them sparingly, because the batteries were quite weak. Mostly, they had just rowed completely blind, feeling their way along when they would occasionally bump into the sides of the cavern. Trevor took out one of the flares and lit it. He then pitched the waterproof pyrotechnic into the water where it lit up their location as it gently bobbed alongside. The light revealed nothing new, black walls of jagged lava rising to an apex 100 feet above their heads. Brice reached over and retrieved his pack. Opening it, he extracted two granola bars, two chocolate candies (Snickers, his favorite), and one of the bottles of water. He handed one of each of the food items and the water to Sam. They lay there motionless and speechless while munching on their plastic-wrapped feast and sipping the stale water. Sam snuggled up to him and fell fast asleep. Seeing no reason not to join her, he shut his eyes as the light from the flair slowly faded.

An hour later, the stench that entered Brice's nasal cavity woke him like a giant brass gong. The toxic cloud had already reached them. Samantha, still asleep, was starting to wheeze as the available oxygen in the area was slowly being poisoned.

"Sam, wake up! We have to go," said Trevor in a voice weak from fatigue and the onset of oxygen deprivation. Sam was already starting to be overcome. Trevor grabbed her shoulders and began to shake.

"Wake up!"

He slapped her cheeks, desperate to revive her. Slowly she came to a half conscious, almost drunken state. Trevor struggled to sit up, his head spinning. He lit a flare to establish their position and tied it to one of the aft ropes so it would drag behind them. At this point, light was as important as oxygen. Grabbing a paddle, he began rowing at a frenzied pace. Occasionally, he splashed the cold salt water over the bow and onto Sam's face, all the while yelling at her to wake up. It worked, but it worked slowly. She eventually started to squirm and then started to cough as her lungs purged themselves of the deadly gases. They entered an area where the height of the ceiling dropped about half. For a time, this would trap the forward movement of the noxious cloud of vapors. Sam had finally returned to a full state of awareness and was opposite Brice, rowing for all she was worth.

Finally, Trevor stopped and sat down in the bottom of the raft. Sam kept up the pace until he reached over and pulled her down with him.

"Take a break," he said, clearly winded.

Several minutes passed before Trevor spoke up, "So Dr. Allison, noted vulcanologist from the Hawaiian Volcano Observatory and all around wonder girl. Where the hell are we, and where does this take us, besides away from the fumes and hot lava?"

"Oh, good question! I've been thinking about that to keep my mind off my aching back. My first assumption was that this passage ran pretty much straight to the ocean, five or six miles. But, shit, we have already rowed for over three hours now."

The raft bumped into the passage wall. Sam rolled over the edge of the raft on her belly, leaned over the side and snapped off a sample of loose lava. She slipped it into her backpack. Trevor just shook his head in amazement at her single mindedness.

"What I am now thinking is that this passage is a part of the southern rift, although an ancient part. It probably was covered over thousands of years ago, and the present rift just formed a short distance away. Ok, assuming that I am correct and that is the case and we are traveling parallel to the current rift, we could have a very long way to go. As the crow flies, the distance between Pu'u 'O'o and the ocean is, I don't know, 50 to 60 miles?"

Trevor covered his face with his hands and lay there in silent thought.

"Let's say that we're covering five miles each hour. That would put us 15 or 20 miles from where we were and seven hours from where we need to be. Looks like it's going to be a very long day."

What he did not verbalize was the thought that since no one knew how the submarine had gotten in, it was extremely unlikely that the entrance was even visible from the water. Somewhere the passage would stop and disappear under the water. What then? "What then?" was the key the $64,000 question. He didn't like not being able to answer that one simple question. He took his paddle, raised himself up and resumed the trek. "What then?" continued to roll over in his mind. At the halfway point, five hours from when they started, it was apparent that the shape of the passage had begun to change significantly. It was getting a little less wide, but the top was now considerably lower. Neither of them spoke of this, though each understood. They would occasionally rest, eat a small snack from their dwindling provisions, and Sam would collect more samples, never once considering that she may never get the chance to study them.

Two hours later, the passage had narrowed to the size of a hotel hallway. There was barely room for the paddles to slip down between the sides of rubber boat and the walls. At times they were forced to use their hands to push the raft along as it scraped against the walls. Certainly the water had to be very deep for the submarine to pass. Thirty minutes later, they entered a small room. Brice lit and threw out another flare. The void was only the size of the neighborhood video store. The entry was behind them and slightly to the left was an opening, an opening only about three feet high and 10 feet wide.

"We are not going in there?" Sam said emphatically. "My claustrophobia is bad enough. You are not going to ask me to go into that! Hell, we can't even sit up in there!"

The concern on Brice's face was evident, but his resolve showed through.

"Look. Think about this for a minute. There were 150 Chinese sailors in that sub. They are not there now, and we have not come across any sign of them. They had to get out somehow."

"They may have gotten out some other way," she protested, "Maybe we just missed it in the dark. Maybe they sent another submarine in to get them. Maybe...."

Trevor placed the fingertips of his outstretched hand over her lips. "Remember what I said earlier, there's a lot of time in the future to worry. Right now we have to get out of here, and that's the only exit. Now just take a few deep breaths and relax. Focus on doing what you have to do." He leaned over and gave her a reassuring hug. "Now let's go."

They rowed over to the opening and turned over onto their backs and laid the paddles down beside them, as the rubber raft slipped into the rocky crevice. Light was now an essential. Trevor turned on the smaller of the two flashlights and laid it at their feet. It provided all of the illumination that was required. The roof was just high enough to allow them to propel themselves along by pushing the ends of the paddles against the crags in the ceiling. The pace was much slower now, but the size of the tunnel did not fluctuate too much. Occasionally, the claustrophobia would grip Sam like a spider would a fly, and panic would set in. Each time, Trevor would stop as she desperately tried to free herself from the confining walls and close ceiling. As the waves of fear rippled along her flesh, his strong arms and soft words helped to reassure her until the episode passed.

"I now understand what it feels like to be a sardine. Just slather me in mustard and oil and pack me away," she said.

"The oil sounds like fun. I can handle that," quipped Trevor, "but the mustard is just a little too kinky." This made her laugh, and she elbowed him in the side.

They were 45 minutes into the tunnel, and there was no end in sight. The ceiling had gotten lower, and they were now forced to use their hands to keep the raft moving. The texture of the lava was like thousands of little scalpels, each biting and digging into their flesh as they worked their way along the tunnel. They had turned off the flashlight, because Sam seemed to handle the darkness better than when she could see in these close quarters. Not being

# Freedom's Menace

witness to her confinement allowed it not to exist. A sudden change in the texture of the ceiling caused Trevor to turn on the flashlight again. Snagged on the small outcroppings and ragged edges of the lava were hundreds and thousands of strands of fabric, rubberized cloth, a single thread with a button still attached and occasional patches of hair. An icy chill went over them as the discovery of the fate of the missing Chinese crew materialized on their conscious.

"Turn it off, turn it off! Turn off the goddamn light," she screamed.

The reality of what they had just seen was far too gruesome for her to even think about. She reached up into the darkness, dug her fingers into the rock and began to pull the raft along at a furious rate. Brice joined in. One hundred and fifty men ground to death against the course ceiling of the narrow passage. Their rafts and bodies scraped against the surface by the force of the undulating tide like bricks of cheese against a metal grate. Neither took the time to consider when the next high tide would come in, but each understood that they had no plans to be there when it did. They each received the necessary shot of adrenaline they needed to continue. Forty minutes later, fingers bleeding and swollen, the raft floated into a small cavern. Trevor hit the light and sat upright as they both squinted under the glare of the bright blue beam.

In a room only about the size of a one-car garage, but with a ceiling that rose out of sight, this was the end of the ride. Trevor pointed the light in every direction looking for an exit. He then lit one of the remaining two flares and dove with it over the side. A startled Samantha crawled to the side of the raft, and peered into the water. She could see the glow of the flare along the far wall at what looked like 10 feet below the surface. Brice was swimming around looking for an underwater exit. His head popped up, he took in several gulps of air and disappeared below the surface. After 20 minutes, the flare was almost burned out, and Trevor swam back to the raft. He lifted his upper body out of the water. With Trevor's arms flung over the sides and his chin resting on the edge of the raft, by the dull glow of the flare that he left floating in the water, Sam gazed into his vacant eyes and slumped back into the raft.

She finally said what had been unspeakable for the past several hours. "Trevor, we missed the low tide you know?" He nodded. "High tide will be here in about an hour. There's no way we can get back through the tunnel in that amount of time."

They just looked at each other as the flare faded to black.

# 31

## Freedom

"I have no tears left in me," she said, "and I have no fear left in me, either. I am really disappointed that I won't get to examine all of these rocks." She placed her left hand on one of the bags.

"I don't know what to say except that I'm sorry," said Trevor, and he climbed in out of the water, making a plopping sound as he splashed down onto the wet bottom of the rubber boat.

"You don't have to apologize, it was a great adventure. All my friends laugh at how much I like to explore new things. That's one reason I chose to live on Hawaii. It's such a diverse island. Oh, I'm sorry, we already had that discussion."

"No, no. It's all right. Please, continue. What's your favorite place?"

# W. Laurence Willis

"That's not easy to answer," she said. "But if you pinned me down I'd have to say Richardson Beach in Hilo. On a clear day, you can go out there and snorkel with the turtles and the different fishes. Do you know what the state fish is called in Hawaiian?"

"Oh, yes, it's Humu humu nuku nuku a pua'a. Short and sweet. My daughter taught me to pronounce it."

"Oh, very good! Most people would never even attempt that one. Anyway, what I really like about that particular beach is the giant mound of 'A'a lava that's just off shore. You can wade over to it and climb up to the top. There are always people up there sunbathing. But what I like is the tranquility. The ocean is the most incredible blue you have ever seen, and the waves come crashing in, turning the blue water into virgin white foam. You put all of that in contrast with the ebony black of the 'A'a lava, and it's the most incredible site I think I have ever seen. I can just sit there for hours and watch the water flow in and out, rolling over the abstract shapes. I also like to watch the little crabs scatter anytime someone approaches. On the left side is this huge tide pool that fills and empties like an overgrown punch bowl. The waves feed into it from several directions at once. The experience is truly mesmerizing."

"I've never been there," said Trevor, "but I guarantee that I'll go first chance I get. But I still like the volcano the best. That lava flow you showed me yesterday, before we were so rudely interrupted, was just awesome. I have never seen anything like that before. It sort of reminded me of Niagara Falls, but with melted rock. It was truly incredible. I also like Maui. Do you ever spend much time over there?"

"Yeah, some. There's a group of us that go over for Easter sunrise on top of Haleakala every year. It has to be the best sunrise in the world. We then spend several days

276

partying in Lahaina and surfing in Kapalua. It's a great time."

"What about Hana? Ever been to Hana?"

"No, we always talk about taking the drive, but after the trip up Haleakala we're usually ready for the beach and a banana-mango-rum-cream and whatever drink. Is it a good place to see?"

"Yes, I would strongly recommend spending a few days there. If you go, stop at Hana Bay and park next to the concession stand, then try to hike to the lighthouse. The trail is not marked, so you just have to wing it. You can't make it across to the lighthouse anymore, but along the way there is this little red sand beach with all sorts of creatures running around on it. When you finally get as far as the trail will take you, there is this 10-foot gap between the little island that the lighthouse sits on and the spot where you'll be standing. It's a small version of what you described Richardson Beach to be like. With the swirling blue water against the red lava it's just a little bit of heaven."

"Why, Mr. Brice, you certainly seem to know quite a bit about Hawaii. I take it you have been here a few times."

"You bet! In fact, my wife was born right here on the Big Island, in Pahala. We honeymooned on Maui and Kauai. Since then, we have been back to visit the Big Island, and we brought the kids for Christmas and New Years 2000. It was on our honeymoon that we found the trail to the lighthouse. At that time, there was this little bridge that allowed us to cross, and we made it all the way to the top. The view from up there was spectacular."

"You know," said Sam, "I also really like Kauai. Last spring my ex-boyfriend and I hiked the Na Pali Coast. It was fucking awesome. There are wild goats roaming the trail and nude hippies wandering around. We joked that they were probably breeding, but we weren't sure who was breeding with whom. Anyway, you can sit up there and watch the whales as they play just off the coast. But the real bonus is when you get to the end, there is this really nice white sand beach where you can swim and have a bottle of wine and soak up the sun."

"You know, I just may have to move here," Trevor said. "I'm sure that the kids would not object too strongly."

"So tell me, what's a secret agent doing with a wife and kids? Don't you people usually just jet about the globe drinking martinis, playing baccarat, killing evil doers and bedding down with some gorgeous babe at the end of every mission?"

Trevor let out a belly laugh. "Don't Hollywood writers have great imaginations? If it were only so glamorous. I went into the Navy after I left Cornell and was sent to special assignment training. It seems I have certain skills that Uncle Sam finds valuable. But that was not where my heart was. After I met my wife, I quit that line of work and opened a design firm. But, as I'm sure you know, our government is very persistent, so I stay on call as an aide to the President. Generally, it requires phone consultations and occasionally a field assignment. An assignment like this is rare at best. I don't think I care to do too many more like this one."

"So, where did you meet your wife? Is she a spy too?"

"I met my wife while we were both on vacation in New Orleans. Actually we were both there with friends and

# Freedom's Menace

getting blasted on hurricanes at Pat O'Brien's. That's where I first met her, but later that evening I bumped into her again as we were walking down Bourbon Street. My friends and I spent several hours with her friends, roaming the French Quarter, eating too many crawfish and getting way too drunk. Later that night we all went our separate ways, and I didn't see her again. But the next morning, she was the first thing I thought of, aside from my throbbing frontal lobe. I spent the next day looking all over for her, but I never did find her. Of course, silly me, I didn't ask for a phone number. I did, at least, remember her first name and that she was from St. Louis. So I went back to Washington, and she to St. Louis. Am I boring you with all this?"

"No, no, not at all. I love this stuff."

"Ok. Anyway, when I got back home, I could *not* get her out of my mind, but I had a problem. I never got her last name."

"So what did you do? How did you ever find her?"

"One nice thing about the work I was doing at the time was that I had access to all kinds of privileged information. A buddy of mine in the computer department, MIS as it's called now, downloaded the passenger manifest for all St. Louis to New Orleans flights. The list covered a four-week period, since I didn't know when she had gotten there or when she was leaving. I took the list and stayed up until 4:00 that morning, but finally I figured out who she was. And then, of all the stupid things, I got her phone number and called her, at 4:00 in the morning. As you can imagine, she was pissed to the gills that I woke her up.

"Yeah, I guess so," Sam said.

"Well, hell, I was up and had just spent the past 10 hours finding out who she was. It seemed only reasonable to call when I did. Anyway, she hung up on me. And then I did something even more insane. I called in sick and hopped the first flight out of Dulles to St. Louis. I made it to her apartment before she even left for work, but now my better judgment told me not to present myself that early in the morning. Sooo, I…"

"So you what? Come on, you can't stop there. I want to hear the rest."

"So I followed her to her downtown office. I even parked two stalls away and rode the elevator up with her, another benefit of my training, she never recognized me. So, after I learned where she worked, I went down to the lobby coffee shop to think. While I was sitting there, one of her friends that had been in New Orleans came in and recognized me. I was obviously on the spot, so I told her the story, most of it anyway. Danielle had already told her that the asshole from New Orleans had called at 4 am. Her friend thought all this was incredibly romantic and started to gush all over me. She convinced me to meet them for lunch and, boom, off she went."

"I had about three hours to kill and left and walked around the city wondering what the hell I was doing. A couple of hours passed, and I stopped in a little deli that was decorated like a French bistro, outdoor seating, the whole bit. I just went in to get a Coke, but while I was there I saw a sign advertising that they catered for all occasions. So after 30 minutes of begging, pleading and outright groveling, I convinced the owner to set up a table in front of Danni's office and serve lunch for a party of two, complete with wine, flowers and a tuxedoed waiter. It cost me a small fortune. But the look on her face when the two of them walked out of the building was priceless. Half the city had lunch in front of that building that day. I found out later that one of the local news stations was housed next door and had filmed the whole thing."

"Ooooh, how sweet," squealed Sam, rolling over and giving him a hug. "That is just too cool. Did you propose right then?"

"No, but we both knew it was fate. I met her again after work and then I flew back to Washington that night, resigned my commission the next day and was in St. Louis three days later. A month after that, I opened my design firm, and the rest, as they say, is history. A little impulsive, huh?"

The raft bumped into the cavern wall, a sign the tide was rising and causing the boat to drift. Trevor sat up and switched on the light. Their entry passage was now completely underwater. He shone the light upward, but there was still just darkness above. He pressed the button, and the two sat next to each other without speaking another word. The tide was rising and falling at a faster rate, causing the raft to bounce from one side to the other. The force of the tide pushing through the large submarine passage and then being forced into the small cavern caused the water level to change by several feet with each pulse. It was like being inside of a coffee percolator. Before they knew, the boat was being lifted more than 20 feet and then dropping back down with bone jarring force. Trevor and Sam were holding on for dear life. The flashlight flew out of his hand and disappeared into the water. Trevor threw his left leg across Sam, helping to hold her down. They were powerless to do anything; they just rode the wave up and down, all the while banging into the walls.

Suddenly, Sam had a thought, "Are your ears popping?"

"What?"

"Are your ears popping?"

"No, but who cares!"

"Then where is all the air going? Every time we ride this up, the water level should be compressing the air in here. If that were so, then our ears would be popping, just like on an airplane. That's not happening. The air is escaping somewhere and in large enough volume to not cause pressure changes on our ears. Which means there is a big hole in here somewhere, and that may be our one chance."

Still struggling to keep from smashing Sam each time the water level dropped out from under them, he reached for the last flare. He pulled it from his pocket just as the boat slammed back down. The flare fell from his hand and floated to the back of the raft. Trevor released his grip and dove for the opposite end in search of it. The next drop bounced Sam out of the boat. She never released her grip, but was now at risk of being caught between the raft and the wall.

"Trevor, help!"

Brice was back to her in a flash. He climbed over the side and used his feet and legs to keep some distance between the wall and Samantha. She didn't have to be told what to do. On the next drop, she pulled herself up and slipped back into the boat. She turned and pulled Brice in on top of her. The impact was crushing as they slammed back down. The air rushed from her lungs as Trevor's weight knocked the breath from her. Up they went again. Brice rolled to his right, hanging on to her left forearm. Down they went. Wham! He rolled Sam on top of him so that she could have time to catch her breath. It worked. She lay there for a while as she regained her composure.

"Looking for this?" she asked, holding up the flare as the bottom once again fell out from under them.

Trevor lit the fuse and a red, smoky glow lit up the cavern. As the wave lifted them they could see an opening in the wall just above their heads. It could be reached if they stood on the edge of the raft and timed a good jump at just the right moment. Down went the raft and up again.

"Man," said Trevor, "If I wanted to do this for a living I would have joined the rodeo as a bronco buster."

He stood and tossed one of the two backpacks up and into the opening. On the next undulation, he pitched up the second one.

"Ok, your turn," he said.

He threw the flare into the water next to them hoping that it would not burn into the raft before they were safely on the ledge. As the water lifted them, Sam stood up on the edge of the raft, Brice firmly holding the backs of her thighs for support and balance. When he shouted, "GO," she jumped with all that she had in her as he pushed her upward. Down went the boat with only Brice aboard. He was off balance and landed squarely on his back on the rubber bottom. The salt water splashed over his face, burning his eyes.

Sam had made it up to her waist and was pulling up into the opening. Trevor continued to ride the raft up and down to let Sam get clear before making his attempt. Sam scrambled up and into the small opening and then rummaged through her backpack to find the tiny AA cell flashlight she had brought with her. She pressed the button as she pulled it out. Turning around and pointing the beam back to the opening, she discovered Brice hanging on the edge by his fingertips. She stuck the end of the light in her mouth and scooted to the entrance. From a sitting position with her legs spread and heels dug into the sides, she leaned over and grabbed Brice's shirt by the shoulders. Sam sat up slightly and then allowed herself to fall backward, letting her weight pull Trevor up. With his right foot, he found a toehold and pushed himself up to his waist and then crawled up into the opening. Sam looked down at him as he lay in front of her face down and just a little out of breath.

"Well, that was fun," she said. "Want to do it again?"

"No, no. I'll pass thank you. Whew! Any food left?"

"You men, all you ever think about is food and sex."

In reality, she was just as happy as he to find that three granola bars, a chocolate and half a bottle of water had survived. They ate and rested for before Trevor grabbed the flashlight and pointed it into the nothingness that lay in front of them.

"Do you feel the breeze that keeps moving back and forth? Well, it's coming from deep in there, somewhere. I think that it's time to find the source."

The natural shaft was small, too small to even stand in a slumped position. It was going to be necessary to crawl their way out, not welcome news for their hands and knees. Brice took out his knife and cut away the material from his pants just below the knees and cut it into strips to wrap around the palms of their hands. He took material from Sam's pant legs to use as kneepads. Samantha led the way.

It was a slow process considering that they each had 25 pounds of lava samples to drag along with them. Sam had the flashlight in her left hand and the strap from her pack twisted around her right wrist. Very quickly the shaft began to slope downward, and the degree of slope was increasing rapidly. After 20 minutes, they found themselves in a sitting position as they worked their way down the slope, like children on a sticky schoolyard slide. Trevor had already noticed that the air was starting to smell cleaner. The shaft narrowed and the slope increased dramatically. Their hands and legs were outstretched as they crawled down the shaft, which was now angled almost straight down. Blood trickled from the small pricks the sharp lava had made in their fingertips and butts of their hands as they fought to keep from falling to the bottom. Relief soon greeted them as they discovered that the sharp drop was only about 20 feet. Sam let out a long sigh when she reached the bottom and waited for Trevor, who was only a few feet behind her.

"Oh, my God! Oh, my God!" she exclaimed. "Look!"

# 32

## Parting Company

Somewhere up ahead in the inky blackness a small, faint beam of friendly sunlight waved to them. Samantha let out an ear-piercing scream of joy and jumped up on Trevor, wrapping her arms and legs around him and shouting, "Oh, my God! Oh, my God! Oh, my God!"

Her pack fell to the ground, landing on top of his left foot as the flashlight in her left hand struck him behind his right ear. He struggled to keep his balance despite the throbbing in his foot and head and the ringing in his ears from her high-pitched exuberance, but he was as overjoyed as she.

She released her grip, dropped to the ground and headed straight for the sunbeam, leaving Brice standing in the dark with the two backpacks, no flashlight and a sore foot. Chuckling with relief, he picked up the baggage and followed her out into the daylight. By the time he had wiggled his way through the tight passage, Samantha was already frolicking in the surf like a child on her first trip to the beach. The bright light hurt his eyes, and he squinted and shaded them with his open hand resting on his brow.

As Trevor's eyes finally adjusted to the brilliant Hawaiian sun hanging lazily overhead, he found himself standing on a very narrow and rocky strip of shoreline that ran along the base of a cliff that formed one wall of a beautiful horseshoe cove. Samantha had waded 10 feet out and was thigh-deep in the cool blue water of the Pacific, her arms out stretched and her face pointing up at the warm yellow orb. The cliff rising up behind him and wrapping itself all around the cove was well over 100 feet high. In the center of the horseshoe was a large beach covered in fine sand that shimmered with colors of pale green, black and gold. A dozen tourists were either playing in the surf or sunning themselves on the beach, and no one showed any acknowledgement that Trevor and Sam had just crawled out from the face of the cliff looking like castaways from a long lost ship. For the moment, this was the most beautiful place on earth.

"Having fun?" he finally asked Sam. "You're acting like you haven't enjoyed our little adventure and prefer to be out here."

She did not say a word. She didn't need to; the look of pure contentment spreading across her face spoke volumes. Her behavior indicated she was obviously having one of her best days ever. Her looks, on the other hand, considering the matted hair, numerous cuts and scrapes and eyes puffy from fatigue and salt water, revealed someone who had a very rough night.

"Hey, Samantha. I hate to break into your euphoria, but do you have any idea where we are?"

She looked at him as if he had three heads, because it was obvious to her that as long as they were out of the damn tunnel, it really didn't matter where they were.

"The Green Sands Beach. South Point, the southernmost tip of the United States, is about 5 miles in that direction." She pointed toward the cliff directly in front of them.

"This is the only green sand beach on the islands. They're quite common on other volcanic islands, like Iceland, but it is rare in Hawaii. The color comes from the crystal Peridot which is belched out of the volcanoes."

Trevor extended his hand to her, and she walked over to him. The two then cautiously made their way toward the beach, stepping gingerly as they maneuvered across the jagged surface. The path, mostly hidden underneath the water, provided a new adventure with each footfall. The brittle, irregular lava had been eroding here for centuries and frequently broke under their weight. It was all they could do to stay upright while, at the same time, keeping the other from falling. Their hands were sore and wet, but they managed to hang onto each other. A fall would certainly result in numerous stitches, not to mention the unpleasantness of a major cut bathed in salt water. It was a long, harrowing 10-minute trek. Finally on the beach, Trevor laid his backpack down at his feet and surveyed the area including the pervasive cliff surrounding them on three sides.

With a puzzled look he asked, "Ok, for my next silly question. How does one get out of here?"

"Well, it's not easy," said Sam, pointing to the middle of the beach. "See the large rock that juts from the cliff face? Just start climbing from either side of it and you will figure it out as you go. I'm always surprised at how some people ever managed to get down here much less make it back up."

She looked up at Trevor to find his attention was focused elsewhere. Just ahead and to the right were three women, in their early 20s, applying suntan lotion to all those areas that were not covered by very slight, brightly colored string bikinis. As the red head with the emerald eyes removed her top, Sam punched Brice in the mid-section with the back of her left hand. "So excuse me, Mr. Pig, just when will your two daughters start to wear those things?"

Trevor looked at her in mock horror, "Never, ever! Thank you!"

Sam turned them in the proper direction and pushed him forward. Brice took one more look at the topless girl as she fell back on her elbows and teasingly arched her back. Laughter from her two friends wafted across the beach.

Up ahead, sitting around the rock marking the exit, was a middle-aged couple that reminded him of the Jack Sprat nursery rhyme. The man was at least six-foot, two inches and as skinny a person as he had ever seen, while his wife obviously ate no lean. Both had spent far too much time in tattoo parlors and not nearly enough at the dentist. The woman held up a small, disposable camera and began shooting photos of her husband as he posed as if he were in the finals of the Mr. Universe contest. The scene stopped Trevor dead in his tracks.

"Look at that," he whispered.

The man had picked up a can of Spam and was now posing with it, first sitting it atop his tattered Panama hat with the faded red and purple band that served as the storage place for his cigarette pack. The Spam went from the top of the hat to the top of his shoulder, to his right biceps as he made a muscle in his stick-like arm, then the can went into the waistband of his baggy swimming suit. Before he could reposition the world famous canned protein, Sam turned away and leaned against Trevor in a futile attempt to keep from laughing out loud. Brice just stared at the scene in wonder and amazement.

"Gee," he said. "They really seem to love the stuff. If they are that passionate about it in public, I wonder ... never mind."

Sam's hand shot up and covered his mouth. "Don't! Don't say it, don't think it, don't even imagine it!" He just laughed, mostly because he really could not imagine what he tried to suggest.

Looking up at the cliff he asked, "What's up there?"

"Its almost desert-like in this area. It's dusty, the wind is very strong, and it is really hot. The constant force of the wind deforms what vegetation there is. The few trees are bent over at right angles. Just another piece of the unique landscape this island has to offer," she said.

"No point in making the climb if we don't have to."

He removed and lowered his waterlogged pack to the sand, dropped to his knees and unzipped the main compartment. A second later he pulled out a yellow, waterproof case from the bottom. Inside the case were his satellite phone, some money and his identification. He took the phone and punched in a series of numbers, the ENTER key and placed the device against his right ear.

# Freedom's Menace

The twirtle emanating from his desk phone froze President Totten in mid-sentence. He didn't even look at the desk. He just sat there, his eyes and mouth in the same position that they were in as he questioned the secretary of state about his conversations with the vice chairman of the Chinese Communist Party. He just sat there waiting for a second ring to confirm what he had just heard. There were only a few people in the world that could call in on the number that rang with that particular sound. The second twirtle and he was out of the chair, which sat next to the fireplace, in a flash, hopping over the coffee table and diving for the receiver.

"Totten, here," he said with the hope of the world resonating in his voice. "Brice! My God man, you're alive! How are you? Where are you? Are you all right? Are there others with you? Jesus, God, man! I can't believe it!"

"Mr. President, I'm fine. Dr. Allison is with me. I regret to report that we were the only ones to escape. The others were killed. I'm sorry, sir, they were all good men."

The President paused to reflect for a moment. "Where are you now?"

"We escaped through the tunnel that the submarine used, and we are now at a beach on the south end of the island. It's a popular spot. Dr. Allison recognized it right away. "

"Brice, eh...Trevor," the President's voice softened. "I know you have been through a lot. More, I'm sure, than I could ever imagine. We were almost convinced that you were dead. But, Trevor, I have to ask one more thing of you." He paused, waiting for the response.

"Ask away, sir," Trevor said.

"You are a good man, Trevor Brice. I need you to go to China. Can you get in touch with Admiral Hanover?"

Brice pulled the phone from his ear for a moment and looked at it. "I think this thing still has some life in it."

"Good. Hanover already knows the drill. We were planning it while you were down scouting out the sub. Now, listen carefully. I'll give you a thumbnail of what we're looking at. You will be flown to Hong Kong. Ambassador Filsinger, a Chinese-American named Alexandra Wilson..."

Brice interrupted, "Alex Wilson, the archeologist?"

"Yes. You know her?" the President asked.

"I know of her. She did a breakthrough study on the Mayans when she was just a teenager. She's brilliant from what I gather."

"That's her. I'll explain her role in a minute. There is also a General He. The general is estranged from the Lolo regime because of his opposition to Lolo's plans. In fact, there is a price on his head. Your assignment is to get Lolo and..."

Brice interrupted again, "You want me to kill him? Kill a head of state?"

"No," said Totten, "but I do want you to capture him and remove him from the country. Reagan did it with Noriega in Panama and stayed in office. I think I can do it with this asshole and not suffer too much political damage. Look, I need you there to lead the operation. I can only trust General He so far. He has his own agenda, but it's the only card I have that I can play right now. Brice, this is critical. We think that if Lolo is out of the way this whole mess will stop. The other Chinese leaders have confided that they do not have their hearts in this war. It is Lolo's war." Totten allowed a brief pause before he continued. "General He will provide you with the men, the weapons and the equipment. As for Ms. Wilson, she has an intimate knowledge of the building and grounds where Lolo will be staying. When this is all over, there are only three people that I care about and want out of there. You, Wilson and Lolo."

"Ok, sir, but what do I do with Lolo once I have him?"

"As I said, I want Lolo out of China. You will escort him to Hong Kong. We have friends that will meet you there. They will take custody the premier and see to it that he ends up in the hands of the Chinese nationals in Taiwan. They will know how to deal with him. Trevor, I still need to know about the submarine, but not right now. Call me en route. There is a great deal more you need to know about Lolo's plans and why we are doing all of this."

Totten hung up and placed both hands palm down on top of his desk and hung his head. "Thank God. This just might happen after all," he thought.

Brice flinched slightly as the connection disappeared with a sharp crack. He pulled the phone from his ear and pressed five buttons followed by the * and ENTER keys. The screen color changed from green to blue, and a compass rose appeared in the center of the one-inch-wide screen. In the center of the compass rose was a clock face with a sweep hand ticking off the seconds. The sweep hand stopped, and the screen went blank only to be replaced with the exact latitude and longitude of his location. He keyed a few more buttons and the information from the Global Positioning System satellites was stored in the phone's

electronic memory. He then dialed Hanover. After a very
brief conversation, he keyed a few digits and downloaded
his location over the satellite link to the Pearl Harbor
Intelligence Center. He confirmed that the information was
received and concluded the call. He turned to Sam, who was
still enjoying the antics of the tattooed odd couple.

"Dr. Allison, we have a couple of choppers coming for
us. I have somewhere else that I have to go. More martinis
and hot babes, you know. The first chopper is mine; the
second one will be for you. You can go wherever you wish,
but until all of this is over, Uncle Sam will be providing you
with around-the-clock armed protection. My suggestion is
that you consider going to Pearl until this is all over. And it
will be over, one way or another, in just a few days. Might
be a good opportunity to study those damn rocks of yours."

She walked up and put her arms around him and
rested her head against his chest. "Thank you, Trevor. You
saved my life, and I never even said thank you."

"Sam, none of this would have happened without you,
and you saved my life as well, let's not forget. Dr. Allison,
you are truly one in a million."

The sound of the approaching helicopters could be
heard as the spinning rotor blades resonated off of the cliff
face. He gave Sam a hug of genuine affection and held on to
her as the drone of rotating wings filled the isolated cove.
He gave her a kiss on the cheek, wished her well and
promised to let her know how things turned out. As he
waded into the water a red-orange rescue harness was
being lowered to him. Sam waved as her new friend rose
into the air and was pulled into the craft. The chopper's tail
spun around and slightly lifted as they headed out toward
the ocean. As the craft cleared the rocky inlet, it banked left
and disappeared behind the cliff. As he vanished from view

# Freedom's Menace

a second craft approached, casting its shadow over the beach.

The tourists all watched in understandable curiosity, each one thinking of a different scenario that would explain what they were witness to. Before the arrival of the Coast Guard, all had only mildly wondered as to identity of the ragged-looking couple who crawled from the cliff. Many were now thinking that something sinister was going on and that the government was behind it. The large woman with the camera became frightened. She panicked and began dragging her pleading, stumbling husband up the path as fast as her short legs and considerable girth would allow. The camera and the Spam lay half covered in the sand next to their abandoned beach towels and cooler. The topless sunbathers covered themselves with whatever was close at hand and, with the others on the beach, just watched. Sam was now standing thigh-deep in the water with her two 25-pound bags of lava samples. The spinning rotors beat the water into an excited froth. It was like a ceiling fan that had run amuck. Rising up out of the sea while being lifted toward the red and white Coast Guard helicopter, she suddenly felt very alone in the world. A crewman hoisted her baggage aboard and helped her to a seat. After checking the security of her seat belt, he wrapped his shivering passenger in a wool blanket and offered her a cup of hot coffee. Their orders were to take their passenger to Pearl Harbor, but at her insistence, and with concurrence from their superiors, they flew the 50 miles to the Kilauea Military Camp and left her in the capable hands of Colonel Kwiatkowski.

The Colonel and two aides were there to greet her when she landed. Kwiatkowski placed a hand on her shoulder and pointed to an area several hundred feet away. There stood an Army private holding the brown leather leash that was restraining her enthusiastic pet.

"Busch," Sam yelled, dropping to her knees. The private released her grip, and the dog lunged forward and took off toward his owner at full speed. The animal literally bowled her over with his exuberant greeting. The deep sense of loneliness started to fade as the two roughhoused on the dusty landing site. Still wrapped in the blanket and with the dog jumping in cadence with her every step, she was led into the bunker for a hot shower, clean clothes, food and some much-needed sleep.

On board his chopper, Brice placed the heavy crew helmet on his head and wrapped himself in a blanket. With the help of the crewman, he plugged the cord that powered the helmet's headphones and microphone into the receptacle located just under his seat. Admiral Hanover was already waiting to speak to him. Brice provided him a 10-minute synopsis of the events of the past 24 hours, including their escape. Hanover began to brief Brice on the events that would fill his life from this point until he reached Hong Kong. A Navy Lear jet was sitting on the tarmac at the Hilo airport, waiting to fly him to Hickam AFB next to the Pearl Harbor Naval Base. He would have 30 minutes in which to clean up and grab a bite to eat before a Navy F-18 Super Hornet would fly him, at supersonic speed, to a remote landing strip on the northern coast of Taiwan. From there he would transfer to a Chinese charter that would take him to Hong Kong. A remote hangar located at the west end of the old Hong Kong International Airport, which was now being used as a regional cargo hub, would serve as the staging area for the next phase of the mission. It would be in that hangar that he was to meet Ambassador Filsinger and the others.

"Brice, you have done your country a tremendous service. The President asked me to tell you how much he appreciates it," said Hanover.

# Freedom's Menace

"Thank you, Admiral," Trevor said, ending the conversation.

He laid his head back and shut his eyes for the first time in what had seemed like days and enjoyed a 15-minute catnap before he was awakened by the pilot's conversation with the Hilo control tower. The chopper sat down on the tarmac, 50 feet in front of a gleaming white Lear jet with the insignia of the U.S. Navy painted on the tail. The copter was lifting off before his feet even hit the ground. He sprinted for the jet. A very large Marine, dressed in camouflage fatigues and armed with an automatic weapon, stood guard at the door. Without hesitation, Trevor climbed into the cabin of the plane. The Marine welcomed him aboard, followed him up the steps and closed and latched the door behind them. The two idling engines spooled up, and the plane rolled forward. The tower gave them clearance ahead of an Aloha Air 737 that was ordered to brake immediately, an abrupt action that startled the passengers and crew. A Hawaiian Air flight on final approach was waved off as the Navy jet, with Brice aboard, wheeled on the runway, engines at full power, directly in its path. While the airliner banked left to clear the area, the Navy jet lifted off and banked hard right, the landing gear closing directly over Ken's House of Pancakes, alarming the patrons and staff. They climbed out over Hilo Bay, turning north to Honolulu. The agitated captains of both airliners could be heard demanding an explanation from the Hilo Control Tower.

The Marine, sitting across the aisle spoke, "Sir, we have something that I believe belongs to you."

He reached behind Trevor's seat and pulled an orange L.L.Bean duffel with TCB stitched in black thread across the side.

"Where the hell did you find this?" Trevor asked.

"As I understand it, one of the car jockeys at the Hilo airport fought off a couple of Chinese guys for it, a few days ago. The Hilo Police took possession of it after one officer broke up the fight. Seems as if the guys got away. The police then phoned someone based on a number they found on the luggage tag. From that point, I have no idea how it got to me. I just have orders to deliver it to you."

Trevor smiled a weak, tired smile, "However it got here, I am appreciative. If you will excuse me, I'm going to shut my eyes for a bit, it's been a long day."

# 33

## Pearl Harbor

The wing flaps were fully extended and the landing gear had just dropped into place when the Marine escort interrupted Trevor's sleep with a gentle hand on his shoulder. Brice was leaning forward, rubbing the sleep from his eyes with the butts of his hands as the Lear jet touched down on Oahu soil. His fingertips scratched his head at the hairline. He rose and stretched as best he could inside the small cabin. Leaning over, he tried to touch his toes, a generally easy task, but his hamstrings were so tight that he could barely make it to the midway point of his shins. He sat back down, and a steaming cup of hot coffee was placed on the tray in front of him. The small white Styrofoam cup shook like a bowl of gelatin as the craft rolled along the asphalt tarmac. Trevor downed a few sips before they coasted to a stop in front of a hangar where all of the smaller "private" jets were kept. As soon as they stopped, the cabin door was opened from the outside. He reached for his orange duffel, but before he could grab the black nylon handles the big Marine said, "I'll see to that, sir. Looks like you have a welcoming party."

Trevor peered through a small round cabin window and immediately recognized Admiral Hanover. The Air Force colonel next to him was a man he had never met before, yet he seemed to remember seeing him in a photo years before. "Jason Sabolic," he thought.

The two men stepped from the plane, Brice in the lead, coffee in hand. He stopped, turned and stuck his head back inside the jet and thanked the two Navy pilots. He made his way across the tarmac to where the two military officers were standing in the doorway of the hangar. As he reached them he extended his hand to the admiral.

"Good to see you again, Admiral, it's been a long time," Trevor said. The two had met at various Washington functions over the years, but had never worked together.

"Well, let me tell you that it is really good to see you standing here. You certainly had a horrifying experience. How are you feeling, son?"

"I'm none the worse for wear, thanks," he said as he turned to the Air Force officer, "Colonel Sabolic, it's nice to meet you."

The blue and white nametag above the breast pocket had confirmed the man's name. The two shook hands and exchanged a pleasantry or two before Sabolic said, "I have a hot shower and a hot meal waiting for you. Which one would you like first?"

Trevor looked down at his tattered and torn clothing, dyed with dry blood, stained white from the salt water and, though dry, smelling a bit fishy and said, "A shower, without question." He pulled the fabric from his collar up to his nose and sniffed. "You may need to fumigate the inside of the Lear before you allow anyone else back inside."

"I can attest to that, sir," injected the big Marine, standing behind Brice and now sporting a huge toothy smile.

"This man deserves a medal," Brice said jokingly as the four disappeared into the hangar.

Minutes later, a freshly showered Trevor Brice, sporting a blue Navy issue jump suit, stepped into the briefing room. The unmistakable aroma of grilled beef roared through his nostrils like a runaway freight train. His long suppressed hunger turned into a primal ravenous urge. Pangs of hunger pounded inside his stomach like ancient tribal drums, while his mouth started to salivate like the proverbial pooch and his eyes bulged as if they were about to jump from their sockets. An Air Force commissary chief sat the large white plate down on a table just five feet from where Trevor stood. A 10-ounce filet of beef sizzled on the hot plate next to a one-pound lobster tail and a steaming mound of long green beans. On the side sat a piping hot bowl of vermicelli pasta that had been tossed in olive oil and garlic. For dessert, a plate of cubed mango, papaya and pineapple followed. Glasses of red wine and water accompanied the meal. Trevor had no conscious knowledge of anything or anyone else in the room except for the meal that lay before him.

In two steps, he was at the table and seated in front of the much-needed nutrition. He ate his fill without speaking or even looking up from the plate. The others in the room simply watched in awe and with some degree of amusement. The commissary chief beamed with delight. For Trevor, the intense hunger and now instant gratification was leaps and bounds beyond what he had experienced just a few months before when he and his eldest daughter joined 40 others to participate in World Vision's 30-Hour Famine. Fasting for 30 hours had taught the experience of hunger. He now understood, on an abbreviated scale, the combined effects of hunger and exhaustion that many in the world experience everyday. His forthcoming contribution to the World Vision organization increased with each bite of the delectable feast.

Twenty minutes later, he pushed himself away from the table, forearms resting on the hard black plastic arms of the chair and the fork firmly gripped in his right hand. He exhaled. With his left hand, he pulled the plate of pasta toward him and swirled a last forkful of the garlic infused grain around the metal tines and moved the shimmering mound to his mouth. The fork fell to the tabletop after glancing off of the edge of the plate, producing a ceramic ringing sound.

His eyes met those of the appreciative commissary chief, and he said, "Thank you very much!"

"Something sweet?" asked the chef with a mischievous twinkle in his eye.

Brice answered by rolling his eyes to the top of their sockets, extending his belly, puffing out his cheeks and exhaling loudly.

"Mr. Brice," said a young airman who had stepped into view from the back of the room. I am Lieutenant Andrew Cosgrove. I will be flying you to Taiwan. Sorry, sir, but we have to get going."

On the surface, Trevor wanted nothing more than to sleep for at least the next month and the expression on his face showed it. However, just below the surface, he knew what had to be done. He lifted the white cotton napkin from his lap with his left hand, and while he rose from the chair he dabbed his mouth and motioned for the lieutenant to lead the way.

Ten minutes later, Brice, Cosgrove and Admiral Hanover were walking through the hangar heading from the giant doors in front of them. Along the far wall Brice saw the movement of several pairs of legs from beneath the wings and fuselages that filled the cavernous hangar. He could not see anyone from the waist up, but did notice that one pair was covered in blue jean denim and two pair that were a short hairy golden red.

"Dr. Allison?" he asked.

"Yes," responded Hanover, "Seems that dog of hers is pretty important, so we arranged to drop her off at the Kilauea Military Base. We had intended for her to stay under Kwiatkowski's care until she had a chance to clean up and get a few days of rest, but she was anxious to get going. We are going to take her and the pooch to her parent's home in Monterey. Don't you worry; she'll be just fine. I assure you that we will take good care of her."

"I suggest that you do," said Trevor, "after all, she is a national hero."

Brice and Cosgrove crossed the tarmac, dressed in their state-of-the-art pressurized G-suits, heading for the F/A-18 Super Hornet that was now parked in front of the hangar. The pick-up-sized support truck, a fuel truck and a five-member ground support team awaited their arrival. Ten minutes later, the canopy dropped over them and the jet rolled forward.

With after burners blazing, the Super Hornet blasted through 15,000 feet heading for a cruising altitude of 42,000 feet. From the rear seat, Brice dialed in the privileged frequency on the secure radio console. Within 90 seconds, he was in contact with the President. Totten was now sitting on his brown leather chair in the far right corner of the White House Situation Room. The President began the conversation.

"Trevor, we are down to just hours. As you may or may not know, the Chinese have bombed one of our towns and are threatening more attacks. Lolo is the one behind all of this. We are going to take him out. So let's go through the drill once more. Traveling at Mach 2, you should land in Taiwan in about three-plus hours. A Taiwanese transport will meet you there and take you the rest of the way to Hong Kong. Ambassador Filsinger will be waiting for you, as will Ms. Wilson and General He. If all goes well you should arrive in Hong Kong just before 6:00 pm. From that point, you will have only six hours in which to reach the emperor's retreat, capture Lolo and get out. Midnight, no later! You absolutely have to be out of that place by then. Is that understood?"

"Do I turn into the pumpkin, or do I get the girl with the glass slipper," Trevor quipped.

"I'm not in a joking mood!" snapped Totten.

"Ok, sorry. What happens at midnight?"

"You just need to be out of there. No, you **have** to be out of there!"

"Whatever you say, sir," said Trevor.

"Oh, by the way," said Totten. "I have some information you might find interesting. The lady that sat next to you on the flight from St. Louis to Honolulu... She's no dotcom executive. The name Martha Gielow was just an alias as we suspected. In fact, we are still not sure just who or what she is. Our suspicions are that she is a paid assassin. The CIA and most international police organization have been tracking just such a person for the past several years. Just after you arrived in Honolulu, a woman fitting Ms. Gielow's description chartered a private jet to Hilo. It arrived there just 20 minutes before you did. We think she was the one who fired the shots. As for how she got on to you, we know that she got her information through a White House aide. The delivery instructions for the package that I couriered you with the info and photo about the submarine accidentally passed through the hands of the aide just before it left here. I'll apologize now. I gave the assignment to her when my secretary was unavailable. It was stupid of me. Luckily for us, the aide had gone out to see a movie the other night, based on a Willis novel, and began to fear for her life. After the movie she wondered around Georgetown for a while considering what she had done. She got home late to find that her apartment had been fire bombed. She was scared to death and spent the rest of the night wandering around the Mall. Yesterday, she came in and confessed. She gave us a complete description of the woman. Seems the two of them had an affair. She thought her friend was only away on a business trip, but after the fire she went to Ms. Gielow's apartment and found it had been cleaned out. Same old sad story that we warn staffers about all the time."

"As for the phony Ms. Gielow, we got lucky there, too. She was picked up this morning while sipping a Pina Colada at the pool bar of the Marriott - Ka'anapali Beach Hotel on Maui. It must have been a great bust. We had an FBI agent posing as the bartender. She had just ordered a drink and settled in to flirt with another guest when the agent put a shotgun to her head. She spilled the Pina Colada all down the front of her gold mesh bikini. I have an excellent picture of the expression on her face. I will save it for you. She was taken into custody without so much as a whimper. I haven't heard the results of the search of her room and belongings, but I seriously doubt they will turn up anything."

"Thanks for the update. She was good. She fooled me. I should have picked her out myself, but I never had a clue. *(a pause)* Is there anymore business we need to discuss?" Trevor asked.

"No, Trevor, that's all. Is there anything else that you need from me?"

"Yeah! My wife and kids! Where are they and how are they?"

Totten cleared his throat. "This is a bit ironic, but we have them in a safe house on the island of Hawaii. Sorry I could not let you see them before you left, but I need you in China."

Trevor did not answer. His right fist slamming against the inside of the clear acrylic canopy startled Lt. Cosgrove. Brice clenched his jaw, pursed his lips and through the visor of his helmet glared down at the clouds below. At the velocity they were traveling, twice the speed of sound, they were catching up with the sunset. From his vantage point, the sun seemed to be rising in the west, a sight he normally would have studied with great interest and wonder. But at this moment he was pissed!

"Brice?" said the President. There was no response.

"Trevor, listen, I could not permit a personal visit, but I can connect you to them right now, if you wish."

His anger instantly transformed into anxious anticipation. Before he could respond, Danielle's voice saying, "Hi, honey!" flowed through the helmet's earphones. The two simple words were like a warm blanket on a cold night. They talked for more than half an hour. He gave her a brief description of the events of the past few days and promised to give her the complete blow-by-blow account when they were again together. As for the two girls, they were thrilled to hear his voice, and as always, the first question was to inquire what gifts he had gotten for them. They also wanted to know if he was having fun on his trip. He assured them that he was.

"And, oh, by the way, Daddy, we got to fly to Hawaii with Mom on an army plane, and it was really cool except that there were no movies or headphones, but it was sorta like first class because we got as many Cokes and snacks as we wanted." They abruptly concluded with, "Well, bye. Rugrats is on."

Trevor laughed out loud when the radio went silent. Once again, "Tommie" was more important than Dad was. He sat back and savored the conversations.

# 34

## Hong Kong

The advanced electronics packages that were tucked into every nook and cranny of the F/A-18 had lined the Navy jet fighter up with the centerline of the now abandoned Taiwan airstrip. Cosgrove had turned off every navigation light and flashing beacon an hour before. They were flying "black." At the present time, they were flying just 50 feet above the waters of the Strait of Formosa while traveling at 675 mph, just under the speed of sound. Cosgrove was totally focused. There was absolutely no room for error. The time was approaching 6:00 pm in that part of the world, and the sun was just starting to fall below the horizon. Behind them, the full moon was already high in the sky. This would be a problem when Brice and his team attempted to break into the retreat. The long shadows from the nearby trees fell across the runway as the wheels touched down without so much as a squeak. Cosgrove had to brake hard as the jet rolled to a stop at the far end of the old, narrow asphalt strip. There was nothing or no one to be seen. The canopy opened, and Brice climbed out.

Freedom's Menace

On the ground, he surveyed the area once more before removing the pressurized G-suit. A small compartment, at eye level just below the cockpit, held his change of clothes, backpack and equipment. He squirmed his way out of the blue jumpsuit and donned an ensemble of all black, including black Nike athletic shoes. The shoes, made expressly for the Navy SEALs, included the famous swoosh, but it too was jet black. He removed the backpack, his Glock 9-mm and a Bushmaster assault rifle from the compartment. He laid these items on the ground and stuffed the G-suit and jumpsuit into the compartment. From there, he carried all of the equipment off to the side of the runway before returning to the plane. Climbing back up to the cockpit, he thanked his driver.

"You do have enough gas to get you out of here, don't you?" he asked.

"I don't have much, but there is a KC-135 waiting for me at 15,000 feet and 100 miles east of here," said Cosgrove. "I should have no problem rendezvousing with them. Mr. Brice, I don't know who you are or what your assignment is, but I wish you well. I do know that a lot of people are depending on you. Good luck, sir."

Brice patted his shoulder and climbed down. With a flip of a lever, he watched as the three small steps closed up into the side of the plane. Reaching into a breast pocket, he pulled the soft, sponge rubber ears plugs from their plastic case. He inserted them into his ears while sprinting to the side of the runway. He picked up his gear and rapidly made his way toward the tree line. As the two powerful turbines spooled up to full power, he cupped his ears for added protection and shielded himself from the forthcoming engine blast. The very short runway forced Lt. Cosgrove to perform a carrier style take-off. It wasn't until the engines were at full power and the afterburners had been ignited


309

that he released the brakes. The fireball that had trailed the jet down the brief path was now rising vertically at incredible speed. Cosgrove killed the afterburners at 9,000 feet and disappeared in the darkening sky.

As the day grew darker, Brice continued to search the area for any sign of activity around the old airstrip. Finding none, he gathered his stuff and headed out through the trees toward the old abandoned terminal building. The small tin building sat between one older, still standing hangar and the remnants of two others. The structure of the standing hangar was more of a lean-to affair, constructed with three sides of rusted corrugated metal and an open front. From his position in the woods, he could make out the nose, wing tip and one engine of what he assumed to be an old, abandoned aircraft.

Under the cloak of partial darkness, he crept toward the structures. Rounding the corner of the terminal, the white beam of a flashlight enveloped his face. A harsh command was spoken to him in Chinese, a language he did not understand. Another harsh order was given; so in deciding that discretion was the greater part of valor, he raised his hands into the air and slowly dropped to his knees. Although the powerful light was trained on his face, Brice could make out the features of two uniformed men moving cautiously toward him. The bright full moon behind him was working to his advantage. These two behaved like cops or security guards. He relaxed a little, but then a long-barrel revolver was thrust in his face, the cold business end pressed against his upper lip, just below the nose. He looked the two in the eye then peered down at the gun and then to the ground behind them. There were five moon shadows. The man with the gun, the man with the light, his own and two new dark figures. From the shadows, he could see the two recent arrivals bringing the butts of their rifles down to impact on the base of the skulls of the two local police officers who were investigating reports of strange sightings at the old airport. Just as the weapons were about to strike, Brice dove to his right and backwards. The sound from the gunshot resonated in his left eardrum as he lay on his back looking up at the brilliant Taiwanese moon. The two ebony figures stepped forward and stood at his feet, looking down at him with their rifles now hanging, innocently, down at their sides.

"You, Blice?" asked one of them in the stereotypical accent of combined Chinese/ English speech.

"I am," Trevor said, returning to his feet.

"Come!" instructed the man as he turned and began walking rapidly toward the one remaining hangar. The second man waited and fell in behind Brice. Trevor turned to study the rear guard. All appeared to be normal, but he sensed that something was amiss.

Inside the hangar sat an old, a very old transport plane. The twin radial engines hung from the stubby wings, 12 feet in the air. The fuselage looked like a railroad boxcar with a slightly rounded nose and sloping back end. The aluminum skin was battered and scraped and was riddled with holes from missing rivets. The two large balloon tires were mostly bald, and there were patches where the polyester cord was starting to show. The large three-bladed propellers looked as if they had been used to chew up concrete and black streaks of oil ran down the cowling. Brice just stopped and stared at the dilapidated hulk that sat before him. He had seen better trash in the junkyard. And he was expected to fly for two hours inside this piece of shit!

As he stood there contemplating this, the right engine slowly began to spin. The decrepit starter strained and howled, as the force needed to turn the three-foot diameter mechanical dinosaur was almost too much for it to handle. Yet the speed of the propeller slowly increased as the cylinders coughed and sputtered. The engine finally fired with a loud pop and then abruptly died. Inside the cockpit the pilot turned the ignition switch again. It sputtered once more and then backfired, belching two four-foot-long columns of flame from its exhaust pipes. The big engine finally chugged to life, sounding very much like a Model-T Ford with rheumatism. With tremendous reluctance, Trevor walked to the cabin door located under the left wing and stepped inside. He swung the door shut and threw the handle to the closed position just as the left engine began to grind away.

The condition of the inside of the plane was about two steps below the exterior. In the front sat the pilot and co-pilot; the two men he encountered earlier were standing on the right side talking to three others that were sitting on a four-foot wooden bench fastened to the cabin wall. Everyone was dressed in black, similar to Brice. Each man carried an AK-47 assault rifle, a side arm, an ominous looking knife strapped to his leg just above the ankle and a parachute. The parachutes, at least, had the appearance of being new, as was the lone spare that sat on the floor behind the pilot. Trevor considered the possibility that they were to jump into Hong Kong rather than land. Considering the condition of the plane, he did not find this to be one bit objectionable, not one little bit. "That's if this piece of shit ever gets off the ground," he thought.

He was thrown backward as the engines revved up and the plane began its forward movement out of the hangar. A similar wooden bench located just behind the pilot's seat was the only remaining seating. Trevor took the end nearest the door. He looked around; there were no seat belts. The man whom Brice had determined to be the leader

# Freedom's Menace

(There had still been no introductions) and the other man joined him on the bench seat. The leader sat in the middle, his AK-47 between his legs, butt on the floor and muzzle pointing straight up. As they taxied, he studied the rest of the interior. The inside of the plane could easily hold a modern minivan and about a dozen people. The back end of the fuselage, which slanted up from the floor about 30 degrees, was made to drop down like the tailgate of a truck, thus allowing the ease of loading. It could also serve as a jump platform for parachutist or cargo drops.

The old craft shook worse than he expected during the take-off roll and initial climb to altitude, but eventually they were in the air and the creaks and groans and rattles faded away. They climbed to an altitude that he estimated to be about 10,000 feet, leveled off and banked left out over the open water. Hong Kong was now two hours away, and midnight was a little more than five. He sat and considered timelines. Ninety minutes to Hong Kong, 90 minutes to the emperor's retreat and two and a half hours to break-in and kidnap the leader of China. "Nothing like a little challenge," he thought.

As soon as they were off the ground, the leader began asking Trevor a series of pointed questions about his plans to capture Lolo. Considering that he had no plans at this point, he answered in the vaguest of terms, indicating that he would have to consult with General He to determine the best course of action. His sense that things were not right was growing ever stronger. His response seemed to satisfy the man as he sat back and shut his eyes while folding his arms across his chest and the muzzle of his rifle. The other four were doing the same. When in Rome, Trevor shut his eyes and began to consider the design plans for the Blue Hawaiian Hotel project. While most people in a similar situation would be fretting over their predicament, Trevor found this type of mental exercise to be very stimulating. It sharpened his mental edge as well as provided him some deep relaxation. A keen mind and relaxed body were going to be of vital importance in the next several hours. Occasionally, he would open his eyes and study his fellow passengers. For the most part, they just sat back, eyes shut, hands on their rifles. At times, one or more of them would light up a cigarette, but they never spoke to each other.

# 35

## The Flight From Hell

Sixty minutes into the flight, Brice's wristwatch softly vibrated to let him know that they were only a half an hour out. He stood to stretch, a pretense that permitted him to see out of the front window. The lights of Hong Kong were glowing in the distance. They were starting to experience light turbulence, a condition that would only worsen, because the heat from the city would rise up and exacerbate the effects of the unstable Asian air.

Brice sat back down and began thinking about the next few hours. Ten minutes had passed when the leader tapped his elbow and started a new round of questions. Clearly, he was trying to determine just what Trevor knew. His senses hit the full "red alert" condition when he was questioned about the volcano. Questions began running through Trevor's consciousness. Who were these men? Whose side were they on? And what was going to happen next? Considering that the man knew something of Kilauea, Brice decided to respond as affirmatively as possible. He explained that they had found the sub and that the crew was missing. He also explained that the eruption had caused them to abandon the search of the cavern and that they never discovered the purpose of the sub. He also explained that they had climbed up out of the volcano just before the eruption blocked their escape. A lie for sure, but he didn't need to be completely truthful. The man wasn't buying it, and Trevor knew it. The ability to read people was critical to his staying alive and this man was making him very nervous.

The leader stood, walked to the front of the plane and held a brief conversation with the pilot. Completing the discussion, he reached down behind the seat and picked up the one remaining parachute. He walked over and dropped it at Trevor's feet. Brice looked at the black nylon bag, up at the man and then back to the parachute. He reached down and flipped it over so that the side that opened up was facing up. Before he could examine it, the leader placed his left foot on top of it.

"I packed this one myself. I can assure you that all is well with it," he said with a smile so phony that Trevor felt he could reach up and peel it right off. "The pilot has received instructions from the ground. The People's Liberation Army is waiting for us to land. We cannot risk being caught, so we will parachute to the meeting place."

Trevor smiled up at the man without letting on that he was in anyway concerned or suspicious. He picked up the parachute by the left shoulder strap and swung it over his arm. His right arm slipped into the other strap and he fastened the clips around his chest. Pretending that the straps were improperly adjusted, he removed it and began making adjustments, all the while watching the others. When he got the chance, a brief couple of seconds, his right hand slipped in under the flap that covered the parachute release pins, which were attached by a small cable to the ripcord. There was only time for a quick feel, but it was all the time he needed. He stood and put the chute back on and secured the clasps again. He picked up the Bushmaster rifle and slipped his right arm and head through the shoulder strap so that the weapon rested across his chest. The parachute prevented him from wearing his backpack as normal, so he disconnected the shoulder and waist straps and secured the bundle around his waist and left thigh. He was ready for something, but was not sure what. The release pins that attach to the ripcord had been bent completely over; his chute was never going to open.

As he had anticipated, the turbulence was increasing. The simple act of standing was becoming singularly difficult. Brice sat back down next to the leader and held on to the bench. The co-pilot turned his head and spoke to the passengers. The leader looked across to the man at the right end of the opposite bench and gestured with his right hand and a snap of his fingers. The man handed his rifle to the one in the center and stood. Holding on to a rope that ran down the fuselage wall, he worked his way toward the rear door. A brass lever was mounted on the side of the wall, even with the location where the rear door was hinged along the floor. The man reached the lever and moved it to the down position. A hydraulic motor, mounted above his head in the center of the fuselage, began to release the cables that allowed the door to open. The entire back end of the plane started to fall away, revealing the moonlit night sky and the edge of the city lights below.

The leader stood and indicated that it was time for Brice to join him and lead the way. This was fine because it gave him a chance to put a little distance between himself and the others. As Brice reached the center of the rear doorway/ jump platform, he turned to wave goodbye with his left hand. Before the hand ever reached shoulder level, the Glock was out of the holster and two shots had taken

out the men still sitting behind the co-pilot's seat. The
leader's anticipation of Brice's actions was too late to stop
the first shots, but he dove across the fuselage and kicked
the gun from Trevor's hand before the third shot could be
fired. The gun flew up from his hand and hit the upper
corner of the cabin. It fell to the floor and bounded on to the
jump platform, a latticework of raised aluminum stiffeners
that formed a skeleton for the outer skin. It came to rest in
one of the small rectangular pockets. Brice was one step
ahead and grabbed the man's pant leg and threw him to the
floor. The assailant was also well trained and spun around
from the prone position, knocking Trevor's legs out from
under him. He landed on his back just as the plane hit an
air pocket, dropping about 20 feet. For a brief moment,
everyone was weightless, an opportunity that Brice used to
roll over to his stomach just before colliding, face down,
with the platform for the second time. Another empty
pocket of air, and again the plane dropped, leaving
everyone floating inside the cabin. Trevor grabbed at one of
the aluminum stiffeners as the body of one of the men
whom he had shot earlier drifted past him, floating out into
space. This time, when he came down, everything below his
waist down was dangling off the end of the platform. The
leader was on his feet, pistol in hand when another jolt
threw him up to the roof. The impact left the man dazed
and lying face down on the floor. The pistol flew from his
hand and bounced toward the cockpit.

Brice was now completely out of the aircraft, holding on
to one of the rear door retracting cables with his left hand.
The 200-mph wind created by the plane's forward
movement was whipping him about like the tail of a kite.
Throughout, the platform operator had somehow managed
to hold on to the rope and had now shoved the control lever
up to the closed position. The hydraulic motor began to reel
in the cables and close the platform door. A few more
bumps and Brice had his right leg back over the end of the

platform. The opening was only a meter wide now. With his right hand, he reached out for the Glock and just got his fingertips on the butt of the gun when the next impact hit. It was only a minor bump, allowing the operator to maintain the upward force on the closing lever, but the Glock rose a foot into space. Brice thrust out his hand and had it in his grip. His first shot severed the door operator's hand at the wrist. The lever fell to the neutral position with just enough opening left for him to climb back inside.

The leader had been on his hands and knees scrambling for a weapon when, facing the front of the plane, he rose to a kneeling position and turned to engage Brice. He was just lifting the automatic rifle as three bullets entered his neck. Brice pulled himself into the plane and rolled down the platform. The co-pilot was climbing out of his chair and had turned to face him when Brice put a bullet through his chest. It was a great shot considering the awkward position that his body was in and the way that the plane was bouncing, but his timing stunk. The dead man fell backward, landing against the control yoke and then slumping into a heap, his body wedging itself between the yoke and his seat. The nose of the plane pitched over into a steep dive. Brice climbed back toward the partially open rear door. He threw his legs over the edge, loosed his grip and flew out into the night. The pilot struggled to pull the co-pilot's body out from where it lay while frantically pulling back on the controls in a futile attempt to lift the nose of the plane.

Instantly, everything was silent. Trevor tumbled through the cool night air as he fought to read the altimeter that was attached to the parachute; 2,600 meters (8,500 feet). He unbuckled the three clasps that secured the parachute to his upper body as he plummeted to the earth. He slipped his right arm out of the shoulder strap while clinching the left strap in the crook of his left arm. He lifted the protective flap and confirmed that all of the release pins had been bent over. He pulled at the connecting cord to no avail. Reaching into his right pocket, he found his red Swiss Army knife. He pried open the smaller blade with his teeth. Then using his fingers as a makeshift depth gauge to minimize damage to the chute, he jabbed the sharp point into the nylon fabric of the parachute pack along the left side of the flap. He cut a long slice down through the nylon, exposing the outer layer of his airborne life preserver. In one smooth, rapid move, the knife was closed and put back into his pocket. His right hand was now full of parachute silk as he started to pull the material through the slit. The knife blade had cut into the top of the drag chute hindering its function of pulling the rest of the chute out of the pouch. Trevor kept pulling handful upon handful of silk from inside of the pouch and releasing it into the air stream. The more he pulled, the more there seemed to be. Finally, enough material had been freed to allow the drag chute to function. As the cords began to unfurl, he threw his arms around the pouch in a crushing bear hug and held on. The soft tug from the chute finally opening gave him a moment to exhale, and he did so with great enthusiasm. He looked down and found that he was a mile from the airport, above the dimly lit shanty villages that surround it. He did not look at the altimeter, but it read 250 meters, less than 800 feet. He had been just 12 seconds from slamming into the earth.

The winds were in his favor, but he needed to reach the control ropes. He pulled himself up by the harness and hopped on the pouch like a cowboy mounting a saddle. He took the wooden handles of the control ropes and guided the chute toward his intended destination. He was absolutely certain that his arrival would go unnoticed as all attention around the airport was now directed at the fireball at the far perimeter. The old transport had crashed into an abandoned warehouse. The airport fire trucks were already racing to the scene, sirens blaring, lights flashing. As the night wore on the local authorities were certain to find a great deal of carnage because that part of Hong Kong was poverty stricken and populated by scores of homeless people.

Ambassador Filsinger and his entourage, General He and Alexandra Wilson had come out of the old maintenance hangar when they heard the explosion from the cargo plane crashing into the warehouse district. As they all watched the flames leaping more than 100 feet into the air, Brice approached them from the rear. No one saw a thing until General He was grabbed from behind and thrown against the trunk of the ambassador's limousine.

With the barrel of his Glock under the man's chin, Trevor said, "Hello, general. My name is Trevor Brice. Are you surprised to see me?"

Brice completely ignored the embassy guards that now had automatic weapons trained on his skull as he stared deep into the eyes of the fugitive Chinese officer. A calm and diplomatic Ambassador Filsinger stepped through the crowd of anxious Marines and placed his hand on Brice's shoulder.

"Mr. Brice," said the Ambassador, "the men who picked you up were not sent by General He. We just learned an hour ago that the transport we sent for you was shot down before it ever arrived in Taiwan. We summoned the local Taiwan authorities to look for you."

Brice continued to glare into the man's eyes as he considered this information. He finally released his grip and lowered the gun, but was still not 100% convinced.

"Sorry," he said. "I thought that you tried to have me killed."

"Apology accepted," said the general tartly.

"We have to get moving," said Brice, in no mood for formalities and moving swiftly toward the hangar entrance while holstering his weapon, leaving the others just standing back and looking for someone else to be the first to follow.

# 36

## The New Mission

Filsinger inhaled and lead the others in following Brice
into the building. The group spent the whole of 10 minutes
inside, just enough time for cursory introductions, a run
through the equipment checklist and a five-minute preview
of the grounds and floor plans of the emperor's retreat.
Brice was the first one back out of the hangar and into the
awaiting U.S.-made Bell Jet Ranger helicopter, a late 1970s
model that was likely procured from Iran after the
expulsion of the Shah. Brice climbed through the side door
and crossed over to the far side of the cushioned bench seat,
where he buckled himself into place. General He took the
middle of the bench, and Alex Wilson strapped herself into
the far right. As the copter lifted off, Brice looked at his
watch. It was 8:15 pm. Shit! He unrolled the drawings of
the retreat grounds and spread them out on the small cabin
floor in front of them. General He and Alex started giving
Brice an in-depth review description of the grounds and of
the proposal for creating a diversion that would allow them
to slip into the retreat.

# W. Laurence Willis

The 10-acre compound was a basic rectangular shape, with three of the sides surrounded by a seven- meter high stone wall and the back protected by a shear cliff that dropped more than 800 meters into a lush green river valley. The stone wall was two meters thick and hand built centuries ago from hand-hewn limestone. The entrance was sealed by a massive ornamental iron and bronze gate situated directly across from the retreat's main entrance. Eight large emerald-shaped gardens lay end to end between stone drives leading to the fountain, seven-meters in diameter, centered in a circular drive that graced the front entrance. Rising from the center of the fountain was an obelisk, five-meters tall, of polished virgin white granite. The obelisk was roughly the shape of a lava lamp with a bulbous bottom tapering to a rounded top. It was three and a half meters wide at the lower end and a third meter in diameter at the top. The stark white surface was highlighted with the embedded flecks of gold that naturally occurred in the stone. The symbolism was unusual in the Chinese culture, and it's meaning was unknown. According to Alex, the big sister obelisk formed the centerpiece of the grand foyer, only it was 10 meters high with a four-meter diameter base.

On first entering the gate, a service drive connected on the left and followed the wall around to the servant's entrance on the left side of the building. The service road was screened from the retreat by a continuous row of trees, bushes and flower gardens. More gardens filled with vegetables, herbs and flowers decorated the landscape on the left side of the estate. The road terminated at the service parking area just to the left of the helicopter-landing pad.

A front lawn, two-acres large, was an immaculate, uninterrupted field of green grass. The right side of the property was landscaped with lush gardens raised to different and contrasting elevations. Fountains, winding paths layered in crushed white stone and a massive elliptical pool near the edge of the cliff was designed for tranquility and meditation. A natural spring twisted through the raised beds of the garden as it trickled over small falls and continued to polish the rocks as it had for hundreds of years. Eventually the water fed into a basin that sat a meter above the pool. A two-meter semicircular waterfall filled the oval pool. The waters finally flowed out from the opposite side and cascaded over the cliff through the nostrils of two hand-carved Fu dogs that sat on opposite sides of a small balcony with a wall, just below chest high. The balcony, cantilevered about three meters over the edge of the cliff, provided a stunning panoramic view of the surrounding country. A line of low-cut evergreen bushes on either side of the Fu dogs separated the pool from the cliff, providing a safety rail for guests. Nowhere else along the edge of the cliff were there any railings or walls.

"Sounds pretty," said Trevor tersely, "but how do we get in?"

"Here," said the general, as he pointed to the cliff side of the right hand wall. "Using climbing equipment, we can work our way around the wall. Once inside the perimeter, we will move to this point."

Making a small circle with his index finger, the general pointed to a doorway that appeared to serve as a basement entrance, midway down the length of the right-hand wall.

"The distance from the wall to the door is approximately 120 meters. At night, the pool is very well lit from the blue underwater lights. The gardens are not so well lit, but the pool is right in the path of the door. There will be no avoiding it. It will be very risky. It is also the only way in."

Brice looked across at Alex, who confirmed the general's assessment with a nod of her head.

"Just how sure are you about getting around the wall? Are there no guards patrolling that area? Why not just scale the thing and come over the top?" Brice asked.

"There are guards on the outside, yes, but there is a small path, here, along the edge of the cliff that is somewhat protected from view by boulders and bushes. We have sent in scouts within the past few nights to confirm that it can be accomplished. In fact, they have already made their way around the wall and into the compound. We have already driven pitons into the rock and strung the necessary safety ropes. The guards on the outside of the wall are very predictable and slipping by them should be no problem. *(a pause)* I assure you," said the general.

"Like you assured me of a safe flight from Taiwan," said Brice pointedly.

General He bristled at this snipe, but continued without comment, "The routine of the guards inside the wall is far less predictable. This is where we must use extreme caution."

"Obviously, we will need a diversion to get past the pool and into the building. What are your plans for that?" asked Trevor.

"I have a squad of 100 men hiding in the hills awaiting our arrival. We are not well armed and have but a few vehicles. There is one armored troop carrier that we will use, and one tank. Our plan is to stage a mock offensive on the compound. This will only serve as a diversion to allow the three of us to slip into the retreat. First, my men will move on the front gate, right down their throat. Just like they are coming to pay a visit. Here is where they will use the armored vehicle. It is old and expendable. It will be filled with explosives and detonated it in front of the gate. This will be followed by an attack on their left flank. The outside guards will be eliminated, and 30 men will scale the wall. I plan to permit them to not allow my men to enter the compound. As the left flank is pushed back, the frontal assault force will retreat as well. They will drive us back, and my men will once again disappear into the hills. By that time the three of us should be inside. Once there, we will be on our own."

Brice considered the plan. It had some serious holes in it. Despite staging attacks on their left flank and the main entrance, some members of the retreat's guard unit would have the presence of mind to not allow the right flank to go unprotected. Of course, if they got past the outside guards without being detected, the exterior guards would report to those inside the wall that the right flank was secure. Once they receive a confirmation, hopefully their leaders would leave only a few men to keep watch. But they would still have to be very cautious. Based on the description of the gardens, there were too many places for the guards to hide and wait.

"General, I don't like the situation on the right side. Here is what I want you to do. After we are in position on the back side of the wall and the front and left attacks are launched, I want a compliment of 10 to 15 men to attack the right flank, eliminating the outside guards and lobbing hand grenades into the right front corner. That should take their eyes off of the pool area long enough for us to get to the building."

The general readily agreed, but Trevor saw the reluctance in his face. He did not trust this man any further than he could throw him.

"Ok," said Trevor. "Where do we go once we are inside?"

Alex reached down and pulled the building floor plan from beneath the bottom of the pile. The drawings were only crude hand sketches and omitted a large number of details, but the basics were there.

"The reason I am joining you on this endeavor," she said, "is because I know most of the inside layout of the retreat. Unfortunately, there are a great many areas that are either inaccessible simply because the doors are always locked or, like the third floor of the residential wing, there are guards at the top and bottom of the stairways. Not even the servants are permitted into those areas."

"Where will these steps take us?" Trevor asked, pointing to the area they planned to use as their entrance.

"They lead down to a storage room on the basement service level. The groundskeepers primarily use it as a storeroom, but there are other assorted items kept there as well. It's a very large room, extending the full depth of the house. There are only two outside entrances; the one we discussed, here in the middle and this one at the right rear corner. The middle door is usually unlocked, but the rear one is always latched from the inside. While the middle door has steps, there is a ramp from the basement up to this rear door. It's for the gardeners to push their wheelbarrow and handcarts up and down. Once we are inside, there's a door leading to the servant's passage, and it is always locked from the other side. We will somehow have to overcome that."

"Doors are not a concern to me," said Brice. "Guns. Guns are a concern! So, what's on the other side of the storage room door?"

"You are not going to like this," she said. "It opens into the main servant's passage. Usually there are no guards down there, but they do have a rest area that is accessed from the kitchen stairs, at the far end of the corridor. Halfway up those stairs is a doorway on the left that opens onto a stairwell. The guards always disappear into it, and there is usually a guard posted just inside. I know that the steps only lead down. It is not a room, only a stairwell. I've been told that it is the entry to their sleeping quarters and equipment storage, but I was never allowed in there. There are about two dozen doorways along the servant's passage. Keep in mind that the retreat is over 80 meters long. Some of the doors open into empty rooms, and some are always locked. There are also three staircases; the one leading to the kitchen, the first that we will encounter, goes up behind the grand staircase in the foyer, access is through a hidden door, and the last one goes to the first floor hallway on the main level. The hard part is that we have to get to the first floor in order to get to the second and third levels. Now, there is a stairwell from the kitchen that hits all three floors, but it is always guarded, and as I said earlier, the third floor was off limits."

Trevor picked up the sketch and studied it for several minutes. He was feeling very uneasy about all of this. It was comparable to breaking into Camp David. After all, the leader of the Chinese people was a frequent occupant and his safety was of utmost concern, particularly now considering the situation with the United States. He started to run the plan over in his mind. It was plausible, but not ideal. He picked up another drawing that showed the second floor and studied it for a while. He turned his head to the left and stared out into the night sky. Alex

Wilson was still an unknown to him, but he felt that she was trustworthy. He had not yet learned how she became involved in all of this and why she had such knowledge of the retreat's design. *No matter.* As for General He, the more Brice was around him, the less he trusted him. There was no way in hell he was going to turn his back on this man.

He leaned forward and turned to Alex.

"I want you to give me a verbal layout of each floor. I want to know where the doors are, where the steps are, where the guards are posted, the location of the bathrooms and where every crack in the floor is located. I want it all. Start where you left off in the servant's passage. Is there anything else down there that could be useful?"

Alexandra thought for a moment before beginning. "Most of the doorways have deep recesses in the corridors. I had to hide from an amorous guard one night, and he ran right past without seeing me. There are usually three steps down into the adjoining room. The doors are all made of heavy wood probably six inches thick. They all have cast iron hinges and locks."

She spread her fingers to illustrate what six inches was to the general, who was listening intently.

"There is a small room under the grand staircase with a servant passage leading to the basement. The doorway is hidden, in that it blends into the marble walls, but it really is not hard to spot if you are looking for it. The stairs at the far end lead right to the heart of the kitchen. You will reach the stairs to the upper floors just before the kitchen entrance."

"And, you have only been permitted onto the second floor? Not on the third," Brice asked, confirming what she had been saying earlier.

"That's right," she said, "there has always been a guard posted at the base of those stairs. On the left side of the second floor, there is nothing but office space. On the right are three studies and lounges. Lolo frequently uses these to relax, read and entertain guests and heads of state. The first two rooms are separated by another primary stairway, which connects the second and third floors."

"So, what do you think is on the third floor?" asked Trevor.

"The rumor is that it is all communications, but that is only a rumor. I have no real first-hand knowledge. Sorry," she said.

"That's all right. You're being a big help. Please continue," he said, looking at his watch.

"At the end of the hallway is the foyer, and it is truly magnificent, one of the most unusual features of the building. Everything is classic Ming-era influence, except the foyer. It is almost classic Jeffersonian, with the round rotunda and domed roof. There is a seven-meter fountain with the obelisk, 10 meters tall, in the middle. The rotunda portion, with its three-story ceiling, extends from beyond the front of the building to about the center of the retreat. A grand hallway extends to the rear of the building and out onto a balcony that can comfortably entertain 50 people. On the right side of the entry is the grand ballroom. It's 20 meters wide and runs from the front to the back." She paused to let them study the detail a bit longer.

Placing her left index finger on the sketch, she continued, "Just beyond the fountain is the grand staircase. It forms a semicircle starting on the left side and rising to the second floor. The second floor continues back to a small rear balcony. The ceiling is two stories tall in that part of the retreat. On the second floor, directly above the ballroom, is the formal state dining room, with the rear third of the building being Lolo's bedroom. Across the hall from the bedroom is Lolo's private office and study. Access can be gained from either a hidden door directly across from the bedroom doors or the main doors in the second-floor hallway. The second-floor hallway is right above the first-floor hall. The hallway provides access to the guestrooms that are on both the front and back of the building. There are eight rooms in front and six in the rear. And again, in between the front guestrooms are the stairs to the first floor, servant's passage and the third floor. At the end of the hall, the stairs to the kitchen and the third floor."

Trevor spent the next half-hour quizzing her about specifics. Where were the doors? Which ones were normally locked? Unlocked? Guarded/ unguarded? The guards' routines? The number of steps in each stairwell? Other hidden doors or rooms? Location of light switches? Any idea as to the location of the primary circuit breakers? Where were the bathrooms and closets? Number of staff present in the late evening; the time that they would be in the retreat? General He did not participate much in the discussions, but was listening intently at every word. The layout of the retreat was now firmly cemented in the minds of both Brice and the general. Alex had given them all the details that she knew. Well, almost; she did not trust the general and withheld certain aspects of the layout, like the facts that the hidden door into the premier's office was frequently latched from the inside and the service stairs to the third floor frequently went unguarded in the evening hours.

# 37

## Meeting the Troops

The nose of the Bell Jet Ranger pitched forward ever so slightly as the pilot began his descent. A feeling of fullness in his ears alerted Brice to this fact. Looking out from his side window, Trevor could only see the vague outlines of the terrain under the light of the moon. An occasional village would display the glow of electric light or a small outdoor fire burning. It was nothing like flying over the United States where the landscape was dotted with the lights of cities and towns from coast to coast. The nose pitched over even more as the forward speed slowed. They dropped to treetop level to avoid detection as the distance to the emperor's retreat lessened. Ten miles from their destination, the craft settled into a valley and landed in a small clearing. The headlights of a few dozen vehicles welcomed their arrival. A group of armed men all dressed in black approached. They stopped just a few yards away and raised their weapons. Alex let out a gasp.

The general patted her knee and said, "Do not worry. These men are mine. They are just being certain of who is arriving. They do so only as a precaution."

The doors on each side were flung open, and the barrels of two AK-47s greeted them. General He calmly spoke, the rifles were lowered, and the welcoming party backed away. One of the men waved his hands above his head, and all the headlights were extinguished at once. Alex breathed a small sigh of relief. The three passengers debarked as the helicopter engines were shut down. A somewhat elderly man approached and spoke to the general. Alex understood him to say that two platoons of men were already in position in the hills across from the retreat. The general was asked whether he wanted to review the attack plans once more. He answered affirmatively, and after asking Trevor and Alex to wait there, he left for a tent on the edge of the clearing. A guard was instructed to the keep a close eye on the Americans and not to allow them to wander. Alex spoke to the guard, even flirted a bit in an effort to ensure that he could not speak English. Once satisfied, she turned to Brice.

"I want you to know that I did not tell you everything that I knew about the retreat. I do not trust the general. There are many hidden doors and passages in there that I did not tell you about," she said.

"Alex, you have good instincts, and I agree with you. He cannot be trusted. I surmised that you had left out a great deal. I am aware that most cultures built hidden passageways into their palaces. I assumed that the Chinese were no different. We are just going to have to play this one by ear," he said.

Taking a small radio receiver from a zippered pocket on his right side, Trevor held it up for her to see.

"I see that you are wearing a whisper radio, also. Tune to channel 'C,' like this." He demonstrated the operation of the controls. "It will allow you to speak only to me if and only if, you are pressing the button on your chest just above the heart. Take your hand and you can feel it through the fabric with your finger tips."

"Got it. This is just like those badges on *Star Trek*," she said. Alex then pulled the radio from its pocket and dialed in channel "C." "How does this work?" she asked.

Brice tucked two fingers into his mock turtleneck and turned the cloth inside out. "There is a small microphone built into the collar, and it presses against your throat. All you have to do is whisper very softly, and the radio amplifies the sound and sends it to our earphones."

He reached up to her shoulder and slipped the tiny earplug from its pouch and gently inserted it into her right ear.

"Can you hear me?" Brice asked in a whisper that was so low that it likely could not have even been heard with his mouth to another's ear. She nodded. "You try it," he said.

It took her a few tries to get accustomed to speaking so softly. "This is really neat. Where do you buy these things?" she asked.

Trevor laughed. "When you are the United States government, price is no object, so don't even ask. While we still have a little time, tell me how you got involved in all of this and how you know so much about the retreat."

Alex went through her story very quickly, but took the time to provide a few of the details about the secrets of the retreat. She had to stop prematurely when the moon cast its blue-white rays over General He, as he and two others came back into view. The general spoke to Alex in Chinese, something that he had not done before. She responded accordingly, but then advised Brice using the special button. They both knew that this was some sort of test, but neither was certain what, if anything, it meant. Maybe he was only trying to see if she would pretend that she did not understand. But this made no sense considering that He was well aware of her role on the retreat's staff. Brice noticed her uneasiness and whispered to her that the general was only trying to rattle her, hoping that she would make a serious mistake later. Trevor told her to relax and just go with the flow.

A Jeep pulled up next to them and Brice, Wilson and He climbed aboard. Twenty minutes later, they found themselves looking over a hillside, peering at the retreat through military issue field glasses. Brice took 10 minutes to survey the area. He quickly spotted the guards that were outside the stone perimeter wall. There were only four guards outside and to the right of the wall, the area where they intended to breech the security. The boulders and scrubs were by no means close to providing the cover General He had promised. There were wide gaps between them. This would require that the three of them slip undetected between the natural hiding places. Trevor did take note of the fact that the guards did not frequent the edge of the cliff; rather they tended more toward the roadway leading to the front gate. Still, this was going to be far more risky than they had been led to believe. When the general left to issue final instructions to his men, Brice took the opportunity to speak privately and candidly to Alex.

"Ms. Wilson, I appreciate all of your help, but this is where you get off. I cannot risk having you with me. It's just too dangerous," he said.

# Freedom's Menace

Alex struck back like a rattlesnake. Her right hand shot out, grabbing Brice above his left breast digging her finger nails into his flesh through the black cotton fabric.

"Listen to me, you son of a bitch. I have spent the past seven years trying to discover the truth about Dr. Scott's death. It took months before I even got the chance to get inside of the retreat, and when I did, I almost had to screw that fuck Lolo. Then, I had to kill two of his guards to keep from being killed myself. I have put too much of my life into this. I'm going with you. The secrets of the Library are somewhere inside of that palace, and I am going to find them."

Brice was impressed by the strength of her convictions, but was equally strong willed. "Look, this is not about some archeological project. This is life and death. It is going to be extremely dangerous in there. I may not even make it to the wall. If I get lucky and get into the compound, I have no idea what to expect. I don't need some amateur spy tagging along. The security and well being of the people of the United States is at stake here. That includes you. You are here of your own fruition. I'm here because the President sent me in to do a job. I cannot let you go. It just will not work. I'm sorry," Trevor said.

"Fine," she said in mock disinterest. "You can find the buttons that open the secrete doors all by yourself."

"What buttons?" Brice demanded.

"Buttons? Oh, did I forget to mention that part?" she cooed innocently.

"Alex, this is serious business..."

"Excuse me all to hell. I am so sorry that I cannot grasp that little detail. I have only watched as my friends and coworkers have been killed and the secret covered up. Our government turned their backs so they would not offend the Chinese. No one cares but me. I may not get in there with your help, but I will get back in there!" she asserted.

Before Brice could respond, the general returned.

"We are ready," He said. "All of my men are now in place. We must get to our positions."

Alex was the first to jump to her feet. Trevor, knowing that he could not stop her short of a knockout punch to the jaw, decided to capitulate. The general led them down the hillside to a place where a small bridge spanned a drainage ravine. They crossed under the road and through a field of elephant-size boulders before finally reaching the edge of the cliff. General He radioed their position and advised that they would now be going to radio silence. Watches were synchronized, and the invasion of the emperor's retreat was officially underway.

It took 20 minutes for the three of them to reach the wall. It was not quite as difficult as Brice had anticipated. The only frightening moment was when the general slipped and fell as he made his way between two large rocks. The sound of him hitting the ground had attracted a guard's attention, but the general was the consummate solider and remained motionless until the threat passed. A shallow recess in the earth provided him with all the cover required, keeping him out of the guard's line of sight. One of the guards continued to check the area, making the last 30 meters the most difficult. Fortunately, the contour of the ground formed a shallow trench, allowing them to stay low. Each time the guard's flashlight panned the area, the beam went right above their heads. Finally, reaching the wall, they discovered, just as the general had promised, the mountaineering gear was in fact there. Trevor was pleasantly surprised at this, but he checked the security of the pitons nonetheless. All was as it should be. Obviously, the general had a need to be inside and wanted their help in doing so.

# 38

## Ready or Not, Here We Come

With Trevor in the lead, they each hooked their carabiners to the rope and, one at a time, swung out over the edge of the cliff. Brice pulled himself along the two-meter wall until he had a view of the other side. All was clear. Small clumps of bushes were situated one and a half meters from the edge, providing a small platform on which they could perch, regroup and remain hidden from view. As soon as Alex and the general joined him on the precipice, Brice peered through the bushes and scouted the area. It was all clear and surprisingly quiet. He scanned the gardens for any sign of movement, but saw none. The blue hue from the pool lights was more intense than he imagined. Anyone near the pool would stick out like a sore thumb. A small wall separating the pool deck from the gardens would provide a small degree of protection in the event they had to dodge gunfire, but there was really no place to hide or to run. He checked his watch. Another minute and all hell was going to break loose.

"Sixty seconds. Stay low and follow the wall on the far side of the pool," Brice said into his whisper mic.

Alex and the general positioned themselves to make a run for the side door. Before the sound from the first small explosion had fully registered in the ears of the others, Brice had darted ahead like a runner sprinting away from the blocks in the Olympic 100-meter dash. He had reached the pool before the others had even cleared the bushes. The sound of intense gunfire and small explosions filled the night air while bright light flashed like strobes at a rock concert. Brice stopped short at the far corner of the pool deck and waited for his team before proceeding across the wide-open green space.

"I'll go first. When I get to the door and open it, Alex, you will follow. General, it's up to you to keep her covered. Once she's safe, you follow. Ready everyone? Here we go," Trevor said.

Brice took one more look before stepping out into the open space. He was to the door in short order and held his breath as his thumb pressed down on the catch. It clicked open, and he pushed the handle away from him. The door opened without resistance. Looking over his shoulder, he saw Alex moving rapidly toward him and the general, weapon poised and ready, preparing to follow her. As she reached the door, Trevor pulled her inside. The general was running toward them when Brice entered the doorway. He and Alex raced down to the bottom of the steps, where he paused and turned, expecting to see the general close behind. There was no one there. Brice allowed a few seconds to pass before dashing back up the steps, fully expecting to find the general's body lying in the grass. Instead he found the door had been pulled shut. Slowly, he opened it again and looked out. General He was nowhere to be seen, but a dozen guards had now come into view and were crossing the grounds heading for the wall. Cussing under his breath, Brice closed the door and secured it with the sliding bolt.

Standing at the bottom of the stairs, Alex saw Trevor's face as he shut the door and knew that General He had abandoned them. She quickly moved across the room, maneuvering through the disorganized accumulation of gardening tools, wheelbarrows and bags of peat and topsoil. A lone incandescent bulb hung bare from the center of the ceiling, providing her only a sparse amount of light as she made her way up the three steps to the door connecting the servant's passage. She waited there for Brice to catch up. When he reached her, he slowly pulled on the door handle, and, as expected, it was locked. He studied the hinges to determine the best way to blast their way in. Alex, meanwhile, lay down on her stomach and peered under the door. Coming down the steps at the far end of the passage were eight pair of legs, soldiers, each with automatic weapons and running at full tilt in their direction. She reached up and tugged on his pant leg.

"We have company coming!" she said. Brice dropped to the floor next to her to see for himself.

"Where's the latch? How do I lock this damn thing?" he demanded.

"This door doesn't lock on this side," she said.

"Oh, shit!" Brice exclaimed. "We have to hide. Is there another door that you didn't tell me about? Another room, stairs, anything?"

"No, just the other outside entry," Alex said, her voice slightly quivering.

"We have to go back out," he said as they moved in the direction of the ramp that led to the far door.

He slipped the strap of the Bushmaster assault rifle from around his neck and shoulder and released the safety. On reaching the ramp, he turned and shot out the bulb with a single bullet. They darted up the ramp and were about halfway along when the guards burst through the door. It wasn't until Brice hit the outside door and it flew open, flooding the room with moonlight, that the guards knew their location. Reacting mostly on instinct, two soldiers pointed their guns in the general direction and opened fire. Alex was showered with bits of the stone foundation as the hail of bullets homed in on their target, but she slipped past the jam just as the projectiles reached her. Brice had his left hand around her right wrist and yanked her outside.

He looked up the side lawn to his right. Three guards were just rounding the corner at the front of the retreat. With the Bushmaster in his right hand, he released three short bursts of fire, sending the guards sprawling to the ground. Muzzle flashes from the soldiers in the garden sent a spray of lead just over their heads. Brice returned fire striking one unseen guard in the face. Alex wrestled her wrist from his grasp as she slipped the strap from the Bushmaster that she carried over her head. While Brice concentrated on the garden, Alex kept the three soldiers at the front corner at bay. Trevor and Alex headed across the lawn directly into the bright blue light of the pool. It was his full intention to work his way back across the end of the wall and disappear into the night. As they approached the pool deck, Brice spotted something moving in the bushes next the corner of the wall. General He had set them up. Brice did not know why, and right now he didn't much care.

For reasons completely unknown, he pushed Alex toward the Fu dog balcony that overhung the cliff. Taking a quick glance over the edge, he saw, to his relief, a small ledge, only about two feet wide. Grabbing Alex around the waist, he climbed over the edge and ducked below the short wall. He stuck the barrel of the Bushmaster over the rail and randomly released several volleys, in short bursts. Alex had already looked over the edge and saw nothing but empty darkness below. She was on her hands and knees on a ledge that was only a half-meter wide, with nothing below her for more than 700 meters. A shutter of brief panic quaked through her body before she caught herself and refocused. Brice looked over as well, only to see the same sight. Voices of men and their thundering footsteps could now be heard heading in their direction.

Grabbing a handful of the ornamental stonework, Trevor leaned out over the edge to get a better look at what, if anything, was beneath them. To his amazement, a small balcony jutted out from the cliff, about 20 feet below. It only extended a few feet from the side of the cliff and was about five feet wide. To reach the small landing a person would have to hang onto the ledge and swing in toward the cliff face and blindly drop down onto it. This was the one and only option that was open to them at this point. Alex was behind him, and both were facing in the same direction. Brice had to stand to turn around. Pulling two of his six hand grenades from his belt clip, he removed the pins with his teeth. One at a time, he tossed the small explosives over his head onto the pool deck.

"Hold on," he whispered to Alex. "There're going to be a couple of loud explosions."

The first grenade exploded a foot in front of the first of the guards as they reached the balcony; the second bounced on the stone deck and went off in midair, taking out four others. This stopped the advancing soldiers for a moment as the rest of them dove for cover.

Brice quickly stood, turned around to face Alex and said, "Just trust me."

. He bent over and grabbed her right hand as he pushed her over the edge with his left foot. She let out a blood-curdling scream as he swung her into the cliff face and released his grip. The scream was exactly the reaction that he had hoped for. He prayed his aim had been on the mark, if not. Brice then slipped over the side and, holding on to the edge with both hands, swung once, twice and let go. In mid-flight he hoped to land on the balcony and not on top of her. Trevor landed hard, but feet first on the stone porch. Alex was curled up in a corner, shaking like a puppy after its first bath. Pressing the button on his chest, he told her to keep absolutely quiet so that neither General He nor the soldiers, only six meters above, could detect whether or not they were still alive. Brice dropped to his knees and leaned over and pressed his forehead against hers in reassurance that she was fine.

The excited voices of the soldiers could be clearly heard. Alex and Trevor did not move or speak for several minutes. Soon all sound from above disappeared. No one could see the small balcony from above without standing on the small ledge and leaning way over. None of the soldiers even considered it.

"They think that we are dead," she said pushing Brice away and rising back up to her feet.

"Just trust me, you said! You asshole!" She kicked him in the right shin. "You scared the shit out of me!"

Bending over in pain, Brice apologized for his abrupt and unannounced action. "I'm sorry. I realize it was a bit empty, sort of like 'The checks in the mail.' I'm sorry."

"No, it was more like that other crude saying you men have," she retorted as she kicked at him again. "Now what do we do?"

"Let's figure out where we are," he said, still rubbing his shin.

Brice slipped off the rifle and turned on the barrel-mounted flashlight. In front of them, hanging by its one remaining lower hinge, was a large wooden door, three-fourths of the way open. Beyond the door were three steps leading down to a long narrow passage that had been hand carved out of the solid rock centuries ago. Before stepping off the balcony, Trevor changed the frequency of the radios so they could freely communicate again. As was common for most structures built that far in the past, the ceiling was very low, forcing Brice and Wilson to stoop as they walked through the ancient corridor. The flashlight of Alex's rifle was also turned on, and the two blue-white beams danced off the walls, floor and ceiling as they slowly made their way forward. The floor was covered in thick slippery mud, and the air was layered with a foul odor. Alex abruptly stopped and placed her hand on Trevor's forearm.

"Why is the roof moving?" she asked.

"What?"

"Why is the roof moving? Look!"

The arched ceiling had a brown, lumpy appearance that gently moved in random motions.

"Oh, it's just bats," he said.

"Bats! I hate bats," Alex exclaimed. "Why are there bats in here?"

"I suspect that they like it here," Brice said, not the least bit sympathetically.

"Well, I don't like 'em and I don't think they should be here," she said in defiance.

"Look on the bright side: if they weren't here, then we wouldn't have all of this delightful bat guano to march through," he said with a laugh.

"Oh, and all over my new Nikes," she said.

"They are not your shoes, they belong to Uncle Sam. Aside from that, don't you think we have more important things to think about other than bat poop?"

"Maybe so, but I still hate bats," she said, getting in the last word.

The bats began to squeak as they passed under them. Alex was crouched in a duck walk position, her eyes and light fixed on the little creatures above her head. Every time one squeaked, she flinched. The passage quickly ended at a right turn, a point that Brice concluded was somewhere below the pool. A few short steps later they found themselves at the top of a staircase at the entry to a very large square room. In the center was a circular stone ring. Broken and rotted wooden tables, chairs and benches littered the floor. The walls on either side had three levels of small rectangular cutouts with iron bar doors that now dangled from rusty hinges or were lying on the floor below in corroded heaps. They climbed down the steps and walked over to inspect some of the cages. An audible gasp arose from within Alex as the beam of her flashlight illuminated a human skull. Human remains were found in several of the 60 small cages. Each cage was only large enough for a human to lie in a semi-fetal position; the people who had been imprisoned here could not sit up or fully stretch out. On the floor of each cage lay hand-forged chains that were fastened to the rear wall. Among the bones broken fragments of simple earthenware bowls were scattered about.

"My God," said Alex, "this is the equivalent of a medieval European dungeon. I never knew that this kind of thing existed in this culture."

She peeled off her backpack and collected a few of the bones and pieces of broken pottery. An iron hinge that had survived the assault of time also went into the pack. Brice had wandered over to the circle in the center of the room. He picked up some of the dark dust that filled the stone bowl and rubbed it between his fingers. The color black from carbon dust confirmed his notion that this had once been a fire pit.

"This is absolutely fascinating! Oh, I could spend weeks studying this site," she said.

Brice laughed to himself, thinking that yesterday he was trapped under a volcano with a driven vulcanologist and today he was in an ancient Chinese dungeon with an equally driven archeologist.

"We have to keep moving," he said. "Have you looked at the floor? There are no footprints. No one has been in here for what, a thousand years?"

Steps on the opposite side of the building led up to a door that was only opened about an inch. Curling his fingers around the old wood he pulled, but the corroded hinges had formed into a solid mass of unyielding metal. Waving Alex back, Trevor placed his right foot against the jam and pulled with both hands; the brittle iron snapped, and Brice and the door came tumbling back down the steps. Alex stepped forward and broke his fall, while using her body weight to pull him away from the heavy slab of wood as it bounced down the stone steps past them.

"Thanks," he said as they stood and brushed off the thousand-year-old dust.

"No problem. Let's see what's behind door number two," she responded.

The beams of their flashlights unveiled a long corridor as narrow, short and dark as the one leading from the balcony. Brice took the lead. The passage was lined with small alcoves, some with the remnants of crude tables and stands. Alex suggested that they were probably used for placing lamps to light the way. At a distance that Brice calculated was under the main section of the retreat, they came to another door and a set of steps leading to it. Three more steps.

"What's with the three steps all the time?" he wondered out loud.

W. Laurence Willis

# 39

## Captured

A dim light shone from the gap under the door. They
extinguished their lights. He looked through the wide gap
and saw the interior of a small, dimly lit room that
appeared vacant. He listened, no sounds. Alex climbed up
and pressed against the door. It did not budge, but did
produce a soft a clanking sound. Examining the door more
closely, they discovered the long iron latch had been shoved
into place. The door had been locked from *this* side!? That
was curious. Alex speculated that one of the small alcoves
contained a hidden passage. Trevor slid back the single
latch and pushed open the door. They ascended the steps
and into the room. Just as Brice was about to step through
the doorway, the unmistakable smell of cigarette smoke hit
him in the face like a brick. His right hand went for the
Glock, but it was too late. A retreat guard leapt from behind
the door and leveled a Chinese assault rifle at his surprised
guests. The young soldier snapped at them in a harsh,
commanding tone. The tone told Brice to give it up. He
released his grip on the pistol and raised both hands above
his head. Alex followed suit.

# Freedom's Menace

"This guy is scared to death. I can hear it in his voice," Alex whispered through the microphone in her collar. Then speaking out loud in Chinese, she tried to reassure their captor.

"We are here to help. The premier is in trouble, we have come to help," she said in a calm voice.

Nice effort, but it didn't work. The guard was too scared to even hear a single word that she had said. At 17 years old, he had been "drafted" into the military six months earlier and now spent his days guarding the helicopter pad from Lord knows what. When General He's men stormed the front gate and the other guards had rushed out in response, he fell back and hid from the fighting. Brice and Wilson had the misfortune to walk into the very room in which he had taken sanctuary. A miraculous change of fate had now permitted him to capture two of the insurgents, and for this daring act, a reward of significant measure was certain to be bestowed on him.

Alex translated his next order, and she and Brice dropped their weapons and removed their backpacks. They then moved to the door on the left, Alex in the lead. Up the short stack of steps and through the door, they found themselves in a long narrow room. A long table with wooden benches on either side filled half of the space. The table and benches were littered with overflowing ashtrays, half-eaten food, spilled containers of tea and newspapers. The walls were adorned with the foldouts from dismembered editions of Asian *Playboy* magazines. Pegs for clothes hangers lined the room and held a variety of military issue shirts and jackets. On either side of the door in which they were standing stood shelves and racks for the storage of guns, ammunition and a generous supply of hand grenades. Their youthful captor marched them through the room, out the far door and into the connecting hall. Trevor was certain that they were still in the sub-basement because nothing matched Alex's earlier descriptions. The soon-to-be hero directed them to the next room on the right. They stepped inside and the door slammed shut behind them, followed by the sounds of the two sliding bolts being pushed into place. The next sound they heard was his footsteps as he ran down the hall.

"Alex, when we turned down the hall, did you notice the door at the far end?" asked Trevor.

She thought for a moment, because this was a curious question considering their circumstance.

"I did see that it was not one of the normal wood doors. It looked like it was some kind of metal. There was also an electrical panel next to it. Right?"

"That door was a high tensile steel security barrier. The electrical panel is a hand print identification station complete with a magnetic card reader. Are you sure that you have told me everything?" he asked.

"I'm positive! I have never been in that hallway. But you know, I used to hear helicopters several times each day, but rarely did I see them land. I have no idea where they came from or where they went. I also remember seeing people that I am sure didn't arrive through the front gate," Alex said.

"There is more to this place than meets the eye," said Trevor, now having a faint idea why an escape by midnight was so critical. He looked at his watch. It was 10:40 pm. He turned away from the door to take in their new prison cell. The large room was at the same elevation as the hall, not sunken by three steps like the others they had seen.

Curious. He looked around. They were in a storeroom! Construction equipment filled the expanse, mostly the kind that was required to move and position heavy equipment. There were steel rollers, high capacity hydraulic jacks, heavy timbers, steel cables with giant hooks, long pry bars and an assortment of sledgehammers. Four carts were lined up along one wall. Each held cylinders of compressed gases oxygen and acetylene, used to fuel the blowtorches for welding and cutting steel. Brice was now convinced that the retreat hid a secret military complex deep within its bowels. The young guard had chosen the wrong place to try and imprison Trevor Brice. This was going to be just too easy.

He began dragging the heavy timbers across the room one at a time and lining them up, end-to-end. Alex just watched as he moved the first two and then joined his efforts, having no idea what he was trying to accomplish. After he had built a string of timbers completely across the room, he started a second row a foot apart and parallel to the first. When they finished the second row, Alex sat down for a rest atop of a stack of bagged cement.

"What the hell is this thing that we just built?" she asked.

Trevor walked over and sat down next to her. He explained that what they had just built was a track for his newest invention, an unguided missile.

"Remember as a kid, you would blow up a balloon and let it go? It then flew all over the room. You see those silver cylinders over there? Those contain compressed oxygen, a lot of compressed oxygen. If you break off that little brass valve on top, the cylinder will take off like a rocket. The timbers are to guide it along the way. We are about to make a big hole in that wall over there."

They were both startled by the sounds of the door latches sliding open. As the door swung inward, Brice and Wilson saw three figures standing in the doorway. Two were obviously military officers and, with them was the boy soldier, who was beaming with delight. The officers were truly surprised to see that there were, in fact, two prisoners locked in the room and one was a Westerner. In an unusual display of emotion, the senior officers broke out in wide grins, one of them slapping the youth on the back as a congratulatory sign. One officer spoke to the young guard as he reached in and pulled the door shut. As the latches slid back into place, Alex raced over to the door in an effort to hear what they were saying as they walked away.

They led the young hero next door to the guard's lounge. One of the officers removed a flask of distilled spirits from his satchel and offered it to the boy. The young soldier proudly accepted and took a long shot. He immediately began to cough as the alcohol burned his throat; his eyes filled with liquid, and he desperately tried to maintain a manly posture. The older men laughed and encouraged him to drink more. The second shot went down more smoothly. With the pint-size bottle in hand, he took the only available chair in the room and sat down, leaning back against the wall. He took a third small sip and placed the bottle between his legs. The other two moved to the opposite end of the room, out of earshot, to discuss the boy's short future.

Brice ran to the oxygen cylinders, cut the hose on one and rolled the silver bullet over to the track they just had built. He laid down his missile and walked over to select the heaviest sledgehammer that he could find.

"They are going next door to decide what to do with us," said Alex as she walked toward Brice. "I think that they are really going to screw that kid to the wall and take the credit for our capture for themselves."

"Well, won't they be surprised when this thing comes flying into the room?" said Brice. "I want you behind that stack of concrete just in case this thing doesn't pierce the wall and starts to fly around in here. Be alert!"

The old stone wall offered no more resistance to the flying cylinder than a plate of glass offers a hammer. The projectile passed through the stone and struck the wide-eyed boy soldier in the upper chest before falling to the top of the long table. The speed at which the oxygen-propelled missile shot down the length of the table was too fast for the two officers to even react. The man on the left caught the impact full force and was crushed against the wall. The cylinder fell to the floor and bounced into a corner, where it danced about like a fish in the bottom of a canoe. The lone remaining soldier darted down the length of the room, stumbling over benches, chairs and clutter, desperately trying to reach the hall door. The cylinder freed itself and turned 180 degrees as if it were homing in on its target as it jetted along the floor. The man's left ankle was shattered by the impact, and he fell sideways, his head striking the sharp corner of a bench. Having completed it mission, Brice's missile hissed its last breath at the base of the steps leading to the hall.

As the dust cloud settled, Trevor squirmed through the jagged hole in the wall and surveyed the carnage. Satisfied all was secure, he signaled for Alex to slip in behind him. As he went to check the hallway, she ran to the adjacent room to retrieve their weapons and backpacks. Brice raced down the hall in both directions. Finding that all was clear, he returned and stepped back inside the room and shut the door. Alex had laid the equipment on the table next to the bodies of the two men.

# 40

## Time to Meet An Lolo

"So, where do you think we are?" Trevor asked. "There is a staircase at the end just before the steel door. It was the only obvious way out of here that I could see."

"That has to lead to the kitchen steps at the end of the servant's passage," said Alex.

"Well, let's go," he instructed, slipping an arm through one of the straps of his backpack. Before leaving, he darted to the far end of the room and slipped six hand grenades into his belt.

Out the door, they quickly moved to the stairs. Alex tugged on his sleeve, "Remember, there is always a guard on the landing."

Brice nodded and pulled the Glock from the holster. Silently he ascended the steps and using a polished stainless steel mirror that was hidden in the cuff of his left sleeve, he peered around the corner. A guard stood at the entrance of the kitchen stairwell, his back facing them. Brice holstered the gun and drew the 90-inch combat knife from the scabbard strapped to his right ankle. He stepped around the corner and silently crept up on the man. As his left hand covered the guard's mouth, the stainless steel blade punctured the man's heart from the back. A few seconds passed before he poked his head back around the corner and signaled for Alex to join him. She rounded the corner and briefly hesitated at the sight of the guard's lifeless body lying face down on the stairs. A thin river of blood cascaded down the stone steps. Slowly, she stepped past him and joined Trevor on the small landing. Together they sailed down the remaining steps and went racing along the servant's passage. Suddenly a door shut, and the woman with the fireplug build exited a room on the left. All three froze in their place. The woman immediately recognized Alex and was so surprised she was struck dumb. Alex smiled a broad smile and with the heel of her open palm landed a punch squarely in the center of the woman's nose. Madame fire hydrant landed flat on her back, down for the count.

"A friend of yours?" asked Trevor, as they resumed their jog down the hall.

"She was in charge of the servants. I was just repaying a favor," said Alex.

"It must have been some favor. You'll have to tell me about it some time," he said, just before stopping at the stairwell that Alex had previously described as the one leading up to the back of the grand staircase.

"Keep going. There is another passage that I didn't tell you about," said Alex, turning to see why he had stopped. Entering the last alcove, she paused to wait for him to catch up. "This goes to the second floor dining room," she said as she passed through the entry.

They climbed the 40-step spiral staircase to a tiny 4-foot by 4-foot room. Faint beams of light shooting through the three peepholes provided the only illumination. Leaning over, Brice peered through one of the holes to check out the room. There were four guards standing next to the double entry, two each by the bay windows leading to the balconies and five posted in a straight line across the double doors of Lolo's bedroom, for a total of 13 heavily armed men.

"We have a small army waiting for us in there," Trevor told her. "We are going to need a diversion, but first, I need to know a few things. Can the doors be locked from inside? If we can get the soldiers in the dining room out into the entry hall, can we lock the doors and keep them out there? Am I correct in assuming that Lolo can lock himself into his bedroom?"

Alex thought for several minutes before responding. "The bedroom doors have more locks than a New York City apartment, and the doors are six inches of solid wood. The dining room doors are lockable and fairly thick. They won't stop a determined group for too long, but they will slow them down for a while. As for a diversion, how about just tossing a few of those hand grenades out into the hall?"

"That would work, but how do we do it?" Brice asked.

"Easy. This panel folds down. It is used for passing the food and trays to the waiters and hostesses." She placed her hand against the wall behind them.

Trevor lifted the clasp and slowly lowered the serving shelf a crack, just enough to afford him a view of the second-floor landing. There were three additional guards

posted outside the double doors and a lone soldier at the
head of the grand staircase. From what he could see, the
rest of the floor was vacant. He closed the opening, thought
for a long minute and then got down to work. He slipped
the Bushmaster over his head and leaned it against the
wall. From his pack came a black nylon case that resembled
a daub kit. Both items were laid on the floor. Trevor took
two of the Chinese grenades and handed them to Alex, but
she did not reach out and take them. Instead, she
contemplated the meaning of using them. She just stared as
they sat in Trevor's palm. She had spent her entire life
reluctant to kill anything. Well, anything with the
exception of spiders, which she hated even more than bats.
The killing of the two guards just days before was an act of
impulse caused by fear, desperation and self-defense. If she
used these, it would constitute an intentional act. That was
completely different.

"You're concerned about killing. I understand. As a
father, I struggle with some of the things I have done in the
name of defending my country. Alex, Premier Lolo has
already killed 25,000 people in the United States and
promises more death. Even my own life is expendable if
given in an effort to stop people like him."

Without another moment of hesitation, she took the
small orbs from his hand and asked, "What do I need to
do?"

"The drill will be a reverse three count. Three, open the
shelf door with your right hand; two, with the grenade in
your left hand, pull the pin with your right thumb; one,
pause; and zero, toss it toward the doors, not too hard; it
will bounce real well on these marble floors. Close the shelf
and count to 30, and then do it all over again. Ready? On
my mark."

She looked at the two explosives in her hand and then up to Trevor. "Alright, let's do it!"

Trevor picked up his Bushmaster, released the safety and chambered a round. He checked the Glock as well. A check through the peephole found the guards in pretty much the same positions as before. He lifted the latch on the door to the dining area and nodded to Alex.

"Three," she whispered and quietly dropped the shelf. Four seconds later the opening was again closed, and a second after that, an explosion reverberated throughout the cavernous, marble clad foyer.

The guards' response was entirely predictable. They reacted with initial shock, followed by fear, panic and confusion. They all started to yell orders to each other as to what to do, but, other than clustering together in a mass of gyrating bodies, not much happened. The one clear head in the room was guarding Lolo's door. He bolted across the room, pulled open the door and began ushering the other soldiers into the hall. He ordered three guards to remain at Lolo's door and one at each balcony entrance. As planned, the second grenade exploded with the door wide open. Smoke and shrapnel went in all directions. Bodies of the dead and injured fell to the floor while a river of blood poured from their wounds and pooled in an ever-widening crimson sea. Brice burst into the room, bullets streaming from the end of the Bushmaster's barrel like angry hornets from a nest. The three soldiers at Lolo's door went down first, then the two at the balconies and finally the few that remained standing in shock at the main entrance. Alex and Brice tore across the room and dragged the dead bodies out of the doorway. They threw the doors shut and secured the locks.

# Freedom's Menace

Trevor raced back to collect his pack and the small black bag. Sprinting toward Lolo's door, he peeled back the Velcro flaps of the bag and removed a three-inch brick of plastic explosive. Dividing the brick into six equal pieces, he pressed them against the hinges. He connected the timer and detonation wires. Alex, who was just standing there watching the speed and accuracy of Brice's work, was almost knocked off of her feet when Trevor ran over and grabbed her around the waist. He lifted her off the ground and carried her to the nearest corner, sheltering her with his body. The six simultaneous explosions were surprisingly quiet, but they both jumped when the massive double doors hit the floor.

Brice leveled the Bushmaster and charged into the bedroom. Alex followed a second later. The room appeared to be empty. Trevor circled the bed and began checking for telltale signs like toes sticking out from under the curtains or anything else that seemed out of place. He poked at the piles of covers and pillows. Nothing!

"Are there any hidden passages in here?" asked Brice.

"No! Not that I'm aware of."

Brice knew Lolo was in here, he felt his presence. Carefully, he studied the room, slowly turning and examining everything. Without warning, he fired a single shot, causing Alex to jump. The projectile hit its mark; the top of the four-meter-high floor mirror in the left corner. Glistening shards of glass twinkled down like falling snow in a night sky. In the midst of the shimmering pool of silver-coated glass shards and directly behind the mirror's frame stood a very nervous An Lolo. With an air of defiance, the Chinese premier tightened his posture and puffed out his chest. He set his jaw and glared at the intruders. A momentary sense of accomplishment was draping itself over Brice and Wilson, when an explosion from the end of a rifle barrel pierced their ears. The bullet struck Lolo squarely in the forehead. Gray matter exploded from the back of his skull and splashed on the wall and silk drapes behind him. As a stream of blood ran down the end of his nose, the premier's body fell forward, coming to rest face down across the mirror's wooden frame, surrounded by a pool of twinkling glass.

Alex and Trevor wheeled around. Just five feet behind them, with the smoking gun in hand, was General He, flanked by two of the Retreat's elite guards.

"What the fuck was that all about?" barked Trevor.

"Mr. Blice, you had your job to do, and I had mine," said General He.

The general allowed time for this to sink in before saying, "Your lady friend was unaware that I have been here many times over the years. I know all of the little secrets of this place. I also know many of the guards. They once reported to me, and some have remained very loyal. Now, will you please drop your weapons and follow the guards?"

Hardly before the words passed his lips, the butt of Brice's rifle slammed into the general's head, just above the left eyebrow, sending a spray of blood into the air. His guards raised their automatic weapons, but Alex let go of a short burst from her rifle and dropped them both where they stood. General He lay unconscious on the floor next to them.

"This way," said Alex, heading for the main hall doorway. Brice fell to the floor on his stomach and checked for shadows under the door. They then opened it just a bit, enough to provide a view into the hall. A dozen men were clustered at the dining room door making every effort to break into the room. Brice pushed the door shut.

"Where, exactly, is that hidden door?" he asked.

"Directly across the hallway," said Alex.

Brice cracked the door again. The wall was a completely homogenous flow of ornately decorated polished marble. It took several seconds for him to spot the opening, thanks to the slightly dull patch left from years of human touch. The accumulation of oils contrasted with the marble's otherwise shiny surface.

"What kind of lock does it have, and where's it located?" he asked.

"It's like most of the doors in the place, a sliding bolt just below waist high on me. You push the door on the right side to open it," Alex answered.

Down the hall, the guards had decided to blast open the door to the dining room. They were too focused on where the enemy had been instead of thinking were they could be now. Most of the guards were crouching down behind the carved marble balusters of the grand stairwell. Two men were left to secure hand grenades to the doorknobs and blast through the inner locks. Brice knew that as soon as the men pulled the pins and began to run, he and Alex had best be doing the same. The explosions would give them the few seconds they needed to cross the wide hallway and get into Lolo's private office.

"Get ready," he said.

# W. Laurence Willis

Trevor grabbed Alex's left sleeve just above the elbow like a father holding a child at a busy intersection. As the first guard broke for the security of the stairwell, Trevor threw open the door and dragged Alex behind him, out into the hallway. He leveled the muzzle of the Bushmaster at the area of the secret door where Alex had told him the security bolt was located. The bullets met their mark, sending chips of marble flying through the air like shrapnel. After the marble facade was blown away, the thick wooden interior splintered into a million toothpicks. They were halfway across the hall when the office door popped open, but at that very instant a thunderous explosion ripped through the main foyer.

The general's troops were pressing forward with an all-out assault on the door of the state dining room, unaware that their leader lay unconscious in Lolo's bedroom. A well-placed tank shell had blown through the front doors and exploded when it hit the base of the white obelisk. The 10-meter pillar of white granite suffered extensive damage. Brice and Wilson were blown off their feet by the concussion from the explosion. The second tank shell hit the outer wall, just above the entrance, blasting a two-story hole in the front of the retreat. A third shell hit the base of the fountain. The base of the 10-meter, 25-ton statue slid off of its mount toward the front of the building as the tip fell toward the back of the building. It crashed onto the second floor balcony just outside the dining room entrance, dropping the floor out from under the feet of the soldiers. The second floor structure continued to buckle under the weight of the impact and began collapsing. As one small section of the floor broke away and the next section crumbled in quick succession. Like a great white shark biting at the water while swimming after its next meal, the great white obelisk began eating away at the floor in two-meter-wide bites.

# Freedom's Menace

Stunned, Alex and Brice lay directly in its path. She was on her belly facing the oncoming menace and began screaming and pushing away with her hands, sliding backward across the floor. Brice jumped to his feet, clutched Alex's right ankle and started to run. He dragged her away and off to the side just as the floor disappeared in front of her face and the glistening white tip vanished below the level of the floor. The entire building shuddered as the obelisk crashed onto the first floor. Large pieces of floor continued to break away and fall to the level below. When the dust finally settled, Alex and Brice were left standing on a three-foot-wide marble ledge. Backs to the wall, they gingerly made their way the 15 feet to the door of the private office. Once inside, they fell against the closed door and breathed a sigh of relief as they each threw a glance at the other.

Her heart was pounding inside her chest like it never had before. The vision of the white granite column chewing its way through the floor on its way to devour her kept flashing through her mind, her chest heaving with each breath.

"That was like living in a Spielberg movie. I was lying on the floor and that thing was coming at me, coming to get me, but everything was moving sooo slow. Wow! What a rush," she exclaimed.

"Glad you enjoyed it. But can we regroup and get the hell out of here?" Trevor asked.

"Oh, sure. There may be a secret door behind Lolo's desk. Awhile back, I was in here cleaning up after the premier had tea with some of his staff and a guest. I left the room and realized that I had left one of the place settings and came back in to get it. As I reentered the room, I heard a noise like a door shutting and noticed that there was one less person in the room. I had only been gone a few seconds, and the aide who had been behind the desk was gone. I assumed that he left through a passage somewhere near the desk, but I never got the opportunity to investigate."

Without another word between the two of them, they made a beeline for the desk. An inspection of the walls did not reveal any hidden secrets. The war that was being stage outside was intensifying. Sounds from the tanks continuing their pounding of the building rang out through the structure. Screams of the injured could be heard as rifle and small arms fire filled the acoustic voids between the exploding tank shells. Alex was searching the desk as Brice looked for hidden switches behind the priceless Ming vases and other antiquities. It was Alex who finally spotted the shining gold tooth in the mouth of a golden serpent perched on a column to the right of the desk. The left fang was brighter, a bit more dazzling than the other. Like Lincoln's nose in front of his Springfield tomb, the fang was polished from constant daily touch. She reached it in two steps and wiggled it between her thumb and forefinger. It moved. With her index finger she pulled it toward her. The result was a faint click from somewhere behind the wall.

# 41

## Discovery & Horror

Trevor looked at her, then turned to study the wall. A small door in the wall to the left of the desk was now slightly ajar. Gently, Trevor pressed against it. It was heavy, very heavy, requiring both hands to push it open. Alex was right behind him, pressing against the door to force it open. They entered a room that was surprisingly large. It measured about 15 meters across. A spiral staircase that dropped to the lower levels was directly in front of them. Four oil lamps mounted on the walls provided the only light. A stack of nondescript storage boxes lined the wall just below an oval window, the only disruption in the stone wall. They slipped inside and closed the door behind them.

A single peephole adjacent to the door provided a panoramic view of the entire office area, an advantage that Brice did not let pass. As he looked into the room, four guards entered in search of refuge from the shelling. From their actions and mannerisms, they obviously were not in search of anyone. They were only looking for shelter. Trevor watched closely for several minutes until he heard a series of unexpected sounds that interrupted his concentration. The sounds of whimpering, sniffling and eventually outright sobbing flowed from his radio earpiece. He turned to look at Alex and found her standing in front of the pile of storage boxes, tears pouring down her face. Raindrop- like tears fell onto the glass front of a picture frame that she was now clutching in both hands. The look on her face sparked some rare male instinct, and he approached her with great care and compassion. At first he did not speak, but rather walked slowly up behind her and stole a peak at the picture mounted in the frame.

"It's me with my mother and sister. This is the photo I was carrying with me on my expedition with Dr. Scott. It always sat on my desk at the excavation sites."

She choked on her tears as she fell to her knees and wept openly.

"These boxes contain all of the personal possessions of the expedition party. This glass clown belongs to Karen. This broken watch was Jeff's. Only the minute hand ever worked. That's probably why he always showed up to things a week late. Steve's yo-yo." She held it up. "He was always playing with the damn thing."

The emotion of discovering the possessions of her friends and fellow explorers became too much. This was the evidence that she had been searching for all these months and years. The fact that their possessions were intact was evidence enough that the Scott party had been kidnapped and herded, like lambs to the slaughter, onto the fatal flight. She had no doubt that they were dead. All of this had been kept to prevent anyone from finding out what secrets the Library had provided. She unzipped her backpack and spilled the contents onto the floor. With the exception of the bones, clay pottery and rusty hinge, the remainder of the items were brushed aside.

"I know that I can't take all of this with me, but I am going to take one thing from each person's belongings and return it to their families," said Alex, her composure gradually returning.

Trevor checked his watch, 11:40 pm.

"Oh, shit!" he thought.

"Alex, we have very little time." She ignored his words and kept rummaging through the boxes one at a time. "Alex, we have to go!"

Having his words again fall on deaf ears, he began to lift the boxes and situate them so she had better access to the contents. It was now 11:43 pm, and she had finished her task except for a large wooden box sealed with a large brass padlock. Alex reached over and pulled Brice's Glock from the holster. With trembling hands, she took aim at the lock. Seeing that she wasn't going to hit a thing, Brice took the weapon, pointed it and squeezed the trigger, blasting away the lock, creating a four-inch hole in the front of the case. Alex reached out and nervously lifted the lid. She let out a gasp, placing her right hand over the center of her chest. To Brice, there was nothing startling inside the crate. But to Alex, it was a gold mine. She reached down and lifted Dr. Scott's leather bound journal and his Apple PowerBook laptop computer from where they were nestled in the soft fabric of his clothing.

At 11:45 pm Brice decided that time had run out. He scooped up his companion's backpack and zipped it shut.

"Your bag and I are leaving. If you wish to join us, then do so now," he said sternly and headed for the spiral staircase.

She understood and was on his heels in an instant. Racing down the worn stone steps, Alex began to say whatever crossed her mind, "The computer and laptop belonged to Dr. Scott. He was a little quirky. Everything that went into the computer, he duplicated in long hand in the journal. Computers were not his thing, but he understood their usefulness," she explained.

The circular staircase ended at more conventional stone steps somewhere below the main level. A heavy metal security door to the right and the stone steps to the left give them two options. Brice gripped the handle of the door and pulled, then pushed. It did not budge and there was no sign of locks, hinges or any means for opening it. Their options were now down to one. The aged stone beneath their feet had been hand hewn from solid rock centuries before. The box-like stairwell design had no handrails, and the opening in the center disappeared into blackness somewhere far below. Hugging the wall, they briskly climbed down, heading to wherever the path took them. Two more stories into the depths of the retreat and they came upon another gray steel security door. Just as they reached it, the clatter of a sliding door latch snapping open rang in their ears.

Brice moved quickly past the opening, pulling Alex past him. An Asian man wearing a white lab coat stepped from the door, head down, his mind buried in the notes attached to a well-worn clipboard. As he started up the steps, Brice was on him in a flash rendering him unconscious. Alex grabbed the door to keep it from closing as Brice tore the man's magnetic ID card from where it was clipped to his lapel. They both slipped into the doorway. Slowly he allowed the door to swing closed, but dropped one of the backpacks in its path to prevent it from re-latching. They were now in a small vestibule with a second steel door containing a small window. Together they looked in.

Their eyes fell on the most appalling and horrific sight either of them could have ever imagined. A long glass wall separated two rooms. The first was a well-equipped chemistry lab with laboratory benches covered with test tubes, beakers of multicolored boiling liquids, Bunsen burners and Erlenmeyer flasks. A dozen white-coated men busied themselves at their assigned workstations, measuring powders, pouring one liquid into another and filling a tray of hypodermic needles with a pale green subsistence.

Beyond the lab and on the opposite side of the windowed wall was a room with 100 steel wire cages, each a meter square and stacked four high. Alex placed her hand over her mouth as a rush of bile erupted from her stomach. Brice staggered back into the wall to his left. Inside each of the steel mesh cages were what had to be apparitions, the grotesque living remains of what at one time had been and, to some unimaginable degree continued to be, human beings. Male, female, young, old, adult and child, most horribly disfigured, were curled into lifeless fetal balls of grayish pale human flesh. They all peered out into space, drool dripping down their chins and pooling onto the floor of the cage, all looking out at the small world around them through dead lifeless eyes, many motionless, some twitching from involuntary muscle spasms.

"Oh, dear God, that's Dr. Scott! The man in the forth cage. Oh my God, no! They're all in there. You bastards, what have you done!?!" Alex shrieked.

She began pounding on the door with both fists. Trevor reached for the handle and pulled on it several times. It did not budge. His blood was already past the boiling point. He shook the handle violently, startling the lab technicians inside who turned and stared at the strangers in disbelief. Remembering the magnetic card he took from the lab technician on the steps, he waved it in front of the black scanner next to the door. A ding sounded, and a panel opened in the wall above the scanner to reveal a small numbered keypad. Brice glared at the gray square buttons as if they were responsible for the situation beyond the door. He stormed out to the stairwell and yanked the semi-conscious technician to his feet and went nose to nose with him, his eyes burning holes through the man's head, the Glock pressing against the soft tissue under his chin.

"Tell him I want the code," he said to Alex.

She asked and received an immediate response, which she relayed to Brice. Holding onto the collar of the lab coat, he dragged the man back into the vestibule and punched in the code. Alarms immediately began to wail and a red light above the door started to pulse like a slow heart beat. Brice loosened his grip, giving the technician an opportunity to escape. He pushed away and bolted out into the stairwell, climbing up the steps three at a time. Brice pulled the Glock, rushed out after him and leveled the weapon at the base of the man's head. Alex grabbed his forearm and pushed it and the gun into the wall.

"You are about to cross a line. Don't do it," she yelled. He turned his head and looked at her incredulously, then lowered the weapon.

"They are doing human experiments in there," he bellowed at the top of his lungs. "Oh, dear God! It's incomprehensible. This is beyond deplorable."

He paused, scuffing the sole of his shoe across the rock floor, desperately hoping for an answer to pop into his head, a way to help those people, a way to take back all that had been done to them. Quickly, reality arrived. He exhaled a long calming breath.

"Now I understand. Now I know why they wanted Lolo alive. Our government knows, or at least suspects, what's happening here."

His last words were a revelation. He looked at his watch, 11:53 pm.

"We can't do a thing here. It's too late! We gotta go, now!"

He snatched up the backpack and pushed Alex through the door and down the steps. The stairwell below them was still a pool of black.

"Just keep going, don't stop, don't let up," he said with a hint of panic in his voice. The stone steps were getting moist and slippery from seeping water, but they pressed on, taking two or more steps at a time when they could.

A faint light finally came into view, but still seemed to be a long ways away. Finally, five stories later, they found themselves at the base of the steps, another security door on the right and an open stone passage to the left. Brice waved the magnetic card in front of the scanner, but nothing happened. They turned and quickly moved along the passage. Two hundred meters ahead the twinkle of stars from the night sky greeted them. They slowed their pace as they approached the end of the passage. The long corridor looked as if it opened on to a natural cutout in the rock. The wall to their left continued to the cliff face another 50 meters out; the right wall stopped 20 meters from the edge. Brice was looking around the corner even before he reached it. He just passed the edge in full stride, but immediately slammed on the brakes and put himself into reverse, almost knocking Alex over in the process.

"What's going on? What's out there?" she asked.

He pulled the stainless steel mirror from his left sleeve and handed it to her. Her mind almost did not comprehend the sight that was reflected in the tiny polished surface. The opening in the cliff wall was immense, a grotto in the center of the cliff wall. At more than 70 meters long, 30 meters high and just under 30 meters deep, the expansive natural void now served as a heliport. In the center sat two Russian Kamov Ka-62 helicopters situated end to end, the first just 15 meters away. Between the two aircraft and the wall were a dozen lightly armed guards and pilots sitting at a long table eating, talking and playing a game of some kind, all oblivious to the activities 10 stories above their heads. No one saw Brice when he briefly ran out into the open. Trevor looked at his watch; there was no time to plan or even to think. The clock only provided time to act.

"We are going to take one of those choppers out of here, and those guys are going to try and prevent it from happening. The only things that we have in our favor are the element of surprise and a shitload of bullets. Alex, get your gun. It's time to ride into the sunset," he mused.

Brice charged ahead, leaving Alex to struggle with slipping the strap from the rifle over her head. The Bushmaster in Brice's hands was already spraying a swarm of lead at the guards and pilots when Alex followed him around the corner. He continued to distract all attention from her by rapidly moving across the floor toward the first aircraft, spraying bullets into the cluster of panicked guards and pilots. Alex simply stepped around the corner and opened fire.

The element of surprise had worked. As the guards ate and chatted, their weapons had been carelessly left leaning against the wall or edge of the table. They never even had a chance. The ones who were still armed or had pistols were firing at Brice when Alex entered the fracas. It was all over in a matter of a few seconds. Except that one of their bullets struck a hand grenade attached to the belt of one of the guards. The bullet struck just where the safety-release pin attached, dislodging it and arming the small, but deadly device. Four seconds later, as Alex and Trevor were surveying the situation, the grenade exploded, sending Brice diving for cover and leaving Alex almost too shocked to move. Most of the shrapnel found a home in the bullet-riddled bodies of the guards, but one of the fragments pierced the aluminum skin of the closest chopper and punctured the fuel tank, sparking a small fire. The ensuing flames followed the stream of liquid fuel as it flowed down the side of the forest green aircraft and began pooling on the floor. Fortunately, jet fuel is not as volatile as gasoline, and there was no immediate explosion. But as the outside of the fuel tank became hotter from the fire, the fuel would vaporize in the tank, making an explosion imminent.

"Let's go!" shouted Brice.

Alex looked at him, then at the fire, back to him, then to the mound of dead and finally back to Brice.

"Move!" he yelled, and she did, her long athletic legs making increasingly longer strides as she ran for the second helicopter. The pool of fire was starting to engulf the first helicopter as she and Brice ran past. As he directed her toward the passenger door, the rear cargo door slid open and a lone soldier leaned out and started to level his rifle at the two of them. Brice had the Glock in his right hand and dropped the man before he could even think about taking aim. His body fell half in and half out of the cargo hold.

Inside the cockpit, the identification placards for the switches and controls were all written in Chinese. This did not deter Brice. All that was required was for him to start one of the twin turbine engines and get the hell out away from that mountain. The rest really did not matter at this point. Fortunately, there is a basic logic for all aircraft design. He quickly found the main power switch and flipped in to the "ON" position. Bells, chimes and whirling noises filled the cockpit as small LEDs flashed on, gyroscopic instruments started up, and the beast came to life. Brice ignored most of the formalities like turning on the navigation lights, beacons and radios because they were certainly of no use to them right now. He located the two starter switches and turned the first one slightly clockwise. The electric starter clicked into position and began spinning the turbine rotor. This was followed a few seconds later by the crack of the igniter as it lit the fuel/ air mixture in the engine's combustion chamber. The low bass drone from the burning fuel and exhaust and the whine of the jet as it spun up were the sweetest sounds that Trevor Brice had heard in a long time. He had already decided to go with only one engine; the other he would start en route.

"Is this where I should ask if you know how to fly one of these things?"

"As long as we are not plummeting toward the earth, you don't need to ask," he said in a deadpan voice while engaging the rotor transmission.

The long limber blades began to spin over their heads. She was not sure what he meant and nervously watched his every move. At this point, considering all that they had been through, worrying about his ability to fly was a little silly, but flying always made her uneasy. With his left hand he twisted the throttle to increase engine speed, causing the blades to spin at an increasing rate. He gently lifted up on the collective until the vibrating craft slowly became airborne. With his right hand on the yoke, he moved it to the right, and they left the confinement of the grotto. He twisted the throttle to the full open position as he pressed the right rudder pedal to swing the tail to the cliff side and pushed the yoke forward. They were finally free.

He turned the other starter switch and lit off the second engine. As the helicopter speed increased to full, the fuel tank of the first chopper exploded, sending shrapnel and flaming liquid flying in all directions. Their escape craft shook violently as jagged particles of aluminum punctured the side of their craft. They held their breath. Brice's eyes scanned the instruments; all was normal. The vibrations quickly ceased, and the Russian helicopter settled back into normal flight. The time was 12:01 am. Trevor continued to maneuver the chopper away from the cliff and the emperor's retreat in a straight line and as fast as possible.

"LOOK OUT!" Alex screamed.

Brice looked up, and in the faint light of the midnight moon he saw something dead ahead. His mind had no idea in what direction it was moving or if it were moving at all. In fact, these thoughts did not even enter his mind until after he slammed the yoke hard to the right and forward while slamming down on the collective. The craft made a hard right turn while seeming to fall right out of the sky. Alex screamed as she went weightless and was thrown about the inside of the cabin. Brice never let his eyes lose sight of the object as it screamed past, missing them by only a fraction. He looked up as they dove toward the ground and saw another dark streak whiz by, followed by a third. He leveled the chopper in a hover position, kicked the left rudder, turning to face the retreat.

"What the fuck were those?" Alex asked, obviously shaken.

"Those are cruise missiles," he started to say, but the words never completely cleared his throat before the side of the cliff lit up like Yankee Stadium during the World Series. Two seconds later, two more explosions. The first two missiles hit the center of the grotto, and the third hit halfway up to ground level.

"Look," said Alex, pointing out her side window. A fourth cruise missile screeched by at 700 mph, followed five seconds later by a fifth rocket.

Number four hit the cliff face 50 feet below the retreat and the last hit squarely in the center of the retreat's first floor. For a moment nothing happened. Suddenly, the entire cliff appeared to shudder, and then the rock wall started to give way. The roof of the grotto collapsed, then in a slow cascade, layer upon layer of mountainside fell in on itself. Like a wave of dominos the rest of the cliff collapsed. The emperor's retreat and grounds looked like a planned urban demolition as it gently folded in on itself and slid down into the crevasse and finally to the valley floor below. Explosions from the small cache of bombs and weapons hidden in the bowels of the retreat provided a dazzling light show as the tons of rock and marble cascaded down the cliff face. The natural spring that had once flowed through the gardens and fed the pool carved out a new path, gracefully cascading over the rim of the newly formed crater. Nature so effortlessly adapts itself to change.

# 42

## Going Home

Twisting the throttle and pulling up on the collective, Trevor lifted the craft to a safe elevation above ground level. With the rudder pedals, he spun around and aimed for Hong Kong. A sense of sadness cloaked them. They stared out of their windows as they passed over the rubble of what had once been a magnificent structure. It had also been a house of unspeakable human abuse and torture.

"For the people, your friends and the others, in those cages, maybe there was some mercy in what just happened. I can't help but believe they are now better off," said Trevor.

Alex did not respond. She just gazed out at the distant light of her mother's village, her mind completely void of thought.

Brice reached for his backpack and the secure satellite phone inside. He had to call the President and report. It was a very brief conversation, but Totten was quite pleased with the outcome and very happy that Brice and Alex had made it out alive. For the next 90 minutes not a word was spoken. Privately, they each reflected on the events of the past several days and hours. Brice was on the brink of mental and physical exhaustion. His thoughts filled with visions of caged humans with lifeless eyes, volcanoes, underground escapes, caged humans with lifeless eyes, submarines, open warfare, caged humans with lifeless eyes, dead soldiers, hidden passages and exploding mountains and those caged humans with their lifeless eyes.

The government had asked a lot of him over the years, but this assignment was more than all of those others rolled up as one. He struggled to contain the intense mental imagery that kept racing through his mind, completely against his will. It was a struggle that he knew he could not possibly win. Finally, he succumbed and allowed his mind to go wherever it chose. But first he found the autopilot and flipped it on. He then sat back and squeezed his eyes shut. His mind relived every gory detail over and over and over until it finally tired of all the negative thoughts and slowly begin to give way. It began to allow a trickling of thought about his wife Danielle and their two girls between flashes of all those empty faces. He mentally relived their lives and began to consider their future.

Slowly the subconscious adversity in his head subsided. He relaxed a bit and envisioned the reunion with his wife and kids and a trip to that Hilo beach Dr. Allison had suggested, with its blue waters and white froth on ebony lava. He started to think of a thousand things that he wanted to do right then and there, forcing the harsh imagery into visions of beaches, bikinis, sunshine, banana/orange/mango blended fufu drinks, with a gallon of rum in each, and making love to his wife on the beach with the waves of the Pacific Ocean crashing only feet away. Snorkeling in tide pools filled with starfish, turtles and anemones after hours of body surfing in the emerald blue

# Freedom's Menace

Hawaiian waters. The thought of his girls screaming at the sight of the crabs peeking from under rocks brought a smile to his face. A day spent kayaking with the dolphins in Kealakekua Bay was always an incredible experience and something the whole family loved doing. Then there were the hours he could spend with his head buried in his sketchpad. The Blue Hawaiian Hotel & Casino suddenly popped back to the surface. He mentally erased all of the designs that had been produced thus far, as an entirely new concept came into vivid view, a volcano rising from the Nevada desert. A romantic dinner with Danielle, a great bottle of red wine, some killer appetizers, all under the shelter of swaying palms at the Palm Café. He laughed to himself with the realization that his thought processes were behaving as if he had been away for a year. It had only been a few days, but, wow, what a few days!

Alex was far too overwhelmed to process all that had happened that night, much less the past several days. She had lied, cheated, stolen, killed, and almost been killed.... She just sat quietly hugging Dr. Scott's journal to her breast and began thinking of her lost friends and co-workers and the evil that was perpetrated on them. Periodically she reached down and touched the backpack containing their few belongings, just to be sure that it was still there. She had finally accomplished what she had set out to do seven years before, determined to discover the truth behind the death of the Scott party. It was finally over, and now the normal letdown was washing over her. Her focus had been so intense, and now she had to regroup. The journal would tell her of the missing month from the time she left for the wedding to the time of the "accident."

What secrets had the Library revealed that were not reported? The early stages of an archeology dig were as important as any aspect. Initial observations paint the picture; retrieving the artifacts simply sharpens the image.

She would know all very soon. The doctor was meticulous in his documentation and record keeping. Because there had been no time for casual conversation with Brice, she still did not know that the diamonds had come from under Kilauea and not somewhere inside the Library. This was something that Brice would tell her before they departed company, and the journal would confirm it in the weeks that followed. She anticipated seeing her parents again; it had been almost a year. The smells and flavors of her mom's pot roast tickled her senses.

Her nephews, Joseph and Mark, were now two and four, certain to be hell on wheels. She couldn't wait to see how much they had grown and wrestle with them on the living room floor. Pursuit of her chosen occupation had been derailed by her quest. It was time to get back into life and return to her love of studying ancient civilizations. Her sister and her husband had a small cabin in the hills overlooking Lake Tahoe. This is where she would go to regroup, study Dr. Scott's notes and let the wounds, physical and mental, heal. She thought of cool mountain air, crystal blue skies, the outdoor hot tub, a bottle of wine and the emerald waters of Lake Tahoe. Perfect!

As the light of Hong Kong appeared in the distance, Brice turned on the navigation lights and red rotating beacons. He lowered his altitude to 500 meters to avoid other air traffic, as well as the local airport radar as much as possible. Skimming over the rooftops of the shanty village, he sat the getaway craft down next to the old hanger where they had all met earlier. A previously placed radio transmission had alerted Ambassador Filsinger of their return.

A sleek black limo complete with driver and two armed U.S. Marines awaited their arrival. Alex and Trevor climbed into the back seat and found, to their great amusement, a silver ice bucket, two long-stem glasses and a freshly opened bottle of Dom Pérignon majestically setting before them. A note of thanks from Ambassador Filsinger was tied around the neck of the bottle with a blue silk ribbon. Trevor filled the glasses and offered a toast, his first real words since leaving the destroyed retreat. During the drive to the embassy, his phone rang, and Trevor answered it, but quickly handed the receiver to Alex so the President of the United States could thank her personally. The mood was much lighter now, and throughout the remainder of the drive they talked of their plans when they left Hong Kong. The events of the night were never discussed.

The long black car pulled into the embassy compound, and the ambassador was standing there to greet them. After the formalities were over, he took Brice aside for a few moments of private conversation. Trevor returned to the car to bid Alex farewell.

"I have a plane to catch. The ambassador has secured me a seat on a State Department jet heading for Hawaii. My family is there. I hope that the journal and computer files bring some closure to you. You have been on a long journey. I wish you well in the future."

She leaned over and kissed him on the cheek.

"I will be just fine. I think that I'll just stay here for the night for a hot bath and comfy bed. Thank you so much for your help. These files and personal effects will mean a great deal to a lot of families. I promise to give you equal credit for their return."

Filsinger interrupted because Brice had to leave immediately. They said their good-byes as the ambassador led Alex into the embassy.

"Ms. Wilson, you may stay here as long as you wish. There is no rush."

"Thank you, but I'll try to catch a flight to San Francisco tomorrow," she said.

"Very good. There is a Singapore Airlines jumbo jet that departs at 1:00 pm. I think that first-class accommodations, complements of Uncle Sam, are certainly appropriate."

# 43

## The White House

Communist Party Secretary Sin Bin Lu, as with other top Chinese leaders, had been concerned for some time about the mental state of Premier Lolo. However, few dared to share their concerns openly. The few bold men who were willing to risk speaking out did so only in broad generalities and always in private. Mostly they tried to ferret out the feelings and concerns of the other man. Not until the destruction of Darnestown did any of the political insiders or those close to the premier fully comprehend or appreciate Lolo's plans for total world domination. As the fury raged in the United States about the bombing, leaders throughout China began to talk among themselves, in small groups at first, sharing the bits and pieces of the confidential information entrusted to them by Lolo. As the true picture unfolded, the awareness that they had poked a stick at the tiger was becoming clearly evident, as was the depth of their leader's madness. Lolo knew that once hatched, rapid execution of his plan was imperative. All the pieces had to fall into place before internal Chinese political pressures forced him to back away. The 72-hour ultimatum had been vital to his plan.

With knowledge that Lolo had gone to the emperor's retreat and with the clock rapidly ticking down, Party Secretary Lu hurriedly planned and organized an appropriate response to Lolo and a reversal of his plan. To the Chinese, who were a stubbornly proud people, saving face was of paramount importance to the Secretary. It never occurred to the Secretary to simply try to surrender, apologizing and offering reparation. Instead, Lu decided that he could work out a way to tone down Lolo's demands, soften America's outcry, avoid retaliation and still gain significant control over the United States. Possibly a United States government with Chinese leadership injected into key positions for oversight? Life for the American citizens would not change too dramatically. They could, after all, still be allowed a car and home, but most of their productivity would be generated for the benefit of the long-suffering Chinese people. Lolo had not been completely mad; the time had come for China to take a definitive leadership role in the world. With the help of the Kilauea diamonds, that opportunity had presented itself. But it could all be handled without the messy business of war. The potential for accumulating great power rushed through the veins of Sin Bin Lu like a raging river through a ruptured dam. It had been Lu who had sent General He to assist the Americans in capturing Lolo.

Even before Brice landed on Chinese soil, Secretary Lu was on the phone to President Totten to discuss the terms for the United States surrender and to discuss the transfer of power. Lu had tried to be very sensitive to Totten and the plight of American people, but he was completely taken aback by the vehement rebuke he received.

# Freedom's Menace

A few hours and a phone call from Brice later, it was Totten's turn to phone China with his list of terms and conditions. This phone call the President was going to enjoy. It was in no way going to be a two-way conversation. The leaders of China were in for a rude awakening. Totten twirled a Macenudo cigar between his thumb and middle finger as he waited for his communications personnel to make the satellite telephone connection between Washington and Beijing. His feet were nonchalantly resting atop the oak panel desk in the White House situation room. The prescribed 72 hours had come and gone. Lolo was dead and could not order further attacks. Most of the White House staffers had been in that room since the beginning. All showed physical signs of exhaustion soiled and wrinkled clothes, mussed hair, dark circles under the eyes, smeared mascara, four days of beard growth and the distinct odor of unwashed bodies. After receiving Brice's call from the helicopter, Totten granted himself the privilege of a shower and shave. If he pulled this off, he was not about to appear before the American people looking like he had been run over by a shit wagon.

"Mr. President?" said a female voice. "I have Secretary Lu on the line."

"Hello, Mr. party secretary," Totten said, his voice calm and relaxed. "A great deal has happened over the past few hours since we last spoke."

"Yes, it seems so. Have you spoken to your leaders and decided to agree to our terms?"

"We have talked," said Totten. "I'm sure that you already know what our answer is, which of course is no. We will not even consider your demands. Why don't I tell you about the demands of the United States of America?"

Sin Bin Lu was silent for a brief moment. "Mr. President, you are in no position to bargain with anyone. Do you not understand the gravity of your situation?"

"Oh, I beg to differ, Mr. Secretary. I am in a very good position," said Totten, his voice as relaxed as when he first took the call. He wetted the end of the cigar. "It seems that Premier An Lolo is no longer with us. In fact, I understand that your own General He had the honor of killing him. As for the general, I'm afraid that he is buried somewhere in the rubble of what once was the emperor's retreat." a pause "I'm sorry, I forgot to consider that you might not have, as yet, been informed that the Retreat is now lying at the bottom of the valley. That's regrettable; I heard that it was a beautiful place. The premier and the general have joined all of the unfortunate men, women and children your country was using as lab rats. It is my sincere wish that they may all rest in peace."

Lu bristled, but maintained his composure, although his voice became noticeably tighter. "You are telling me that you have bombed the sovereign nation of China and killed our premier and a general in our army. What, sir, makes you think that we will allow this to stand? What makes you think that we will not carry out the rest of Lolo's plans and release our vengeance on your country?"

Totten made a gesture toward General Persi, who was standing across the room with a red telephone in his right hand. At the President's signal, he lifted the receiver to his ear and issued the order for the prearranged military strike.

"Look, Mr. secretary, I really didn't call to have a conversation. China has committed an act of terrorism on our country, and we know about your country's support of the global terrorists these many years. The rein of terror is now finished. It ends tonight, right now! If you please, allow me to list the demands of the American people. First, you will return all of the remaining diamonds, which you have stolen from us. We found your submarine and the remains of its crew. We will set up a payment plan for China to reimburse the American people for those diamonds that you have already sold or are being held as collateral. Second, the Chinese government will make full and complete restitution to the families of all those whom you killed when you bombed our country."

Sin Bin Lu started to protest, but Totten talked right through him.

"Number three, you, your under-secretary, your top ministers and all direct subordinates for five levels down in the Chinese government will resign immediately. It is time for fresh and youthful blood to manage the Chinese affairs of state. Lastly, by this time tomorrow you will publicly address the people of the world. In that address you will confess all, and you will apologize to your own people and to the world. Do you have any questions?"

Before Secretary Lu could respond, Totten added, "And, by the way, I need your answer in…"

He looked at his watch, then to Persi who flashed the five fingers of his right hand three times.

"…in 15 minutes. I'll hold."

"You arrogant American bastard!" shouted Lu. "What makes you think that I will even consider doing what you ask? Do you not understand that we have the means at our disposal to do great damage to your country? I have stopped what Lolo had planned and offered you the olive branch, as you say. What I get in return is this?"

# W. Laurence Willis

"What are you going to do, sir? Release the gas canisters in Magnolia, Arkansas? Incinerate Pittsburgh, Pennsylvania? Divert the Mississippi River above Baton Rouge by sinking those 20 barges? Oh, I know, your six Akula submarines, you are going to launch missiles from them. Sorry, but four of them are now resting comfortably on the ocean floor and the other two have already turned and run, but we will get them, too. Shall I continue? You now have twelve minutes."

The cigar returned to Totten's mouth as he awaited the reply.

"You think you know so much, but you do not know all of our capabilities. I was prepared to make this easy on you, but instead you mock me. How dare you!" Lu said in clear defiance.

"How dare I indeed, sir! You now have 10 minutes."

"Ten minutes. What is 10 minutes? You cannot hurt me. I..."

Totten broke in; " You seem to think that you have plenty of time for explanation. Ok, but let me tell you this. We found the entire list of towns you planned to destroy. All threats have been eliminated, and, for good measure, the residents were evacuated. The Internet attack. Sorry, but AOL, Microsoft, Prodigy, Yahoo and all the service providers are aware of the threat and are on alert. At the first hint that you are trying to flood our systems, they will voluntarily shut down, and when they do, 43 super-computers in universities all around the free world will retaliate in the same manner. We will shove that ball right back down your throat. Eight minutes, Secretary Lu, eight minutes remaining. Let's see now, we have covered the

390

booby traps in all of our small towns, that Internet thing,
your submarines. What have we missed? Ah, your
ingenious anti-missile system. Not bad! It took our guys a
while to figure it out. Very good, you should compliment
your scientists. You have six minutes, 30 seconds."

Totten stood for the first time, threw the half-chewed
cigar on the desktop, sat the phone down and adjusted his
tie. He then picked up the receiver and continued.

"Mr. secretary, correct me if I am wrong. You are
presently standing behind your desk at party headquarters
with 40 or 50 of your closest advisors gathered around. Am
I right?" a pause " Never mind, it doesn't matter. In one
hour, I have a press conference scheduled to talk with the
American people. I will either be advising them of the
complete and unconditional surrender of China and your
agreement to meet all of our demands, or I will tell them
about the eight Tomahawk cruise missiles that landed in
the center of Communist Party headquarters in downtown
Beijing. On that last point: it will happen in just about five
minutes if I don't get a satisfactory answer in the next two
minutes. You see, it takes a little time to divert that many
missiles from their target."

Seventy-five seconds later, Totten smiled and tossed
the telephone receiver onto the desktop. Looking at Persi,
he made a slashing gesture under his chin with the thumb
of his right hand. General Persi, telephone already at his
ear, called off the attack. Seven of the Tomahawk rockets
ran out of fuel 50 feet over the Yellow Sea and fell
harmlessly into the water, but as planned, one "errant"
missile landed and exploded in the lake behind the summer
retreat just north of Beijing. Sauce for the goose. There
would be no misunderstandings.

# 44

## Closure

"Get Brice on the phone, please," Totten ordered, thoughtfully looking at a painting of Teddy Roosevelt that hung on one wall. Eighty seconds later, he was connected to his special agent, who was riding in a State Department Gulfstream G-4 jet, 32,000 feet above the Pacific Ocean.

"Good news, Trevor. The Chinese have agreed to a complete surrender. Thanks to you, we have finally severed the head of the snake. The death knoll for terrorism has sounded. Another six months and we can put this all behind us. You did a fine job and I wanted to thank you again. Your plane should be landing in Honolulu in a few hours. We have a helicopter ready to take you on to Kona. There, you will be reunited with your family. We have secured a quiet little Polynesian hut for you at a very exclusive resort. It's a favorite spot of Betty and mine, and I'm sure that you will fine it very relaxing, not that you have any need for relaxation." a laugh "You can stay there as long as you wish. Uncle Sam owes you that much."

"Thank you, Mr. President. While I have you and if you can spare an extra minute, I have a few questions."

"Go ahead, my boy. For you, I have all the time in the world," Totten said.

"The volcano and the sub. Has the navy found the entrance yet?" Trevor asked.

"Yes, yes indeed, thanks to your escape. I have not seen the official report yet, but Admiral Hanover gave me a thumbnail earlier today. It seems that there is this very large and very deep hole in the ocean floor just off the south end of the island, very close to that Green Sands Beach. That's not news, we have known about it for decades. What we discovered is that if you drop down toward the bottom of the hole, the cavern entrance stares you right in the face. We don't know how the Chinese ever found it in the first place. One supposition is that they were nosing around in our waters and had to hide in the hole to keep from being detected by one of our routine patrols. We're still investigating, but it may have been as simple as dumb luck on their part."

"That's an incredible story. What's the situation with Dr. Allison and Alex Wilson?" asked Trevor.

"Dr. Allison is still in protective custody at her parent's home in Monterey, and Ms. Wilson is flying home later today. She, too, will be protected until this all settles out. But they both should be able to return to their normal lives very soon. Trevor, if you will excuse me, I'm scheduled to speak to the nation in just under an hour and I have to get ready," said the President before remembering one more tidbit.

"Oh, and one other thing, that Ms. Gielow, our international assassin. Well, she escaped! Took out six federal agents in the process. She didn't kill anyone, thankfully, but four of them will be in a Maui hospital for a few more days. They should all recover quickly, their injuries weren't too severe. We did get some very interesting pieces of information about her, though. She made a purchase at one of those ritzy shops in Whaler's Village and arranged for the purchase to be shipped. It was a birthday present for her sister in Schenectady, New York. As I told you, international authorities and intelligence agencies have been looking for her for the past several years without so much as a clue. Now they have lots of clues. They don't have her, but they have a lot of clues. Her real name is Beth Neuwirth. We now know where she was born, where she went to school, her best friend from high school, her favorite rock group, the name of her husband and ex-husband and what size underwear she wears. Turns out that sending that present was a huge mistake. We still don't know where she lives now and have no guarantee of ever catching her, but it's a start. I don't think that she will cause you any more trouble. She was well paid by a government that has fallen flat on its face. But keep your eyes open, just in case. Well, I've got to go, my friend. Enjoy your rest. You deserve it."

Television screens across the country flashed the gold letters "Breaking News" against a black background while the disembodied voice of the announcer said, "Ladies and gentlemen, we interrupt our normal programming to bring you this breaking news story. We take you now to our nation's capital and our new chief White House correspondent, Dixie Makepeace." The picture flashed to an image of Ms. Makepeace standing amid the trees on the lawn of the Executive Mansion, the towering white columns of the front entrance in clear view over her right shoulder,

# Freedom's Menace

the large carriage lamp gently swaying in the late afternoon breeze.

*"Good afternoon, everyone. In about 30 minutes from now, President David Totten will be addressing the nation. It is believed that he will announce a surprisingly quick end to the tensions that have gripped this country over the past several days. I have had the privilege to view the inner working of this administration during this time of crisis and can tell you that the well being of this country and its citizens has been the only consideration. Everything possible was done to avoid a costly and bloody war. What I have witnessed over the past 48 hours has impressed me. Our leaders have acted coolly, confidently and decisively to bring an end to an already disastrous situation."*

*"For these past few days, I have used my position as a journalist in an act of deliberate subterfuge in a willful attempt to help President Totten outwit the leaders of China. Our global news channel was the perfect conduit through which to launch a misinformation campaign. The Chinese aggression has ended so abruptly that I am not sure just how effective or beneficial my efforts were, as there was only time for two fictitious telecast. Regardless, in our efforts to deceive, we also had to mislead the American people. On behalf of this news station and from me personally, I apologize to each and every one of you. The subterfuge was carried out on the condition that once the crisis was over we could reveal the truth."*

*"Just over three days ago, the People's Republic of China destroyed the town of Darnestown, Maryland, killing 25,000 of our citizens, our friends, our families. Our leaders quickly identified 83 other towns, scattered all across America, which potentially stood in harm's way. To save lives, the people of those communities were temporarily evacuated from their homes and transferred to safe*

395

*locations. I was called upon to dupe the Chinese into believing that all was well in those small and mostly rural towns. You may have seen my story on our* Travel Weekend *program about Oblong, Illinois. Oblong was one of the eighty-three and was completely uninhabited on the day we aired that piece, but from your perspective everything looked normal."*

*"The President has authorized me to set the story straight. I can tell you that the evacuations were the correct course of action. Exhaustive searches were conducted throughout each of the towns. In most cases, nothing was found. However, several dangerous devices were found around the country, and each one was set to inflict additional devastation on this country and kill more United States citizens. Heartfelt thanks go out to those unnamed U.S. Special Forces personnel from all branches of our military who risked their lives to seek out, identify and remove the dangers that threatened those towns and our way of life. As I speak, buses are already returning people to their towns and homes where they can once again feel safe and secure."*

*"The loss of our families and friends in Maryland only highlights how dangerous the Osama bin Ladens, Adolph Hitlers, Pol Pots and An Lolos are to the safety and security of the human race. The terrorist regime of An Lolo slipped through our defenses and badly injured this great country. We are sad, we are angry, but we are not broken. It is the President's place to tell you how we have responded and what the future holds for the people of the United States and China. I only wish to remind you that we live in a great country, one with strong, honorable leaders and brave men and women watching over it."*

*"For now, we will resume our normal programming, but I will be back on the air following the President's address*

# Freedom's Menace

*and will be sitting with him in the Oval Office for an unprecedented one-hour open conversation about the events of the past few days. Our viewers will have the opportunity to ask President Totten questions by logging onto our website at CNN.com. I look forward to you joining us."*

*"Thank you, and see you back here in just a while."*

W. Laurence Willis

# 45

## Reunion - Kona, Hawaii

The Kona sun ladled its warm relaxing rays over the
leeward side of the Big Island. Trevor Brice was standing
knee-deep in a small tide pool examining the starfish that
his youngest daughter had found clinging to a rock and
desperately wanted to keep as a pet. Trevor sat down next
to the two girls and explained how the starfish moves using
water pressure instead of muscles, pointing out the water
intake valve on the top center of the unusual creature. He
flipped it over and showed them its six flexible legs and
hundreds of tiny feet. Studying the other starfish in the
pool, they were learning how the animal conforms itself to
whatever shape it desires while moving, very slowly, in any
direction without having to turn around. The lesson was
going quite well until a small black crab the size of a
quarter crawled across Kelly's foot. The older child shrieked
and ran from the water and across the snowy-white beach
to her mother. Trevor howled with laughter as he left Pam
Marie to her aquatic exploration.

# Freedom's Menace

He waded out of the water and crossed the sands to the two-man hammock that lazily swung between two palm trees in front of their Kona Village Resort oceanfront Hawaiian hale, or hut. He paused for awhile and reflected. A thatched tropical hut absent of telephones, TVs and radios, a hammock, his wife and kids, and the blue waters of the Pacific Ocean. This was truly paradise, a little piece of heaven. Danielle was there, stretched out in grand repose, a Pina Colada in one hand and a paperback novel in the other. He picked his drink from where it rested in the sand and was taking a long sip from the banana-pineapple tropical freeze when he saw the package lying on the hammock next to her.

"What's this?" he asked as he gingerly lay down beside her and picked up the package.

"I don't know. The front desk delivered it while you were out playing with the girls."

The box was only about four inches square and six inches deep. It was wrapped in Hawaiian motif paper and tied with a palm leaf bow. There was no card or any indication from where or whom it came. He held it to his ear and shook gently.

"Go ahead and open it," Danielle said, trying to usher him along.

Trevor twisted his mouth in a contorted manner, giving carefully consideration to his wife's request. He gently tugged at the green palm leaf and pulled it until the bow came undone. Slowly, he pushed open the top and looked inside. Nestled in a bed of white tissue paper was a lump of jet black A'a' lava that glistened with gold and purple as the sunlight reflected off its porous surface. Growing impatient at his meandering progress in searching the contents, Danielle took the box and pulled out the tissue paper. Two, native Hawaiian women, clad only in the smallest of thong bikinis and showing their ample assets stared out at her from the front of a postcard, which had certainly been purchased from a local tourist trap. Danielle gave her husband a look of suspicion and flipped the card over to read the other side.

In bold flowing lines, the blue ink scrawling across the card read, *"So, Mr. Brice, Remember the red head at the Green Sands? How much longer until your two girls can wear these?"* It was signed, *"Ha, ha! Samantha Allison."*

"Ok, buster, would care to explain this, and while you are at it, who is Samantha? Isn't she that girl you were trapped with under the volcano?" Danielle asked.

Trevor was too busy laughing and fishing through the bottom of the box to bother answering. He pulled out another note. This one was written on fine stationary stock with the letter "A" embossed at the top center. He read the note twice to himself and then out loud to Danielle.

*"Trevor, I don't have a lot of good memories from inside Kilauea except that I did meet a new friend. Thank you again for saving my life! I kept a small souvenir that I thought you might like to give to Danielle."*

Trevor removed the next layer of tissue and found the golf ball sized diamond that he had picked up from the volcano floor and had first offered to Dr. Allison for examination. He lifted it from the box and found that someone had sliced away a nickel size section revealing a crystal of deep blue color. He went back to reading Danielle the note.

# Freedom's Menace

*"A friend of mine, a gemologist in Hilo, examined this little find for me. In his opinion, it's as near perfect as you can ever get. He also thinks that if you have this cut into an emerald shape it will yield a stone of about 35 carets! Not a bad souvenir of your little Kilauean adventure in Hawaii. To the best of my knowledge, the National Park Service has no regulations against taking mineral samples from your visits, so this should be yours to keep. My best to you and your family. Keep in touch, Samantha Allison."*

Danielle went wide-eyed and snatched the stone and card from his hands.

"Can we really keep this? Oh, my God! Won't this look wonderful as a necklace?"

She ogled the diamond in the rough, disbelieving that it could really be hers and laying it against her chest as she envisioned what it would look like when cut.

"I could check with the Park Service to..."

"Oh, don't you dare, mister."

Suddenly, from the dense foliage to their right came the sounds of heavy footsteps crashing through the lush green gardens. Instinctively, Brice leapt out of the hammock and onto his feet, ready to resist the unknown if it proved to be a threat. So quickly did he jump up the hammock became unstable sending Danielle airborne, her drink, the diamond, the box, postcard, and tissue paper, all landing in a heap atop the soft sand. Trevor rushed toward the sound, but stopped short at a sight that took him completely off guard. In the background he could hear Danielle raising hell at his impulsive behavior. Twenty feet ahead a figure burst through the vegetation. It was a male member of the resort staff, 16 years old at the outside. The youth broke into the clearing and immediately tripped over a large coconut that the girls had fished out of the ocean the day before. He fell face down in the sand; the cell phone that he was carrying flew from his grip and landed at Trevor's feet. The boy was up in a flash and scrambled over to where Trevor was standing.

"Mr. Brice, Mr. Brice," he said excitedly and almost out of breath. "You have a phone call, sir. It, it, it's the President of the United States. He's calling you! The President is calling you!"

By this time he had made it over to the spot where Brice was standing and retrieved the phone from the sand. Brushing it off, he handed it up to Trevor, his eyes flashing in amazement and anticipation, his chest heaving as he tried to capture his lost breath.

Trevor did not take the phone, rather, with a smile, he turned and walked over to the hammock and retrieved two $1 bills, brought them over and offered them to the young man.

"Do me a favor," Trevor said. "On your way back the office, please ask the bartender to deliver two more of those drinks that we ordered earlier, Pina Colada and a banana-pineapple freeze."

Speechless and confused at first, the boy just stared back at Trevor; the cell phone still gripped in his out stretched hand. Finally finding his voice, he said, "But, sir, it's THE President. He's on the phone and wants to talk to you."

Trevor smiled and said, "Tell the President that I will call him back."

He turned and walked back to the hammock and rejoined Danielle. He lay down next to her, rolled over and gave his wife a long, deep kiss.

As if his feet were locked in clay the boy just stood there, unable to move or speak. Finally, he flipped open the cellular phone and nervously held it up to his right ear, his hand trembling from fright.

"Uhhh, hello?"